THE LAST
PARADISE

ALSO BY ANTONIO GARRIDO

The Corpse Reader

The Scribe

THE LAST
PARADISE

ANTONIO GARRIDO

Translated by Simon Bruni

Text copyright © 2015 Antonio Garrido
Translation copyright © 201/ Simon Bruni
All rights reserved.

Previously published as *El último paraíso* by Editorial Planeta in Spain in 2015. Translated from Spanish by Simon Bruni. First published in English by AmazonCrossing in 2017.

Published by AmazonCrossing, Seattle

www.apub.com

Amazon, the Amazon logo, and AmazonCrossing are trademarks of Amazon.com, Inc., or its affiliates.

ISBN-13: 9781503941885
ISBN-10: 1503941884

Cover design by Michael Heath

Printed in the United States of America

For my parents, Antonio and Manuela,
with all my love.
Just a handful of words, but I'd need a book
without end
to tell them how much I love them.

1

Winter 1932
Brooklyn, New York

Jack Beilis ducked into the narrow streets of the Williamsburg neighborhood with the desperation of a cornered jackal. Now and then, the weak light from a streetlamp illuminated his gaunt face emaciated by hunger, his blue eyes showing no sparkle. As he walked on, he rummaged in his pockets for a crumb of stale bread, a vain gesture so often repeated. His stomach protested. In the year he'd spent in Brooklyn, his savings had enabled him to avoid the charity lines, but the Depression had eaten away at those funds just as it had eaten away at his body until he was down to his last ounce of fat. He cursed the Ford Motor Company and Bruce Tallman. Especially Tallman.

Harried by the rain, he escaped through a doorway and climbed the rickety staircase that led to his father's apartment. He stopped on the fifth-floor landing. As he searched for the keys in his pants, he could taste helplessness at the back of his mouth.

He opened the door and hit the light switch without much confidence. Fortunately, the bulb flickered on. He shed his raincoat and traded it for the blanket he found on the couch. Then he walked through to what had been the dining room, before his father, Solomon, turned it into a dumping ground for old shoes, scraps of leather, and scattered awls. From the hall, he heard snoring. Entering the bedroom, he found his father asleep on the bed as if he'd simply collapsed onto it, fully dressed and giving off the pungent smell of alcohol. Beside him stood a near-empty bottle of bourbon. Jack covered the old man with the blanket and snatched the bottle. Back in the dining room, he lit the menorah, the seven-armed Jewish candelabrum that rose up from the table. When his father woke up, he'd be pleased to find it burning.

That night, it took Jack a while to get to sleep. His feet were swollen from so much walking, and he was numb with cold. Lying on his back on the threadbare couch, he longed for the days when he would arrive home from school and his mother would welcome him with freshly baked buns that melted in his mouth with their warm butter glaze. Days that would never return. He opened a drawer in a nearby side table and took out a picture faded by time. It was a photograph of his mother, Irina. He contemplated it nostalgically. He could almost feel her soft, delicate face, and see the deep, dark eyes that seemed to protect and advise him: *Keep going, son. You have to look after yourself . . . and look after your father.* He'd been trying to do that since he'd returned from Detroit.

But Solomon wasn't cooperating. His only concern was to secure his daily ration of drink, as he'd been doing since the day Irina fell ill.

Jack grabbed the bottle and took a long draft. The liquor burned his throat but comforted him. For the first time in a long while, his stomach was filled with something warming. He closed his eyes to enjoy the feeling. The remaining gulps raised his spirits enough to give him a flicker of hope. Unlike his father, he was young and strong, with two skilled hands and an ardent determination to find a job that would save them from ruin. For a moment, he considered himself lucky, comparing himself to the thousands of destitute living in shantytowns across the city. At least he and his father still had a solid roof over their heads. For as long as Kowalski allowed it.

2

He looked at his mother's portrait again. Five years ago, when times were still good, Solomon had moved his shoemaker's store to a more central location on Broadway. But shortly after Solomon's Shoe Works opened, the dreadful symptoms of disease began to appear. The cancer didn't just end her life. It exhausted Solomon's life savings, leaving him only debts. Jack was working in Dearborn. By the time they'd told him she was sick, it was too late. When he asked his father for an explanation at the funeral, Solomon was barely able to murmur that he'd merely fulfilled his wife's wishes. Irina had not wanted her son to know of her illness and to suffer because of her.

The bourbon eased his sorrow, though he attributed his change of mood more to the medallion he wore around his neck, an ancient seal of Hebrew characters that his mother had given him for his tenth birthday. Since her death, he hadn't removed it; it was all he had to remind him of that happy time in his life. Which was why he squeezed the medallion between his fingers before sleep overcame him.

The cold of dawn woke Jack as if he'd slept out in the open. He looked at the window. The wind had torn the newspapers that covered the broken panes, turning the room into an icebox. He loosened his muscles, went to the bathroom, and stood in front of the mirror, contemplating the cadaverous set of features his face had become. He took a deep breath before dunking his head in a basin of icy water, then dried himself with a ragged towel and used little pieces of soap to plug the cuts he'd made shaving. He looked at himself again. With each day, he found it more difficult to accept that the deep rings around those blue eyes belonged to the same young man who a year before had provoked sighs of admiration from the girls at the Dearborn Dance Society. But he had long ago stopped being the attractive Ford Motor Company supervisor who wore French jackets and frequented the best clubs in Detroit. And that reality ate away at him.

He preferred not to think about it. Lately, thinking only gave him stomach cramps. His most pressing concern was to find a job, or he and his father would be forced to wander the streets and sleep under cardboard boxes in Central Park, surrounded by beggars and criminals.

He opened the wardrobe and took out his only smart shirt, a classic-cut white cotton number. The garment still had the tag from the Abraham & Straus department store where he had purchased it. He delicately stroked the buttons with his fingers before slipping it onto his fibrous body. He put on a woolen vest, and on top of that, the worn raincoat his father had lent him—he'd traded his own the week before for a little lard and a pound of potatoes. He left the coat unbuttoned because it was small on him, and picked up his Bulova watch, which he'd tried to sell so many times; no one had offered him more than a bowl of soup for it. Before fastening the band, he looked at the engraving on the case back: *Ford Motor Company Worker of the Year.* He gave a bitter smile. Last, he donned his hat. He looked at himself in the mirror again. The shadow of the brim hid his drawn face so that nobody who saw him would know how bad things were. Numb with cold, he rubbed his hands, turned off the light, and exited the room.

He was about to leave the apartment when a soft voice stopped him.

"Where're you going?"

When Jack turned around, he found himself face-to-face with what was left of his father. The old man's hair was as disheveled as a used scourer, remains of food still clung to his gray beard, and his eyes were half closed, as if they refused to fully see the ragged body hidden under a stained T-shirt.

"To work," Jack lied. He disliked lying, but he didn't want to trouble his father any more than necessary.

"Dressed up like a dandy?" The man hawked as he tried to squeeze a last drop from the empty bourbon bottle. "Damned headache. What time is it?" he sputtered.

"Early . . ." It was getting late. "Have you had your syrup?"

Solomon Beilis didn't respond. He scratched his armpits and stood looking at his son with glazed eyes, as if searching his brain for the right answer. He didn't find it. He sat on the couch and turned to Jack.

"Kowalski was here yesterday."

"Again? And what did he want?" he asked for the sake of asking. Kowalski always wanted the same thing.

"The low-down Polack doesn't listen to reason. He says he's sick of waiting for us to pay the electric bills and has people waiting to move into our apartment."

"He must've gotten up on the wrong side of the bed. I'll speak to him. There's still some mashed potato in the pot. I'll see if they'll give us some bread on credit at the bakery later. Now, put on some clothes, or that chest will never get better."

"And how about a little something to drink?" the old man replied. "It's a day of celebration. I'll have to go out and find a drop or two."

Jack shook his head. He still couldn't understand how his father managed to get his hands on alcohol, with no money and in the midst of a prohibition. He watched his father stagger as he headed toward the menorah to light one of the wicks that had gone out. After a couple of attempts, the old man managed to light a match, but it slipped through his fingers.

"You'll wind up burning yourself, Father. Come on, I'll take you to your room."

"Get your hands off me! The Christians have their damned Christmas, and we have our Hanukkah, so I'll be darned if I'm not going to light this sacred candelabrum. And I'll light you with it if I have to, boy!"

As he tried to shake his son off, the old man splashed Jack's vest with wax. Seeing it, he mumbled something like an apology, but Jack ignored him. He cleaned himself up as best he could and left the apartment.

Outside, the wind howled between the buildings, picking up dust and dead leaves. Jack wrapped himself in his raincoat. For days, the sun had remained hidden, as if ashamed to cast light on that landscape of grief and desolation.

He lifted his head to look around him. The apartment where he now lived with his father was on South Second Street, three blocks north of the Williamsburg Bridge, in an old tenement house mostly occupied by Jewish immigrants who had arrived from Europe at the turn of the century and had settled in the area for safety in numbers. Many had Americanized their surnames to make integration easier, but Solomon Beilis was proud of his Russian roots. That was why he had made sure his American son learned the language of his forefathers. Those were different times. Now the hustle and bustle and the children's laughter that once filled the Williamsburg streets had evaporated, and the neighborhood had become a wasteland of deserted alleyways and barren parks.

Jack saw some people on the streets in spite of the cold, and he stopped reminiscing. He had to hurry, or by the time he arrived at the market, the earliest risers would have torn off the job offers that were sometimes pinned to the notice boards.

He had no luck at the market, or at the building site for the new line on the Independent Subway System, or at the Brooklyn docks, where corporations like Esso, Pfizer Pharmaceuticals, and D. Appleton & Company hired dockhands from time to time. For hours, he walked from factory to factory, receiving the same shakes of the head as the rest of the throng of unemployed that surrounded him. Even the vast dry docks of Red Hook had limited the number of workers they were taking on, allocating the vacancies to the Italian immigrants who paid protection money to the Mafia families that controlled the docks.

At midafternoon, the businesses closed their gates, and the jobless set off home with their pockets empty, their bones creaking, and their spirits crushed. It was the worst moment of the day, when hunger's claws were the sharpest.

On the way back to Williamsburg, Jack stopped at the house of charity at Brooklyn Bridge to gaze at what New Yorkers had christened "the breadline." That day, the line of people hoping to raise a bowl of soup to their lips stretched around the block and disappeared out of sight. Jack recognized Isaac Sabrun, the storekeeper whose furniture business went bust not long after the stock market crash. He was dragging his feet, his gaze absent. A little farther back, he saw Frank Schneider, the River Street lawyer whose sizable investments turned to dust overnight. The poor man said that he joined the breadline after his wife died, but everyone in the line knew that, when he lost everything, she'd run off with a wealthy rancher from Nebraska. Behind Schneider, he spotted the well-known journalist Dave Leinmeyer, who reportedly lived under the bridge, and who'd let his beard and mustache grow so that he wouldn't be recognized.

Jack pitied them though his own stomach grumbled, imploring him to join them. He wondered whether he should listen to it for once. He hadn't had a hot meal in weeks, yet something inside him stopped him from accepting charity. Doing so would have been to admit he had lost all hope as well as everything material.

He walked on, head down. He didn't want anyone to see him gnaw at the scrap of bread he'd surreptitiously picked up from a coffeehouse table earlier that morning.

While he devoured his meal for the day, his mind turned to the landlord and the unpaid bills. Until now, he'd managed to keep him happy with the promise to return the money owed with interest, but if, like his father said, Kowalski had tenants ready to pay up front, it wouldn't be long before he took action.

Jack despaired. The odd shift unloading goods wouldn't remedy the situation. He needed money, and fast. For a good while he pondered what he might do. Finally, he rummaged through his wallet until he found his last five-dollar bill. It was all he had, enough to feed himself for three weeks, but nothing like what he needed to save him and his father from being turned out onto the street. He crumpled it up in his fist in anger, then stepped into the nearest grocery store and asked if they had a telephone. The storekeeper wiped his hands on his apron, assessed Jack's appearance, and shook his head, until he noticed the bill in the young man's hand. Without a word he took it, opened the cash register, and gave Jack change. Then he gestured at the device that stood on a corner of the counter. Jack eyed it. He wondered whether to make the call. Finally, he picked up the receiver and dialed a number he knew from memory. When the conversation was over, he prayed that his idea would work.

He had time to spare, so he went to the entrance of the American Sugar Refining Company thirty minutes early.

Built on the East River docks, ASR continued to process more than half of the sugar the country consumed, and it employed hundreds of workers to stow, handle, and transport its product. Jack knew that securing a job there was a difficult task, but if anyone could help him do so, undoubtedly it was his friend Walter.

It was beginning to rain, and the American Sugar watchman had been out a couple of times to tell him to move away from the entrance. Jack muttered something but grudgingly obeyed. He waited impatiently in the rain for his friend to appear.

Though they'd once been best friends, he hadn't seen Walter Scott for some time. For years they had shared a desk at the Brooklyn Technical High School, and they had been inseparable. He recalled those days. Though feeble and sickly, Walter always seemed to be in a good mood; he enjoyed hunting lizards, and his laughter was infectious. His comedic gifts were matched only by his ability to get himself into trouble, forcing Jack to stick up for him against whoever lashed out at him. At the time, Jack's physique was beginning to make him conspicuous among his classmates, since he now stood almost a full head taller than the rest of them. His arms were strong and his hands skilled, earning him the boys' respect and the girls' admiration. Sometimes Walter envied him, but Jack always pointed out that, despite his strength, his grades in lettered subjects were not as good as Walter's. Fortunately, Jack found a way around his limitations when he began to study mechanical engineering. He interpreted designs, analyzed mechanisms, and fixed faults as if they were a child's puzzle. As he learned, his fascination with any contraption that he could dismantle, figure out, and repair grew. A bicycle, a cash register, a lock, a gramophone . . . He didn't care what it was or where it came from. The more complicated it was, the sharper he became, and the greater his satisfaction when he managed to bring it back to life. Walter, on the other hand, took an interest in politics. At sixteen, he spent his spare time reading books on the violent events transforming Europe. Sometimes he asked Jack for his father's opinion on the Russian Revolution, but Solomon never spoke of such matters.

Despite their differences, their friendship grew as solid as a redwood. Together they enjoyed their first cigarettes and went to their first prom. They fell in love with the same girls, and when those girls rebuffed them, the disappointment lasted no longer than an old umbrella on a windy day. Over six long years, they forged a bond that they swore would never break. But on graduation day, an incident marred their friendship forever. Jack had just turned eighteen, and his whole family was on the top floor of the Hotel Bossert to celebrate the occasion. The partygoers included his uncle Gabriel and his cousin Aaron, whom he rarely saw because they lived in a wealthy neighborhood on Manhattan Island—and because Solomon disapproved of the way they made a living.

After their arrival in America, the two brothers had gone their separate ways. While Solomon persevered as a shoemaker, Gabriel worked in a pawnshop of dubious reputation before establishing his own loan office.

However, given the occasion of the graduation, Irina had persuaded Solomon to invite Gabriel to bring the family together for the benefit of their son. Jack had also convinced his father to accommodate Walter, whose parents did not have the means to pay for their child to attend the ceremony.

Perhaps that was why Walter ate like a man possessed and drank the punch as if he'd just crossed a desert. When the alcohol began to take effect, he became bolder, and when he learned that Jack's cousin drove his own car and had a liveried servant, he started in on him, calling him a filthy capitalist.

That was the first mistake leading to the life-changing tragedy. The second was Jack's: trying to separate them, he inadvertently caused Walter to send Aaron falling down a flight of stairs. When his uncle Gabriel found his son motionless, he cursed Jack as if the accident were his fault. Aaron never walked again, and Gabriel Beilis broke the weak bond that still tied him to his brother, Solomon. As punishment, Jack's father barred him from any contact with his friend Walter.

The incident forever tainted Jack's relationship with his father. For years, Solomon had imagined that one day his son would inherit his little workshop and carry on the family trade, but though Jack worked hard from dawn to dusk, his interest in footwear ended as soon as his father pulled down the shutters at the end of the day. So when Brooklyn Technical High School's head teacher, Theodorus Rupert, offered Jack the opportunity to secure a position at the gigantic factory that the Ford Motor Company had built in Dearborn, Michigan, he jumped at the chance.

The idea of losing his only assistant angered Solomon, but Jack was determined. In Dearborn, not only would he receive a salary four times what his father paid him as a shoemaker, but he could also advance by earning promotions. Jack promised that he would send his parents half his earnings every month, but Solomon continued to refuse until his wife intervened. Irina insisted that neither Solomon's nor the shoe store's interests would be put before those of her son. After all, she reminded him, in their youth they had also left their parents in Russia to immigrate to America in search of a better future.

With his mother's blessing and his father's resigned acceptance, Jack packed his bags, bought a bus ticket, and moved to Michigan to enjoy what destiny had in store for him.

For a while, he heard news of Walter Scott through the old classmates with whom he corresponded from time to time. They told him that Walter had moved to Long Island, where he was a union man, helping disadvantaged workers. Then, as the years went by, Jack gradually lost contact with his classmates and his connection to Walter. He regretted it, because he missed their friendship. On some of his visits to New York, he was tempted to try to find him, but he never dared to go against his father's wishes concerning Walter Scott.

A decade had passed since the ill-fated graduation dinner that left his cousin Aaron an invalid. Now, aged twenty-eight and in dire need of help, Jack was directly disobeying Solomon for the first time with respect to those wishes.

When Walter finally appeared, Jack barely recognized him.

His old friend still had his scruffy intellectual mien, with the same shabby tortoiseshell spectacles perched on his nose, and his characteristic red scarf knotted around his neck. Yet he was thin, and his once smart clothes were now little more than rags. Jack's surprise was so great that he didn't know what to say. Walter was speechless, too. Finally, they clasped each other in a long embrace.

"It's so good to see you, Walter! You look . . . You look great," he lied.

"Oh, come on, Jack, there's no need for flattery," the young man said with a smile. "Things have changed since we were at school together, huh? But I suppose I can't complain. But look at you! Quite the man about town. Are you still a hit with the girls?"

"Believe me, women are the last thing on my mind."

"There's always time for dames, Jack. Always!"

Jack could see that, though Walter had lost much of his hair, he hadn't lost any of his optimism. His smile lifted Jack's spirits. But his appearance didn't really suggest that he was someone in a position to provide him with employment. He didn't want to seem self-interested, but it was raining hard and they were getting soaked, so he asked, "What should we do, then? Should we go inside?" He pointed at the refinery entrance.

"There? What for?"

"I don't know. When you mentioned this place, I thought—"

"That the job would be here? God, no! At American Sugar they hang union guys from the chimney! No. I suggested meeting here because it's close to a coffeehouse I know. Come on, let's get going before we freeze to death!"

On the way to the coffeehouse, Jack wondered how he'd pay for their drinks—he needed every last cent that he possessed. Walter seemed to read his mind.

"It's on me. They still give me credit there." He laughed self-assuredly and put his arm around Jack's shoulder.

When they walked into the establishment, Walter smiled and greeted the other customers. Jack was pleased to see that his friend was still the same affable, talkative guy he had been, the kind of person whose mere presence could brighten up a wake.

They made themselves comfortable at a table by a window and ordered coffee. Jack asked for a large one. They could barely breathe with the cigarette smoke, but it was warm and comfortable, and the music from the wireless was an invitation to believe that happiness still existed in some corner of the world. Jack sipped his coffee nervously. It was burning hot, and though he detected a hint of chicory, it tasted no less delicious.

"Well, thanks for coming, Walter. I guess my call surprised you? I bet you're wondering why I've suddenly appeared, after so much time and . . . Well . . . it might sound like an excuse, but I would have found you sooner had my father allowed it. I never blamed you for what happened to Aaron. But for my family, it was a big blow. You know how these things are . . . Then the years went by and, well, what else can I say? I've missed you, old buddy."

"Oh, come on! You don't have to apologize, especially for something that was my fault." Walter downed his coffee, and his eyes came to rest on the tabletop, as if he could see the past on its surface. "Believe me, I've gone over and over it, and I still don't understand why I behaved like that. I don't know, I was sore . . . That cousin of yours, he was so young and full of himself. He had everything, and I couldn't even pay for my dinner. The drink went to my head, and when he poked fun at my clothes, I lost my cool and—" He looked down and fell silent, before adding, "I asked after you and Aaron a few times. They told me he never recovered."

"It's true. Ah well, let's change the subject. How about a toast, to us?"

"This damned Prohibition! Toasting with coffee. What the world's come to, eh, Jack?" He touched his empty cup against his friend's with a smile.

"So you're still living on Long Island?" Jack asked.

"Surviving, shall we say? But tell me about you. I heard it was going well for you in Detroit. Someone even said you got yourself an apartment. Your parents must be proud of you."

Jack's face darkened. Looking at him, Walter remembered how close Jack had been to his mother.

"I'm sorry. I forgot about your ma. My parents died, too. But it's a fact of life. We just have to pick ourselves up and carry on."

"It was like a prelude to this goddamned depression. First I lost my mother, then . . . then everything else." He sighed.

Jack couldn't stop himself remembering the afternoon of March 23, 1931, when Bruce Tallman called him into his office at the Ford factory in Dearborn. At that time, Tallman was foreman of the stamping area, where they shaped the gleaming metal coils into doors and fenders for the Model A. Jack presumed he was calling him in to promote him. Despite the economic crisis, the assembly lines were at full capacity, and there were rumors among the workers that an innovative new vehicle was about to go into production and take the market by storm.

As Jack walked into the office, Tallman asked him to sit down and offered him a cigarette. Jack was suspicious—the man was never this friendly. He accepted the cigarette all the same. But before the first puff reached his lungs, the foreman had taken a piece of paper from his drawer and held it out to him without saying a word. Jack recognized the document immediately. For a moment, he thought it must be a mistake, but Tallman continued to hold out the letter of dismissal until Jack took it from him. After reading it, he sat in silence. The document announced the termination of his contract without specifying a reason. As he looked up, he saw a hint of a smile on the foreman's face, a smile he could happily wipe off with a thump, he thought to himself. But assaulting him would only get Jack locked up, and he wasn't going to give Tallman that pleasure. After slamming the door on his way out, he headed to the trade union offices, where they informed him that there was nothing they could do. Henry Ford, the factory's owner, had personally ordered every Jew to be dismissed.

"They must have added my name to a blacklist, because I found it impossible to find work anywhere in Detroit. When my savings ran out, I had to leave my apartment, so I came back to be with my father, who wasn't in a good way. He hadn't told me, but the shoe store's debts and the cost of treating my mother's illness had ruined him. For a while, I worked in a repair shop, fixing flat tires and washing cars for a miserable salary until the owner sold the business. Then I did a bit of everything: mechanic, lathe operator, electrician, docker. But unemployment spread through New York, and by the end of the summer, I found myself on the street, broke. It's nothing you haven't heard already! And the ironic thing about all of this is that my father still thinks I'm working. He's sick, and I don't want to upset him. Which is why I thought to call you.

I reckoned that seeing as you're a trade union guy, you might be able to help me. I hope I'm right."

"The filthy rats! I could imagine it happening to pretty much anyone, but not you. And at Ford! Those fat cats! Things are bad. Really bad. I'm serious. You should have formed a union." He stood up from the table and gesticulated at the other patrons of the coffeehouse. "Workers need to defend themselves against the vultures. They need to band together to help one another. Do you hear? This is how the capitalists grind us down!"

Jack was embarrassed. He'd forgotten how vehement Walter could become, and he tried to calm him down; he didn't want them to be thrown out, and he was even less keen for word to get around that he was one of those hotheads who goaded the jobless into rising up against the employers. Fortunately, the few customers in the coffeehouse continued with their conversations without paying much attention. Jack got the feeling it wasn't the first time they'd listened to one of his friend's rousing speeches.

"There you go," Walter said, slumping despondently back into his chair. "Spineless, all of them! The jobless just sit around waiting for someone to come down from the heavens and help them, and the employed bless themselves and keep their heads down to wait for the storm to pass. To hell with this country!"

Jack felt uncomfortable. Walter had been his best friend, but that didn't mean Jack had to share his radical views. In fact, Jack remained convinced that the United States offered endless opportunities and that if a man worked hard enough, sooner or later he'd escape the misery. His fear was that it might not happen before he starved to death.

He kept his thoughts to himself and refocused on Walter.

"So, you're just a trade unionist?"

"Well, let's say I used to be. The printer's where I worked went bust, and the bastard in charge let us all go. The trade union thing gave me enough to survive on for a while, but no longer. But we sure as hell gave that bloodsucker his comeuppance!" He smashed his fist into the palm of his other hand.

"So, you're out of a job, too?"

"Who isn't? Wake up, Jack! Why do you think I'm wearing this patched suit?"

Jack took a deep breath. As nice as it would've been to reminisce about the old days, it was time to speak frankly. When he asked him about the kind of work he had in mind for him, Walter gave him a mischievous smile, adjusted his spectacles, and from his raincoat took a newspaper clipping that he unfolded on the table.

"Relax, Jack. I have everything under control." He pushed the crumpled clipping toward his friend.

Jack picked up the piece of paper and smoothed it out with care. As he read, he went from confused to astonished.

"Walter, if this is some kind of joke, I'm not in the mood for—"

"A joke? Are you serious? This is the solution to all our problems!" He pointed at the scrap of newspaper again.

Jack had to read the *New York Times* advertisement twice to convince himself that Walter was serious.

THE AMTORG TRADING CORPORATION
OFFERS AMERICA'S UNEMPLOYED THOUSANDS OF JOBS
IN THE FACTORIES OF THE SOVIET UNION

"Have you lost your mind?" He stood, visibly disappointed. "Do you really think I'm going to leave the country where I was born to go back to the hell my parents escaped from?"

"Listen to me, Jack! Things aren't like they were before. Now the Soviets are offering—"

"You're serious, aren't you? For the love of God, Walter! We're Americans! Have you forgotten that those Bolsheviks are butchers? That they killed the tsar and everyone else who got in their way? Even our own government has questioned the legitimacy of their leaders!"

"Please, Jack, calm down and listen! I was at Amtorg yesterday, and everything advertised here is true. You should've seen the lines of applicants, from all over the country: Texans, Southerners, Californians . . . entire starving families, looking for a better life."

"I'm sorry, Walter, but you can count me out."

"Oh, come on, Jack! You speak perfect Russian. And there's work for you there. Do you know how much they're paying in their factories? A hundred and eighty dollars a month! Do you hear me? How much would you get here now, if you could even find a job? Four dollars? Five, maybe? And that's not all. In Russia, they'll give you a free home! And medicine. And paid vacation. Look, just last year they received over a hundred thousand applications from Americans like you and me. A hundred thousand, Jack! With your skills and my contacts, we'd be kings of the world."

Jack shook his head in disapproval.

"Russia . . . You must be crazy."

"Crazy? Me? Have you stopped to look at yourself recently?" Walter fell silent for a moment. "Do you really think you're going to trick anyone with your raincoat that won't even button up? Tell me something: When was the last time you ate a hot plate of spaghetti? Or a hamburger? Or pork chops? How long will you last like this? What has this country done for you that makes you think it's so great?"

Jack wasn't sure how to answer, but the one thing he did know was that in Detroit he'd had a chance to enjoy life. Though he had lost everything he had worked for, something told him that he could get it all back.

"I'm sorry. I can't accept, Walter. I knew that you were wrapped up in all this stuff at school, but I never thought you'd go this far. I don't know. Maybe it's my fault for thinking you were talking about a normal job. Thanks for the offer anyhow. If you end up going, I wish you all the luck in the world." He rummaged around in his pocket for the money to pay for the coffees himself.

"Wait a minute, Jack. Don't you see? We used to be inseparable, and now you've shown up as if it were meant to happen. I don't speak a word of Russian; I'd feel like an orphan out there. If it's the Bolsheviks who are the problem, I can promise you that—"

"It's not just that. I told you, my father's sick. I can't just leave him."

"And what will you do for him here? Start begging to pay for his hooch?"

"Watch your mouth, Walter! I won't allow you to insult my family!" Jack's voice turned threatening. He left twenty cents on the table and turned around to leave, but Walter held him by the arm.

"It's common knowledge. That drunk's sucking you dry, and you just let him do—"

A fist stopped Walter midsentence, making him crash into a table. Jack froze. He realized how out of proportion his reaction had been. He tried to help Walter up, but his friend refused the gesture.

"I'm fine, I'm fine," Walter said, acting as if it were nothing as he tried to reassemble the spectacles that Jack had just broken. "I don't believe it, Jack. At school you protected me from the bullies, and now you've turned into one of them."

Jack couldn't find it in himself to apologize. He just put on his hat and left. As soon as he was out on the street, the rain whipped his face. He regretted punching his friend, but Walter had asked for it. His problems with his father were his own, and no one, not even Walter, had the right to rub salt in the wound.

2

Back in Williamsburg, Jack noticed two squat figures sitting on the steps at the entrance to his father's apartment block. They were cloaked in the smoke from their cigarettes, but as he approached, he recognized one of the figures as his landlord, Lukas Kowalski. The other man was one of his goons. When the landlord spotted Jack, he stood with a snort.

"Hey, kid, nice of you to make an appearance. You Jews have been playing hard to get lately," he said.

"Good evening, Mr. Kowalski. I'm sorry, but I don't know what you're referring to."

"Oh, you don't? Well, let me explain it, then."

Kowalski made a gesture, and before Jack could do anything, the thug grabbed his arm and twisted it. Jack let out a groan as he fought to free himself.

"Relax, kid," Kowalski whispered in his ear. "I ain't stupid enough to leave you crippled, not just yet. I just wanted you to know that I'm done waiting, so tell your pop to stop hiding away like a cockroach and pay me what he owes, or I'll smash the door down and drag him out myself."

Jack couldn't understand Kowalski's rage over a couple of electricity bills. When he pointed it out, the landlord turned red.

"To hell with the bills. I want the money he owes me for the rent and the whiskey I've given him. And this ain't a request!" he yelled. "Make sure your father understands. Tell him I don't care if he doesn't open the door. If I don't have my hundred dollars in my office by tomorrow, I'll come for the two of you and break some bones."

Kowalski signaled the goon again, who shoved Jack toward the door. Then they turned and disappeared into the rain.

Jack straightened his torn raincoat. He'd have liked to have told the landlord just what he thought of him and his family, but everyone in the neighborhood knew that Kowalski's men were always packing heat. He brushed the dust from his hat and climbed the stairs to the apartment. The steps creaked. When he arrived, he went to speak to his father to find out what was going on. Seeing him, Solomon grumbled.

"You're making a face. What, they didn't pay you today?"

Solomon always asked the same question. Jack ignored him.

"I bumped into the landlord downstairs."

"You did? The bastard tried to come in here, but I didn't open the door. I'll be damned if I'm going to let that lowlife in."

"Why does he swear that we owe him a hundred bucks?"

"What? How should I know? You know that bigmouth, always talking garbage." He looked away. Then he headed toward the kitchen and grabbed a bourbon bottle.

"Father!" Jack persisted.

"He *swears* . . . He *swears* . . . I'll pay him! Haven't I spent my whole life paying my way?"

"What do you mean you'll pay him? What happened to the money I've been giving you for the rent?"

Solomon, gripping the whiskey, fell silent. Slowly, he put the bottle down on the table and lowered his head. Jack couldn't believe what his father was confessing with his silence.

"You've g-g-got to be kidding me. Tell me it's not true," he stammered.

"Didn't you hear me, damn it? I told you I'll pay him!"

Suddenly, Jack felt a stab of terror. He turned and ran to the sideboard in the kitchen, opened a drawer, and took out a small cigar box, praying to God that he was wrong. But when he lifted the lid, his suspicions were confirmed. He waved the empty box in front of his father's face.

"Where's Mother's bracelet? What have you done with it?"

"Do you not have eyes in that head? It's not there," he muttered. Then he slumped into a chair.

Jack threw the box to the floor. He had an unstoppable desire to punch the person who'd pissed away their last flicker of hope. For a moment, he felt sorry for his father, but the prospect of finding himself out on the street hardened his heart. He looked around the apartment in desperation.

"All right. We'll sell the menorah. It's solid bronze; perhaps the shylock who bought our other belongings will give us enough for it to keep Kowalski off our backs until—"

"Never! I'll sooner sell my soul!" Solomon roared, standing between Jack and the candelabrum.

He said it with such feeling that Jack was certain that he'd make good on his threat. Even so, he tried to make his father reconsider.

"Those men aren't joking. If we don't pay them, they'll throw us on the street with our legs busted into more pieces than we can count."

"I said *no*! Do you hear me? Sell whatever you want. The tables. The chairs. The shoes. But don't even think about touching my menorah, or I swear on your mother's memory I'll make you regret it."

Jack clenched his teeth. He wouldn't even get three dollars for all the junk his father mentioned. He tried to reassure him, promising him that hocking the menorah would only be a temporary measure, and that they'd get it back when he'd found a decent job.

"And when will that happen?" Solomon replied, beside himself. "Since you got back from Detroit with your tail between your legs, you've been talking big about finding a job, but the best you've come up with is changing a few tires at some dump of a repair shop."

Jack couldn't believe what he was hearing. He'd used up all of his savings to look after his father, and this was the thanks he got for it. Even so, he tried to keep his cool.

"Let's leave it for now. We can talk later, when you're sober."

"No, we'll talk now! I don't need a clear head to know who's to blame for all of this," Solomon went on. "You and your delusions of grandeur! If you'd stayed at the shoe store, none of this would've happened."

"Let's leave it, Father. Now's not the time to—"

"And when will be the time? When *you* decide? Oh, of course. I forgot . . . It's high-and-mighty Jack who decides when we speak and when we don't. High-and-mighty Jack doesn't have to be a miserable shoemaker like his father. In fact"—he stood, puffing and panting—"high-and-mighty Jack is so important that he had to leave his family and go off to live on the other side of the country while his mother was dying and his father worked himself to death mending shoes."

Jack felt a dagger pierce his heart. He hadn't abandoned anyone. In fact, he had never forgiven Solomon for not telling him when his mother fell sick. And while he was in Dearborn, he had sent half his salary to his parents each month. He was consumed with rage.

"Everyone has the right to choose what they do with their lives! At least I lived well, and not like some poor wretch as you would've had me living!"

"How dare you? Get out!" yelled Solomon, turning away. He tried to get a last swig from the empty bourbon bottle, and seeing that not a drop remained, he smashed it on the floor. "I took care of you and your mother. If we don't have anything now, it's because—"

"Because you blow the money on booze!" Jack blurted out.

"Go! Get out of this house. Nobody wants you here anymore."

Jack clenched his fists. Then he headed to his bedroom, threw his remaining clothes into his suitcase, and closed it, leaving a shirt cuff hanging out. He picked up the photograph of his mother and looked at it. He considered what to do. Finally, he put the case down on the bed, went out, and crossed the living room.

"Where're you going?"

Jack didn't answer. He left the apartment and slammed the door, making the entire stairway shake.

As he prepared himself for a terrible night's sleep curled up in the hallway, he made out his father's muffled voice behind the door, sobbing. "Please, son . . . Don't leave me now."

As Jack progressed north through Manhattan, the old brick buildings gradually gave way to taller, more modern structures, before finally being replaced by brand-new stone colossi, the streets between them seething with pedestrians and vehicles, which, despite the blight of the Depression, seemed to broadcast that New York remained the center of the universe.

The hands on his watch were not yet pointing to noon when he stopped to examine the towering complex of buildings that made up Rockefeller Center. Some of the real estate was still under construction, but the main tower was already a vast edifice of concrete and steel that rose defiantly as far as the eye could see. Jack stood admiring it. It may not have been as high as the Empire State or as elegant as the Chrysler Building, but even before its official opening, the Rockefeller could boast something that no other structure could: inside, America's richest men decided the world's fate. He imagined his uncle, Gabriel Beilis, was one of them.

He took his time to find a way into the building. After skulking around the area, he discovered one of the entrances where a continuous stream of office workers went in and out. For a moment, he envied them. Their immaculate suits and narrow ties reminded him of his days in Dearborn. But he pushed those thoughts away. He knew that if he tried to intermingle with them, he'd be discovered and, most likely, arrested. Fortunately, he saw a group of workmen heading toward the entrance. Without a second thought, he took off his hat and helped the last worker with the joist that he was carrying.

Once inside, he moved away from the workmen and hid behind a pillar, from where he could marvel at the sumptuous entrance hall. He'd never seen anything like it. The lobby glistened with dozens of golden murals that contrasted magnificently with the black marble of the floor. He looked for the elevators, which he found strung along an endless corridor. He counted fifteen. In reality, he didn't know exactly where he had to go, but when two office workers headed toward one of the doors, he took the opportunity to follow them. When he was about to walk into the elevator, a uniformed security guard grabbed him by the shoulder.

"Pardon me, son, but I don't believe I've seen you around here before. Do you have an appointment?"

"I sure do," Jack lied.

"Right. Well, in that case, do me a favor and check in at the desk," he said doubtfully.

Jack shrugged off the security guard, brushed his jacket down in an attempt to recover some of the dignity that he felt he'd been robbed of, then headed to the huge timber desk crowned with an impressive polished marble countertop. Behind it, a middle-aged receptionist wearing flawless makeup turned to greet him.

"How can I help you, sir?" The woman smiled, barely looking up.

"I wish to see Mr. Gabriel Beilis. Spelled B-e-i-l-i-s. Of Schwalbert and Associates."

"Which building?" The receptionist slid her thick-rimmed glasses to the tip of her nose so that she could observe the newcomer over

24

them, but when she saw Jack's disheveled appearance, her friendly smile changed to a grimace of disapproval.

"I couldn't say. All I know is that he works here."

"Sir, this is a large complex of buildings . . . Forget it, I'll take a look for you." She opened a folder and searched for the surname. "Beilis . . . Beilis . . . Oh yes, here it is. Beilis, Gabriel, of Schwalbert and Associates. You're in the right lobby, forty-fourth floor. Do you have an appointment?"

"No, it's a courtesy visit," he lied again.

The woman arched an eyebrow, but replaced the receiver.

"What company do you work for?"

"Excuse me?"

"What company do you represent, sir? I need to know so that I can announce you."

"Solomon's Shoe Works. The name's Jack," was the first thing that occurred to him.

The receptionist dialed the extension. After a few seconds, she hung up.

"I'm sorry, but there appears to be a problem with the line. Would you be kind enough to step to the side so that I can attend to the next visitor?"

"It's urgent; please try again," he pleaded.

"Sir, I'm afraid that I can't help you until the line's working again."

"Sure. Do you know when that will be?"

"I don't know. Step aside, please. I'll let you know as soon as the line's free."

Jack was about to insist, when the guard who had stopped him approached the desk.

"Is there a problem, Beth?"

"Oh, I don't think so, Tom. The young man was about to leave." The woman gave Jack a challenging look.

"Look, miss. I've walked here from Williamsburg, and I'm not moving until—"

"Right, that's enough, kid!" The guard grabbed Jack by the shoulder. "Let go of me!"

The security guard held Jack with a clamp-like grip and moved him away from the line that had formed behind him, forcibly leading him toward the exit. He was about to throw him out, when a man stepped between them.

"Wait a minute, Tom. Jack? Is it you?"

The guard recognized the suited man and immediately let go of Jack.

"I'm sorry, Mr. Deniksen. Do you know this gentleman?"

"Ben? Ben Deniksen?" Jack looked at him disbelievingly. Then he clasped him in an affectionate hug. When they separated, he looked at the man with surprise. It really was old Ben Deniksen, a close family friend he hadn't seen for ten years. His hair had grayed, but he wore the same sideburns and bushy mustache. Ben worked as Gabriel's accountant.

"Jack, little Jack . . ." A smile spread across his face. "God! I barely recognized you! You're a head taller than me, and you were still in shorts last time I saw you," he exaggerated. "What're you doing in New York? I thought you were in Michigan. I haven't seen your father for some time. You know . . . things aren't the same with him." He screwed up his face. "Anyway, what brings you to the Rockefeller?"

"Well, I came to—" He broke off for a moment. "I wanted to speak to my uncle Gabriel."

Benjamin frowned in disbelief. "Whoa, Jack." He shook his head. "I don't think that's a good idea."

"I don't really care whether it's a good idea or not, Ben. I need to speak to him."

Benjamin could see the desperation on his face. "All right. Come with me. I'll see what I can do."

Jack followed Benjamin down the long corridor. Finally, they reached another lobby containing four elevators. They took the first. Jack had never been in such a modern contraption. The elevator traveled at an incredible speed and eventually stopped on the forty-fourth floor. Benjamin told him to wait at the secretary's desk and disappeared through a door, over which a bronze plaque announced:

SCHWALBERT & ASSOCIATES

GABRIEL BEILIS, CHIEF EXECUTIVE

While he waited, Jack wondered whether coming to Rockefeller Center had been a good idea, but he had no choice if he wished to protect his father. The door suddenly burst open, and Benjamin, with a cautious expression, invited him to go in. Jack straightened his raincoat and smoothed his hair back with his hand. Despite his height and piercing blue eyes, he had quickly learned that, without money, a man's looks dissipated like a puff of smoke on a blustery day.

Inside the office, sitting on an easy chair upholstered in sumptuous red velvet, a man with white hair at the temples and pronounced wrinkles was perusing the report that lay on his desk. Jack stood in silence beside Benjamin until the accountant coughed, causing Gabriel Beilis to look up from the report. The man observed Jack.

"All right, Ben. You can leave us now."

Benjamin obeyed.

Alone facing his uncle, Jack took a deep breath. Gabriel Beilis stood, revealing an impeccable dark suit that looked newly bought. He had aged, but he still had the eyes of a wolf. The two of them remained silent long enough for Jack to feel uncomfortable. In the end, it was the young man who broke the silence.

"It's been a while . . . ," he began as he held out his hand. Gabriel didn't take it. Instead, he went to the window and looked defiantly out at the sky.

"Come, take a look," he said in a tone that made every syllable an order. "See that there? Central Park, once the green pride of New York, now a vagrant-infested pigsty. Twenty years ago, you could take a pleasant stroll there with your children. Now, those creatures would strip you to the bones." He shook his head in a gesture of disapproval. "So," he said, finally turning to his nephew, "tell me, to what do I owe the honor of this visit?"

Jack swallowed. He wasn't sure where to begin, or how to express the extent of his desperation. In the end, he just blurted it out.

"They're going to evict us."

The man stood looking at him without replying. He opened a box of cigars, lit one, and took a long pull, savoring its flavor.

"That's it?" He wandered around the office. "After ten years, you show up here and have the nerve to say to me, 'Uncle Gabriel, they're going to throw us out onto the street.' Not even an apology. Nothing." He took another puff on the cigar. "Tell me something, Jacob, or *Jack*, as you call yourself now. What am I supposed to say in reply to that? Pretend nothing happened? Put aside my anger and help? I don't even understand how your father could've sent you here."

Jack was unsure how to respond. He still couldn't grasp why his uncle blamed him for the accident that Walter had caused.

"My father doesn't know I'm here. If he'd known I was coming, he would've stopped me."

"So why go against his wishes?"

"I told you. We have nowhere to go."

"I see. Well, evictions are common these days. Life's tough. For you, for Solomon, for everybody."

Jack contemplated the luxury that surrounded him. "Tougher for some than others." Until that day, he had underestimated the progress that his uncle had made.

"True. For instance, you can still walk, and my poor son can't."

Jack moved closer to the man who seemed to be taking such pleasure in his misfortune.

"Forget about me and think of Solomon. Your brother needs you, sir."

"That man's not my brother!" he yelled. "For God's sake, I don't even know why I'm talking to you!"

"Please, Uncle. You're flesh and blood, and our religion obliges us to—"

"What? You dare to come here and talk to me about religion?" He turned around, fixing his eyes on Jack. "You, Jacob, who calls himself Jack because he's ashamed of his Jewish roots? You who ate whatever he pleased and never observed the Sabbath? No, *Jacob*. If you'd cared about your religion, you'd have learned that a Jew never attacks another Jew."

"I was only trying to separate them," Jack said in his defense. "I wasn't the one who pushed him. In fact, it was you who ignored Prohibition and turned up at the party with barrels of punch."

Gabriel snorted. He adjusted his jacket and took a long pull on his cigar. Then he went to his desk, opened a drawer, took out two tickets, and held them out to Jack. "Here. They're for the new show at the Radio City Music Hall. Have a great time. It's all I can do for you."

If Jack didn't throw the tickets in his uncle's face at that moment, it was only because his powerlessness was stronger than his anger. He took the tickets, said good-bye, and left the office in despair. He was about to take the elevator, when his uncle's accountant called to him.

"Jack. I'm sorry. I couldn't help overhearing." He looked down, unable to hold Jack's gaze.

"Don't worry, Benjamin. It was my fault, really. It was absurd to think that my uncle—"

"He's a very strict man. He works day and night, and he has suffered a great deal with his son," he said in an attempt to excuse Gabriel. "I don't know what to tell you."

"I know. Well, thanks anyway. It's been great to see you again. Are you all well?"

"Yes, we're all well. All—"

"I'm really pleased to hear that. Give my regards to your wife and children."

"Jack, you know how fond we all were of your father . . ."

"Yeah. Everyone used to be fond of him. Anyway, good-bye, Ben. Take care."

He hugged him.

"You, too, son."

Back on the street, Jack sat on the steps leading up to the complex. He couldn't go home empty-handed. While he tried to think of something, he fiddled with the tickets that his uncle had given him for Radio City Music Hall, the magnificent theater that everybody was talking about and that had yet to open. He thought they were neat. They announced the premiere of a show called "the Rockettes," with Caroline Andrews as the diva, and a performance by the Flying Wallendas circus act. Seeing on the reverse that the theater was located just behind Rockefeller Center, he headed there to find out what the tickets cost and inquire whether it would be possible to return them for a refund.

As he reached the box office, he had to pinch himself when he saw that each ticket was worth nine dollars, an outrageous sum compared to the quarter that it cost to go to the pictures, or the dollar twenty-five to watch a baseball game. The eighteen dollars from his two tickets would be enough for a month's rent with some left over. The problem was they did not accept returns.

He decided he wouldn't give up so easily. He remembered how, in Detroit, he had sometimes bought tickets for Tigers' games at Navin Field from touts—for double the normal price. If he could find the right buyer, he could make a tidy sum.

The opportunity presented itself when, after he had hung around outside the box office for several hours, a Duesenberg twice the length of a normal car parked up under the Radio City Music Hall's impressive neon signs, and a well-dressed couple stepped onto the sidewalk. The man must have been about forty years old, with slicked-back hair and a thin mustache, fashionably trimmed. He was accompanied by a stunning young woman, whom he was obviously trying to impress. He went straight to the box office and argued for a few moments with the clerk, before turning to consult with his girlfriend. The young woman made a face when she learned that the best seats were taken. The box office clerk could only offer them seats on the third balcony. The man had turned up his nose as if he had just been offered a piece of garbage.

Jack waited for the couple to retreat from the theater. Right when they were about to climb back into their car, he rushed up to offer them his tickets. At first, the wealthy man looked at him with scorn, but then he considered Jack's proposal. He took the tickets and examined them more closely.

"These wouldn't be fakes, now, would they?"

Jack's only response was to wave them at the box office clerk, who confirmed their authenticity.

"Sir, I can assure you that, had my wife not been taken ill, nothing in the world would've stopped us seeing this show, on the opening night," he improvised.

"And you say you're selling them for thirty dollars?" the man tried to barter.

"The cream of New York will be attending. You and the young lady will be shoulder to shoulder with Jean Harlow, Douglas Fairbanks, Kid Chocolate . . . As you already know, the best seats are sold out. But if you can't afford thirty dollars, that's understandable."

"Douglas Fairbanks?" the young woman cut in, wide-eyed. "Oh, please, darling! Buy them! Please say yes!"

The man stoically withstood the girl's arm-twisting, but he eventually shook his head in resignation. He counted out the bills and handed them to Jack.

"You're sure Douglas will be here?" he grumbled.

"Absolutely," lied Jack as he said farewell with his best smile.

◆ ◆ ◆

On the way to Brooklyn, he rued having argued with his father. Though the anger was always short-lived, it wasn't the first time that, in a fit of rage, Solomon had ordered him out of the apartment. But at least now his father would have cause to be happy. Despite his father's drinking problem, Jack was convinced that sooner or later everything would return to normal, and the best way for that to happen was to start paying some of the rent they owed Kowalski. Then he would find a job doing whatever he had to and find a way to make Solomon give up the booze. They would get through it together, he and his father. He was certain of it.

By the time he reached South Second Street, it was almost night. People who still had somewhere to live would be in their homes as it was Christmas Eve, which was why he was surprised to find a crowd gathered outside his father's apartment block. Wanting to know what had happened, he picked up his pace. As he approached, he saw women sobbing and wailing. One of them gave him a look filled with pity. His pulse quickened.

He made his way through the crowd until he reached a ring of men busy trying to resuscitate a bloody body. Jack assumed someone had been hit by a car, but a number of people were pointing up at an open window on his father's building. Jack's heart stopped. He tried to shoulder his way through, until finally one of the men tending to the unfortunate person moved away to call for help, revealing a devastating sight.

Flat on the road's surface, atop a spreading pool of blood, lay the lifeless body of Solomon Beilis, clutching his beloved menorah.

3

The cemetery on Bay Parkway was the final stop for Brooklyn's destitute—a landscape of blackened gravestones permeated by misery, tears, and desolation. Jack hadn't set foot there since his mother's death. Now, wearing a borrowed black tie, he stumbled along in the rain with the other pallbearers under the weight of a cheap pine coffin, its edge digging hard into his shoulder.

As he walked, he suffered the irritating silence of the handful of mourners who had attended the burial, imagining their eyes fixed on his back. He was convinced they all blamed him for his father's suicide. When they stopped in front of the grave, Jack once again regretted arguing with him, though he was certain that his words had not caused the tragedy. He knew exactly whom to blame. At the vigil, a neighbor from the same landing had sworn that she had heard Kowalski and his goons hammering on Solomon's door the night of his death. They had banged on the door viciously, again and again, but Solomon hadn't opened. Instead, he had thrown himself from the window. The woman wasn't surprised. He hadn't been the first and he wouldn't be the last to take his own life during those desperate times.

Jack kept his emotions in check as the grave swallowed what remained of his father. Though there were no prayers because the Law of Moses forbade them for suicides, he said a few words of his own. Then he cast the first shovelful of earth. When the gravediggers finished their task, Jack laid a stone on his father's grave. Tears escaped his eyes as he said good-bye.

On the way out of the cemetery, Jack received condolences from Benjamin, whom he had last seen the day before at Rockefeller Center. The man lowered his head when he tried to justify his boss's absence, claiming some unavoidable commitment. Jack didn't believe him. He was certain that his uncle Gabriel was the kind of person who could cancel a meeting with the company president, spit in the face of his partners, and still make more money than he had before. With tear-filled eyes, the accountant said how sorry he was that he'd been unable to help Jack's father.

"He was stubborn . . . You know what he was like," Benjamin said.

Jack nodded. Solomon had always been stubborn.

The funeral-goers gradually filed out until Jack was left alone. He stood quietly for a while, letting the rain soak him, until someone approached. Jack looked at him in silence. It was Walter, his spectacles mended with surgical tape. Jack felt ashamed. Yet his old friend spoke to him as if nothing had happened, resting an arm on his shoulder.

"Come on, Jack. Let's get you home."

Jack wondered what home he meant.

The last person he imagined he'd find waiting at the entrance to his building that day was Lukas Kowalski. The man was sheltering himself from the rain in silence on the steps leading into the hallway, flanked by two of his thugs. As soon as Jack saw him, a surge of anger filled his chest.

"You son of a bitch. What the hell are you doing here?"

"Hello, kid." There was malice in Kowalski's voice. He didn't even look at the young man as he took a puff on his cigar. "I wanted to get into *my* apartment . . . but you have the key."

Walter managed to stop Jack just as he went to leap on Kowalski, who continued to smoke undeterred. He merely gave the younger man a condescending smile, as if dealing with a small child.

"Look, kid. It's cold and this place stinks, so I advise you to—"

Jack didn't let him finish. He shook Walter off, took out the money he'd earned from the sale of the theater tickets, and threw it in Kowalski's face.

The landlord raised his eyebrows as he inspected the bills that had fallen at his feet. Without deigning to pick them up, he turned to Jack.

"Thirty dollars? What do you expect me to do with that, kid? Buy myself a hat?"

"I'll have the rest next week," Jack replied. "Now, get out of here before I kill you."

Kowalski sat in silence, as if considering the offer. Finally, he struggled to his feet.

"Next week . . . next week . . . It's always the same old story! And then it's the next, and then the one after, and then, surprise surprise, you suddenly disappear and make a fool of me." He came down the steps until his face was almost touching Jack's. "Tell me something, boy, do you think I look like a fool?"

Jack stepped back to get away from the stench of stale sweat the landlord gave off.

"Look, Kowalski, I don't want any trouble. Take the money and come back tomorrow. If I haven't got what I owe you by then, I'll pack up my things and—"

"I don't think you've understood me, kid. I ain't here for spare change. I've come to take what belongs to me . . . as well as all your belongings."

"Damn you, Kowalski! I said I'll—"

The landlord held his hands to his head.

"Why is it you Jews never do what you're told?" he said, raising his voice. "Who *knows* what might happen tomorrow?" He took a long puff on his cigar, savoring it. "Why don't you just ask your pop?"

"Son of a bitch!"

Jack threw himself on Kowalski again, but before he could reach him, the nearest goon stepped in and knocked him down. Walter went to help his friend, but the second thug stopped him dead with a knee to the stomach.

The two young men writhed on the ground.

"The key!" Kowalski demanded.

Jack was trying to get up when a kick to the ribs sent him flying against the handrail on the steps. Walter, immobilized by pain, looked on helplessly.

"Leave him alone, you bastards!" he bawled.

The two men turned on Walter and kicked him mercilessly. Jack, bent over the handrail, took the chance to grab a loose metal bar and smash it against the shin of his nearest assailant. The man howled and collapsed on the steps, his leg shattered. Seeing this, the thug kicking Walter left him and turned his attention to Jack. Before he could pounce, Jack moved away just enough to be able to drive the iron bar into the goon's belly. Then he ran to help Walter.

"Watch out!" his friend warned him.

Jack turned in horror to find that the hood he'd just struck was pulling out a revolver. He leapt on him and grabbed his arm before he could take aim. The two men struggled, the revolver dancing in the air until, suddenly, a gunshot rang out in the night.

For a moment time stopped. Jack and his adversary froze, looking at each other. Then they loosened their grip and slowly separated as, a few yards away, Lukas Kowalski's body lay lifeless on the steps.

"Boss!" sputtered the goon.

Walter approached his friend from behind.

"Let's go!" he urged him.

Jack remained motionless, gazing at Kowalski's blood-soaked chest.

"But I . . . I . . . ," he stammered.

"For God's sake, Jack. Run!"

Jack and Walter fled down a deserted alleyway, stumbling and bumping into things as they dashed across Williamsburg's avenues, trying to get out of Brooklyn as quickly as possible. Jack followed Walter blindly, certain that Kowalski's men would appear at any moment to riddle them with bullets. Every so often they heard far-off voices, sirens, or the squealing of brakes, making them duck into porticos or crouch behind trash cans. Whenever they stopped to catch their breath, Jack tried to remember at what point the gun had gone off, but Walter wouldn't let up, pushing him to keep running. As they got farther away from the scene of the crime, the streetlamps became less frequent, and the avenues turned into a maze of backstreets and alleyways that Walter snaked through as if he'd been born there. Jack thought they must be close to Long Island, the neighborhood where his friend lived, but he couldn't be sure. Finally, they stopped in front of a doorway that, judging by the rust covering it, seemed as if it had been closed for years. Walter took a key from his pocket, opened the padlock on the iron shutter, and tried to lift it.

"Come on! Don't just stand there! Help me before they find us!"

Jack was still struggling to get his breath back, but he pulled with all his might and the shutter rose with a metallic screech. Walter ducked under the half-raised shutter and turned toward his friend to usher him in. When Jack was inside, Walter lowered the shutter, and they were suddenly in almost complete darkness. Jack remained on the alert. He could barely make out his friend's form, but he could hear his agitated breathing. A few seconds later, there was a crackle, and a flame appeared in Walter's hand. Jack looked around. The intense smell of ink and damp, coming from an old Linotype, told him that they were in an abandoned printer's. At his feet lay dozens of packages of old newspapers with long-forgotten headlines, while the walls were plastered with moldy posters that seemed to come to life in the flickering flame of Walter's cigarette lighter.

"It's the printer's where I worked before I was laid off," he informed his friend. "When it closed down, I kept a set of keys, and since then I've used it as a union meetinghouse."

"Is it safe here?"

"Safer than your house."

Jack fell silent. He couldn't get Kowalski out of his mind.

"Do you think he's dead?" he asked Walter, hoping his reply would be no.

"I don't know, but he was bleeding like a stuck pig."

"Shit! We should go to the police."

Then they heard a noise, and Walter shut off his lighter. Jack felt his heartbeat quicken. A moment later, Walter relit, and his spectacles glistened a handbreadth from Jack's nose.

"Shhh . . . rats!" Walter whispered.

"They've found us?"

"No. Actual rats." He kicked a creature that went flying with a shrill squeak.

Jack sighed with relief.

"I was saying that we should go to the police. We can't stay hidden forever. Sooner or later Kowalski's goons will find us."

"Are you kidding? If that bastard's dead, they'll send you straight to Old Sparky."

"That guy was going to kill us. You saw it, Walter."

"Of course I saw it! But what do you think those tough guys will say to the judge when he asks them? That it was *their* gun that went off? And anyway, those people have contacts, Jack. How else do you think they've gotten rich while the rest of us are starving to death? Corrupt capitalists . . . ," he muttered.

"Damn it! But I didn't kill him," he insisted.

Walter surveyed Jack's anguished face. Sweat pearled on his brow.

"Let's not get ahead of ourselves. We don't know if he's dead."

"All right . . . So, what're we going to do? Shit! I can barely breathe. Those assholes must've broken my ribs."

"I don't know. Let me think . . ." He moved away from Jack, searched around on top of a workbench, and returned with a candle in his hand. "We should stay here until things calm down. There's a washbasin with running water out back, and a lavatory. We could—"

"Wait. And my things? They're all at the apartment."

"For God's sake, Jack. You're not saying we should go back . . . The police will have been called by now. They'll be looking for you, or waiting."

"I don't care! Everything I have is there."

"Listen to me. All you have left now is your freedom."

Jack fell silent. He knew that Walter was right, but as insignificant as they might seem to his friend, he couldn't accept losing the last traces of his life.

"My photographs are there," he replied.

"Photographs?" Walter grimaced in disbelief.

"Of my parents."

"You're joking, right? We've got to get away from here, and all we need for that is our driver's licenses."

"What?"

"We'd need them to get a passport. You do have your license on you, right?"

"I already have a passport. But why the hell would I need it?"

"Hey, I can't force you to leave the country, but if Kowalski's dead . . ."

"Damn it, Walter! You said yourself that we don't know if he is."

"All right. Let's keep calm." He lit a crumpled cigarette and inhaled. He offered one to Jack, who readily accepted. The smoke tasted of ink. "OK. Give me the keys!"

"Huh?"

"Give me the fucking keys! I'll go to your father's apartment and pick up your things."

"Are you nuts? I ain't gonna let you put yourself in danger. I'll go myself."

Walter put his hands in Jack's pockets and snatched the keys.

"You can't so much as move. Anyway, do you think I'm an idiot? I'll only go in if the coast's clear." He cleaned his glasses and pulled his hat down to his ears. "No one in that neighborhood knows me. If I get the chance, I'll ask about Kowalski. Maybe the slug just scratched him."

"All right. But be careful. I couldn't bear to lose my only friend."

"Don't worry, Jack. We'll get out of this, you'll see."

4

Jack gazed at the rays of light filtering in through the holes that the rust had bored through the metal shutter at the entrance. He clenched his teeth. His head felt as if it had been stomped on, but the cause was neither the ink fumes nor the blows from the goons. He went back to the chair where he'd spent the entire night thinking about the tragic death of Solomon Beilis. He might not have been the most caring of fathers, but he had been the only father that Jack had. He kicked a bundle of newspapers, which flew in all directions like leaves in the wind.

He looked at the rays of light again. Walter had assured him he'd be back before dawn, but that was already a couple of hours ago. Jack began to consider the possibility that his friend had been caught.

He decided to light what remained of the candle and conduct a cursory inspection of the premises, something he'd avoided doing in the night, fearing someone might notice the light and discover him. When the wick flared up, a weak light illuminated the space, revealing a clutch of machines that looked unusable, posters strewn on the workbenches, dried-up ink rollers, and rusty guillotines. He examined a few of the posters, and seeing that they consisted entirely of anti-capitalist screeds, he left them where he'd found them. Heading to the cubicle where Walter had told him the lavatory was, he discovered an open drain in the floor. Beside the lavatory was a little window closed with a shutter. He gave it a couple of whacks, and the lock flew apart, the hatch coming away from one of its hinges. He peered through the cavity. The window looked out onto a small well. He breathed with satisfaction, knowing that, if necessary, he could jump outside. He blew out the candle. The morning light was coming in through the window, brightening the room. His stomach complained of hunger.

He allowed the hours to pass—six more than he'd agreed with Walter. His watch showed twelve o'clock. He paced from one corner of the room to another. He was beginning to consider making his escape, when suddenly he heard some quick footsteps that stopped at the entrance. Jack pricked up his ears and stood in silence. Then he gave a start when he realized that the padlock was being handled. He prayed for it to be Walter but retreated to the window, fearing it could be the police. Slowly, the shutter was lifted. Fixing his eyes on the metal screen, Jack felt his pulse surge. When it was halfway up, he threw caution to the wind. "Walter?" he asked. But no one answered. He decided he had to escape.

He was about to jump out of the window when a soft voice told him to stop. Jack slowly turned. When his eyes had become accustomed to the light, he could not believe what he saw. At the entrance, silhouetted against the clear day, stood the slender figure of a young woman.

Once inside, she told him her name was Sue and that she was Walter's fiancée. Before Jack could utter a word, she lowered the shutter and added that Walter had sent her to help him. She took a loaf of bread from her worn purse and handed it to him.

Jack didn't respond. As he tucked into the bread, he stole a glance at the newcomer. She might not have been a classic beauty, but she was the kind of vivacious girl who would attract the gaze of any young man.

She was a redhead, her age probably close to his own, though she could easily have been younger, slim as she was. He suddenly realized that he had forgotten the most important thing.

"Where's Walter?" he finally asked.

"To be honest, I don't know. He said he had to take care of some business; that's all he'd tell me." She smiled.

Jack swallowed the last mouthful of bread and licked the crumbs from his lips. He asked for a cigarette, but Sue didn't have any with her.

"And did he tell you when he'd be back?" He didn't want to be more explicit—he was unsure how much the girl knew about the fight with Kowalski's men.

"No, but I don't think he'll be long. Truth is, he was being pretty mysterious, and my Walter isn't like that. Did something happen?"

Jack tried to change the subject. New York girls loved to talk about their boyfriends, so he steered the conversation in that direction. Sue was true to form and chattered away. She told him that she'd met Walter four years ago, at the diner where she served coffee, and that since then they'd been inseparable.

"Moody's was out there, opposite the printer's. Walter had breakfast there every morning, and sometimes, when I served him, he'd tell me wonderful stories about equality between races and peoples." Her freckled face lit up. "He was so interesting . . . so different from the other oafish guys. But that was before they closed the diner. Well, Moody's and every other restaurant in the area," she complained. "Now I clean stairways for a pittance."

Jack believed her. It was obvious from her threadbare stockings, the ladders of which she'd tried to mend with little success. The young woman fell silent for a while, and then said, "Has Jack told you about our plans?" Her pearly eyes were bright with joy. "He must have. Walter tells everyone. We're going to leave this damned country soon and go to a place where happiness isn't just for the rich. We're going to Russia . . . the last paradise—"

Jack struggled to his feet and limped to the shutter, cutting the girl short. He looked through a crack. "Well, I hope it works out nicely for you," he said tersely before locking the shutter from the inside with the padlock and going back to his chair.

"Wow, you're quite the talker! Not like my Walter, he—"

"Are you sure you don't know where he is right now?" Jack cut in. Sue's smile froze.

"I told you. He had to take care of some business," she replied, clearly irritated. "He said to me that we shouldn't worry, to wait for him to get back."

"Very well. We'll wait."

Jack picked up some pamphlets, planning to pass the time reading them.

It was two hours before the screech of brakes tore him from his thoughts. He immediately ran toward the window, but Sue, who had already gone to the shutter to peer through a crack, reassured him.

"It's Walter."

"Walter has a car?" He was surprised.

"Come on! Help me with the shutter."

Jack ran to assist her. As they lifted it, Walter's face appeared, looking troubled under his large tortoiseshell spectacles.

"Make some space! We have to hide this old clunker!" he said.

Jack couldn't imagine where Walter had found a car, but he supposed it must be part of his escape plan. He and Sue moved aside the junk that blocked the path, and Walter accelerated the old Studebaker until it almost hit the Linotype. Then he leapt out of the car, and together with Jack, lowered the shutter.

"What happened?" Jack stammered. Walter's face was flushed as he took Jack's arm and moved him away from Sue.

"Bad news," he whispered as he looked back to check that the young woman wasn't listening. "Kowalski . . ." He shook his head and clenched his teeth.

"What?" Jack felt a knot form in his stomach.

"He died this morning."

"Oh God!" He slumped into a chair.

"We have to disappear, Jack. Take a ship to Russia, right now. It's that or we'll both be off to the gas chamber."

"For Christ's sake! How many times do I have to tell you? I don't want to go to Russia," he growled.

"Then you should reconsider. Anyway, they're not just after you; they're searching for me, too," replied Walter. "I've risked my neck to help you, but if you want to throw your life away, I won't try to stop you. Your things are on the car seat."

Jack didn't reply. He went to the automobile and opened the door. There was little there worth keeping: a couple of changes of clothes, a worn-out overcoat, a folder containing various documents, a broken old phonograph, and the splintered picture frame with the photograph of his mother, which he contemplated as intensely as the semidarkness allowed.

"And my passport?"

"It wasn't there, and I didn't see much else," Walter said apologetically. "When I arrived, the door had been kicked down and the apartment turned upside down. That was all they left. I put a chest of stuff in the trunk. Here. Your driver's license. Now you can go and ruin your life."

Jack didn't hear him. His hands trembled, clutching Irina's portrait. Then he cursed himself. The only option he had thought up involved fleeing to Canada via Buffalo, but for that he probably needed a passport. It was as if Walter read his mind.

"I could get you one," Jack heard his friend say. He looked at him in silence and understood that he was at his friend's mercy.

"The Amtorg offices close at five. Come on, honey, finish with that blusher—it's a fair way to go from Long Island to Fifth Avenue!" Walter said to Sue.

Jack was certain that going to the Soviet trading corporation was a mistake, but he had resigned himself to going along with Walter's idea.

Inside the Studebaker, the three of them went over the plan before leaving. Walter, knowing the Soviets' interest in broadcasting the virtues of their revolution to the capitalist countries, would apply to join one of the overseas propaganda units run from Moscow. He would highlight his affiliation with the Communist Party USA, as well as his experience as a printer. Sue would offer herself as a librarian and sympathizer to the cause.

"And you, Jack, you'll be my assistant. Since you speak perfect Russian, I'll tell them that I need you as an interpreter."

Jack pulled his hat down as far as it would go, and squeezed the iron paperweight that he'd hidden in his pocket to use as a weapon in case of an emergency. He remained unconvinced, but he had decided to trust his friend.

"OK. Crank her up."

The Studebaker shuddered as Walter hit the gas. As they crossed the Queensboro Bridge heading toward Manhattan, Jack turned to watch Brooklyn's buildings disappear from view. Then he turned back and looked ahead, trying to persuade himself that all he was leaving behind was the grayish smoke that the Studebaker kicked out through its exhaust pipe.

It was 4:50 p.m. when traffic forced them to slow almost to a stand-still. Walter snaked between the mass of vehicles, swearing and honking the horn as though his life depended on it, until a delivery truck stopped dead and forced him to swerve. Finally, somewhere between the Flatiron and the Empire State Buildings, he parked the car. Sue waited in the vehicle to avoid a parking ticket, while Jack and Walter got out and dashed into 261 Fifth Avenue. Jack didn't even pay attention to which floor they were heading to. His friend dragged him along, not giving him much chance to stop and think. They both took a deep breath as they waited for the elevator to reach its destination. When the elevator doors at last opened, they found themselves at the back of a long line of ragged creatures that led to a door with a plaque over it:

Amtorg Trading Corporation

Amerikanskoe Torgovlye

Jack felt a tremor in his stomach. It was the second time he'd seen a Russian text that week. The first was the epitaph that he had commissioned for his father's gravestone.

The enormous line did not dampen Walter's spirits. He handed Jack an Amtorg pamphlet to read while he waited, and cut the line, ignoring the insults and accusations directed at him.

While he waited, Jack noted that the applicants in front of him looked much like the poor wretches he saw on the breadline every morning. The main difference was that, while few women went to the soup kitchens, entire families waited in the Amtorg line. He listened to the families chatting merrily about the beautiful cities they'd visit, the salaries they'd receive, or the homes they'd be provided with. Some workingmen clutched documents that qualified them as miners, electricians, or builders. A couple of them even carried their own tools.

Jack was surprised to hear that the Quaker family in front of him had sold its land in Illinois to pay for the voyage after some neighbors did the same and were now enjoying a new life in Leningrad. And that the woman with thin hair holding her sick child in her arms had been promised that the Soviets would provide her with the medicine they lacked in America. He was impressed. Men and women who had lost even the dignity of believing they were human beings smiled with optimism and held their heads high again.

To pass the time, he opened the promotional booklet that Walter had handed him, and began to read it closely.

Sue's sudden appearance interrupted his reading. He was glad to see her. The young woman had climbed the stairs, and the effort had caused her face to flush red, making her glow with vitality. She took Jack's arm as if they were a couple. It made him feel a little uncomfortable, but he allowed Sue to grip him while she peered through the crowd of people waiting in line. He explained that Walter had introduced himself to a receptionist and slipped into an office.

"And why did you come up?" Jack asked.

"I was bored." She assured Jack that she'd persuaded the parking attendant not to give them a ticket. "Look, Jack, there're even Negroes waiting," she said, amazed.

Jack had seen them and had also been surprised. Yet the two men seemed unaware of the stares from the rest of the line.

At that moment, an Amtorg representative, squeezed into a suit two sizes too small for his large frame, appeared, and shouted out to the applicants that the office was closing for the day.

"We will see you tomorrow, with number assigned to you," he added in a strong Russian accent.

Jack did not take the hint until the large man insisted that they leave the office.

"We're waiting for a friend. He's inside."

"We don't have friends in Amtorg," the Soviet official replied.

Walter then appeared through a door and gestured to them to go in.

"Well, that *is* a shame," Sue said with a smile to the official, and she pulled Jack into the room.

Once inside, Walter introduced them to a well-built man in his fifties with a serious face, his eyes sheltered by thick, wiry eyebrows.

"This is Saul Bron, head of Amtorg in the States. For all intents and purposes, he's the Soviet ambassador," Walter added smugly.

Jack noticed an expression of satisfaction on Walter's face that he had never seen before. Sue let go of Jack and held her hand out to the senior official.

"Pleased to meet you," she said, and improvised a ridiculous bow.

"Right," said Saul Bron, taking his seat behind the giant mahogany desk that dominated the office. "You must be Mr. Scott's friends. Please, make yourself comfortable. Mr. Scott tells me that you wish to join the honorable cause of our beloved Soviet Union." He indicated the portrait that hung from the wall behind him.

Sue nodded with a picture-perfect smile, while Saul Bron waited for Jack's confirmation. At that moment, he was preoccupied by the stern-looking man with a large mustache who appeared in the portrait. He recognized the figure as Joseph Stalin—it was the same photograph he had seen in booklets at the printer's.

"And you?" the head of Amtorg insisted.

"Me, too," was all Jack said, with all the emotion of a waxwork.

Saul Bron cleared his throat, opened the file that lay on the desk, and looked over the document.

"Walter has already told me about Sue. With regard to you, Mr. Beilis, he said your parents were Russian."

"That's right. From Saint Petersburg."

"You mean Leningrad."

"Sorry, yes. From Leningrad," Jack corrected himself, remembering that, following the revolution, the Soviets had renamed the city after the Bolshevik leader.

"Do you still have relatives in Russia?"

"No. My grandparents were Ukrainian, from Odessa, but I never met them. They died soon after I was born."

"And in America? Do you have family?"

"No, not here, either." Walter had warned him against mentioning his capitalist relatives, and anyway, his uncle, Gabriel Beilis, was dead to him.

"And tell me, Jack. Why did your parents immigrate to the United States?"

"Hunger, I suppose." His expression hardened.

"Do you know whether you are related to the Beilises of Kiev?"

"Not that I know of. It would be the first I've heard of it. Why do you ask?"

"Just curious. There was a Menahem Beilis in Russia accused of murdering a child. A notorious case. He was tried and found innocent. He lives here now, in the United States, and has written a book on the outrages perpetrated by the Russians on the Jews. You will understand why I ask. We don't want to have any misunderstandings."

"As I say, I don't know anything about that."

"Good. One final question. Was your family associated in any way with the tsarist forces, the nobility, the bourgeoisie, the White Army, or the Orthodox Church?"

"No. Not at all. My father was a Jewish shoemaker, my mother was . . . well . . . she played the piano. They came to this country like thousands of others who immigrated, searching for the opportunity that Russia had denied them." He paused. "But, it seems, things have changed now." He looked at Walter, as if seeking approval.

"Indeed. They have changed, a great deal. Very good. In that case, I will summarize the situation for you." He stood to address the three applicants. "The Soviet Union is a generous nation that opens its arms to all oppressed peoples, regardless of race, religion, or nationality. Our struggle is that of the weak, of the poor, of the slaves of capitalism, of the world's outcasts. Walter, whom I have known since he was a trade unionist, has told me of your plans, and I assure you that nothing would please me more than to be able to help you. However—"

"However?" Walter broke in, removing his tortoiseshell glasses.

"However, things are not so simple now," he went on. "Hundreds of jobless citizens come to this office each day: cooks, clerks, electricians, pilots, salesmen, chemists, storekeepers, librarians, dentists, even undertakers, in search of work. Our staff can barely keep up with the workload. We've processed over a hundred thousand applications, and the number of vacancies is beginning to shrink."

"But wait a minute," Walter cut in. "Last time we spoke—"

"Last time we spoke, I explained that we were overrun with applications." He took out a bundle of newspapers and spread them over the table. "Here: Roy Howard of Scripps Howard, Karl Bickel of United Press, the correspondents Eugene Lyons, William Chamberlin, Walter Duranty, Louis Fischer . . . everyone! They're all talking about the Soviet Union as if it were Eden rediscovered. Even the US Chamber of Commerce has published a bulletin encouraging citizens to travel to Russia!"

"Yes, but you promised me that you'd deal with our application personally."

"And I will, Mr. Scott. I give you my word that I will, but not with the haste that you are demanding of me. Right now, there just aren't places for everyone."

"So, what about all those people waiting in the line?"

"We can only accept specialized workers. The rest must wait their turn, just like you."

"How long are we talking about?" Jack asked.

"I don't know. Let me see . . ." The Amtorg boss studied the reports on his desk. "Five months. Maybe six. Certainly no sooner. The ships are full, and, to be frank, with all the publicity we've received, propaganda workers like you are a low priority. Of course, as soon as an offer that fits your profile comes up, I will bear you in mind." He walked over to the door to invite them to leave.

Walter and Sue got up, but Jack remained in his chair.

"And what about the Avtozavod?" Jack inquired.

"Pardon me?" Saul Bron fixed his eyes on Jack.

"You know, the Ford Motor Company in Russia. This pamphlet of yours says that they urgently need workers for the production plant that Henry Ford is building in Gorky."

Saul Bron grumbled like a bear as he snatched the document that Jack held out to him and saw the news for himself.

"That's right. But I don't know what this has to do with your application. This offer is for highly qualified automotive operatives and—"

"Yes. I've read it. So it's true that they need skilled workers urgently?"

"True enough. Should we find them, they'd be setting sail tomorrow."

"In that case, you have your men right here," Jack replied with his best smile.

Back at the printer's, Walter hugged Jack until his ribs creaked, and he let Sue give his friend an enthusiastic kiss on the cheek. Neither could believe what had happened. Jack had persuaded Saul Bron to have Intourist, the Soviet travel agency, process three last-minute tickets, and to promise them jobs when they arrived in the Soviet Union.

"I don't know how you wangled it, but that thing about me being the best student at the Brooklyn Tech must have sounded convincing," said Walter. "Thank you, Jack. You've saved my life."

His friend shook his head. "If you spoke Russian, you would've persuaded the Soviet official yourself. After all, what I said was hardly a lie." He raised an eyebrow. "I just forgot to mention that in the last two years, you've traded your mechanical engineering classes for *canteen politics.*"

"Jack, I don't know what they're expecting of you in that Russian factory," said an openmouthed Sue. "But to cough up dough just like that, they must really value your work. Free tickets!"

"Well, not exactly *free*." Walter took off his glasses and rubbed the lenses with his shirttail. "When I spoke to the administrators, they explained to me that, once in the Soviet Union, they'll deduct the cost from our wages. Still, you can't deny it's a godsend." He put his spectacles back on no cleaner than they were before, and gave a self-satisfied smile.

"Oh! Of course, of course," muttered Sue.

"And it wouldn't have been right if we had accepted a preferential deal. Would it, Jack?"

"I suppose not," he replied. For a moment he'd imagined that the Soviet Union might really be the paradise Sue and Walter had fallen in love with.

Walter gave Jack a celebratory slap on the back.

"And what about me? How can I thank my new husband?" Sue smiled mischievously as she approached Jack, swinging her hips.

"Hey! That's quite enough of that!" Walter laughed, and he moved Sue away with a kiss that did not prevent her from continuing to gaze at Jack. "For the record, I didn't take kindly to that stunt. Why in hell's name did you decide to say that Sue was your wife?"

"Oh, give it a rest, Walter. I've already told you three times."

"Well, I do apologize, but since she's *my* fiancée, you might have to tell me again!"

"OK, OK." He stood to dramatize the story. "That Soviet official who interviewed me, he was mighty suspicious. When I informed him in detail of my old position at Ford, he seemed persuaded, but with Walter, it was more difficult. In the end, he reluctantly approved his application, but he refused to allow Sue to come with us. I didn't know what to do, so when she whispered to me to tell the man that she was my wife, I didn't think twice."

"And, Sue, why exactly didn't you whisper to him that it was you and I who were married?" Walter reproached her.

"I don't know. I was nervous. In the moment, it was the first thing that came to me. I guess I thought that, as the wife of the indispensable engineer, they'd be less likely to make it difficult for me. You didn't say anything at the time. And anyway, what does it matter? Don't the Soviets advocate free love?" She winked.

"Huh? Well, the two of you can get divorced right now—we're still in America!" Walter added, and they all roared with laughter.

To celebrate their good fortune, they opened a bottle of soda they'd just bought and warmed a can of sausages over an improvised fire of posters and pamphlets. Jack was hypnotized by the scene. Walter and Sue were a model of happiness. He couldn't see himself, but he knew that if disillusionment had a face, it must be much like his.

"We won't need these anymore," Walter said, throwing another poster on the fire. "To the last paradise!" he toasted, raising the bottle.

"To the last paradise!" repeated Sue, waving her sausage.

After finishing his snack, Jack suggested making an inventory of their belongings, to compare it with the customs list provided by the Amtorg clerk, which cataloged the items that the trading company recommended taking, as well as those that would be confiscated by Soviet customs. The banned objects included everything from cameras, weapons, and musical instruments, to jewelry, toys of any kind, books in languages other than Russian, and medicine not prescribed by Soviet doctors. Walter noted with irony that the jewelry rule was unnecessary, for no wealthy capitalist would ever immigrate to the Soviet Union, while Jack wondered what would happen to a sick person with no knowledge of Russian who needed urgent treatment and did not have "Soviet" medicine.

As for the recommendations, the list advised immigrants, in addition to the relevant visa, to pack canned food, cookies, dry confectionery, nuts, warm clothing, winter footwear, fur hats, and tobacco. The Amtorg official who gave them the list also informed them that their US dollars would be exchanged for Soviet rubles at the border, which was of little concern to Jack, given that his cash reserves totaled little more than nothing.

"I don't know what we're going to do. Where will we get the money for our travel costs?" Sue slumped on the floor, suddenly deflated. Her pout reminded Jack of a little girl whose doll had just been stolen.

"Oh, come on, Sue! There's plenty of stuff we can sell here," Walter reassured her as he rummaged through his belongings. "Let's see. A nickel silver cigarette case, a wristwatch . . . Look! My Emerson wireless! We also have an old Underwood typewriter that works, I think, the pen you gave me when we got engaged, and my old bicycle. At home, there's some furniture in good condition, and you have the vacuum cleaner that you bought when you worked at the diner. And you, Jack?"

"Same as you. Trash," he muttered.

"You're kidding me, right?" Walter turned on his friend as if he'd been shoved. "Just the wireless cost seventy-five dollars! All right, it doesn't work, but I bet you it just needs new valves. And the fucking bike cost seven dollars." He gave Jack a kick. "She paid twenty for the vacuum cleaner. If you add everything together . . ."

"Don't waste your time, Walter. I've tried selling junk like this before, and I know what I'm talking about. Take my phonograph. When I went to sell it, they laughed in my face. We won't get ten dollars for this heap of scrap. The only thing that has any value is the Studebaker, and it's not ours."

"Then let's sell it!" Sue blurted out.

"What?" Walter couldn't believe what she was saying.

"You always said your neighbor was an exploitative capitalist, didn't you? So let's sell his car. I bet he just buys another."

"For pity's sake! You can't just put up an advertisement for a stolen car and sell it to the first sap that walks by," Walter sputtered. "But it isn't a bad idea. Shit! Maybe it ain't! Let me think . . . Hang on a minute! Jack, you worked at a repair shop, didn't you?"

"That's right, but I don't see what—"

"So you must know the right people: mechanics, taxi drivers, traveling salesmen . . . Maybe one of them will take it off our hands."

"And have the cops on our backs? Are you crazy?"

In the absence of alternatives, Jack suggested they put aside financial matters and concentrate on organizing the journey. Walter and Sue agreed.

When they came out of the Amtorg offices, Walter had called an old contact to make sure that Jack's fake passport would be ready that night. To avoid unnecessary risks, they decided that Jack would stay hidden at the printer's while Walter picked up the passport and returned the Studebaker. Then he would drop by his lodgings to collect his warm clothes, spend the night there, and head back to Amtorg early in the morning to have their visas stamped. Sue, who had handed her key back to her landlady, would stay at the printer's to help Jack with the luggage. In the morning, the two of them would go to the docks, where they would buy as many supplies as they could afford. Finally, Walter would meet them at the port to exchange their Intourist vouchers for tickets.

Having split up the tasks, Walter located the Linotype he would use to print a false marriage certificate, to which Jack thought he could give an air of authenticity if he stamped it with the Hebrew characters from the medallion that hung from his neck.

"It was my mother's," he said in a low voice, squeezing it between his fingers. "I don't know what it means, but we'll tell the Russians it's a rabbi's seal."

Shortly after sundown, Walter cranked the Studebaker and lowered the window.

"You behave now," he joked to Sue before putting the car in reverse. "And you," he said to Jack, "take care of her. I'll see you both tomorrow at the docks."

Jack sighed with relief as the beat-up automobile clattered into the distance. His friend had done a good job, and the marriage certificate that traveled with him in the glove compartment looked as genuine as the old pay stubs that he had given Walter as proof of his time at the Ford Motor Company. He closed the shutter and got back to work.

As he organized the rest of his documents, Sue packed their clothes and wondered how many supplies they'd be able to buy with the thirty dollars they'd designated for food. However, as time went by and Jack said nothing, she set the suitcases aside and began painting her nails, humming a tune. Then she walked up to Jack and placed her hands between his face and the papers he was working on.

"What do you think?" She showed him her fingers tipped in bright red as if they were jewels. Though they were a handbreadth from his nose, Jack merely glanced at them.

"I preferred the sausages," he mumbled.

"Oh!" Sue snatched her hands away, embarrassed, as if she'd just discovered they weren't pretty. "What're you doing?" she asked, trying to change the subject. She gave Jack a mock smile.

"I'm doing my accounts," he said with sarcasm, and pushed the papers aside.

"Well, I've finished packing." She stood and swiveled around in an improvised dance move, during which her smile regained its splendor. "Oh, Jack! Russia! This is all so exciting; I don't know how I'm going to sleep! On the subject of sleeping, what're we going to do?"

Jack continued to stare impassively at the table.

"I don't know about you, but I reckon I'll close my eyes and wait for dawn."

Sue's joy froze over.

"Why are you being so sharp? I'm only trying to be friendly."

"I'm sorry. I'm just not in the mood for conversation." He tensed up. "Going to Russia might be your dream, but it sure ain't mine, so don't expect me to get excited by the idea of rotting in a country where, no matter what I do, I'll always be a nobody without a dime to my name."

"Oh!" Sue's expression hardened. "And what exactly are you in America, if you don't mind my asking? A world-famous down-and-out?"

Jack looked at Sue as if she'd just slapped him.

"I said I'm sorry," was all he could say in response.

"I don't get you, Jack. There's no future here. You were lucky and made some real money at Ford, but that time's over. This awful depression's never going to end. You should forget what you were and make do like the rest of us, rather than blind yourself with vain pretensions."

Jack turned away to shut her out. He'd have liked to have told her just what he thought, but he had enough to worry about, without having to justify himself to some obnoxious brat who would never understand. What did *she* know about life? Who was Sue to tell him to forget about the good fortune he once had? Perhaps moving to another country was the solution to all of her problems because her only aspiration was to marry Walter and produce children. But if that was so, then it was Sue's ambition, not his. And anyway, his success at Ford had nothing to do with luck. No. The comfortable life he'd lived in Detroit was the kind of existence he had striven to achieve for as long as he could remember. He had worked like a dog for that life; he had turned his back on his family for it; he had sweated and suffered for it. All to create a future for himself that was cruelly and unjustly snatched from him.

He finished spreading the blankets over the chairs and stopped to examine himself.

He, who had once worn cologne, now had to put up with the stench that his body gave off because he did not even own a bar of soap with which to wash. He yearned to wear tailored suits again, and not the rags that covered his body, and he longed to taste a tender steak, even if just once more, at a restaurant with linen tablecloths. And Sue reproached him for it? Why? What right did anyone have to fault him for dreaming that he might one day get back the little luxuries for which he'd fought so hard? Nobody had just handed them to him then, and no one would do so now. *Delusions of grandeur* . . . Maybe his dreams seemed frivolous compared to Sue's, but was it so awful to want a good job again? To feel wanted and admired? What was so bad about that?

The wail of a siren in the distance pulled him from his thoughts. Jack ran to the shutter to look through the cracks, fearing it was a police car, but beyond the light from the nearby streetlamps, all he could see was darkness. As he pressed his eyelids against the shutter, the sound gradually faded. Turning around, he found Sue in front of him.

"Something worrying you?" she asked him.

"No. Just looking."

"It's not unusual to be woken by sirens in this neighborhood. There're more backroom distilleries here than there are jobless folk." She paused. "We should rest. We have a long day tomorrow."

Jack nodded. There weren't many places to choose from, so he curled up in a corner and covered himself with his raincoat. From there, he saw Sue take the candle and head to the row of chairs that he'd put out for her. Then she blew it out, and the darkness swallowed her.

Jack tried to sleep, but the night's silence bellowed in his ears. He thought of his father. He remembered him when his hair was still dark; when he was still sober and enjoyed telling stories about the far-off country of his birth; when he hugged Jack as a boy and made toys for him from shoe scraps, or when they went together to synagogue. Deep sorrow washed over him as he reflected on his failure to help Solomon. When the memory faded away, he turned his thoughts to Walter and Sue. He was unsure why he found it so difficult to feel grateful toward them. After all, they were the only friends he had left. The only ones who'd helped him. They might not share his dreams, but theirs were pure and simple, whereas his were selfish. And though he knew it was wrong, he could not help envying his uncle, Gabriel Beilis, the only person who seemed immune to the Depression. He imagined him smoking a Havana cigar and laughing at the world from his Rockefeller Center office. Jack hated him for it, and hated that his uncle would never suffer hardship the way he and his father had. That was when he swore to himself that from that moment on, he would do everything within his power to pull himself up from the gutter.

5

Maybe it hadn't been such a good idea.

From the first light of morning, the North River docks had been abuzz with sailors and stevedores emptying the bellies of gigantic cargo ships. The yelling of foremen haranguing their workers intermingled with the cries of fish auctioneers, the sirens of the steamships leaving port, and the high-pitched squawks of seagulls as ravenous for food as the unemployed men who milled around the warehouses looking for work.

And where there were jobless, there were always cops.

Jack scanned his surroundings but didn't spot any police. He helped Sue drag their luggage through the crowd, negotiating goods and passengers, and they filled their lungs with the intense salt air. He had improved his appearance by carefully shaving, and had used a touch of blusher that Sue had insisted on spreading over his cheeks, aware that they needed to look healthy in order to get past the tuberculosis checks. Even so, Jack, whose main concern was to go unnoticed, walked bent over to disguise his height and hide his features.

When they reached the wharf from which the American Scantic Line ships operated, Jack had to raise his voice to make himself heard over the cranes' incessant screeching.

"Right. This is where we agreed to meet Walter," he yelled, leaning their bags against the wall of a hut. "You should wait here while I buy the supplies we need." He looked at his fistful of grubby bills and searched around for a marketplace. "Watch out for pickpockets. This place is swarming with them!"

Sue gave Jack a defiant look.

"Trust me, I ain't gonna let some rat ruin the best day of my life," she replied, and she sat on the suitcases, adopting one of the most determined poses that Jack had ever seen.

He left behind the crowds that had gathered at the entrance to the offices of the shipping company that ran the New York–Copenhagen–Helsinki route, and made for a vast warehouse where a sign over the door announced that it sold the finest salt fish in the city. As he walked in, the smell of sea and salt guided him to the stall of a fishmonger who was shouting himself hoarse, extolling the virtues of his herring. Yet, instead of succumbing to the man's crowing, Jack stood motionless, his eyes fixed on the elegant young woman wearing a hat who was examining goods at a nearby grocery stall.

It had been a long time since he'd seen such a distinguished lady; the young woman looked straight out of one of the lounges of the Waldorf Astoria. Hypnotized, he slowly approached the stall and saw that the woman, dressed in an elegant fur coat, was inspecting a can of Petrossian beluga caviar. Jack observed the young woman's gloved fingers caressing the overpriced cans as if they were jewels. With no premeditation, he positioned himself beside her and picked up a yellow can from the counter.

"Don't be fooled. You'd do better to buy this Avruga. They make it near here, in Delaware. It's cheaper and tastes delicious," he advised her, surprised at his own gall.

The young woman looked him up and down.

"Are you a fishmonger?" she asked with a scowl.

Jack blushed. For a moment he'd imagined himself in Detroit, flirting with a secretary he could dazzle with little more than the sound of his convertible.

"No. I'm afraid not, but everyone knows that Delaware caviar is just as good as the—"

"On the contrary, young man: what everyone knows is that the sturgeon in the Delaware River all but died out twenty years ago, and since then they've sold substitutes. I'll take six cans," the young lady said to the stallholder. "Of the Petrossian," she added.

Jack gazed at her as she walked off, spellbound by the surreal image of a siren among dockworkers. Then he looked at the exorbitantly priced cans of Petrossian caviar and compared it to the cheap substitute he had recommended. He figured there was as much difference between those two cans as there was between the women whom he had until then pursued and the elegant young lady who had just walked away.

When Jack, bearing a supply of kippers, arrived back at the spot where he'd left Sue, he found her with her arms around Walter, smothering him with kisses like a teenager with her first summer love. He fended off a stab of jealousy as his friend greeted him, waving the tickets that would get them out of the United States. Jack examined his ticket and saw that the reverse side showed the name and a photograph of the ship SS *Cliffwood*, along with its astronomical price of $180. He could not help gawking when he considered that the sum was the same as a year's rent on the apartment from which he'd just been evicted.

"Here. Your passport."

Jack looked over the forged document that Walter handed him. Jack ran his fingers over the imitation-leather cardboard. The material seemed genuine, but the official stamp that validated the photograph wouldn't fool a child.

"The guy who made it assured me they'd only pay attention to the Amtorg recommendation in the Soviet Union," Walter said, seeing Jack's skeptical expression.

"I'm relieved to hear it." Jack clenched his teeth. "And I guess that guy will be sitting comfortably on his sofa when I have to explain to the Russians why I'm trying to enter their country with a passport that looks like it was won in a raffle."

"Oh, come on, Jack. Give me those kippers to carry, and stop being such a wet blanket. I promise you, compared to the trouble you have here, any problems you encounter in Russia will seem like a blessing." With a smug expression, he pushed Jack toward the SS *Cliffwood*'s gangway.

While they waited to embark, Jack looked doubtfully at the dilapidated hull of the ocean liner and sighed. Despite its impressive size, the only thing about the ship that resembled the photograph on the back of the ticket was the black paint that covered it. None of the passengers in front of them seemed to notice the ship's imperfections. On the contrary, the emaciated workers wearing donated suits chatted excitedly, their smiles disguising the scars that hunger and desperation had left on their faces.

At twelve o'clock sharp, the sailor guarding the entrance unknotted the rope that cordoned off the gangway and blew his whistle, prompting the impatient line of passengers, with their trunks, bundles, and cases of belongings, to start moving like a caravan of peddlers. Jack, Walter, and Sue got ready. The line climbed toward the deck at a sluggish pace until, when Walter was just a few yards from showing his ticket to the ticket collector, some yelling made him stop unexpectedly.

"What's happening?" asked Jack. He looked ahead but couldn't see anything unusual.

Walter, who as a precaution had positioned himself a couple of places ahead in the line, could see that there had been an altercation.

He turned to Jack to warn him that a police officer was present and had begun to request passports.

"They're saying they caught someone trying to stow away. If we try to board now, we'll be arrested," Walter whispered. His eyes were bright with fear. Jack saw more cops arriving, and he placed his hands on his friend's shoulders to calm him down.

"It's too dangerous. If we leave the line now, we'll arouse suspicion. We have to carry on."

"What about your passport? Shit! It might pass as genuine in Russia, but we'll get busted for it here."

"Pass me the kippers and let me take care of it. Sue, you go with Walter."

Walter sputtered something but obeyed. Jack took his friend's place in the line and whispered something into Sue's ear. Then he slung the kippers over his shoulder, gripped the passport between his teeth, and with a determined stride, pulled on the trunk that contained his belongings.

"Come on! Keep moving!" yelled the policeman checking documents.

Jack strode up to him, and after laying the trunk on the floor, he took out his ticket with his free hand. When he held it out, the uniformed cop fixed his eyes on Jack's and narrowed them.

"Your passport," he demanded.

"Huh? Oh, sure, my passport . . . ," Jack stammered through his teeth, keeping the document in his mouth.

At that moment, Sue stumbled into Jack, making him drop the kippers, which fell onto the ground along with the passport.

"Oh shit! I'm sorry, officer," said Jack as he knelt to pick up the fish and the passport. "Excuse my wife. It's the first time she's been on a ship, and she's nervous. Here you go." He handed the policeman the document opened to the page with his photograph. The cop took it from him and studied Jack, showing little sympathy. Jack felt his heart thump in his chest. He disguised his nerves as he knelt to finish picking up the kippers. The cop frowned.

"Nice way to ruin a new passport," the officer finally said, brushing off some fish remnants that had stuck to the fake stamp. "Your wife should be more careful if she wants to stay married. Here you go. Now move on, please."

Once on board, Jack finished cleaning off the kipper he had pressed against the stamp when he'd bent down to pick it up from the ground.

"You dirty crook! You did it on purpose?" Walter exclaimed. "The stumble . . . the kippers . . ."

"And I was his accomplice," boasted Sue, taking Jack's arm. "Clearly, Walter, this young man's worth his weight in gold. You should take note."

Walter's smile froze on his lips.

"Oh I should, should I?" He dragged the luggage to the place where the rest of the passengers were congregating.

An impeccably uniformed American Scantic Line officer led the group to its quarters belowdecks. On the way, the officer informed them that the SS *Cliffwood* had been used as a freighter by the navy during the Great War, and that, after the armistice, it was acquired by the Moore & McCormack shipping company, which fitted it out as a combined cargo and passenger ship. That was why it had only a limited number of individual cabins, reserved for the most well-to-do passengers, and a communal sleeping area for the second-class passengers.

"Your attention, please," said the officer. "As you know, weather permitting, we will arrive in Helsinki in five days. During the crossing, you will be able to go on deck whenever you wish. Up top, near the bridge, you will find a small canteen selling cigarettes, food, and beverages. The latrines are at the rear of the hold."

"Compared to the *Aquitania*, this rust bucket's what a donkey is to a mustang," said a passenger, spitting on the floor.

"I heard you, sir," said the officer, unruffled. "This ship may not be a luxurious ocean liner like the one you mention, but neither do the jockeys that ride Thoroughbred racehorses resemble the rustlers who ride donkeys." He tipped his hat by way of a good-bye and turned to return to the deck. "Access to the hold is strictly forbidden. Anyone found contravening this order will be punished."

At two o'clock in the afternoon, gripping the handrail on deck, Jack listened to the whistle that announced the departure of the SS *Cliffwood*. He looked around at the other passengers as they waved good-bye to the friends and relatives who'd come to see them off. Some cried; others gazed vacantly at the huge buildings they might never see again. Jack contemplated them, too, while the cold East River wind stung his eyes. As the ship left the wharf, Jack remembered what Walter had given as his reason for staying belowdecks. *Sue and I are staying down here to watch the luggage, Jack. You should do the same. Stay on guard and keep your most valuable things with you if you don't want them to be stolen.* And that was what he'd done: gone up on deck to imprint in his mind the image of New York and keep it with him so that nobody could ever steal it.

6

The third day of the crossing was the worst.

Shortly after the ship weighed anchor, Jack had begun to feel unwell, but he stayed on deck long enough to flush out the memories that tormented him. But the constant heave of the rough sea, foreshadowing the imminent storm, had made the passengers seek refuge on the mattresses of their bunk beds. Sue and Walter passed the time in the communal dormitory, fantasizing endlessly about their future lives. She imagined herself in her little Soviet house with a garden and swings for their little ones, while Walter saw himself as a future representative of the American workers. However, his friends' dreams excited Jack about as much as watching paint dry. In Russia, there would be no luxury cars to own, no elegant suits to wear, no jazz clubs in which to have a good time. With luck, his greatest achievement would be having the opportunity to work like hell for a miserable salary for the rest of his days. He took a deep breath and rolled over on his bed. The ship's constant heaving was making him queasy. Finally, he got up to wander around the dormitory and stretch his legs.

As he strolled, he noticed that one of the portholes that looked into the hold had been left ajar, so he approached it to get a better view. He was trying to make out what was inside the containers stacked on the other side of the bulkhead, when an arm pulled him unceremoniously away from the window.

"May I ask what you are looking at?"

Jack gave a start when he found himself face-to-face with an angry, white-bearded man. He was one of the Russian workers who appeared every now and then to go down into the hold to check on the cargo.

"Oh, I was just being nosy," Jack explained.

"Yes . . . well, in Soviet Union, we don't like nosy people," the man said with a strong Russian accent.

Jack guessed that the furrowed face in front of him did not belong to a simple workman. He didn't want any trouble, but neither would he let some stranger bully him.

"As far as I'm aware, this ship doesn't belong to the Soviet Union."

"Maybe ship, no, but cars in hold, yes." The Russian's voice sounded authoritative.

Jack tensed his muscles. He was about to respond, when Walter came up behind him and pulled him back toward the bunks. As he retreated, the white-haired Russian challenged Jack with his eyes.

"They're all yours!" Jack muttered under his breath as he let Walter drag him away. "Frankly, I'm about as interested in those crates as I am in your sister!"

The man ignored Jack's taunt. He simply closed the porthole, checked that the door to the hold was locked, and returned to the deck. When he had gone, Walter stood in front of Jack.

"Have you lost your mind? Do you want to make us enemies of the Russians before we've set foot on Soviet soil?"

"Did you see what that guy did to me? I was just looking, and he pulled me away like I was a dog pissing on his boots."

"Then put up with it, for Christ's sake! After everything we've been through, I'm not going to let you get us sent straight back to America because of your pride."

"Those crates were from Ford."

"Huh?"

"I'm telling you, those massive containers were from the Ford Motor Company. It was printed on them in red ink: 'Ford Motor Company. Dearborn, Michigan, USA.'"

"So what? What does it matter if they were from Ford or General Motors? Some American engineer probably ordered a couple of cars to take his girl for a ride."

"That's what that Soviet operative wanted me to believe, but those crates don't contain cars. I worked at Ford for nine years, and I promise you that no car from that company is as big as a bus."

"Then whoever's bought them must have a lot of girls, and needs a bus to take them out. What does it matter?"

Suddenly, a large wave hit the side of the ship, making it lean. Jack managed to grab a bunk bed to keep his balance, but Walter rolled off along the floor. An alarm on deck announced the storm's arrival.

Jack helped Walter get back to his bunk. Gradually, the persistent pitching of the SS *Cliffwood* grew more severe until it became an eruption of creaks, lurches, and shudders. Before long, luggage was scattered across the floor, its owners able to do little more than scramble after it and cry out in fear. Jack realized how dangerous the situation was when one of the passengers lost his balance and hit his head against a pillar. The people around him screamed. He quickly took off his belt and used it to secure Sue to her bunk. Walter copied him and did the same with his own belt. Jack, meanwhile, gripped the bars, trusting in the strength of his muscles, while the storm battered the ship mercilessly.

Amid the chaos, passengers called out for help to the crew members who had come down from the deck to secure the cargo in the hold. But before they could do anything, a violent wave made the ship's bow rear up, and after a few eternal seconds suspended in the void, the liner smacked down against the surface of the ocean with a great crash.

Jack lost his grip and was thrown from the bunk, stumbling forward until he crashed against the door to the hold. When he managed to sit up, he saw how the ship's lurches were tossing passengers and luggage around like rag dolls. A trickle of blood from a cut over his eyebrow blinded him. He wiped his eyes as well as he could and looked around, searching for a way to get back to his friends, when he heard a piercing scream behind him. He turned around. It was coming from the hold. Through the porthole, he could make out a crowd of men trying desperately to move an upturned container. Someone appeared to be hurt. Another scream made his blood run cold. Without a thought, he opened the door and went in, finding himself in front of a group of Russian workers frantically trying to pull away the remains of the container and extract the screaming man, who, he now saw, was trapped under a huge machine. Jack recognized the contraption as a Cleveland press, a steel monster that must have weighed more than thirty tons. Through the mass of workmen, he saw that the machine had crushed the man's left arm, so that in order to free him, it had to be lifted. But in the manner they were attempting it, they would never pull it off him.

He was trying to think of a solution, when he heard the Soviet he had argued with moments before suggesting they amputate the man's arm.

"If we do not, he will die," he said in his heavily accented English.

The trapped man shook his head and screamed at them to keep trying to lift the machine. The workers obeyed, but another big wave hit the ship, pushing the machine onto the man's elbow. He bellowed as if he'd been split in half. The workers froze, but one bent down to pick up a rusty saw. Seeing this, the injured man found his voice and yelled like a lunatic.

"If anyone so much as tickles a muscle, I swear I'll kill him," he said in perfect English.

The workmen looked at one another, hesitating, but the one with the saw approached the man.

"Wait!" Jack broke in. "I think I know how to get him out!"

They all stood motionless, except for the white-haired Soviet.

"Busybody American! Get out of hold, right now!" He shoved Jack violently back.

"I'm telling you, I know how to move the machine! I know the Cleveland like it was my own child!" he countered.

The Soviet made as if to strike Jack, but the trapped man's commanding voice stopped him. "Damn it, Sergei! Let him approach," he bellowed.

The white-bearded Soviet mumbled something in Russian before stepping aside, and Jack was able to kneel by the injured man. He didn't seem Slavic. His features, dripping with sweat, were a picture of despair. Jack guessed he was well into his fifties.

"You really think you can free me?" the man asked.

"I believe so, sir." Jack assessed the position of the trapped man in relation to the position of the machine. "I'll need a couple of hex keys and a hammer."

"Yeah? OK, kid. I hope you know what you're doing. Didn't you hear him?" he screamed. "Give him what he wants! Quickly!"

Once Jack had the tools in his hands, he set about the machine with feline agility. He began unscrewing some thick bolts, removed a cam, and gained access to a hatch, through which he inserted another hex key. He worked as quickly as possible, but the hold's constant jolting in the storm made progress difficult.

"Shit!" complained Jack when one of the keys escaped his grasp. "I need someone to help me. You! Come here!" he called to the Soviet workers surrounding him, but they merely looked at him in a daze. Jack repeated his request, but nobody responded. "You damned morons!" he bellowed in Russian. "Don't just stand there watching. Give me a hand!"

Hearing the order in their own language, the workers gave a start, and, ignoring the creaking bulkheads, they rushed to help Jack. He grabbed the hex key again and continued barking out instructions in Russian to the astonishment of the trapped man, who watched their attempt to save him through a face disfigured by pain. A final screw popped out, and the machine divided into two blocks, as if it had been decapitated.

Jack took a deep breath before turning to the workmen.

"Now! All together!" he ordered.

At his command, the workers grabbed hold of the section that still crushed the man's arm, tensed their muscles, and, with a Herculean effort, tried to lift it. But the machine didn't budge. Jack kept trying until he felt faint.

"It's useless!" Sergei complained. "We couldn't lift it with a hoist. Vasil, fetch the saw."

Jack looked at the injured man as he tried to get his breath back. He felt for him. He was starting to walk away so that he wouldn't have to witness the butchery, when suddenly he stopped.

"Wait! How many cars like this are there in the hold?" Jack pointed at a black automobile lashed to a bulkhead.

"Twelve," the injured man said in a tiny voice.

"That'll do," said Jack, and he dashed off toward the vehicles. A few moments later, he ran back, carrying six car jacks. "Quickly! Get them under. Find firm resting points. There," he said, pointing, "and under that plate, there."

A group of workers positioned the devices as instructed, and on Jack's command, they began to operate them simultaneously, while the rest of the men kept the machine from tipping over. Jack told the men to get ready. He warned them that they would have only a couple of seconds to get the injured man out before the machine came straight down again.

"Now!" he yelled.

As one, the workers pulled the man out from under the machine, just before another wave made the machine lose its support and smash to the ground.

When Jack had recovered his breath, he rubbed his bruised hands, then turned to see what state the man he had just saved was in. He couldn't: the medic had already taken him away.

7

At breakfast, the conversation among the passengers revolved around the damage caused by the storm, and Jack's heroics. While some were amazed at the willowy young man who, it was rumored, had lifted up a steel machine using only his bare hands, others wondered what kind of person spoke perfect Russian and was able to dismantle such a complex industrial contraption. A few branded him a fool for having entered the hold despite the explicit orders not to do so.

Walter chatted merrily with the passengers, offering details on what had happened as if he had been involved himself, celebrating the feat as he shared the bottles of vodka that a Soviet officer had given them as a reward for Jack's help. When Walter didn't know what else to add to the story, he stashed the cigarettes he'd sweet-talked from his audience, finished off the bottle, commandeered another bottle that was half full, and returned to where Jack was savoring the second of the cookies that constituted his breakfast. He took out a cigarette and offered it to his friend. Then he waited for Jack to have his first puff before asking him who the injured man had been.

"I have no idea," he insisted as he enjoyed the feel of the warm smoke. "But he was American. Of that I'm sure."

Hearing this, Walter let out his frustration with a kick to his bunk. For a moment he had thought the man Jack had saved might have been an important Russian official who could reward them with some kind of plum position.

"American . . . ," he grumbled, and he took a long swig. "Well, those chumps took the bait." He showed Jack the handful of cigarettes he'd coaxed from the group of passengers. "Can you imagine the headlines we could've got in *Pravda*, Jack?" He traced an arch over his head with both hands: "'American immigrant saves Soviet dignitary.' Now *that* would have been a good way to make our entry into the Soviet Union!"

"Truthfully, I'm more worried about arriving with a pair of healthy hands," Jack said, rubbing his bruises. Then he looked at Walter and saw just how intoxicated his friend had become, his halfway-closed eyelids barely concealing his glazed eyes. "And you'd do well to go easy on the vodka. You're swaying more than you were yesterday in the storm."

"It must be someone important, or those Russians wouldn't have gone out of their way to help him," Walter insisted.

Jack was surprised by the comment. After all, if the Russians were as egalitarian as Walter proclaimed, they would have made the same effort to save the man had he been a lowly peasant.

Noticing Jack's expression, Walter tried to defend his words. "Of course, all I mean is, he must be an influential figure, that guy. Not necessarily a rich man, but a journalist who sympathizes with the regime, or maybe an important American Communist. We should make the most of this." He took another swig of vodka and gave Jack a slap on the back.

Jack raised an eyebrow. He didn't know whether the man he'd saved was really someone important. But even if he was, Jack was wary enough of these people to know that it was best to keep his distance.

He was about to sip his coffee, when Sue appeared. She'd been up on deck for some fresh air. Walter offered her the bottle, but she refused.

She sat between the two of them and put her arms around them to bring them closer.

"You won't believe this."

"Believe what?" answered Jack and Walter, almost in unison.

"The man you saved, Jack. I've found out who he is," she boasted with an anxious smile.

"He's Russian, right?" Walter put in.

"No! Much better than that. He's Wilbur Hewitt, the general manager of the factory we're going to!"

"Are you sure? It can't be!" A nervous smile spread across Jack's face.

"Hear that, Jack? I told you. We've struck gold! You saved our future boss's ass." Walter's little eyes were bright under his spectacles, as if he'd just unwrapped his birthday present.

"But that's not all," Sue announced.

"It's not? What else is there? Come on, out with it!" Jack pressed her.

Sue paused for dramatic effect, aware she had the full attention of the two young men.

"All right." She looked at Walter, and then Jack. "Are you ready? Mr. Hewitt has invited Jack to join him for lunch on the bridge today!"

"What do you mean?" Jack thought she was joking.

"Ha! Didn't you hear her?" Walter stood and attempted a series of ridiculous dance steps as he tried to drink from the empty bottle. "This is incredible news, Jack! You have to win him over! Tell him about us. We have to make the most of this." He slapped Jack on the back again. "No. Even better: ask him for a reward for saving him! One for you, and one for us for bringing you here!"

Jack burst into laughter at Walter's outlandish behavior. He was clearly drunk. When he'd managed to control his emotions, Jack asked Sue how she'd found out about it. The young woman explained that she'd overheard a white-bearded Soviet talking to the ship's captain. Apparently, he wasn't just an ordinary worker—he was some kind of official that the Soviets had assigned to Mr. Hewitt to escort him during his stay in Russia.

"I heard them call him Sergei Loban," said Sue.

Jack listened to Sue's story with the enthusiasm of a boy reading *The Adventures of Tom Sawyer*. After a few seconds, he took a sip of his coffee to make sure he wasn't dreaming.

"Well," he replied, "in that case, I guess we should celebrate. Coffee?" He offered his cup to Sue. However, unexpectedly, Walter stopped him.

"Sue doesn't drink coffee. You should . . ." He barely had control of his tongue. "You should know by now that Sue doesn't like coffee. Ain't that right, *honey*?" His voice had turned from cheerful to bitter.

Jack was shocked at Walter's outburst, but he kept silent.

"And you should know that I don't like other people deciding for me," Sue said reproachfully to her fiancé before accepting Jack's cup. Walter was wide-eyed with disbelief in spite of his drunkenness.

"Ha! But you do what *Jack* tells you to do, huh? Why doesn't that surprise me? Oh, of course! Because Jack's having lunch with the big shots! Eh, Jack? You'll be someone important soon," he mocked. His glazed eyes seemed to have difficulty focusing. He turned toward Sue and looked at the coffee that the young woman was about to drink. "Leave that, honey. If you want coffee, I'll make you one," he sputtered, and he tried to snatch the cup from her, so clumsily that the coffee spilled all over her beautiful orange scarf.

Sue was silent for a moment. Then, red with rage, she smashed the cup against the floor, and, cursing Walter, she left the dormitory in the direction of the deck.

Jack watched the scene without knowing what to say, unsettled by Walter's possible misinterpretation of what had merely been a friendly gesture toward Sue.

"I'm sorry, Walter, I didn't mean to—"

"Really?" he shot back. "If you really were sorry, you wouldn't flirt with my girl at every opportunity," he blurted out, holding on to the bunk bed to stop himself from falling over.

"You're kidding me, right? Anyone can see I was just trying to be friendly." Jack couldn't believe what he was hearing.

"Then be friendly to your bunkmate, or dance with the captain, or go feed the dolphins . . . but stop horning in on *our* life." He looked at Jack as if he were speaking to a stranger. "Do you think I haven't noticed? Always playing the big man . . . And why the hell did you say you two were married, huh?" He kicked the coffee cup. "Shit! I don't even know why I helped you."

Jack looked at his friend. It was obvious that he'd drunk far more than he should, but that didn't excuse his nasty tirade. He tried to make Walter take a step back, but he managed only to infuriate him even more.

"Save your smooth talking for some other woman!" Walter bellowed. "We're not at school anymore, and Sue isn't one of those teenage girls you stole from me."

"Walter, please. Everyone's staring at you."

"Oh, I see! Well, when you hit me in that coffee shop, you didn't mind me being stared at. Don't like it when you're not the center of attention, do you?" he jabbered.

Jack knew it was just the vodka talking, so he decided to put an end to the conversation and get away from there. But when he went to walk off, Walter stopped him, grabbing him by the arm.

"Let go of me!" Jack growled, shaking Walter off. "Have you looked at Sue? You must be deluded if you think she's the kind of woman I'd lose my head over!"

As he said the words, Jack realized how cruel his response had been. He considered apologizing, but pride gripped him. Instead, he looked down in silence, sat on the bunk bed, and sank his head into his hands. When he looked up again, he found Sue, watching the scene from the stairs, tears in her eyes. He felt like a tyrant. It had been a reaction to being provoked, but neither Walter nor Sue had deserved his harsh words.

At five minutes before noon, Jack looked at himself in the mirror one last time. For a fleeting moment, he saw himself as the attractive young man who'd conquered Dearborn. He adjusted his jacket, checked his shave, and put on the felt hat that Harry Daniels, his bunkmate, had lent him. To his mind, his getup was the mark of someone respectable enough to at least not be branded a pauper. He made a final correction to his tie, checked the time, and contemplated his companions' empty bunks. He regretted they weren't there; he'd have liked to have shared the moment with them, but it had been a while since they'd disappeared. Finally, he picked up the invitation that a crew member had delivered to him, took a deep breath, and headed up to the deck. He had no idea what his meeting with Wilbur Hewitt held in store, but he was determined to make the most of any opportunity that presented itself.

On the bridge, he found Sergei Loban, wearing a green dress coat with red epaulets, his expression that of a dog ready to defend its bone. The Soviet official grunted something like a *good afternoon* in English, and without saying another word, led him to the adjoining room where lunch was to be served. Once inside, Jack saw that it was an old cabin that had been beautifully and painstakingly refurbished. The damask-lined walls complemented the beige upholstery of the chairs, and the table, covered in an ostentatious ivory lace tablecloth, was set for six with porcelain crockery and an army of forks, spoons, and knives. Jack was surprised to find the dining room empty, but he gave nothing away to Sergei. Instead, he stood and waited with the Soviet until, a few minutes later, the ship's captain and his boatswain appeared, impeccably uniformed, along with a stranger in a brown suit and a red bow tie almost as striking as his bushy mustache. Finally, with his jacket unbuttoned and his left arm in a sling, Wilbur Hewitt, the man Jack had saved, made his entrance.

As he took his seat, Mr. Hewitt eyed Jack through his gold monocle, before erupting into an effusive display of gratitude.

"So this is the young man to whom I owe the honor of waking this morning attached to my left arm!" he bellowed. "Wipe that funereal look off your face and smile a little! If it weren't for you, those Russians would've turned me into an amputee."

Between grimaces of pain, Wilbur Hewitt made the introductions himself. Nicholas Raymeyer, the captain of the SS *Cliffwood*, with more than twenty years' service in the American Scantic Line, and his boatswain, Mr. Jones, congratulated Jack on his timely intervention. The man with the red bow tie turned out to be Louis Thomson, the renowned journalist of the *New York Times*, a newspaper of which Hewitt confessed to be a fervent reader. Of Sergei Loban, all he said was that, considering he was the liaison officer that the Soviet authorities had provided him, his English was terrible.

"Still, rough manners aside, I have to admit that he performs his duties with surprising efficiency. As for me"—he removed his monocle and pushed out his chest, inserting the thumb on his healthy hand under his armpit—"you've probably heard who I am by now. My name's Wilbur Hewitt, industrialist and graduate of the Massachusetts Institute of Technology, financier and head of operations for the launch of the Gorkovsky Avtomobilny Zavod, more commonly known simply as the Avtozavod, the greatest car manufacturing plant in the Soviet Union." Then he offered Jack a business card on which, under the letterhead, appeared the title "General Manager for Foreign Affairs of the Ford Motor Company, USA."

"Shall we sit?" the captain suggested.

His tone told Jack that the question was just that, a question, not a suggestion. From his chair, Wilbur Hewitt looked at the seat that remained unoccupied.

"Yes, yes. What're we to do? Let's start. As you can see," he addressed Jack again, "one word from me, and I can mobilize five thousand workers to screw bolts for ten hours, but when it comes to my beloved—"

At that moment, the sound of the dining room door opening interrupted his soliloquy.

"I'm sorry to be late," a voice said.

Instantly, the men who'd just sat down stood up. Wilbur Hewitt smiled from his chair, filled his glass, and raised it in a toast, giving a giant smile.

"Jack Beilis, I have the pleasure of introducing you to my pride and joy, my only niece, Elizabeth Hewitt."

Jack managed to stammer, "Pleased to meet you." Then, he waited for the others to sit, and without taking his eyes off her, he did the same. At the first opportunity, he took a sip of water to try to loosen the knot that gripped his throat. Discovering that the person for whom the all-powerful Wilbur Hewitt was waiting was his niece certainly came as a surprise, but what had really left him speechless was realizing that the young woman of intoxicating beauty who had just walked through the door was the same woman who'd captivated him at the salt-fish market.

Though the surprise was mutual, Elizabeth Hewitt seemed less pleased by their reunion than Jack. The young woman kept her composure just the same and took her seat next to the guest of honor. Jack, meanwhile, barely dared look at her, still embarrassed by his ridiculous performance at the market. He doubted she recognized him, and if she did, it was just a matter of time before she made a mockery of him. Fortunately, at that moment Wilbur Hewitt asked Jack about his skills, making him forget his fears.

"You might not believe it, but this young man is a diamond in the rough," Hewitt said about Jack. "Kid, I still don't know how you managed to dismantle the machine I was trapped under. You said you had mechanical expertise, but, by God, in twenty-five years of running factories, I've never seen anything like it!"

"Well, to be honest, it was a coincidence, sir. I knew that machine because we repaired a similar model in the workshop where I was employed." Jack lied about his past in Dearborn to prevent anyone from connecting him to the murder of his landlord.

"A coincidence? Don't be so modest, kid! That machine was the latest Cleveland model, a technological marvel, and I'm told you dismantled it like someone taking the chain off a bicycle. A guy winning the lottery without buying a ticket would've had less luck than me. What do you think, Elizabeth? Am I right or wrong when I say this kid's a diamond?"

His niece examined Jack with an air of self-satisfaction and smiled. "Uncle dear, I think the morphine they've plied you with is making you indulgent. Judging by his appearance, this workman's more rough than diamond." She smiled again.

They all laughed at her witty remark. But the tone in which she'd said the word *workman* cut Jack to the core. For him, working with one's hands was something nobody should be ashamed of. On the contrary, he was proud to have started out as an operative, just as he was proud to have worked harder than Wilbur Hewitt's niece could ever imagine. He considered answering back but decided to remain silent. Had it been a man, he would have made him blush with shame for saying those words, but as at the market, her mere presence perturbed him.

The lunch consisted of fresh sea bream dressed in lemon, French wine, and clams. Jack would have preferred a succulent Montana beef hamburger and a cold beer, but he appreciated the elegance of his surroundings and the delicacy of his meal all the same.

For all the shiny silver cutlery, fine crockery, and fragile glassware, what fascinated him the most was Wilbur Hewitt's niece. Observing her out of the corner of his eye, Jack admired her polite gestures, the exquisiteness with which she handled the cutlery despite the ship's lurching, and the elegance and distinction of her language. It was an elegance that contrasted with the riotous spontaneity of her uncle, who, though obviously an educated man, expressed himself as if he'd grown up among Brooklyn's longshoremen.

As he savored the delicious champagne sorbet that the waiters served between courses, Jack imagined himself enjoying the same luxurious life that Wilbur Hewitt led. He examined the executive: his gold monocle, his matching cuff links, his tiepin . . . His impeccable suit alone probably cost more than a year's salary at Jack's old job, and the pocket watch he wore on his vest probably double that. Despite his apparent familiarity, Jack got the impression that Hewitt was the kind of man who was not only in complete control of his own life, but also comfortable deciding the fate of others. And he admired that. He didn't mind admitting that he was attracted to luxurious watches, exotic delicacies, and tailored clothes. But what he really envied was something that only men like Hewitt possessed, and that he longed for with a passion: position. Because if there was one thing Jack had learned from the Depression, it was that, even if the world turned into a wasteland overnight, Hewitt's kind would never find themselves in Jack's position: jobless, up to his neck in debt, on the verge of begging for crumbs. That was why ordinary men envied people like Hewitt. For his unobtainable position. That was why they admired and respected him. Jack looked at Elizabeth and took a deep breath. It was also why he was prepared to overcome any obstacle that got in his way to win the respect of others.

He was still absorbed in his thoughts when Elizabeth Hewitt called the waiter over and said something into his ear. The waiter nodded with a severe expression and then disappeared, before returning a few minutes later with a tray of ice, upon which lay a plate of caviar.

"I couldn't resist." She gave her uncle a mischievous look, as if waiting for approval that she didn't really need. "I hope our guest likes beluga." She smiled.

Jack blushed. For a moment he thought Elizabeth was going to ridicule him by recounting the embarrassing episode at the fish market, but to his surprise, not only did she not do so, but she graciously served him a spoonful.

"Thank you," was all he managed to stammer.

He ate as he listened to a conversation on the marvelous deeds of the Soviet regime. Again, Wilbur Hewitt mentioned the Avtozavod, the gigantic factory that he was going to run and the difficulties that he would have to overcome. The latest inspections had revealed that the majority of the machinery being transported in the ship's hold had been rendered unusable, and Dearborn had informed him by radio message that no new supplies would arrive for up to three months.

"And then there are the disappointing production figures I've been shown, so you can see why I'm concerned. I'm not questioning the Soviets' organizational capacity"—he looked at Sergei as he spoke—"but we're talking automobiles here, and I get the feeling they need an American with the guts to get what looks like a school yard the size of Wisconsin in order," he crowed.

Sergei finished chewing a piece of fish he'd just put in his mouth.

"In our defense," said the official in his Slavic accent, "I should say that Soviet Union is a young, inexperienced country, but full of energy, and like all hotheaded young persons, its enthusiasm sometimes take it down tortuous roads." He wiped his mustache with his napkin. "We make mistakes, sure, but we can admit them, and then, fix them. Our hospitality and generosity for all who want to build future is great. But do not doubt it, Mr. Hewitt, I repeat, do not have any doubt whatsoever, that our leaders could not be more determined to ensure that Soviet people progress until inequality and poverty are wiped from face of earth."

Wilbur Hewitt was silent for a moment, as if pondering Sergei's prophetic words. Then he raised his glass.

"Well, I'll toast to that."

They all repeated Wilbur Hewitt's toast in unison, raising their glasses as one. Sergei smiled as if he approved of the industrialist's gesture, but Jack had a feeling that if hyenas could smile, they would undoubtedly look just like the Russian.

After dessert, the diners congratulated Jack, before leaving the room for their own cabins. Elizabeth, who was waiting with her uncle, held out her hand to Jack for less time than he would've liked, and she left with the same gracefulness that had captivated everyone when she came in. For a moment, Jack stood in a daze, unaware that Wilbur Hewitt was waiting to say good-bye to him. He only realized when he heard a little cough behind him. Jack, who had already put his hat on, took it off again.

"Mr. Hewitt." He cleared his throat. "I can't tell you how grateful I am for giving me the opportunity to share a table with you. It's been an unforgettable experience. I would—"

"Kid, save your soft-soaping for another time. If you get like this over lunch, I dread to think what you'd have done if I'd invited you to my house in the country."

"Pardon me, sir?"

"All I mean is, if there's anyone here who should be grateful, it's Wilbur Hewitt, the man who, thanks to you, can still get himself dressed in the morning. The man who still has his own two hands. Tell me something, kid: How did you do it? How in hell's name did you know what parts to dismantle to take apart a thirty-ton machine in five minutes? And where did you learn Russian?" Hewitt stood waiting for a reply from Jack, who was slow to answer.

"My parents were Russian. And I worked at a Buick supply workshop, sir," he ad-libbed.

"Buick? Look, kid. I know those turkeys well, and they wouldn't know a kingpin from a kingfisher. It's all right," he grouched, "if you don't want to tell me, don't. But I don't like owing favors to anyone." His hand went to his wallet, and he pulled out a hundred dollars. "Here."

Jack flinched, as if he'd been offered stolen money.

"I . . . I can't accept that, sir," he stammered.

"Don't be a fool, kid. If you don't think it's enough, you're an idiot, and if you think it's too much, well, I can assure you my arm's worth much more. Take it. It's not the first time I've traveled to the Soviet Union, and I can tell you without fear of being mistaken that you're going to need every last dollar you can find."

"I don't understand, sir."

"Oh, you will, son. You will . . ."

The five-thousand boiler horsepower generated by the SS *Cliffwood*'s mighty GE Curtis turbine snorted away, driving the vessel at a speed of ten knots through the icy waters of the North Sea on the final stretch of the crossing. Wrapped in his jacket, Jack strolled around the bow deck, enjoying the light drizzle that landed on his face. With each spatter, he imagined the water washing away the misery that had clung to him, making him a new man, clean and different. Because that was how he now felt. He could still taste the salty flavor of the caviar and the champagne's delicate sweetness. Remembering the lunch, Jack saw himself among the elite, accepted by all of them, speaking as an equal with those he envied, admired by them and receiving their praise. It was an intoxicating feeling, more so than anything he'd felt before, than anything he could have imagined.

His watch showed five o'clock in the afternoon and it was pitch-dark. He decided it was time to return to his friends and share his experience with them.

As soon as he entered the communal dormitory, the noxious smell given off by the dozens of scrawny men, women, and children tore Jack from his daydream. He was surprised, because he hadn't noticed it before. In fact, since their departure, he would have sworn that they were eating enough, that they traveled with dignity, and that their lives were moving toward a brighter future. But after experiencing the sumptuous luxury of the officers' dining room, after savoring the succulent delicacies and enjoying exquisite company, he could see the true face of his reality. A squalid existence, a world of poverty, hunger, and misery, a world of immigrants without hope. *That* was the world he belonged to.

He found Sue and Walter gnawing at some salt herring next to a porthole through which they looked out at the blackness of the sea. As soon as she noticed Jack, Sue turned away. But Walter stood to greet him and offered him a piece of fish.

"I . . . I don't know what to say, Jack," he admitted. "Anyway . . . I'm sorry for this morning. Really, I don't know what came over me. I'm not used to drinking like that, and from what Sue tells me, I behaved like a chump."

Jack was pleased to see Walter back to his usual self. He accepted the herring and sat down beside him.

"We all make mistakes. Me more than most." He looked at Sue to make sure she was listening. "You're a fantastic girl," he said apologetically. "I was angry, and I blew a gasket. Any man would be lucky to have you. I'm—"

"That's enough of the schmaltz!" Walter feigned a serious expression. "If there's one thing everyone in New York knows better than the Yankees' lineup, it's that my friend Jack Beilis is king of the chuckleheads." He gave Jack a wink and hugged him.

As they ate the fish, Jack gave his traveling companions a detailed account of his meeting with Wilbur Hewitt, immediately arousing the interest of Joe Brown and the Smith brothers. His fellow passengers' eyes were wide, eager for gossip, but Jack, who knew the hardship they suffered, avoided mentioning certain details of his lunch, such as the abundance of food and the high quality of the dinner service.

"So, this Hewitt really is the big boss?" asked Walter at the first pause.

"So it seems."

"And do you know if he'll be able to help us?"

"Well, I didn't have a chance to—"

"Did he say anything about workers' salaries?" Joe Brown cut in.

"Did he say whether we'd get a house and medical care?" put in Brady, a miner whom they all called Silicosis.

Jack shook his head. When he admitted he hadn't found the right moment to bring up those subjects, he could see the disappointment in their faces. He looked at the rags that hid their starving bodies and lowered his gaze.

"But he assured me that Americans with guts would be needed to get that factory working like it should." He raised his voice. "And we're going to be those Americans!"

That night, Jack was unable to sleep. They were a day's sailing from Helsinki, and he sorely regretted wasting the one opportunity he was likely to have to better his situation. He should have followed Walter's advice to make the most of his meeting with the executive, but instead, he had allowed himself to be bewitched by the man's niece, and failed to make any kind of approach. Now it was too late. After they disembarked in Finland, their chance of running into the executive again would be remote at best, though as Hewitt himself had mentioned, he and his niece would remain in Helsinki until his injuries had healed.

Jack tossed and turned in his bed, thinking of Elizabeth's perfect face and wondering where she had come from and why she was accompanying her uncle to such a far-off country. Was she promised to anyone? What did she like? What were her motives? He sat up, despairing. He had a thousand more important problems to deal with, and instead of trying to solve them, he was spending his time getting worked up over a woman who'd barely noticed him and whom he barely knew. What he did not doubt was that, because she saw him as nothing more than a worker, he would never know her.

He was sick of the straw mattress. He took off his only blanket and got out of bed in the middle of the night, trying not to make any noise. Walter snored nearby, hugging his pillow like a child. Sue did the same in the top bunk. He hoped that their peaceful sleep might be at least in part due to the hundred dollars he'd shared with them. As he'd done before, he headed to the hold door to look through the porthole, and observed the containers destroyed by the storm. Standing there for a long while, until the cold began to make his fingers numb, he contemplated the machines that had been rendered useless. Suddenly, his heart started thumping. Perhaps it was madness, but he had to take a chance. He opened the door and snuck into the forbidden hold.

8

The Port of Helsinki woke to a sky dark with menacing gray storm clouds, like inhospitable guards that glared watchfully at the passengers of the SS *Cliffwood*. From his hiding place, Jack breathed in the clammy smell of fish and petroleum. While he waited under the tarpaulin that covered the lifeboat, he rubbed his grease-covered fists. Disobeying the order that all passengers were to remain in their quarters until the ship had been moored, he had gained access to the bridge in the hope that he would find Wilbur Hewitt. But he had been freezing to death for an hour without any sign of the industrialist. He observed that the ship was being tugged burdensomely through the foggy waters by a minuscule barge that deftly dodged the many islets that dotted the bay. The image of that giant of the ocean led by a miserable packet boat made him think that, together, the destitute of America who had been forced to leave their country might be able to play a key role in the development of the Soviet Union.

"Sorry, kid. I'm busy with the unloading now."

"Pardon me, sir, but what I have to say is very important," he insisted.

"Are you deaf?" Sergei intervened, irritated.

"Mr. Hewitt, at lunch I forgot to tell you, but I'm traveling to Gorky, too, to work at the Avtozavod, and I want to make you an offer," Jack yelled, trying to make himself heard over the noise of the cranes.

"An offer? You? And what would that be?" Hewitt asked in astonishment. He gestured to Sergei to let the young man speak.

"I'd like to work for you directly."

"Shucks!" He raised an eyebrow. "If that's the way you do business, you aren't going to get very far." He turned back to the boatswain to continue directing the unloading of the machinery.

"Sir, you said that production would be delayed by three or four months, until a new consignment of parts arrived, did you not?"

"Sure, that's what I said. But what does that have to do with—?"

"I can fix the machines."

Wilbur Hewitt looked up from the cargo list and fixed his gaze on Jack.

"What did you say?"

"The damaged machines. I can repair them," Jack repeated. "The Cleveland press. The one you got trapped under. I worked on it all night, and it's almost fixed. If you hired me, I could—"

"You fixed the Cleveland?"

"I sure did. Well, a few heavy parts require assembly, but the main issues have been rectified now. With a little soldering, it'll run good as new. As for the other machines that were damaged in the storm, if you could provide me with a winch, a milling machine, and a few workers to help me, I could repair them all in three or four weeks."

"I don't know why you listen to this charlatan," Sergei broke in. "We run late and—"

"Please, be quiet for a moment!" said Hewitt, before turning to Jack. "Look, son, I'm extremely busy, but I'll spare a moment to ask you this one question: Are you saying you could get that heap of junk in the hold working?"

"With total confidence, sir."

Hewitt frowned and scrutinized Jack as if seeing him for the first time. He cleared his throat before continuing. "All right. Then answer me one more thing. Why would a simple operative like you know more than the Soviet engineers who've assured me those machines are beyond repair?"

"The thing is, sir, if I may be so bold, I don't give a damn what the Russians say. I know those machines, and I can fix them," he replied.

"Hmm." Hewitt clenched his teeth, as though judging Jack's nerve. Finally, he turned to the Soviet. "Sergei, please order your men to examine the Cleveland machine that trapped me and determine whether it could be fully repaired without having to wait for spare parts."

"Sir, that inspection already was carried out, and our experts decide—"

"Then do it again!"

Sergei shot Jack a murderous look before complying with Wilbur Hewitt's order.

While they waited for the report, Hewitt turned his attention away from Jack and focused on checking the cargo inventory. He verified the number of containers still to be unloaded, counted the freight cars to which they'd be transferred, and went over the customs control records while Jack waited by the gunwale. Within a few minutes, Sergei returned, escorted by a Soviet technician Jack hadn't seen before. The stranger, a timid-looking man, scrutinized Jack with disdain before bending to say something into Hewitt's ear. When he'd finished, the executive turned to Jack with astonishment painted all over his face. He scrutinized the young man in silence for a few seconds.

"OK, kid. It appears you have ability as well as nerve. I might even consider offering you a contract. But there's one thing I'd like to get to the bottom of."

Jack took a deep breath, convinced that Hewitt would make him reveal where he acquired his skills. He felt his heart pumping. Hewitt narrowed his eyes and smoothed his mustache.

"Why would you risk going against the ban on entering the hold to try to fix some machines that, as far as you knew, could have been irreparable?"

Jack tried to control his nerves while he considered his response.

He fixed his eyes on Wilbur Hewitt's and replied, "Because, like you said, sir, this country needs Americans with guts, to get things working."

Back in the dormitory, he found Walter and Sue killing time until they could disembark.

"Where the hell have you been? We thought you'd gone overboard!" Sue scolded him.

Jack quickly gathered his belongings, deciding to make up a story until he could find the right moment to tell them all about his meeting with Wilbur Hewitt.

"I got distracted up on deck by the scenery. It's freezing out there." He cleared his throat. "We should put on every bit of clothing we've brought."

"And what do you think we've done?"

Jack, who hadn't noticed earlier what they were wearing, bellowed with laughter. His friends were wrapped up like mummies. While he finished packing, he saw two families, the Danielses and the Millers with their children, standing nearby.

"What are they waiting for?" Jack murmured into Walter's ear.

"The Danielses? They seemed a bit lost, so I invited them to travel with us. The Millers heard and asked if they could join our group as well. I couldn't exactly say no," answered Walter with a serious look.

"You invited them? And what did you tell them? That if they came with us, they'd all be given Christmas turkeys?" he whispered. "Think for a second! It's not just that they'll make the journey more difficult, which they will; if they come with us, they're putting their fate in the hands of two guys wanted for murder." He shook his head.

"So, what would you have had me do?" replied Walter. "Remind them that we're Americans, and that Americans don't help one another? After all, that's why we're here, isn't it? Because no one in our country helped us. Damn it, Jack! They won't be any trouble. Look at their eyes . . . They're excited! They know you speak Russian and that you have a rapport with Hewitt, so they thought you could help them. Ah, well. You're the one who's got their hopes up, so you decide."

Jack turned to look at the Danielses and Millers, and couldn't find even a hint of the excitement that Walter mentioned on their faces. On the contrary, all he could see was desperation in the dark rings around their eyes and on their famished bodies. He let out a sigh and cursed. These people would be more than an inconvenience, but if nobody took care of them, they would struggle. He took a deep breath and gripped his trunk. "You big softy! All right. Tell them to gather their things and follow us."

An icy wind stabbed at the faces of the passengers descending the gangplank of the SS *Cliffwood*, making them huddle together like a row of icicles molded together by frost. Jack was the first to set foot on the Helsinki paving, a wharf like any other, except that ice glazed its surface and snow whitened its little red buildings. Sue suggested they leave their luggage with another passenger and take the opportunity to visit the city, but Jack and Walter thought they'd better save their energy and head directly to the railroad station.

The station was an exquisite art nouveau building on two floors, insignificant compared to New York's Grand Central, but with a waiting room large enough to accommodate all the frozen passengers. Jack rushed to get ahead of the emigrants in front of him and settled his group on some wooden benches near the ticket office. After stacking the luggage against the wall, he looked around. The station thermometer read twenty below zero. He didn't need to convert it to Fahrenheit to know that it was an inhuman temperature. Fortunately, the waiting room was clean, and the locals who looked at them with interest wore clothes of obvious quality, attractively made, suggesting they didn't need to worry too much about thieves. Everything seemed new and well tended, except for the poor souls who had just disembarked. Jack adjusted his threadbare overcoat, missing the deerskin jacket he'd used in the winter in Detroit. Still, when he looked up and saw the rags that covered the Miller children, he couldn't help feeling sorry for them. He sucked in air and contemplated their troubled faces. Despite the cold and the hunger, the two youngsters endured in silence. Without saying a word, Jack took off his overcoat and held it out to Mrs. Miller, who, immediately gripping it as if someone were about to snatch it from her, ran to wrap it around her children. Jack answered the woman's expressions of gratitude with a forced smile, and moved to one end of the bench to plan his entrance into the Soviet Union.

During the voyage, he had seen that two types of emigrants traveled on board the SS *Cliffwood*: a handful of lucky ones who would arrive in Russia with a contract in their hands, accommodation arranged, and train tickets paid; and those left to their fate, traveling on tourist visas. But the case was different for Walter and Jack. Since their applications had been rushed through, Amtorg had given them only an authorization that they would take to the Council of the People's Commissariat for Trade and Industry in Moscow to exchange for a proper contract. They had no transportation or hotel; they would have to make their own arrangements. The Danielses and the Millers were among the jobless families that would enter Russia as tourists, so they would travel with them until Leningrad, at least. Jack sighed. It was going to be a long and arduous journey.

He was pondering this when Walter approached to tell him that he had just held a *committee meeting* with his *comrades in arms*, as he referred to a group of American emigrants with whom he'd struck up a friendship.

"In the end, we agreed that, given your privileged situation, you could ask Hewitt for favorable treatment for all of us. You should've seen their faces, Jack. Even Bob Green, the Wisconsin carpenter who introduced you to his children on the ship, was saying that you were the best thing that had happened to him since they left home. I promised them you wouldn't let them down."

Jack swore. First it was the Danielses, then the Millers, and now the Greens. At this rate, soon he'd no longer be Jack the mechanic; he'd be Jack the Moses, leading his flock to the Promised Land.

"Walter, how could you have? You know what our situation is. Hewitt's an industrialist who looks out for himself. And who knows what kind of arrangement he has with the Soviets?"

"Get outta here, Jack. You saved him. He's an American like us. He can't hang them out to dry."

"He can't? Like I say, you can bet he has his commitments. In fact, he's on the way to a hospital now, Christ knows where. When these people boarded the ship, they knew what they were getting into. And anyway, most of them will get work as soon as they arrive. That's what you've always said, isn't it? That there are jobs falling from the sky. That there's work for everyone."

"Oh, come on, man. I'm not saying it's absolutely necessary, but you know as well as I do that any help will be welcome. We'll find out where he's being treated. Hewitt has an obligation to repay you."

Jack was silent. He looked at Walter and lowered his head. "He already has."

"What?" Walter took off his glasses to improve his focus, as if wanting to make sure that Jack was saying what he thought he was.

"You heard me. I spoke to him before disembarking, and he offered me an assistant's position. They were going to send the machinery that was damaged in the storm back to Dearborn, but I persuaded him that I could fix it, and now they're going to transport it to Gorky."

"Seriously? Well, that's fantastic! Why didn't you say so before? So, did you tell him about us? Did you tell him you're traveling with two friends who would also be useful to him?"

"Of course I told him."

"And?"

"I'm sorry, Walter. I tried, but his reply was that the position was just for me."

"What? Who the hell does he think we are? A bunch of bums? I bet he didn't know we were traveling with guaranteed jobs. So what did you say? God! I would have given my last dollar to see his face when you turned down his offer." He gave a proud smile.

Jack fell silent. Then Walter saw that Jack's face showed the same expression that his boss had adopted when he laid him off from the printer's.

"Jack? You did turn him down, didn't you? You wouldn't have said yes . . ."

"I tried. I insisted he had to make the two of you an offer as well, but he said I had two choices: accept his proposal and start building a promising future for myself, or turn it down and work on an assembly line for the rest of my life."

"But if we separate, how will Sue and I integrate? You're the one who knows the language. The one who can help us." Walter put his spectacles back on with such anger that he almost broke a sidepiece. "What're *we* gonna do?"

"I don't know, Walter. I don't know how things work here. When it comes to the Soviet Union, you were always the one who had all the answers."

Jack found a bench outside the waiting room. He felt indebted to Walter and Sue, but he didn't know how to repay them. The two of them had gone off for a walk. Jack didn't wish to see anybody. Some passengers who knew he spoke Russian had pestered him to translate leaflets and tickets for them, but he needed time to ponder how he could make amends with his friends. He couldn't come up with anything, until he thought of the passengers who kept badgering him for translations. Finnish and Swedish were the languages of Finland. Signs at the ticket counter indicated a Russian-speaking and a French-speaking clerk, but none who spoke English.

He stood with purpose and checked the price of international journeys on a nearby information board. After making a few notes, he headed to a group of passengers and started to gather them around. He made them an offer they couldn't refuse: he would buy their tickets from the Russian-speaking clerk for them, saving them the hassle of communicating in a foreign language, and he would give them a 5 percent discount on the official price for journeys to Leningrad.

"Just like that?" asked a bearded man with a doubtful expression.

"Just like that, friends. Don't let anyone tell you we Americans don't help one another," he said, remembering Walter's words.

Some were suspicious, but most agreed to it. They gave him the money, and Jack, after handing each emigrant a makeshift receipt, headed to the ticket office where, to his surprise, he saw Elizabeth Hewitt, along with a maidservant, discussing business with two Soviets.

While he waited his turn, Jack couldn't help overhearing the conversation that Miss Hewitt's maidservant was attempting in her rudimentary Russian. However, Elizabeth captured most of his attention. She was wearing a red leather coat with fingerless gloves, along with an *ushanka*, the famous Russian hat with earflaps, which made her even more attractive. Jack tried to go unseen, but the young woman noticed his presence. His pulse quickened. Between glances, he daydreamed about what her interests might be. Perhaps she rode or played tennis, spoke French, or played a musical instrument.

As he moved forward in the line, Jack concentrated on counting the money that some fifty passengers had given him. If his calculations were correct, even after giving them a discount of 5 percent, he would make a decent profit, since the offer for large groups was for 25 percent off the standard ticket price. When it was his turn, he bought the tickets, checked the change, and stealthily hid the profit in the secret pocket he'd sewn into his pants to avoid being robbed. He was turning around, his hand still down the front of his trousers, when he found himself face-to-face with Elizabeth Hewitt.

"Ah!" exclaimed the young woman with feigned astonishment. "Handling machinery again, Mr. Beilis?"

Jack's hand shot out from his pants as if it had been seared with a hot iron.

"Miss Hewitt! What . . . what a pleasant surprise! I was just . . . I was . . ." To hide his embarrassment, he showed her some rubles that he had received as change.

"Oh! A novel way to mint money! But he can spare us the details, can't he, Gertrud?" she said.

"Miss Elizabeth! I should remind you that Mr. Hewitt doesn't want you to speak to strangers. Not to mention"—she gave a grimace of distaste—"strangers who go around . . . touching themselves in those parts!"

The young woman gave her maidservant a smile, revealing teeth radiant as mother-of-pearl.

"Don't be alarmed, Gertrud. Jack's an old acquaintance, and as far as I know, he's very much to my uncle's liking."

"I'm glad you think that, Miss Hewitt," Jack said, still flushed but trying to put his best foot forward.

"Well, Jack, that you're to my uncle's liking doesn't mean you are to mine." Her intense gaze unsettled him, because her eyes seemed to contradict her words.

Jack managed to regain his composure. He smoothed his jacket down with his hands and tried to relax. He didn't want to waste an opportunity that might not present itself again.

"I understand you're staying in Helsinki for a few days," he said.

"I see that news travels fast even on this side of the world. That's right. We'll stay until the doctors decide how bad my uncle's injury is. And if all's well, we'll move on to Moscow, where he has some business to take care of. So it would appear that this is where you and I go our separate ways."

"Maybe not. We're taking the next train to Leningrad, but then we're traveling on to Moscow, to hand in some documents. Who knows? We might meet again there."

"Oh, I don't think so. Moscow's a big city. We're about as likely to bump into each other there as a polar bear and a Pygmy. Farewell, Jack," she said, and moved to walk away.

"In that case, which would I be? The bear or the Pygmy?" He took the liberty of holding her back by the arm, offering her his best smile.

Elizabeth returned it, making him think for the first time that she might eventually succumb to his charms.

"The bear, I suppose."

"And could that bear dance with you next Friday at your party at the Hotel Metropol in Moscow?" he said.

"How do you know—?" She was left speechless.

"I'm sorry. I couldn't help hearing your conversation with your maidservant. The party, it's for your birthday, right?"

"Oh! I see . . . All right, Jack, let's get a couple of things clear." She gently freed herself from his grip. "Maybe there's been a moment or two when I've thought you seem like a fun guy. Sure. You're gutsy. Sharp. Good-looking, even. But look at you." She surveyed him from top to bottom, as if adding together the price of each garment he wore. "I can promise you that you're not even close to the kind of guy that a Hewitt would introduce to her friends."

Jack watched Elizabeth Hewitt disappear into the crowd. When she was out of sight, he stood motionless, entranced by her image. He remained there for some time, until the station clock's bell reminded him he had to get back to his friends. But he didn't rush. He checked that their train tickets were in a safe place, and then strolled to where his compatriots were waiting for him to finish the transaction. As he walked, he forgot about his profits for a moment, turning his thoughts back to the industrialist's niece. Perhaps he wasn't the kind of man that a wealthy woman like her would step out with. Not at the moment. But Elizabeth Hewitt didn't know he was prepared to do whatever it took to become that man.

9

The gigantic boiler of the October Revolution Locomotive Works steam engine, proudly displaying the five-pointed red star on its side, snorted furiously and spewed out an immense column of steam that filled the station platform. The train shuddered, and, shaking and screeching, slowly began to pull its cars, while the last passengers leapt on, hurried by the trainmen's whistles. Jack was glad he'd been able to get on early, as it had enabled him to strike a deal with the controller to accommodate the Millers and Danielses in a compartment next to the one he'd obtained for himself and his friends. It was third class, but at least they would travel in relative comfort, away from the Finnish farmers, who were loaded down like mules. Walter reclined to rest his back, while Sue made herself comfortable on his lap. However, as they set off, a family of Soviet villagers carrying a consignment of chickens saw the free seats, and greeting them loudly, helped themselves.

Once he'd gotten over his surprise, Jack observed the newcomers. The woman looked like an enormous rag doll that someone had stuffed with wool until its seams had split. As for her husband and sons, they obviously enjoyed the same diet. Fortunately, they were as friendly as they were obese, and not long after leaving Helsinki, they offered around some boiled corncobs and cardamom cake, which, to Sue, Walter, and Jack, tasted like heaven itself.

The villagers had proved to be open and talkative. Between mouthfuls, Konstantin, as the head of the family said he was called, asked about the customs of the United States, and was amazed to hear that Americans could travel from state to state freely without authorization. Then, between bellows of laughter that revealed gums dotted with gold, he bragged that he knew all about the Americans from the documentaries they showed in certain Soviet cinemas. He summarized his wisdom in two clear sentences: baseball was a ridiculous game consisting of whacking a ball with a stick, and the cowboys conquered the Wild West because the Indians always attacked them by running around and around in circles so they could be more easily shot down. Jack listened obligingly, astonished at the speed by which Konstantin emptied the bottle of vodka down his throat. Meanwhile, his wife, Olga, who seemed to be paying particular attention to Sue's clothes and shoes, asked the younger woman about the most fashionable Hollywood stars.

Jack interpreted as well as he could.

"She's fascinated," Jack translated for Sue. "Now she's asking whether you'd trade your skirt for her fur coat."

"Seriously?" Sue replied, unconvinced. "It's worn-out." She looked down at it. "And anyway, I don't know if *he'd* approve . . ." She gestured at the space that Walter had left when he had gone off to have a cup of tea in the buffet car at the rear of the train.

"Nonsense! You've been complaining about the cold since we left. Go for it!" Jack encouraged her.

"You think?" Her tone was like a naughty girl's. "That coat doesn't exactly look my size."

"Ha! And your skirt isn't hers. What does it matter? You can trim off the extra and use it to make a hat."

Despite not understanding the conversation, the Soviet peasant woman took off the fur coat and held it out to Sue with a smile. Sue carefully stroked the garment, marveling at the soft fur. "Will you help me try it on outside?" she asked Jack. "There's no space in here."

"Sure." He took the coat and followed Sue out into the corridor. In a swift movement, she slid an arm into the sleeve and let Jack help her with the other one.

"How does it look?" She posed like a vaudeville showgirl.

"They're going to see you," Jack replied, gesturing at the passengers crowding the corridor. He went to return to the compartment, but Sue stopped him.

"Wait. I still have to give her the skirt."

Without letting Jack respond, she turned toward him, and using him as a screen, she took off the skirt, revealing pale legs topped by tight-fitting white panties. Sue's brazenness made Jack feel uncomfortable, but he couldn't prevent a stab of desire.

"Hurry up," he said, looking away.

Sue quickly buttoned up the coat, and they went back into the compartment, where Olga, mumbling, *"Krasivy, krasivy,"* impatiently snatched her new acquisition.

"What's she saying?" Sue asked.

"That even if it doesn't fit, it's beautiful," Jack translated as he took his seat.

Sue slumped back onto the wooden bench, and her half-open coat allowed Jack to see her thighs. He took a deep breath to shake off the discomfort that was making him flush red, and tried to distract himself by looking at the chickens in their cages. But his eyes disobeyed him, lured by the whiteness of Sue's firm, slender legs, contrasted against the dark of the coat. It had been months since he'd enjoyed the company of a woman. As his breathing accelerated, he forgot his reserve and fixed his eyes on Sue's legs. Nobody seemed to notice what was happening; the two Soviet children dozed, and their parents were absorbed in exploring every last stitch of the American skirt. Jack squirmed in his seat, discomforted by an intense heat that he didn't know whether to attribute to the crude radiator at the window or Sue's exposed skin. He thought of Walter. Finally, he unbuttoned his shirt neck and stood.

"I can't stand this heat. I'm going to see what your fiancé's up to," he said, and left the compartment.

On the way to the buffet car, Jack had to fight his way through the dozens of passengers who filled the corridors, some wrapped in so many rags that they were barely distinguishable from the bags in which they transported their meager belongings. He looked at them with pity. Unlike him, none of them had paid the *provodnik* the five rubles that it cost to reserve a seat, or the five extra for blankets. However, as the train clattered along, what surprised him most was the smell that came from many of the compartments, even the first-class ones, occupied by Russians and Finns.

As he made his way through the rearmost cars, wondering what caused the pungent aroma, he came across Walter, who was returning from the buffet.

"Hey, Jack! I was on my way to let you know. Some locals just told me we'll be arriving in Vyborg any moment now; it's the last stop in Finland. Isn't that incredible? We'll go through customs, and in a couple of hours, we'll be in Leningrad." He took off his spectacles to wipe the mist from the lenses. His face was a picture of happiness.

"That's great." Jack was relieved that Walter, who'd been silent since their falling-out at the station, was speaking to him again. "But we should wait here. Sue's sleeping, and the compartment stinks," he said in an attempt to delay being reunited with the young woman. He was still flustered by the image of her thighs.

At that moment, the locomotive's brakes screeched and the cars shuddered. Slowly, puffing and snorting, the train ground to a halt at Vyborg Station. When the *provodnik* finally blew his whistle, a stampede of Finns alighted and ran toward the food stalls that some peasants had set up on the platform. Jack and Walter braved the cold of the night and got out to stretch their legs. While they walked, Jack marveled at the trails of breath emanating from the crowd of passengers, like dozens of puffs of smoke whitening the night air.

"What're they doing?" Walter asked.

"I don't know. Looks like they're buying food," said Jack, stiff with cold.

Jack saw Konstantin, the man who shared their compartment, haggling with a farmer over the price of a sack of potatoes. He left Walter for a moment and went to speak to him.

"What did he say?" Walter asked on his friend's return, blinking behind the lenses of his spectacles.

"That unless we want to starve to death in Russia, we should spend every last ruble we have on meat and vegetables."

When Sue saw Walter, Jack, and Konstantin returning to the compartment loaded to the hilt, she was speechless. Jack had bought smoked venison sausages, rice pudding, and cinnamon cookies, as well as a packet that smelled as bad as the interior of the car. When she asked Jack what it contained, Konstantin cut in.

"*Klavo, Gvozd.*" He showed her some brown powder and smiled.

"It's ground clove," Jack explained. "That's what the strange smell was. Take some and spread it over yourself. It seems the Russians use it to scare the lice away." As they packed up the food, he explained to them that Konstantin had assured him that it would keep them safe from typhus. "So I bought enough to resell to the other passengers," he added proudly.

Walter gave Jack a disapproving look. "I don't understand where you got the money for all these supplies. How much did Hewitt offer you?"

"What offer's this?" Sue asked.

Jack cleared his throat. The border police were about to come on the train, and he didn't want the officials to find them arguing. "If you must know, it has nothing to do with Hewitt's proposal."

"It doesn't? So where did you get it from? Because as far as I can see, you just bought up half the market."

Jack sat in silence for a moment, weighing whether to let Walter in on the source of his profits. He knew he wouldn't be happy about it, but he had to come clean. "It was from the tickets."

"The tickets?"

"The train tickets I bought in Helsinki. For buying them all together, they gave me a twenty-five percent discount."

"And you took advantage of your fellow countrymen to turn a profit?"

"Oh, don't give me that crap, Walter. I gave them a five percent discount, and as for you two, well, until a second ago, you seemed perfectly happy wolfing down my *profits*." He gestured at the packages of food he'd shared with them.

Sue looked at Jack, then turned to Walter. "Jack's right. We need food, and he hasn't done anything wrong."

"He hasn't? He cheated the others and kept their money."

"I didn't cheat anyone!" Jack's expression darkened.

"Don't get like that, Walter," said Sue. "Jack's right. He just offered to buy the tickets for the passengers at a certain price. If he then got a bigger discount and profited from it, I don't think—"

"Damn it, Sue! Whose side are you on?"

Sue was about to respond, when the compartment door was flung open. A flashlight shone in their eyes. The three of them fell silent.

"There is problem?" the officer finally asked in thickly accented English.

Jack and Sue remained silent. Only Walter defied the beam of light that dazzled him. "No, sir. There's no problem. Not yet."

Jack ignored the persistent rapping of knuckles on the lavatory door and continued the task of hiding bills in his secret pocket. In total, he had seventy dollars, including his meager savings, the profits from buying the train tickets, and those he'd just made from the sale of ground clove to the terrified Americans. He kept out a few notes and the handful of rubles he'd exchanged at the railroad station. He was buttoning himself up when they hammered on the door again. Jack yelled to them to leave him in peace. His hands were as muddled as his mind. He wasn't sure he was doing the right thing. They'd reach the border at Beloostrov at any moment.

He washed his face with a sprinkling of icy water. When he opened the door, he found himself face-to-face with an angry old man who threatened to urinate on him. Jack pushed past him and headed to his compartment, doubt eating away at his insides.

Hours before, the foreign exchange clerk at Helsinki Central Railway Station had warned him that the ruble was not yet a recognized currency, so its value depended on what the international banks chose to pay for it at a given time. The value of the ruble was therefore impossible to predict, let alone guarantee. Konstantin had confirmed as much.

Between swigs, the peasant farmer had explained how he'd been personally hit hard by the frequent devaluations that had depreciated his savings until they were worth less than a handful of snow. That was why he advised Jack to hide his money. The border guards would give him two rubles per dollar, but on the Russian black market, he could receive up to forty-five.

"I've seen you're carrying dollars. I could help you. For a small fee, of course. You just have to know the right people," he'd proposed, before his wife upbraided him for it with an elbow to the ribs.

Jack had been interested. He treated the couple to some of the delicacies he'd bought, and encouraged Konstantin to say more. The man's words exuded the honesty of someone who had nothing to lose because he'd already lost everything. Jack remembered that, after emptying the first bottle, the peasant farmer had told him about his former status as a *kulak*, a prosperous landowner who inherited the land that his parents inherited from his grandparents. Konstantin had taken pride in being an honest employer who treated his workers with respect. Even so, the Bolsheviks branded him an exploiter. He was lucky to survive. He hated the Bolsheviks so much that, given the opportunity, he would have killed them all with his bare hands. Halfway through the second bottle, he explained to Jack that, after the expropriations of the revolution of 1917, he and his family subsisted by working like slaves on a collective farm. For years, they endured the threats and mockery of their former serfs, until in 1921, President Lenin introduced the New Economic Policy, the NEP, that would steer the Soviet Union toward prosperity. For Konstantin, those bland initials offered a glimmer of hope, because, overnight, private property was granted legal status once more. Motivated by rage and determination, he slept little and managed to save enough to invest in a small plot of land. Gradually, suffering immense hardship, he began to flourish again, without understanding that the Bolsheviks would never tolerate individual prosperity, even if earned with blood and sweat. Stalin demonstrated as much when, within three years of coming into power, he abolished the concept of private property that Lenin had approved. However, on this occasion, when the Bolsheviks came to plunder his smallholding, his eldest son fought back, pelting them with stones. He now lay buried under the same land he had plowed.

That was why Konstantin drank, and why he hated them. Since then, his family had made a living selling contraband, traveling from time to time, disguised as peasants, to visit relatives in Finland.

Before returning to his compartment, Jack adjusted his pants. Walter might have justified the actions the Bolsheviks had taken against Konstantin, but he wasn't Walter, and he knew nothing about politics. What he knew well was the language of desperation. He guessed

Konstantin must have heard the same language in him when he shared his secrets with him.

Inside the compartment, they were all dozing. Jack settled into his seat opposite Walter and looked at Sue, resting her head on his friend's shoulder, her new overcoat carefully buttoned down to the knees. He tried to forget her legs and once again questioned whether it was a good idea to hide his dollars from customs. Given that he was about to begin secure employment, perhaps it was reckless, but his decision wasn't just about the desire to enrich himself. The reality was they didn't know what they'd find in Russia, or what terms their contracts would have. In fact, the position promised by Wilbur Hewitt was nothing more than that: a promise. The industrialist's condition might deteriorate, and he could be forced to stay in Helsinki or return to the United States, and even if he did recover as expected, he could easily forget his offer as soon as he arrived in Gorky. Equally, if the customs officers discovered his money, Jack could always feign ignorance. After all, it was only obligatory to declare the dollars he was going to bring into the country; he didn't have to exchange them. Konstantin had explained that, if he decided to keep them, customs would give him a receipt indicating the amount of currency he had decided to hold on to, which he would then have to show each time he went to a Soviet bank to exchange them. With each transaction, he'd be given another receipt indicating the dollars exchanged, so that the government had a record of every last cent.

And *that* he didn't like.

Walter's whisper tore him from his thoughts. "Give me your passport," he said, sitting up with a yawn. Jack handed it to him. The three of them had agreed that Walter would deal with immigration control, since it would take place in English and they trusted that his enthusiasm, ease of manner, and most important, his knowledge of the Soviet regime would help smooth the process. Walter took the document, put it together with Sue's and his own, and looked out of the window.

Lights blinked in the distance. "Our first Soviet city! Let's wake Sue."
He did so by kissing his fiancée on the cheek.

Jack thought that the Soviet customs officials in Beloostrov performed
their duties with the bored efficiency of operatives on an assembly
line. As soon as the passengers were on the platform, they separated
the immigrants by nationality, read out a list of banned items in poor
English, checked their visas, and conducted a thorough search without
any scope for objections of any kind.

They appeared well trained. Noble McGee, a Quaker from Arizona
whose deafness prevented him from understanding the instructions,
was almost arrested when he refused to allow a female officer to frisk
him. Fortunately, his wife's shouting alerted Walter, who persuaded the
old man that in the Soviet Union, women performed the same work
as men. Perhaps it all had its logic, Jack thought, though, to his mind,
there were other cases more difficult to understand. Berthold Finns, a
California physician who had embarked on the SS *Cliffwood* driven by
a thirst for Communist solidarity, found it inconceivable that the customs officers had confiscated his phonendoscope simply because they
did not know what it was. Jack was just as surprised when they forced
Richard Barnes, the lawyer of socialist convictions, ahead of him in the
line, to relinquish his law books because they were written in English.
But what shocked him the most was one of the officers requisitioning a
scooter from a small child and explaining that such a toy would make
less-fortunate Soviet children envious.

When it was Jack's turn, Walter went in front as agreed, their passports in his hand.

Jack observed the young Soviet official while he performed his
duties. About twenty years of age and with a shepherd's red cheeks, he
examined their documents with exasperating thoroughness.

"Wait one moment," he said in something vaguely like English. Then he went away with the passports and whispered something to a man who appeared to be the head of the unit. Jack noticed that the young man was pointing at his passport.

"Is there a problem?" Walter asked.

The older officer who had retained the documents returned with an expression that was far from friendly. "I'm sorry, but it will be necessary we make some verifications." He waved Jack's counterfeit passport in the air.

Jack fell silent. When they performed the relevant checks, they'd discover that he was a fugitive accused of murder. For a moment, he considered trying to escape, but he was in the middle of nowhere and would compromise his friends. Walter seemed to read his mind.

"Look, Officer, we're honorable people." He took off his glasses. "Proletarian workers who—"

"You have something declare? Moneys? Jewelry?" he cut in.

"Huh? No, we don't . . ."

Walter put his spectacles back on and hastily deposited a handful of coins, an old Communist Party USA membership card, and a blunt pencil on his trunk. Sue handed over the marriage certificate they'd forged at the printer's and an old photo in which she appeared in a bathing suit with a friend. Jack offered up ten crumpled dollars and the letter of recommendation from the Amtorg agency. Despite the warning, he kept his mother's medallion. The customs officer glanced at the membership card and recommendation, but held on to the picture of Sue, looking at it with obvious pleasure. "This how woman dress in your country?" He smiled.

Jack snatched the photograph from him, playing the affronted husband. "We Americans have come to the Soviet Union to offer our labor. Got it? Our *labor*."

The man gave a smile and leafed through the passports again. "Jack Beilis. You have curious name."

"Oh? I didn't know a surname could arouse such curiosity . . . What's yours?"

"Mine not your concern." The smile disappeared. "Open luggage."

The officer examined the contents. He said nothing, but he seemed amazed at the quantity of food. When he'd finished his search, he raised an eyebrow, unsatisfied.

"Everything all right, comrade?" Walter said, trying to fraternize with the officer.

"Alexei Petrov and Mikhail Lebedev were my comrades. They die in revolution of 1917," he spat out with a sour expression. "OK. Take your things."

Jack, Sue, and Walter didn't need to be told twice. They bundled their belongings like dirty laundry and quickly obeyed. However, when Jack held his hand out to take his passport, the customs officer refused to return it.

"You must wait. I need make more verifications. Just routine," he assured Jack in a tone that suggested otherwise. "My assistant give you receipt that allow you travel in nation until we resolve matter."

"But what's the problem?" Sue put in.

"In Soviet Union, we don't often have problems. Only, sometimes, foreigners they make them."

Though the journey between Beloostrov and Leningrad took only a couple of hours, to Jack it seemed never-ending. To avoid worrying Sue, he hadn't spoken about his fears, but he was beginning to play out some scenarios in his mind that were less than promising. Still, his only option was to keep going, and the farther from his crime the better.

On the last stretch of the journey, he tried to get some sleep, but to no avail. He thought of Hewitt. His niece, Elizabeth. The incident at customs. Too many events ended with the same feeling: the sense of an uncertain future. As he tried to relax, his hand felt in the pocket where his dollars were hidden. He was relieved they hadn't frisked him, though it may have been down to the misfortune of "Silicosis" Brady. During the inspection, an ill-timed coughing fit had betrayed his condition, and the stir had interrupted the searches. Jack was sorry for him. He pictured him alone and frightened in some dark cell, waiting to be repatriated.

He took a deep breath and looked around.

Dawn was breaking, and through the misted windows, Jack could make out the snowy fields of the former Saint Petersburg. When he wiped the glass, he discovered that the landscape was much like his father had described it to him as a child: clean, virgin countryside, as if freshly painted white, dotted with the occasional dacha, its little garden populated with fir trees, its chimney speckling the sky with smoke. Yet, as the train approached Finlyandsky Station, dark concrete buildings began to appear, one after the other. Konstantin called them the workers' beehives.

"And soon you'll be the bees that live in them."

10

On the platform of Leningrad's Finlyandsky Station, the passengers said their first farewells. Some of the Americans traveling with contracts with the Leningradsky Metallichesky Zavod had spread the rumor that the giant foundry on the banks of the Neva needed extra manpower, and the Millers had decided to end their journey here and try their luck in the former Saint Petersburg. Walter and Sue wished them well. Jack, shivering with cold and busy trying to find the fastest and cheapest way to travel to Moscow, waved to them from a distance.

On the way to the ticket office, he noted the two impressive banners hanging from the station façade, depicting Stalin and Lenin as mythological heroes. They made quite a contrast with the cracked walls, which, like the rest of the building, seemed to be falling to pieces. Yet what worried him most were the dozens of ragged peasants roaming around and looking lost, some with bare feet covered in filth so caked on, it was impossible to guess the true color of their skin.

Jack was finding it difficult to believe that the Soviet Union, proclaiming itself to be the nation of plenty, where there was no shortage of bread or work, was the same country he saw in front of him, like an old photograph yellowed by time. He turned his head to take in the beggars, workers, and peasants who milled around outside. He didn't see a single taxi or motor vehicle of any kind. Not even a motorcycle. Nothing that might be associated with progress. Just people on foot, an old tram, and horse-drawn carriages on the snow-covered paving.

He was about to inquire about tickets, when someone grabbed his arm. Turning, he found Konstantin, visibly panicked.

"Have you seen my son Nikolai?" he asked frantically.

"No, I haven't. The last time I saw him was with you on the platform. What is it?"

"The little devil! He disappeared when we were unloading the chickens, and now we can't find him."

Jack looked around. In a corner, he saw a uniformed man standing guard. "Have you asked that policeman?"

"Ask a member of the OGPU for help?" He spat in disgust. "That guy would grill me with a thousand questions before moving a muscle. You have no idea how things work here, do you? A life's worth nothing here. If anything happens to Nikolai . . ."

Jack felt for the peasant farmer. He still didn't understand why Konstantin wouldn't ask the police for assistance, but he offered to help anyway.

"Let's separate," Konstantin suggested. "You stay with Olga and search the station, and I'll go outside to check the surrounding area. We will meet up in fifteen minutes by the carriages."

Jack nodded, and the Russian rushed outside. Then Jack informed Walter of his intentions and suggested to Olga that she watch the concourse while he searched the platforms.

He climbed onto several stationary trains, running down their corridors in case the little boy was trying to return to the compartment in which they'd arrived, but inside he found only workers and peasants. He ran back to the platform and searched under the railcars, then checked the public restroom, the cafeteria, and the barbershop.

He stopped to get his breath. There was no sign of Nikolai. It was as if the earth had swallowed him up and filled the hole with concrete.

He was about to return to the concourse, when he glimpsed a small child, crouching over a man laid out on the ground, half hidden near the freight platform. The boy was Nikolai. Jack's heart raced. He headed toward the youngster, seeing his hands dip into the man's overcoat and extract something that he stuffed into his little leather bag. Jack quickened his pace, not knowing what was happening. He stumbled across the tangle of tracks, yelling Nikolai's name. He was one track from reaching him when from behind a car emerged the policeman he'd seen on the concourse. In a flash, the officer grabbed Nikolai and pulled him away from the man on the ground.

He prayed that the little boy was unharmed. However, as he approached the policeman, he was shocked to realize that the man on the ground was in fact a frozen corpse.

He was going to thank the policeman for his help, when the officer aimed a pistol at him.

"Are you this boy's father?" he yelled.

"Relax. Please, lower your weapon. I'm a friend of the family. I was actually—"

Without letting him finish, the OGPU officer grabbed the leather bag hanging from Nikolai's neck, tugged it off, and pulled out a document.

"The boy was stealing from a dead body, and he'll be arrested," he said, looking at the child without pity.

Jack was perplexed. He didn't know how to respond. He couldn't understand how, rather than investigating the circumstances around the man's death, the policeman was more concerned with arresting a child. He looked at Nikolai's contrite expression. The officer was holding him in his arms like a trophy. He was about to object to the policeman's behavior, when he noticed Konstantin, hidden behind a pillar. He had no idea why he was hiding, but he guessed there must be a powerful reason. He tried to improvise. "Officer, I don't mean to question what you're saying, but how can you be so sure that the boy was robbing that poor man? I was at the same distance as you, and to me it looked like he was feeling the heart to see if there was a pulse."

The policeman put Nikolai down and holstered his gun, but when the boy tried to run toward Jack, he grabbed him by the arm, shaking him like a doll. "Oh, sure. So I suppose this ration book in the name of"—he took out the document from Nikolai's bag, read it, and showed it to Jack—"Leonard Kerensky, I suppose you're going to tell me it's a death certificate issued by the kid, eh?"

Jack contemplated the document while the officer bragged about his successes catching petty thieves specializing in ration books stolen from the starved or the frozen-to-death. It became clear that it might not have been the first time Nikolai had done something similar. At any rate, his chances of proving the police officer wrong had been reduced to zero. Jack pursed his lips. He looked back at Konstantin, but the Russian was motionless behind the pillar, like a startled deer. He was about to give up trying to defend Nikolai, when an idea came to him. He fixed his eyes on the policeman's and hardened his expression.

"The dead man's not Leonard Kerensky. I'm Leonard Kerensky. The boy must have taken my ration book to play with."

The police officer looked at him with disbelief. Jack's American clothes, not to mention his foreign accent, wouldn't have fooled a blind man.

"Kerensky . . . You're Leonard Kerensky, you say." He looked at the ration book again, then at the frozen dead body at his feet.

"That's right."

"Excellent. In that case, tell me, how is it possible that your ration book states that you're seventy-five years old?" He smiled.

Jack cleared his throat. But he was prepared. "Because that's my age," he assured the officer. "And here's the document that proves it." He dipped a hand into his jacket's inside pocket, rummaged around, and finally held out an envelope containing the letter of recommendation from Amtorg.

"Oh! American . . . ," said the policeman, feigning surprise, and he unfolded the letter that Jack had just handed him. "Recommended by the Soviet agency to perform essential work at the Gorky manufacturing plant," he read.

Jack hoped the information would make the policeman have second thoughts. Suddenly, the officer raised an eyebrow. In the envelope, under the letter, was a ten-dollar bill.

"Do you know the penalty for trying to corrupt a police officer?"

"I'd rather not find out." At that, Jack took out another ten dollars and inserted the bill under the letter that the policeman was holding. "It's very cold out here." He looked at the frost-covered tracks. "You could buy yourself a new pair of boots with that," he added, pointing at the worn regulation footwear out of which the policeman's toes were poking.

The officer looked from side to side, took Jack's money, and stuffed it in his jacket.

"What did you say your relationship was to this little piece of work?" asked the policeman as he looked Jack up and down.

"Friend of the family," he repeated.

"Well, that family should teach the boy that using illegal ration books is considered a crime against state property, and it's punishable with ten years' hard labor."

"Of course. However, you'll agree that the kid hasn't used the book illegally. All he did was pick it up, in all likelihood to return it to the authorities."

The policeman fixed his eyes on Jack again, before finally nodding his head. He was about to go when, without warning, he stopped.

"Take them off," the officer ordered.

"What?" Jack didn't understand.

"Your shoes. It's true. It's very cold out here."

Jack obeyed. He took off the pair of shoes that his father had made for him shortly before his death, and handed them to the policeman. He felt the stones freezing his feet. Fortunately, the police officer took off what remained of his own boots and gave them to Jack.

"One more thing."

"Yes?" asked Jack as he pulled on the tattered boots.

"Don't try that trick on anyone else." He patted the place where he'd stashed the dollars. "You'll probably be shot."

Konstantin embraced Jack again and again, nearly asphyxiating him.

"Leave something for Nikolai," the American said with a smile.

On the way back to the concourse, Konstantin confessed to him that some time ago he had been involved in a serious altercation with the same corrupt officer. "A real son of a bitch," he spat out. "He was a miner before joining the party and working for the OGPU, the government's secret police. They assigned him to the public market, where the Organization paid him a bribe to turn a blind eye to their backstairs activities."

"The Organization?"

"You know . . . *friends* who help one another mutually. You don't think a smuggler could survive in a country like this operating alone, do you? Here, without *blat*, you have nothing to fall back on," he clarified. Konstantin explained that the Organization had provided him with the false passports that he and his family used to cross the border from time to time. "We say we're visiting sick relatives so we can arrange for the goods to be sent. Thanks to *blat*, we can cross the border no problem," he added.

"And what were you saying about the corrupt policeman?"

"Ah yes! That bastard started demanding bigger and bigger bribes, without realizing that the Organization also had his immediate superior on the payroll. One day they demoted him without explanation and sent him to patrol this station. I'd already had an altercation with him at the market, and he blamed me for what happened. If I'd intervened when he caught Nikolai, he would've arrested me and jeopardized the Organization's entire distribution system."

"But he was your son—"

"Of course. And I promise you that if you hadn't resolved it, I would have stepped in." He opened his overcoat, and Jack saw a knife.

Olga burst into tears when she saw her son run toward her and leap into her arms. The tears stopped her seeing Jack saying good-bye.

"I'll never forget what you've done for Nikolai," Konstantin vowed, shaking his hand. "I heard that bastard say that you're going to Gorky. Here." He handed Jack a piece of paper. "Now you have *blat*, too. And one more thing: never trust anybody. In Russia, there's no such thing as a friend."

11

The Moscow-bound train departed from Moskovsky Station, located on the other bank of the River Neva, so Jack and the rest of the Americans had to drag their bags across central Leningrad from one station to the other. The inhuman cold prevented Jack from paying much attention to the impressive French-style palaces and Orthodox churches, which, crowned by gold domes, festooned the city with their exotic onion forms. However, he noticed again that not a single automobile circulated on the streets, as if the inhabitants wanted to preserve the city's old-world charm. Very occasionally, a train of horse-drawn carriages would interrupt the silence with their clatter of hooves on the paving. Yet, aside from that, the city of the tsars seemed to be inhabited entirely by a plague of impoverished vagrants whose rags would have been an embarrassment even to the jobless Americans who begged in the soup lines.

Fortunately, Jack and his friends were heading to Moscow, the capital, which, according to Walter, was a byword for Soviet progress.

The *provodnik* who showed them to their third-class seats apologized for the modest amenities aboard the Moscow-bound train, but assured them proudly that when the *Red Arrow* first took up its route, not only did it cover the distance between the two major cities in less than eight hours, but it was also possible to telephone any part of the world from its restaurant car.

Jack thanked him for the information as he spread the mattress that he'd just rented from him out on the wooden bench. The freight train's fifteen-hour journey time didn't seem so bad to him, especially considering that most of the trip would be at night and he'd be sleeping. He needed rest.

He turned the control several times, but the heating didn't work. The cold forced him to keep his hands in his pockets for warmth, and there they found the piece of paper that Konstantin had given him before they parted. He took it out and read it again in the semidarkness: *Ivan Zarko. Upravdom at 25 Tverskaya Avenue, Gorky.* Konstantin had explained that an *upravdom* was a cross between a landlord, an administrator, and a building superintendent, employed by the state to manage the buildings that the party assigned to him. Jack carefully folded the paper and pocketed it again, while the image of a blood-soaked Kowalski appeared in his mind. He imagined that, by then, the customs officer who'd retained his passport would have sent it on to Moscow. It was only a matter of time before they established that it was false and ordered his arrest.

He looked at Walter, sleeping peacefully next to Sue, unconcerned about what had happened at the station or the danger they were in. According to Walter, it was highly unlikely that they'd detect that the passport was a fake in Moscow for two reasons. First, its tiny imperfections would be imperceptible to anyone unfamiliar with the new American documents. Second, they hadn't retained the passport because they doubted its authenticity. Rather, they had likely confiscated it for the same reason Jack had been questioned at the Amtorg office in New York: the provenance of his unusual Russian surname. Furthermore, that the United States had cut diplomatic ties with the Soviet Union meant, in practice, that the Soviet authorities would never ask the Americans for his criminal record.

But those were Walter's thoughts, not his own.

Still, he wanted to believe that his friend was right. And, now he had *blat*. He didn't know how it might help him, but he had it, even if it had cost him a pair of new shoes.

He looked out of the train window. Walter had spoken to him of the breathtaking beauty of Saint Basil's Cathedral, the formidable walls of the Kremlin citadel, and the impressive expanse of Red Square, but compared to the decadent majesty of Leningrad, the outskirts of Moscow were a gigantic suburb of crude gray buildings, which, far from belonging to a state capital, seemed to Jack like a drab industrial installation, crammed with warehouses that had been haphazardly converted into homes. Walter pointed out that the most iconic buildings were still to come, but at this stage of the journey, all Jack could see were the silent streams of workers whose features and clothing were as gray and as dirty as the districts they wandered through. Finally, at 11:00 a.m., the train arrived at the old Leningradsky Station in Moscow.

Walter was the first to get off. He left his luggage behind, leapt onto the platform, and gazed at everything around him as if laying eyes on the sea for the first time. He smiled, his chest swelling with satisfaction. At last his dream was coming true. Yet for Jack, seeing the station brought no excitement. The same giant portraits of Stalin and Lenin were on the façade of the train station, a carbon copy of the one he'd seen in Leningrad. The building had the same monotone bossage, the same Risorgimento-style windows, and the same central tower with its French clock, the ever-present five-pointed star in its center. Even the cold was the same. As far as he could tell, the only thing differentiating Moscow from Leningrad was the Muscovites. Wherever he looked, crowds of people in fur coats, scarves, and hats walked in silence like automatons whose routes, occupations, and expressions were inalterably fixed.

He noticed a poor woman, bent under a bale the weight of which even a cart would struggle to bear. She walked barefoot, asking for change without anybody so much as looking at her, while what appeared to be her children followed her with gaunt faces and frightened eyes. A little farther on, he saw two soldiers dragging away a crippled beggar who was blaming his misfortune on the revolution, a sign around his neck asking for money to help him survive the winter. Jack clenched his jaw. Too many people and too much poverty.

He was forced to look away. In his adopted role as guide, he had to be on alert in case any of his fellow travelers went astray, so he directed them as they unloaded their luggage, and informed his group that, as soon as they left the station, they would head to the Intourist offices, where those who didn't yet have lodgings could make arrangements. For ten cents a head, he would help them do all the necessary paperwork. They all accepted his suggestion, but Walter approached quietly and interrupted him.

"It's impressive how you can turn a little information into profit," he chided him.

Jack took the comment to be the product of jealousy and didn't bother to reply. It was true that his friend had provided all the details on Intourist, but Jack had offered to share the earnings with him, and Walter had refused.

"And I suppose you'll charge them for taking them to the People's Commissariat?" Walter added.

Jack remained silent. He hadn't intended to charge them, but he couldn't understand why Walter objected so much. Ultimately, he was providing a useful service that the American travelers could accept or reject with no obligation.

"You didn't pay me for the information," Walter insisted.

"You didn't ask me to," answered Jack, and in a bad temper pulled down one of the suitcases jammed into an overhead rack.

"These people have no money."

"Nor do I."

Walter grabbed hold of him. "But don't you see, Jack? This is a different world we're in now. In the Soviet Union, people share their resources and dreams with everyone else. And unlike all of them, you've been promised a good contract."

Jack looked around him. "You know what, Walter? All I see them sharing is their poverty. As for my contract, you've just described it perfectly. It's been promised. Just promised." He turned away and carried on unloading the suitcases.

On the way back from the Intourist office, Jack regretted the way he had spoken to Walter. Perhaps the Soviet Union wasn't the paradise that his friend had prophesied, but that didn't make the fact that Walter had risked his life in New York to save Jack from prison any less true.

He looked at his friend with remorse. Walter, wearing his broken spectacles, was walking in front of him, with Sue close by. He was full of excitement as they headed to a guesthouse. He didn't seem to need anything else. Just the air he breathed, the company of the girl he loved, and the knowledge that he was in a world where there was no place for selfishness.

Jack clenched his fists and looked down at himself. He no longer wore the faded jacket he'd begun the journey with, or the worn, patched-up shirt, or even the tattered boots that the corrupt policeman had given him in Leningrad. With the profits from his activities as a guide, and from the sale of the ground clove, he'd managed to persuade every fellow traveler to sell him his best clothes, until he had an outfit that, altogether, and compared to the rest of his group, made him look like a man of some means.

The situation made him uncomfortable, but he had no regrets. What he'd gained was through his own hard work, like everything he had achieved in life. For as long as he could remember, he had slogged away, worked diligently, and made sacrifices. His life had always consisted of making the effort that would enable him to progress, to climb out of the misery that his father seemed to have predetermined for him. He had gotten up every morning, lamenting his fate and envying others for what they had achieved. His uncle Gabriel, the banker, had been his model. That was why he had continued to grind away when he left his native New York for Detroit. It was why he had fought there to build a future for himself, sweating blood for long, exhausting days, studying every screw, analyzing every cog, and memorizing every process. It was why he had enjoyed the little privileges with which his sacrifice had been rewarded: a car to go out in, a tailored suit, and a beautiful apartment. It was why he hated those responsible for the economic crisis that had snatched from him everything he had worked for. And it was why he was prepared to do whatever it took so that, as little as he might achieve in the Soviet Union, nobody would ever take it away from him.

He looked up and contemplated the buildings in front of him, their façades and balconies cracked as if they were open wounds left by the violence of the revolution. Jack likened them to a cast of old actresses, their beauty faded by time. He looked to the horizon. Everything was strange. To the eyes of someone accustomed to the defiant skyscrapers and tumultuous avenues of New York, Moscow was an inexplicable mixture of antiquity and decadence, vast and provincial at the same time, like an immense medieval town where the fairy-tale palaces and gleaming churches had been forced to breathe in to make room for the gigantic, monstrous new socialist constructions.

It was getting dark and the cold was growing worse.

While they waited for the arrival of the tram that was to take them to the guesthouse they'd organized through Intourist, Jack berated himself for his distrust. For a moment, he saw himself as a bitter man directing all his resentments at the Soviets. He took a deep breath. The air was icy but clean. He could feel that he needed it. The group of Americans that accompanied them had been reduced to five: the four members of the Daniels family and Joe Brown, one of the few black passengers who had traveled on board the SS *Cliffwood*. The rest of the immigrants had decided to hire an official Intourist guide to take them to their lodgings. In total, a party of eight—eight Americans lost in the Soviet Union. Perhaps they were nothing more than a bunch of paupers staying in second-rate guesthouses and traveling third class, but if Jack stopped to think about it, in reality they were privileged. They had traded a miserable life without hope for a new one. Different, perhaps, but new, nonetheless. A life in a country that had opened its doors to them, and whether those doors were older, or more modern, was of little consequence. The most important thing was what waited for them behind those doors: work, prosperity, and hope.

Jack wanted to believe that was how it would be, even though the tram they had to cram into like sardines reminded him that the prosperity he longed for might still be far away.

"Do you really expect us to sleep in this room? It's colder in here than it is outside." Sue turned to Walter in disbelief.

"It is best room, miss," the building's *upravdom* said with a smile, taking off his hat and revealing teeth as black as charred kernels of corn.

Walter dropped his suitcases on the floor of the filthy room for which they'd just paid ten rubles each. It certainly wasn't what he'd expected for that price, but apparently the high cost was due to overpopulation in the Soviet capital. Jack raised an eyebrow. He looked at the crumbling walls, the chipped windows, the panes of glass that looked as if they'd never been cleaned, and an old bed that made sleeping on the floor seem preferable.

"What a pigsty," Walter finally mumbled.

"You shouldn't be surprised. You cried out to the heavens when I told you about the cost of hotels like the Moscow, Lux, or Europa," Jack responded, using his foot to push aside a rug and revealing a hole through which the floor below could be seen. "Could you show me my room now, please?" he asked the *upravdom*.

"This. This is room." He gestured at the dilapidated spring sofa against one of the walls.

As much as Jack tried to make the *upravdom* understand that they'd paid for separate rooms, there was no persuading him. The man explained that he'd had to make last-minute arrangements for a Ukrainian family that had been transferred to Moscow, and there were only two rooms available in the entire building. "If you want, you use this," he said, pointing at a blanket hanging from the ceiling and indicating that it could be drawn like a curtain.

Jack nodded and helped the *upravdom* spread out the blanket. The Daniels family would sleep in another room of the same size, while Joe Brown would spend the night on a mattress that the *upravdom* had set up in the corridor between the two rooms. *I don't mind,* Joe had assured them. *You should see some of the places where I've had to sleep in my life.*

"Well, at least we have a heater in the middle of the room," said Walter, and he gestured at a strange copper contraption standing on the tiled floor.

When the *upravdom* went away, they all sat around what seemed like an old heater, waiting for Jack to light it. He examined it closely, until suddenly he burst into hysterical laughter. "Oh hell! It's a *samovar!* A goddamned tea urn!" It had taken him a while to identify the device because the tap was missing, but it was similar to one he'd seen as a boy at his uncle Gabriel's house. Fortunately, it contained some remnants of tea, which Jack judged to be enough to make a brew. He also found a broken electric stove, which he quickly repaired with a splice and used to heat the samovar and warm the room. Before long, they were sharing a couple of cups of watery tea, while Sue cobbled together a dinner with the supplies that Jack had bought at the border.

They savored it. Jack watched the food that he'd worked so hard to earn disappear. But he didn't care. "Tomorrow we'll have a feast using the meal tickets Intourist gave us," he announced, and they both responded with a smile.

Nobody imagined how short-lived that smile would be.

The next morning, Jack and Walter turned up first thing at the People's Commissariat to have their employment contracts authenticated, as Amtorg had instructed them to do. However, after they had waited two hours in the line, the official responsible for approving foreigners' contracts shook his head and returned them to Walter without even looking at them.

"I am sorry, citizens. Quota of foreign personnel assigned to Avtozavod is filled. You must wait three months for next quota."

Jack looked at Walter, hoping it was some kind of joke, but his friend's stunned expression said otherwise. *The man must have made a mistake,* he thought. At the Soviet office in New York, they had been assured that they would be accepted at the Avtozavod immediately upon arrival. When Jack told the official that they barely had the means to subsist for a week, the man repeated the same sentence without so much as blinking. Jack demanded to see his superior, but the official's only response was to signal to an armed guard, who ordered them to leave the line to make way for the next applicants.

As they left, Jack, filled with indignation, demanded an explanation from Walter.

"There must've been a misunderstanding," answered Walter.

"A misunderstanding? Did you not hear him? The guy basically told us that our contracts are worthless. We have to wait three months. What're we gonna do in the meantime? Starve, or freeze to death? Forget it. I already know the answer: we are going to starve *and* freeze to death." Jack cursed himself for trusting the Soviets. He was beginning to wonder whether Wilbur Hewitt's offer of work would be worth nothing as well.

"Your pessimism won't solve anything. We don't know how any of this works. Let me think . . . I know a Muscovite I've been corresponding with since I was a trade unionist; he has contacts at the People's Commissariat of Heavy Industry. Maybe he can help us."

"Oh really? Well, he'd better. Or I can see us competing with the beggars for space on the sidewalk."

It took them the entire afternoon to find Walter's friend Dmitri, whom they finally located at his home overlooking the Moskva River. The man, a timid Georgian who spoke crude English, said he was sorry for their situation and offered them a cup of hot tea. As they warmed up, he promised them he'd be able to arrange for them to be seen by the commissar for industrial contracts within a couple of days as the man was a great friend of his. One way or another, they'd resolve the matter. Walter hugged the man in celebration. Jack remained unconvinced.

Back at the guesthouse, Walter told Sue what had happened and reassured the Danielses that his contact would find them jobs soon. Jack remained silent. When they finally turned off the light, he lay on the wooden sofa and tossed and turned. He couldn't believe what was happening to them. As much as Walter refused to accept it, they were alone, halfway across the world, cowering in an icebox with their pockets half empty and nothing but unemployment on the horizon. He took a deep breath, which only made him even colder. He wanted to think, at least, that he still had Hewitt's offer up his sleeve. He wondered what the industrialist and his niece were doing. Then he conjured the image of Elizabeth in his mind. With his eyes closed, he felt as if her face were glowing next to his and in some way dissipating the icy cold that penetrated the cracks in the windows. He tried to get to sleep—he wanted to be up early and go out in search of a nice gift. After all, he could hardly attend Miss Hewitt's birthday party empty-handed.

After two hours going from stand to stand, suffering the noise and jostling of the crowds, Jack came to the conclusion that, in Moscow's markets, you could buy any trash that a person was able to extract from a dunghill and deposit on a counter. Scattered all over the market floors were splintered picture frames, scraps of fabric, tattered shoe soles, the completely unusable remains of furniture, dented pots, loose crockery, army uniforms, and pieces of lead piping. In other words, he could search for a year and would never find anything fit for a lady.

He decided to take a break and find a teahouse where he could warm up. The boiling tea burned his lips, but he welcomed it. He thawed his fingers over the steam from the cup and looked around to find that all eyes were on him. A trader with a ruddy complexion approached and offered Jack half his stock of cheese in exchange for his American clothes. In other circumstances he'd have accepted, but he'd worn rags for too long and wasn't going to give up his outfit even for a ton of genuine French Roquefort. However, he took the opportunity to ask the man where he could buy flowers. The cheese seller looked at Jack as if one of his goats had spoken to him. "Flowers? In Moscow? In winter? Nobody sells flowers here." When Jack asked him why, his answer was that nobody would buy something that served no purpose.

Jack shrugged and finished his cup of tea. He was about to leave, when one of the waitresses stopped him. "Ignore him. It's true no one sells flowers at the market, but two blocks on, heading toward the river, you'll find a few stands that practically give them away."

Fortunately, Jack arrived minutes before the sellers gathered up their goods to flee the imminent blizzard. For a couple of rubles he bought a little bunch of violets and white wallflowers that they wrapped up for him in a sheet of the *Pravda*. He looked at the flowers and smiled. The wrapping might not be the best, but at least he could read the newspaper on his way back. Now he just needed to leave the flowers in some water, dress up like a dandy, and head to the Metropol to ask Wilbur Hewitt's niece for a dance.

12

Perhaps Jack Beilis lacked the glamour he would need for a liveried doorman to let him into a hotel just by looking at him, but he certainly knew how to bluff it. Wearing a perfect smile, he got out of the *droshky*, paid the coachman, and sauntered idly through the snow-covered gardens that led to the Hotel Metropol's entrance, endeavoring to make sure that when the doorman caught sight of him, he'd think that the newcomer arriving with an aristocratic manner had come to close an important deal. As he reached the doorman, Jack stopped to take in the beautiful mosaic that adorned the building's façade. "Spectacular! *The Princess of Dreams* surpasses any of Mikhail Vrubel's previous work!" he said, waving his bunch of flowers and addressing the sky. And without giving the doorman time to speak, he strode confidently into the building.

Jack shuddered when he felt the warmth from the heating. Braving the Moscow cold without a coat had been almost as audacious as trying to gate-crash the Metropol, but the short journey on the horse-drawn carriage had been worth it, considering that, for the five rubles it had cost, the coachman had thrown in the detail on the building's façade that Jack had used to impress the doorman.

Once inside the opulent foyer, he greeted any guests he crossed paths with as if he'd known them all his life, headed to the reception desk, where, without looking up, he commandeered a copy of the *Izvestia*, and sat on a gaudy armchair that would have made a much more comfortable bed than the sofa he'd spent the night on.

He was inside. He examined every detail around him. The reception clock showed a quarter to six, so he still had some time to amuse himself reading the news. He turned down the offer of tea from one of the waiters and took a look at the newspaper, noticing that the main differences compared to an American rag were the absence of advertising and the portrayal of all of its contents, even the death notices, as good news.

After scanning a couple of propaganda pieces, he turned his attention to the guests who were beginning to arrive. A mature man, dressed up like a peacock, positioned himself nearby, conversing with another older gentleman wearing a tuxedo and a blue sash. They were joined by a lean young man in an impeccably pressed brown army jacket, who paid his respects to the older gentlemen as if he held them in extremely high regard. Most of the guests appeared to be diplomats, businessmen, and foreign dignitaries, but there were also a number of Soviet military men and political leaders. He compared their garments with the suit he wore and decided to remain seated until he could more easily blend into the crowd.

Gradually, the foyer filled with men and women in formal attire, and the staid conversations turned to lighthearted chatter about the evening's menu, or on the latest trends in Parisian fashion. Finally, at exactly six o'clock, the doors to the ballroom opened, revealing an extraordinary space flanked by brown marble columns with golden capitals, crowned by a multicolored glass dome that left the guests speechless.

Jack paled, not so much due to the magnificent and extraordinary ballroom as to the dazzling figure that approached him holding the arm of a Soviet official.

Elizabeth Hewitt was captivating. When she passed Jack, the young woman gave him a hint of a smile, before moving on without turning her head. Jack waited for a chance to approach her, but the man she was with followed her wherever she went. Jack looked at him. It wasn't that he'd imagined anyone in particular, but the man with the slicked-down hair wasn't the kind of guy that he would have envisioned escorting her. His chiseled features were ornamented by a perfectly crafted mustache almost as impressive as his dark eyes. He must have been about forty years old. Jack served himself some vodka and, keeping his distance, watched the man's movements closely. The official moved energetically, arrogantly, and Elizabeth seemed to be enjoying his company as much as he did hers.

To Jack's distaste, the quartet of Soviet musicians responsible for livening up the evening played nothing but dreary pieces by Tchaikovsky, Prokofiev, and Borodin, which were dutifully applauded by the couples who flooded the center of the ballroom to enjoy the party. Elizabeth and her partner took the first dance.

Jack finished his drink and set about the dish of prawns, beside which he had abandoned his white wallflowers and violets. He wondered what Elizabeth saw in such a mature man.

He poured himself another glass of vodka and sat on an armchair in the ballroom.

The waltzes followed one another at the same rate at which Jack followed one drink with the next. From time to time, Elizabeth would give him a fleeting look, but not as often or with the intensity that he would have liked. Even so, every time their eyes met, he felt a stab in the belly, as if he'd been hooked by a grapnel.

With the bottle of vodka almost empty, Jack began to wonder what he was doing at a party to which nobody had invited him, surrounded by geriatrics with phony smiles and absurd costumes. He considered getting up and leaving, but one look from Elizabeth stopped him.

Why did she keep glancing at him? What was it she wanted?

He was trying to gather his thoughts when a man approached, his face vaguely familiar. He tried to remember where he'd seen it before, but nothing came to him. Fortunately, the man helped him.

"Well, I'll be damned! It's Beilis, from the ship. Isn't it? It sure is a surprise to find you here! You're staying at the Metropol, too?"

His reedy voice enabled Jack to identify him as Louis Thomson, the *New York Times* journalist he'd shared a table with on board the SS *Cliffwood*. Jack stood and greeted him and two men he was with, whom the journalist introduced as colleagues.

"I should tell you that, were it not for this young man, Wilbur Hewitt would now be 'One-Armed' Wilbur," Louis chortled, raising his glass to celebrate their meeting.

Without much enthusiasm, Jack thanked him for the toast while he held out a hand to the other men. He thought he could see their heads dancing on their shoulders and understood that he'd drunk too much. "Yeah, I must admit I quite like playing the hero," Jack said, carrying on the journalist's jocular tone. "In fact, right now I was saving *myself*. From dying of boredom." He signaled for the bottle of vodka and filled his audience's glasses.

Suddenly, without intending it, Jack found himself engaged in an enjoyable conversation, in which the four men were as likely to celebrate the latest results of the New York Giants as poke fun at the pale flesh hidden under the Soviet women's skirts.

Jack savored the moment as if he were taking a long pull on a good cigar after a large meal. For the first time, he felt at home in Russia, enjoying himself like an American, surrounded by Americans. And not destitute Americans, but real ones. Successful ones. As the conversation progressed, he began to talk about the American miracle as if he were part of it, with almost as much energy as he used to criticize the Soviet system. Amid the laughter, he felt like just another member of the privileged few. Suddenly, even the tedious classical waltzes seemed less annoying, though Jack wondered whether the Russian musicians knew a fox-trot that would really get the party going. He decided to ask for one, and his new friends enthusiastically offered to back him up.

He was heading toward the orchestra when he crossed paths with Elizabeth Hewitt. He looked at her as coolly as he could. She was truly radiant, in a tulle dress that, hugging her waist, gave her a swanlike air. For the first time, he found her alone, without the Soviet official. He had been waiting for this moment for so long that, now it was here, he didn't know what to say. For a second, he turned his head toward the bunch of flowers that lay scattered by the dish of prawns, but figured that it wasn't such a good idea. He turned back to Elizabeth and smiled. "I promised you we'd see each other again," Jack finally said.

"I must admit I was surprised." She gave him a cursory examination. "I'd go so far as to say that scarecrow's jacket you're wearing doesn't look too bad on you." She smiled.

"It's a Russian thing. My Soviet tailor's hands froze up." He smiled back. "You, on the other hand, look incredible. By the way, I brought you a gift . . ." He changed his mind and just pointed at what was left of the wallflowers and violets. "But I'll have to leave it for another time."

"A Russian thing?" She smiled again.

"Something like that. How's your uncle getting on? Still in Helsinki?" He hoped he was wrong.

"My uncle Wilbur? In Helsinki?" She let out a burst of laughter that caught the attention of everyone around them. "It's obvious you don't know us Hewitts. We won't be held back by a little thing like an accident."

"Yes, I can see that."

"Oh? What have you seen?"

"That nothing stops you. You wouldn't stop dancing. I was hoping you'd take a break so *I* could ask you for a dance."

"Well, I was having fun."

"Me, too, watching these old fogeys dancing."

"You didn't seem to be enjoying yourself."

"You were watching me?"

Elizabeth smiled. "Well, I have to go now."

"Wait." He took her hand. He didn't feel her pull it away. "You haven't told me how your uncle is."

Elizabeth saw that Jack was swaying a little, and she smiled again. "In better shape than you. He's staying here, at the Metropol. May I have my hand back?"

Jack gently let her go. He waited for her to walk off, but she stood in front of him for a moment that seemed endless. He was about to ask her for a date, when a figure suddenly appeared.

"Sorry for the delay. Political business," said the newcomer, and he took Elizabeth by the arm. "Excuse me. And you are . . . ?"

"This is Jack . . . Jack . . ." Elizabeth quickly introduced him, his surname apparently already forgotten.

"Beilis. Jack Beilis," he added, holding his hand out to the Soviet official Elizabeth had been dancing with. The officer returned his greeting energetically.

"That's it. Jack Beilis," said Elizabeth. "I met him on the SS *Cliffwood*. He's an American immigrant."

"That's right." It bothered Jack that she had introduced him as a simple immigrant and left out the detail about his saving her uncle Wilbur. "An American immigrant," he repeated.

"Beilis . . . You wouldn't have anything to do with . . . ?"

"No. Definitely not," he said, cutting him off. "It's interesting. I've been asked about my surname so often lately that I'm wondering if I should change it. And your name is . . . ?"

"Oh! How rude of me," said Elizabeth. "Jack, this is Finance Commissar Viktor Smirnov. Viktor's a distant cousin of Stalin's. We met on my first visit to the Soviet Union, and he's always been the perfect host." She smiled.

"Elizabeth, darling, with you it's always a pleasure. And anyway, it would be rude not to redouble the customary Soviet hospitality for those who come to our country to contribute to its development." He returned her smile. "And speaking of the perfect host." He paused for dramatic effect, like an amateur actor, Jack thought. "Here. A small gift from our government." He handed Elizabeth a velvet-lined case.

The young woman's eyes opened as wide as her mouth when she discovered its contents. "Oh, Viktor . . . It's . . . it's beautiful." Elizabeth took the almond-sized emerald and went to hang it around her neck. Viktor helped her.

"The necklace belonged to Anastasia, daughter of the tsarina. I took it from her dressing table myself the day we overthrew them." He gave the American woman a smug look.

Jack feigned a smile. He tried to think of a witty remark, but nothing came to him. In any case, seeing Elizabeth overflowing with happiness and Viktor so triumphant, he knew it wouldn't be welcomed. In fact, Jack was certain that, to Viktor, he was nothing more than a ridiculous insect whom he would never see as a romantic rival. He sensed it because Viktor would glance at him from time to time, but not *see* him. Jack looked at Elizabeth, beautiful, smiling, out of reach. For a moment, he'd believed that his stature, his smile, and his blue eyes would distract from his humble thirdhand jacket and mended shoes, but now it seemed obvious that for Elizabeth, it wouldn't be nearly enough.

He decided that he'd better say his good-byes.

He was rejoining his fellow Americans, when the final notes of the last waltz were played, and as if by magic, the musty old Soviet ballroom was transformed into New York's buzzing Cotton Club. Suddenly, the rhythms of a frenetic fox-trot filled the room, and the guests delighted in the change. It was enough for Jack to forget about all of his problems for a moment, and he turned toward Elizabeth. He was forced to swallow his envy when he noticed that the young woman was attracting the glances of the entire room with her sensual movements, while Viktor was flailing ridiculously in an attempt to follow her lead.

He guessed the best thing to do would be to return to his guest-house. There, even if he had to endure one of Walter's boring political discussions, at least the night would be bearable.

He was saying good-bye to the journalists, when he saw a man with his arm in a sling waving at him from the other end of the room. It was Wilbur Hewitt. He said his farewells as quickly as he could, then headed over to Hewitt.

"Well I never, kid! You're the last person I'd have expected to see among this bunch of bourgeoisie-turned-revolutionaries. What in hell's name are you doing here?" asked Elizabeth's uncle.

"It's good to see you, sir. I was chatting with Louis Thomson and—"

Jack wanted to avoid explaining his presence at the Metropol and asked the industrialist about his arm.

"I still have it!" He laughed. "Those Finnish doctors are magicians. Strange methods, but magicians." He clumsily bent his wrist to demonstrate the improvement. "Incidentally, it's a stroke of luck that you're here. I've been looking for you. Remember Sergei, the Soviet official escorting me on the SS *Cliffwood*? Well, they've promoted him to director of operations, and among other things, he's responsible for the Avtozavod's security now. I told him to ask Intourist for your whereabouts, and I was waiting for the results of his inquiries."

The hair on Jack's neck stood on end. Any hint that somebody was investigating him put him on the alert. "And what did he find?"

"If you don't mind, we'll go to the library. What I have to propose to you isn't for blurting out in a Soviet ballroom."

On the fourth sip of strong coffee, Jack began to sober up. But he still couldn't believe what Hewitt was proposing, so he asked him to repeat it.

"It's simple," the industrialist summarized. "If you accept my new offer, I'd be prepared to pay you two hundred dollars a week."

Jack had to clear his throat when he received confirmation that Hewitt's proposal hadn't been a vodka-induced fantasy. He took another sip of coffee and looked at the general manager of the Avtozavod. Eight hundred dollars a month was a Ford Motor Company executive's salary in the United States.

"For six months. A year at most. Then you can work in a normal role befitting your skills, though still well paid," the industrialist added.

Jack smiled. He asked Hewitt what the catch was.

"You know what, Jack? That's exactly what I like about you. You're smart. And you say things to a man's face." He folded the copy of the *New York Times* he always carried with him and left it on the table. "I'll be straight with you. I've been turning over in my head what we talked about when we were disembarking in Helsinki. What I said about the Russians needing some Americans with guts to⊠"

"Sure. To get things working once and for all. But I was referring to the job at the factory, to repair the machinery damaged in the storm, and that has nothing to do with what you're proposing now, sir."

"Forget that machinery, Jack. I know this has nothing to do with that, but what have you got to lose? I'm just asking you to keep your eyes open for me during your day's work as an assembly line supervisor."

"And rat on my fellow Americans?" He was trying to wrap his head around it.

"No. That's not what I said."

"You said someone's been sabotaging production, and you want to offer me a job as a front to find out who's behind it."

"But I didn't say the perpetrators were American. I just pointed out that the Soviets will blame anyone to hide their incompetence. Most likely, it's Russian operatives unhappy with the working conditions. It might be that, or it may simply have been a succession of accidents. And I wouldn't agree with your description of your position as a front, either, considering that your technical skills will be essential to uncovering the cause of the damage."

Jack looked at Hewitt. Eight hundred dollars a month was a lot of money. Perhaps it was too much.

"I doubt you'd offer me a chunk of change like that"—he served himself some more coffee while he weighed up what he should say—"if it didn't come with risks."

Hewitt raised an eyebrow.

"It's like anything in life. You can't get the best views unless you climb the mountain."

"And what if they rat me out?"

"Who?"

"The Soviets."

"Well, let's be straight. You'll have to make sure that doesn't happen. The Soviets don't usually mess around." He paused. "But don't worry. Nobody will know you're tasked with investigating the incidents, and obviously you won't be stupid enough to go around telling people. And anyway, when there's an accident at the factory, they blame the inefficiency of the American equipment, the American workers, or the American procedures. If they suspect anything untoward, they arrest someone, interrogate him, and let him go, but they don't want to hear any talk about sabotage that would prove the existence of anti-Soviet groups. Henry Ford thinks differently, which is why he's entrusted me to get the Gorky factory up and running at full capacity. That's why I'm in Russia, and why I'm offering you so much money."

Jack drank from his cup again. He couldn't think clearly. "And if I don't find anything?"

"That's a risk I have to take. We're all taking risks here, Jack. Your risk is being uncovered. My risk is you finding nothing and me wasting money."

"I see." Jack pursed his lips. Hewitt seemed honest in his proposal, but Jack couldn't understand why he was entrusting such an important task to a virtual stranger. When he asked him why, the industrialist was pretty explicit.

"You really want to know? Well, because I have no goddamned choice, son." Hewitt admitted that he had lined up an engineer in the United States for the job but, just before the SS *Cliffwood* had set sail, he'd suddenly fallen ill. "Appendicitis, I believe. In fact, George McMillan should be sitting where you are right now, and I should be talking to him, not you. Luckily, you showed up. And not only did you save my arm, but you're also bright, know the Ford machinery like the back of your hand, and speak Russian. I couldn't have found a more ideal candidate had I tried!"

Jack tapped his fingers on the table. He didn't know how to respond. It may have been the effect of the vodka, but he couldn't see things clearly. It was too unexpected. There were too many factors. Too much money.

"I don't know, Mr. Hewitt. I'd need some time to think about it." He got up and held out his hand.

"Of course, kid! No problem. You take your time. If you want, we can meet again tomorrow."

"Yes, all right, I'll see you tomorrow."

"Excellent." He squeezed Jack's hand and returned his good-bye. "Hey! Now I think of it, where are you staying?"

"A guesthouse. Well, in reality it's a tenement house, it's—"

"Would you like to stay here?"

"Pardon me, sir?"

"I'm asking if you'd like to stay here, at the Metropol. McMillan's room was paid for in advance, and it's still available. You could have it, free of charge."

"But . . . I . . ."

"Oh, come on, kid! Don't be daft! Sleeping on a soft mattress won't commit you to anything. See it as a gift for having heard me out, and tomorrow morning we'll talk over breakfast."

On the way to his room on the fourth floor, Jack wondered at the size of the function rooms and corridors, their gold fabric-lined walls contrasting with the blue diamond-patterned carpets. The mock Corinthian columns and ebony figures of lions were such a display of opulence that he felt like a thief who'd been given permission to steal whatever he wished.

He checked his room number. It was 428. He was searching for the key in his pockets, when at the end of the corridor, he saw Elizabeth appear. The young woman was alone, looking down at the floor, seemingly deep in thought. Jack watched her closely. She was walking carelessly, with her low-heel shoes hanging from one hand and her crocodile-skin purse swinging gently in the other. Jack thought to himself that he had never seen such a beautiful twenty-two-year-old.

"Hello," he said to her, a yard before she bumped into him. She gave a start.

"Oh! Hello, Jack. Sorry. I hadn't recognized you."

"Yeah. As soon as I take my jacket off, I look like a waiter." He smiled.

She returned the smile, but it was forced. "What're you doing here? This part of the hotel's reserved for guests."

"Yeah, I know."

"You're not worried they'll throw you out?"

"Nope."

"No? How brave! Anyway, I'm exhausted. Wearing new shoes to a ball is the stupidest thing a woman can do."

"Well, the way everyone was looking at you, I'd say it was worth it."

Elizabeth's smile this time, though tired, was sincere. She let herself slump into a chair and gently massaged her feet. Jack gazed at her.

"You still haven't told me what you're doing here," she said.

"I was waiting for you," he lied.

"For me? What for?"

"You still owe me a dance. You promised, remember?"

"I did? I don't know. I've got no shoes on now, and I wouldn't want you to step on me with those big feet. We'll have to leave it for my next birthday."

"I'm very careful," he said in a persuasive tone.

She sat looking at him, then closed her eyes and smiled. "Maybe some other time. It's been a really long day and—"

Jack didn't let her finish. He threw his arms around her and found her mouth. For a moment he felt her abandon herself to him. But it was just an instant, before she pulled away abruptly and slapped him across the face.

"How dare you?" The sweetness in her face had now turned bitter with indignation.

"I . . . I don't know what came over me . . ." Jack didn't know how to apologize.

"Are you crazy? Do you think that smiling at you a couple of times means I'm attracted to you?"

"Elizabeth! Keep your voice down! I told you I'm sorry. Anyway, when I was kissing you, I didn't get the impression you disliked it."

"What? How pathetic! Do you really think someone like me would notice a down-and-out like you? Did you think that I'd like you, and we'd end up frolicking in some dump of a boardinghouse where you no doubt live?"

Jack fell silent, his head bowed, biting the lips that a moment before had savored Elizabeth's.

"You're right," he finally said, withdrawing a few steps. "I've been a fool. And you were also right to think that I like you, and that I believed you might notice a down-and-out like me." He paused for a few seconds. "But you were wrong about one thing, at least." He slowly took the key from his pocket and opened the door to his room. "I wouldn't have taken you to some dump of a boardinghouse. I can promise you that."

13

He wandered around the extravagant room, marveling at every detail. The delicately decorated porcelain coffee set, the satin-lined walls, the beautiful pair of Empire-style armchairs, the comfortable temperature of the heating. He admired the vaulted ceiling, ornamented with floral motifs and a hunting scene. The sense of luxury overwhelmed him. It was a luxury as alien to him and as unattainable as Wilbur Hewitt's niece. He leaned against the radiator and allowed the warmth to imbue his body. The room smelled of clean, starched cotton, as deep and as intoxicating an aroma as the one given off by the shirt section at the Hudson's department store in Detroit. It had been so long since he'd been there, and he still remembered it! He let himself fall onto a bed that seemed to welcome him. What a bewildering life his was! Luck seemed to smile on him or abandon him at random, as if someone were pulling the strings of his destiny at whim.

The velvet bedspread made the hair on the back of his neck stand on end. He imagined it to be like Elizabeth's skin: soft, warm, delicate . . .

He'd kissed her. Though it seemed improbable, it had happened, and the memory of her mouth was so powerful that he could feel nothing that wasn't her lips. Perhaps it was because it hadn't been like any kiss he'd experienced before. The heat from her lips still burned him; he could still taste the sweet flavor that he had savored for that one fleeting moment. But the more he tried, the more difficult it became to remember it clearly, and his thoughts turned again to her half-open mouth, its softness, its trembling warmth, surprised and yielding at the same time. That brief instant during which he'd kissed her had felt eternal until the moment when their lips had separated and stopped a hairbreadth apart, as if they longed to remain touching, and there, almost brushing together, stole each other's breath for the last time, as if to keep it with them forever.

He'd never kissed like that before, and he doubted that she had, either, which was why he couldn't understand the rage with which Elizabeth had slapped him.

He closed his eyes. At some point he dreamed of her. He dreamed that they were dancing together, going to parties and shows arm in arm, dining in posh restaurants, and that Wilbur Hewitt approved. Sometimes, in his delirium, Elizabeth appeared wrapped in linen sheets, writhing with mischief, aware of her beauty and nakedness, rationing every portion of exposed skin to feed his desire, a desire that grew with each insinuation, with each movement.

And then suddenly, Elizabeth's face transformed into Sue's, and Jack retreated, frightened. He saw Kowalski stalking him, threatening to evict him again, approaching with his goons, and Jack gripped the arm that brandished a pistol, and held it with all his might until the bangs echoed in his ears, again and again. Tock, tock, tock.

Tock, tock, tock.

Jack woke with a start, dressed in the same clothes he'd collapsed onto the bed in a few hours before. Someone was knocking on the door. He tidied his hair as well as he could and rushed to open it. Seeing who it was, he was almost as surprised as he was flushed.

"Sue! Er, what are you doing here?"

"I should ask you the same thing!" She strode into the room in a rage. "May I ask where you got to? You were supposed to come with us to the People's Commissariat this morning."

"What? The Commissariat? Oh damn! I forgot. What time is it?" It all flooded back to him. The whole room was spinning.

"Ten." She opened the curtains without ceremony to allow the sun to assail Jack's reddened eyes. "Holy Mother of God! What a room!" she added, dancing around it. "It's bigger than my house! What've you done? Swindled someone?"

"It's a long story." He went to the bathroom to wash his face. "Shit, I'm going to miss my meeting."

"Meeting?" Sue said with surprise, but Jack didn't answer.

He looked himself up and down. His pants were creased; his shirt was, too. He went to the wardrobe and flung it open to find that it was empty.

"What about that chest?" Sue pointed at it.

Jack looked at the trunk that lay at the foot of the bed, which until then he'd taken to be just another part of the furnishings. He confirmed the initials inscribed on it. *G. McM.* George McMillan. He assumed it must be his luggage, and that in the hospital where he was recovering from appendicitis, he wouldn't miss it. Jack needed clean clothes, so he examined the lock.

"Do you have a hairpin?" he asked Sue.

She took one from her hair. "What're you going to do? Pick it?" She gave a nervous laugh.

"Quiet!" he ordered.

Jack took the hairpin and poked it into the lock, moving it until he heard a click. He looked at Sue with an anxious expression, as if waiting for her approval to open it. She nodded.

Jack had hit the jackpot. The chest contained everything a traveler could need and much more than he could have imagined: a folder of assorted documents, a case of cigarettes, a silver lighter, a comb, a shaving set, three bottles of painkillers, two pairs of shoes and two pairs of pants, a suit, three shirts, a magnificent overcoat, and several changes of underwear that Sue handed one by one to Jack, who spread them out on the bed like trophies.

"Will they fit you?"

"I don't know. I think so. Did you see this? The guy even packed cologne." He showed Sue the bottle of Floïd that he'd just discovered. "I'm going to clean myself up." He took the shaving set and a change of clothes and headed to the bathroom. Through the half-open door, Sue watched Jack take off his shirt, leaving his torso bare. "By the way, how did you find me?" he asked as he began to lather his face.

"Joe Brown told me that the bunch of flowers you bought was for a party at the Metropol, so I guessed you'd be here. Who were they for?"

"What?" He cursed Joe Brown for being such a blabbermouth.

"The flowers. Who were they for?" she said as she sat on the bed, stroking the sheets.

"Oh! For Hewitt." He was unsure why he'd lied. "I heard he was recovering at the Metropol, so I brought them as a gesture."

"Flowers for a man?" Sue pulled a face.

"Sure. Here in Russia it's considered a courtesy between men. I explained it to Joe. And how did you find my room?" He tried to change the subject.

"Oh, well, in the garden I saw that guy you saved on the ship. What did you say his name was? Hewitt? Yeah, that's it, Hewitt. He was the only person I knew, so I asked him. You should've seen my face when he told me you were staying here. I think I was as surprised as I was the first time I saw a boy take his pants down. So anyway, I thanked him and came up. Hey! You still haven't told me how you ended up sleeping in another man's room," she said, looking at McMillan's trunk.

Jack didn't answer. Sue imagined it was because of the noise from the shower, which had been on for a while. She got up and went to the bathroom door that Jack had taken care to leave only narrowly open.

"Jack. Can you hear me?"

Sue opened the door a little. Jack, his eyes closed in the shower, didn't notice her. But instead of closing the door, Sue stood for a few seconds looking at Jack's naked body as he let the water wash over his skin. She continued to admire it until he began to turn around. Sue gave a start and retreated.

When Jack came out of the bathroom, dressed, combed, and perfectly shaved, Sue was sitting on the end of the bed again. Jack was surprised to see her lower her head, as if embarrassed. "What is it? Do I look bad?" He tightened the belt.

Sue told him to relax, assuring him that he looked straight out of a Charles Atlas advertisement. She stood and helped him put his jacket on. It was a bit too big, but close enough for Jack to wear without feeling uncomfortable. He thanked Sue for her help and completed his transformation with a few drops of aftershave.

"Come on! That's quite enough dressing up. Walter's waiting for you at the Commissariat with his friend Dmitri, the one who's going to help us."

"Huh? Oh, sure! Damn it, I completely forgot. This . . . I'm sorry, Sue, but I can't go with you," he said apologetically.

"Are you serious? I came all the way here to fetch you."

"I know, but I can't. Would you go and meet him, please? Tell him I'll see him at the guesthouse later."

"No!"

"What?"

"I'm not leaving this room without you! We have been waiting for you without knowing whether you were alive or dead, and I didn't cross Moscow on a flea-ridden tram just for you to say sorry and not come to the Commissariat. We need you, Jack! Us, the Daniels family, and Joe. They're waiting for you, too."

Jack bit his lip. He didn't like letting them down, but an offer like the one Hewitt was making him was a once-in-a-lifetime opportunity.

"Really, I can't. Anyway, you don't need me. There was an English interpreter at the Commissariat, and you have the Amtorg contracts. Walter can sort out everything himself. For God's sake, you can't expect me to do everything for you."

"I can't believe you're doing this to us, Jack!"

The young woman's face was a mixture of astonishment and disappointment, like a little girl who had just learned Santa Claus wasn't real. She retreated to the door. Jack was silent with shame, but remained where he was.

"Think what you want, Sue. I can't tell you what it's about, but trust me, you would do the same thing if you were me."

Hewitt didn't seem to care that Jack showed up wearing an outfit that belonged to his employee McMillan. In fact, when Jack confided to him that he'd found the sick engineer's trunk open, Hewitt not only approved but encouraged him to use the clothes.

"After all, McMillan bought them with Ford Motor Company money, right? If you hadn't taken them, I might've had to buy you something. Anyway, I'll send someone to take care of your belongings later. Have you had breakfast?" He didn't give him time to answer. He laid his copy of the *New York Times* on the table and called to the waiter. "What will you have?"

"I'll have whatever you're having." Though he was Jewish, he didn't follow the religion's dietary laws.

"Good choice! We'll have coffee for two, and bacon, fried eggs, sausages, and French fries. The American newspapers always reach Moscow a week late"—he pointed at the out-of-date broadsheet—"but I can't live without them."

Jack didn't pay much attention to the newspaper. His head still hurt, but he hadn't lost his appetite.

"So. Have you had a little think about our conversation yesterday?" He took off his monocle.

"A little think, sir? Truthfully, I didn't sleep a wink."

"Ha!" He interrupted to allow the waiter to serve them. "And is that good or bad?"

Jack took a deep breath. In reality he hadn't decided yet. "Mr. Hewitt, I must admit that your offer's tempting, but before I decide, there are a few things I'd like to discuss with you."

"Of course! That's why we're here, isn't it?" He wolfed down a sausage practically in one bite.

Jack asked Hewitt about the responsibilities he'd have as supervisor, what his everyday work would be, and how he would report his discoveries. The industrialist explained that he'd occupy the position earmarked for McMillan, and consequently, he'd work directly under him. "Though in theory, under Sergei as well," he added. "As I said, they've made him head of security at the Avtozavod."

Jack choked on the mouthful he was eating. His brushes with the Soviet on board the SS *Cliffwood* did not suggest they would get on well. But Hewitt reassured him.

"Don't worry. It's just bureaucracy. We Americans have important roles, but the factory belongs to the Soviets." He explained to Jack that, three years earlier, when Stalin decided to build a factory in Gorky in the image of the Dearborn plants, they extended every courtesy. "Joseph Stalin is a car fanatic, desperate to motorize the country whatever the cost. Imagine old Henry Ford's joy when the Soviets made him the offer. Not only would Stalin pay him forty million dollars to start manufacturing an obsolete model, but he also agreed to buy the used machinery that Ford had already jettisoned from its factories in Germany." He clumsily wiped his mustache. "Though, of course, the Soviets made sure that, in addition to building the factory and supplying enough parts, Ford would provide the American technicians needed to get the factory up and running. At first, everything was our responsibility, but as work progressed, the Soviets gradually took over."

"Took over?"

"Well, that's one way of looking at it. The fact was, any useless Soviet could be appointed as a boss simply for belonging to the Communist Party, and the next day that boss would hand another position of responsibility to his brother-in-law."

"That doesn't surprise me. Like you say, the factory belongs to them, doesn't it?"

"Yeah, sure, but things worked before. If a nut happened to fall down a crack, they'd damned well make sure they found it and put it back in its place. But now, if you want a Soviet to bend down and pick up a nut, one that he might well have dropped himself, on purpose, half the factory has to be mobilized to authorize it. There are bosses for everything: section bosses, chain bosses, line bosses, union bosses, machine bosses, committee bosses, duty bosses, heads, executives, managers! The few who do any actual work are illiterate peasants from the Caucasus, the Urals, and Mongolia with no initiative and no dreams . . . If it carries on like this, before long, there'll be more bosses than workers."

"But I don't get it. If the factory's Soviet, there are more and more Soviet bosses, and things are done the way the Soviets want, why do you care so much?"

"I just told you. They hired us to deliver a factory that works, and until it achieves the agreed production figures, the contract remains unfulfilled."

"You think that the suspected sabotage could be for political reasons?"

"I'm not certain. It might be. They blame counterrevolutionary elements or attacks from disgruntled workers. But it could also be nothing more than a series of accidents due to the operatives' lack of expertise, or just poor maintenance . . . anything. Either way, it's my duty to find out. Pass the coffee, will you?"

Jack was pensive, looking Hewitt in the eyes. "And what does Sergei have to do with all of this?" He filled the industrialist's cup.

"Sergei? Sergei's your typical tight-lipped Russian. He is a survivor. They assigned him to me this year as a liaison officer, and since then, he's followed me everywhere like a dog." He gestured with his chin, indicating the entrance to the room. Jack looked and recognized Sergei's white beard. He was reading the *Pravda* some distance away. "Although they've promoted him, that shouldn't worry you. Bear in mind that your job will be to supervise maintenance of the production chain, which isn't a position that will arouse his suspicion, and it's something, I'm told, for which you have the necessary skills."

"You're told?" He stopped chewing.

Hewitt opened the *New York Times* with his only good hand, took a folder from the inside pages, and dumped it on Jack's plate of bacon. "Look for yourself!"

Jack, surprised, opened the folder and studied the report he found inside. It was a wire transmission dated three days earlier in Helsinki, sent from Dearborn. "But this is . . ."

"Exactly. Your employee file. I requested it as soon as I was admitted to the hospital. Everything's in there, from the day you started at Ford to the day they fired you: training, promotions, authorizations, what you ate, whom you mixed with, and how long you spent in the bathroom. It would appear that you're a smart guy." He winked.

Jack breathed in. His heart was thumping. He supposed that if Hewitt had dug this deep, he might know something about Kowalski's death. But it was unlikely he'd gotten wind of it, and Jack wanted to do business with him.

"I see you leave nothing to chance."

"I sure don't, kid. You might've impressed me on the SS *Cliffwood*, but I needed to make sure you could repair the damaged machinery.

And now these reports are just what I needed, to know I'm going to pay two hundred dollars a week to the right person."

"Three hundred."

"What did you say?"

"I said, three hundred. Three hundred dollars a week if you want me to take this on. Like you said, there's a lot of money at stake, and there's no one else who can do it. I'm traveling with my wife, and even though you won't admit it, everything suggests it's going to be risky."

Jack fell silent. He hadn't asked for more money out of ambition. He just wanted to check whether Hewitt knew he was wanted for murder. If he did, Hewitt would be the one calling the shots and could make him work for free, if he so wished, but if he agreed to Jack's financial terms, it would mean he had nothing on him. Hewitt stared at Jack for a while. "All right, young man. Three hundred it is!"

Jack didn't wait to start showing Hewitt that he took the job seriously. He hadn't yet finished his coffee before he asked for the factory's floor plans, a detailed inventory of the machinery, the credentials of the Soviet and American machine operators, their shift patterns, and, of course, a comprehensive list of the incidents that had taken place and the workers involved.

"Well, blow me down! All right, I'll try to get all that together for you."

"Perfect. As for my cover story . . ." Jack admitted to Hewitt that he was concerned that if his unexpected appointment wasn't made to seem credible, it would arouse the Soviets' suspicion.

"That won't be necessary," Hewitt reassured him. "I'll tell Sergei the truth: that I needed someone to replace McMillan, that I asked Dearborn for your file, and that you were the best man for the job. The only thing I'll hide is the real purpose of your role. He'll assume you'll keep him up to date with everything you find out, but in reality you'll tell him only what we want him to know."

"So, Sergei knew about the problem with McMillan?"

"There ain't much the Soviets don't know. They always ask for a list of the American specialists that Ford is sending to their factory ahead of time. That's why it makes sense to hire a replacement for McMillan."

"OK. In that case, there's just the matter of my friends."

"I don't understand. What do they have to do with this?"

Jack admitted to Hewitt that he and his friends had come up against a setback trying to validate the contracts that Amtorg had granted them in the United States.

"I'm sorry to hear that, but it's a separate matter. I don't see how I can help them."

"It's simple. There're just five of them: my wife, my friend Walter, Harry Daniels, his elder son, and Joe Brown. They're all qualified, and they would help me integrate as a supervisor. Their presence at the factory would enable me to ask questions without arousing suspicion."

"Five, you say?" He blew out. "Honestly. I don't think it'll be necessary."

"Look, sir. It's not like you're hiring a bunch of good-for-nothings. As I said, they all came with signed contracts, but apparently the Soviets filled their quota and no positions will be available again for three months. All I'm asking is that you speed up the process. It won't be hard for a man of your influence to do that."

"Jack, as well as being difficult, it would be expensive. I'm sorry, but if you want me to hire them, you'll need an argument with more weight than that."

"Is the weight of the machine I lifted off your arm not enough?"

Wilbur Hewitt breathed in and clenched his teeth before taking a final bite of his sausage.

"All right, kid. But don't tell anyone I was the one who hired them."

14

Jack didn't expect his companions to welcome him with applause and confetti, but neither did he imagine that, when he arrived at the guest-house, even Joe Brown would refuse to speak to him. They were all in the bedroom, a funereal look on their faces. He asked what was wrong, but nobody responded. Jack approached little Danny in silence to hand him a cookie he'd taken from the buffet at the Metropol, but when the boy went to take it, his mother pushed it away. Harry Daniels lowered his head. Sue ignored him. When Jack insisted on knowing what was wrong, Walter exploded.

"You still have the gall to show up and ask us what's wrong? *Us?* Ask yourself what's happening with you! Or even better, let Joe tell you, because until the last minute, he defended you, saying that it was impossible that you'd let us down. Or ask Harry, damn it, who went without eating, hoping that you'd finally appear. Or Sue, who went to the trouble to go find you because she was so worried that something had happened to you. Or ask me, your best friend. Ask me why I, while you were having fun at a luxury hotel, went down on my knees to beg the Commissariat to give us jobs. Jobs for all of us, including you!"

"Wow! I see I can't leave you alone for a minute." He tried to put an arm over Walter's shoulder, but his friend pushed it away.

"Some balls you have, Jack! Why don't you keep your goddamned jokes for your friend Hewitt? Maybe he can stomach them."

Jack grasped that it wasn't a time for sarcasm. "All right. I know I should've told you, but—"

"No! It's not all right, Jack! It's far from all right! Our jobs are far from all right! Your passport's far from all right! The food is far from all right! And this fucking guesthouse is far from all right! And while we bust a gut trying to change things, even if it's just to know that we'll still be able to sleep between these four walls tomorrow rather than freeze to death in a park, you decide to spend your time at parties, staying in suites, and abandoning the friends who helped you not so long ago."

"Hang on, Walter. You don't know what happened. I—"

"I don't know? Damned right I don't know! And you know why? Because although Sue asked you at the hotel, you didn't deign to answer her."

"For God's sake! Let me explain!"

"You ain't gonna persuade me with your hot air. Joe Brown and the Danielses know about what you did with the train tickets. They know how you took advantage of everyone. Nobody wants your explanations here. Thought you were a big shot, huh? Jack the indispensable, the man who fixes everything, but of course, only when you pay him enough. Well, guess what? I got jobs for them, free of charge. Do you hear me? Free."

"Well, I'll be damned, Walter! I'm impressed." Irony returned to his voice.

"Look, Jack. I can't even be bothered to talk to you."

"Oh no. Let's talk!" he said in the same sarcastic tone. "You got jobs for everyone, huh? Gee! That's great news! And I guess they're well paid, right?"

"Well paid or not, they're jobs."

"How much, Walter? A hundred and eighty dollars a month? Because that's what you promised us we'd receive, isn't it?"

"No." He lowered his head. "Those wages were for specialized workers with contracts."

"We had contracts."

"Which are no longer valid. They produced them for us overnight, and they weren't confirmed. Don't ask me why, but they're not worth the paper they're printed on."

"Oh! So the wages you promised us were just for specialized workers. And what's Joe Brown? A farmhand? As far as I knew, until the damned depression, he was working at a Kosciusko foundry where he'd been working since before he was out of diapers. And Harry Daniels? Is Harry not specialized? Because as I understand it, in Massachusetts, he handled a lathe like he was riding a bicycle. And his son Jim? Did Jim not study at the Institute of Technology and work at Jason and Brothers Presses? I don't know what you think, but I reckon they're pretty specialized."

"It's not like I thought it would be here. There are more and more qualified Soviets now, and the immigrants who arrive without a valid contract have to make do with—"

"With what, Walter? A hundred and fifty? A hundred and twenty a month?"

Walter didn't respond. Jack looked at everyone else for an answer, but they all remained silent.

"Fifty!" Joe Brown blurted out in the end, spitting on the floor. "Fifty dollars."

"What do you expect for half days? It's better than nothing!" Walter yelled. "What did you get, Jack? What have you got for us?"

Jack looked at them all one by one before replying. "Two hundred. Two hundred dollars a month, for each of you."

◆ ◆ ◆

The transfer to Gorky by railway was much the same as the other train journeys they'd experienced: the same packed third-class cars, the same delays, the same insufferable jolting, and the same snow-covered horizon. The only difference was that Walter wasn't traveling with them. Jack looked at the chipped wooden bench where he'd spent ten hours. Pressed shoulder to shoulder with Sue, he asked her why, in a country that glorified the equality of all citizens, they had three classes of accommodation on trains.

"I guess it's because these cars are from the age of the tsars," Sue replied, trying to rationalize in the same way that Walter would have.

Jack scratched his head. "I doubt it. If that was the case, it could easily be remedied. They could have a single price and allocate the best seats first come, first served."

"Oh, Jack!" She smiled. "I don't understand politics. I bet Walter would have given you a better answer. I don't know. Perhaps they've kept the higher classes for rich foreign tourists. Anyway, what do you care? The important thing is we're about to arrive at the gateway to the Urals!" She stood up to gesture toward the impressive pair of transmission towers visible in the distance.

Jack wiped some condensation from the glass and looked through it at the gigantic twin towers. A shiver ran down his spine. They were just over twelve miles from Gorky and their new life. And though he didn't fear destiny, for the first time, Walter's absence unnerved him. He still couldn't understand why his friend had not gone with them.

The night before they left, Walter had been defiant, declaring that he would never accept handouts from a capitalist pig. It had been no use insisting to him that Wilbur Hewitt had been hired by Stalin himself to help the Soviet Union. Sue said that Walter hadn't grasped just how good a deal it was that Jack had managed to get from Hewitt, and that was why he had decided to stay in Moscow for a few days and find his own opportunities in Gorky through his Muscovite contact. To avoid any trouble, Walter hadn't wanted her to stay with him. He'd given himself a time limit of one week, he told Sue. If he didn't get results, he'd travel to Gorky and accept Hewitt's offer.

Just after midday, the train came to a halt in Gorky Station.

As they alighted, the sixty-eight American immigrants heard the Intourist official responsible for guiding them to the blocks where they would be housed suggest that they load their luggage onto the carts that waited for them by the river, but nobody moved a muscle. After coming halfway around the world, they were not about to separate themselves from what little they still possessed.

Jack rubbed himself in an attempt to retain some of the heat that seemed to be escaping through his mouth with every breath. He looked around. The avenue on which the snow buried both the roadway and the houses was almost deserted. On the station façade, the thermometer showed thirty-five degrees Celsius below zero. He put his arm around Sue, who was shivering like a puppy. No one had warned them that the last paradise would be so cold.

Like a herd of reindeer, the American immigrants followed the Intourist official to the tram stop on line eight, where they were told that it would take them forty-five minutes to travel the seven and a half miles from the center of the city to the suburb where the factory was located. Once they were squeezed in like livestock, the driver rang the bell, and the tram dragged its two cars through Gorky's desolate streets. As they huddled together, Jack could not imagine how the city's freezing inhabitants could know the meaning of the word *happiness*.

Gradually, the last buildings made way for a monotonous, snow-covered upland, interrupted from time to time by lampposts sunk into the snow like harpoons protruding somberly from a great white whale. After half an hour, the tram approached a gigantic complex of industrial buildings protected by dozens of wire fences. Murmurs were suddenly replaced with words of admiration when the passengers saw the impressive size of a site that, at first glance, seemed bigger than the city itself.

Jack was impressed. The Ford factory where he'd worked in Dearborn had comprised assembly and power plants, a foundry, a bodyworkers' shop, an engine factory, and countless warehouses and auxiliary buildings spread over a thousand acres. The Avtozavod not only housed similar installations, but behind the fences there seemed to be an army of armed guards.

When the tram reached the final stop, signposted "Eastern District," Jack was one of the first to enter the registration office that the Soviets appeared to have set up for the occasion in a timber hut. He was received by a guard with slanting eyes under a fur hat almost as large as the overcoat that covered his body. The man shivered behind a little counter upon which lay a cap similar to the one Elizabeth's partner at the dance had been wearing. He wondered to which section of the army the cap belonged. When it was his turn and the employee asked him to identify himself, Jack placed the letter of recommendation from Amtorg and the contract that Wilbur Hewitt had provided on the counter. The man ignored the letter and concentrated on the contract, verifying that, alongside Hewitt's signature, Sergei Loban's appeared. He stamped the document and added Jack's name to a registration book. When the Soviet asked him for his passport, Jack informed him that it had been requisitioned at the Finnish border.

"The officer who retained it assured me they'd send it on to the People's Commissariat of Heavy Industry in Moscow, but when I went to collect it, they told me that they'd forward it directly to this factory."

The guard turned his slanted eyes toward Jack. He looked at the name that appeared on the contract again and searched in his drawer. Jack noticed that it was filled with American passports.

"Jack Beilis. Yes. Here it is." He took it out of the drawer, compared the photograph to Jack's face, and set it down next to the cap. "You come with family?"

Jack remembered that he had shown his fake marriage certificate at customs. At that moment he was glad that Walter had decided to stay in Moscow; otherwise there would no doubt have been a quarrel. "Yes, I'm traveling with my wife." He gestured to Sue to come forward. "She has a contract, too." He showed it to the man.

Sue smiled and gripped Jack as if he belonged to her, making a face when she had to let go to hand the guard her passport.

"All right. Fill out questionnaire, sign, and wait outside until accommodation assigned to you," he said.

"And our passports, when will they be returned to us?" Jack asked.

"Why ask question? To work in Soviet Union, you not need passports."

The Daniels family and Joe Brown also had their passports taken. However, like the rest of the immigrants, they were given a typewritten receipt so that, when the time came, they could retrieve them.

With the paperwork done, the sixty-eight Americans were led on foot across the snow-covered mile and a quarter between the Eastern District stop and what was known as Fordville, or the American village, the complex of prefabricated bunkhouses built to house the Avtozavod's foreign workers.

As they approached, Jack gazed at the apartment buildings. Though newly built, the timber of the walls and roofs, along with their squat size and the wire fencing that encircled the site, made them look like giant stables. They were nothing like the family homes that Walter had described, but taking shelter in a barrel would have been preferable to spending a moment longer exposed to the cold, so Jack ignored the soulless appearance of the buildings and, along with the rest of the workers, sought refuge inside. Finally, after weeks of hardship, laughter and jubilation took hold of the Americans, and the cold and the fear disappeared. Joe Brown asked Jack to pinch him, but Sue got in first and gave him a shove that did nothing to diminish the daft smile spread across his face. The man couldn't believe what he was seeing. In his fifty-three years of life, working from dawn to dusk with no vacation or Sundays off, he had never had so much as a new mattress, and now, in front of him, like a Christmas gift, there they were waiting for him: a new home and a salary of two hundred dollars a month, all for tightening a few screws.

Jack would've loved to go to see the baseball field, the social club, and the other facilities that the veteran Americans who had come to welcome them wanted to show them, but a young Soviet guard appeared and stopped him. He said he had come on behalf of Wilbur Hewitt, and added that the industrialist was waiting for Jack in his office.

Jack understood that it wasn't an invitation. He gave his luggage to the Daniels family to take to his room and said good-bye to everyone.

"But, Jack! You'll miss the welcome party they've laid out for us!" Sue complained.

"Then save me some cake!" he yelled as he went out into the blizzard and headed to the old truck where the guard was waiting for him with the engine running.

The vehicle roared as its heavy wheels turned on their axles, fighting to free themselves from the nasty mixture of mud and snow that the road had become. As they built up speed, Jack could see that the fresh-faced youngster was enjoying squeezing the truck for every ounce of power it had left in it, thrashing it about on the factory's tracks as if it were a giant iron toy. Between potholes, Jack noticed the blue ribbon around the kid's peaked cap, which was different from the one worn by the guards at the gates. He considered asking him why there was so much security, but something told him that curiosity would be about as helpful here as washing his hands in a bowl of acid. Instead, he gripped his seat and allowed the young guard to concentrate on his crazed sprint across the site.

Finally, the vehicle stopped by a guard station with a screech that made Jack think the bearings had breathed their last breath. The driver turned off the engine, waved at the sentry, and after showing his ID, asked Jack to accompany him. Heading through an administrative building crammed with workers, they stopped in front of an office where the sign on the door read:

Sergei Loban

Director of Operations

Jack was silent. He looked at the driver for an explanation, but the youngster just knocked on the door and waited for an answer. When Jack heard Sergei's voice, he could not prevent a slight shudder.

The director of operations received Jack while leaning back in his armchair, with the same dour portraits of Lenin and Stalin behind him that seemed to look over every room in the Soviet Union. By the armchair of frayed felt stood a coatrack from which hung a thick fur overcoat and a peaked cap trimmed with blue ribbon. Sergei Loban put out his cigarette in a half-drunk glass of tea, dismissed the driver, and asked Jack to take a seat on one of two red leather armchairs. Jack obeyed, anxious to find out why he now found himself in that office and not Hewitt's.

"You should trust your hosts more," Sergei replied when Jack questioned him about it. "Mr. Hewitt had to tend to some urgent business, and since you're going to be doing the job entrusted to Mr. McMillan, I thought it would be good to welcome you on board officially."

Jack didn't know whether to believe him. He decided to remain wary, given the first impression he'd had of Sergei on the SS *Cliffwood*. "Please accept my apologies," he said, trying to rescue the situation. "I can assure you that I'm most grateful to the Soviet people, and my intention is only to do the best job I can in the tasks I've been assigned. I was just confused because Mr. Hewitt had told me how much work there is to do, particularly on the assembly line and press shop, and I imagined he'd called me here to bring me up to speed. I found you, and that's why I was surprised."

"I understand. Very well. Wait one moment, and I'll see if Mr. Hewitt's free." He picked up the telephone and dialed a number.

While he waited, Jack noticed a picture frame showing a photograph of Stalin shaking Sergei's hand, at what appeared to be the factory's grand opening. He heard Sergei ask whether the industrialist had finished the business he'd been taking care of. When he hung up, he smiled in a way that Jack hadn't seen before.

"Mr. Hewitt's able to receive you now. As you can see, Jack, we Bolsheviks aren't the ogres that everyone makes us out to be." He stood to bring the conversation to a close and show Jack the exit. "However . . ." He stopped in the middle of the office.

"Yes, Mr. Loban?"

"However, make sure you respect us. This isn't America." His smile was gone.

"Oh, don't let the Soviets' chest-beating scare you," said Wilbur Hewitt as he shook off the nurse who was trying her best to apply iodine to the scars on his injured arm.

Jack watched Hewitt lower his sleeve with difficulty and head to his office armchair. Perhaps he was a presumptuous, eccentric type, but though Jack knew him only from a couple of conversations, he had the feeling that the American executive was the kind of person who could push men to work harder with just a couple of sharp remarks. And he admired him for that. He imagined that nobody in the Soviet Union would dispute his effectiveness as a leader. However, at that precise moment, it wasn't Wilbur Hewitt who had captured all of Jack's attention; it was the young nurse who was gathering her equipment with the care of a mother arranging her sick child's medicines. Jack had been aware of every movement that she'd made since he walked into the office.

He found her very attractive. In fact, she was the first Russian woman he'd encountered who in his view deserved that description, though that was probably because every other Soviet woman he'd seen had been on the street, covered from head to toe to keep warm. Her beauty might not have been like a Hollywood starlet's. On the contrary, her soft, clean features were those of a simple young woman who, though she knew she was attractive, gave off an image of seriousness and reliability.

He guessed she was around twenty-five years old. Perhaps less. Her fresh-looking face without a trace of makeup, her long braids gathered over her temples like two nesting snakes, her emerald eyes, focusing only on the medical tasks for which they'd been trained, and the masculine white coat that looked like it had been washed a thousand times gave her a smart, no-nonsense appearance. Jack was admiring her delicate movements and the name "Natasha" on her badge when Hewitt cleared his throat loudly.

"Excuse the mess, kid. They won't leave me alone. Clearly, these Russians ain't gonna let me die until I've got this factory working."

The young nurse blushed when she realized she was being referred to. She quickly finished gathering her equipment and took her leave from Hewitt, reminding him of their appointment the next day.

"Yes, yes, tomorrow," he said wearily, and he waited for her to leave. "So then, Jack. Have you settled in?"

"Not quite, sir. I was about to move into my living quarters when a guard showed up and brought me here. Incidentally, first he took me to see Sergei's office."

"What? Oh yeah! I told you he was in charge of the Avtozavod's security. Sergei works, eats, and sleeps in this factory. He loves everyone to know that he's doing his job."

"What's with the caps with blue ribbons? Their wearers look as if they think they own the place."

"You noticed, huh? Well, you were right to. Those ribbons are the emblem of the OGPU. So that we're clear, that's the secret police. Some people still call them the Cheka. We have to be careful with them. You can't imagine the headaches they could give us."

Jack remembered the corrupt policeman he'd bribed in Leningrad to rescue Konstantin's son. "Secret? Why secret?"

"A revolutionary thing, I suspect." He lay back in his chair, crossed his legs on the table, and lit a cigarette. "When the Bolsheviks toppled the tsar, they set up various organizations for both domestic and international security. There were foreign powers trying to stop them with all kinds of conspiracies, even backing counterrevolutionary groups who undermined the revolution from the shadows. The Cheka was formed from elements of the Red Army and party leaders, as a kind of state security organization aimed at eliminating their opponents." He lowered his feet from the table and sat up, moving his head in the direction of Jack's ear, as if to tell him a secret. "To do away with anyone who contradicted them, shall we say."

"They sound dangerous."

"Potentially." He sat back again. "I haven't had any problems with them, though I tread carefully. Don't worry about Sergei. All he cares about is giving the factory a veneer of normality, and to do that, he needs to get rid of the saboteurs.

"Anyway, let's focus on what concerns us, which is this dinosaur of a factory." He opened a drawer and took out a brown folder that he placed on the desk. "Here's the information I couldn't provide you with in Moscow: plans, machinery inventory, subsidiary enterprises that work with us, and a file listing the incidents and the workers involved. Like I said, most of the problems have been in the press shop and assembly plant. Unfortunately, I don't have a complete record of all of the employees."

"But you'll be able to get one?"

"I think it'll be difficult. More than thirty thousand people divided into three shifts work at the Avtozavod. And we have to be discreet. If I asked for such an exhaustive list, it could make someone involved in the sabotage suspicious."

"Well, I really only need records for the plants where the incidents have taken place."

"I'll see what I can do, but for now you'll have to make do with this." He pushed the folder containing all of the documents toward Jack and stood to bring the meeting to an end.

"When do I start?" Jack also stood as quickly as possible.

"The first shift's tomorrow at eight. At seven, they'll come to collect you and your friends. By the way, I have to admit that posting your companions to the various locations of the incidents is the perfect way to gather information without attracting attention."

"Let's hope it helps. Like I said, I'll be able to speak to them whenever I need to, and they'll tell me everything they see."

"Great. So we're all set, then. Spend these first few days familiarizing yourself with the factory and making contact with the workers while you oversee the repairs on the machinery damaged during the crossing. Unless you discover something important in the interim, we'll meet again in this office next week."

"Very well, Mr. Hewitt. This . . . There's one more thing. If you don't mind my asking, I was wondering about your niece. In such a remote part of the world, and without knowing the language, maybe she'd like some company."

"Gosh darn, kid! Aren't you married?"

"Yes, sir. Well, no, sir. I mean—"

"In hell's name, explain yourself! You're either married or you aren't."

"The thing is"—he figured it was best to tell the truth—"in order to help my two friends, a couple, enter the Soviet Union, we had to fabricate a marriage. Now that we're here, we've kept up the sham, but I swear that I intend to resolve this business as soon as possible and—"

"Ha! Don't trouble yourself on my niece's account, son. Elizabeth has eyes only for rich guys like Smirnov—that's the kind of man she wants to be with. I doubt my niece would mind spending the rest of her life with you if you were a sultan, harem included."

"I'm sorry. I was just trying to be friendly." He cleared his throat. "One last question." Jack stopped in the doorway. "At the gates, they confiscated our passports. Do you know anything about that?"

Wilbur Hewitt stood in silence while he finished his cigarette. He clenched his teeth and sat down. "I know a little. What I don't know is whether you'll want to hear it."

15

Jack was oblivious to the skidding and jamming of brakes as the truck hurtled him back toward the American village, because in his head all he could hear were Wilbur Hewitt's final words: *The OGPU retains all the Americans' passports because their intention is for their owners never to leave the Soviet Union.* And he'd added, *But don't worry, if you need to get back when all of this is over, I'll help you out.*

When all of this was over . . . But what if things didn't go as Hewitt planned? What if the industrialist returned to the United States before anything was uncovered and forgot about his promise? Or what if Jack simply wanted to start a new life in another country? What would he do then? For the immigrants traveling from the other side of the world to put down roots in a country that guaranteed secure work, it might seem a minor inconvenience to have their passports confiscated, but to Jack, it was as reassuring as taking a nap next to a nest of vipers. Why did the Soviets take their passports? Was there something about the Americans they were afraid of?

Why did he care so much? Right then, not only did he have no intention of leaving the Soviet Union, but for him as a fugitive, returning to the United States was out of the question.

He breathed in the icy air that seeped in through the crack in the window, trying to find a moment of clarity that would allow him to reflect properly on his future. The driver, seeing him, gave a stupid smile, as if he imagined that the jolting vehicle had made Jack queasy and as if that were something to be proud of.

Jack closed his eyes. He should really consider himself lucky, he thought. After all, the country that had welcomed him was the land of his parents, a great and powerful nation of hardworking, hospitable people—at that very moment, a driver was taking him to a hot bowl of soup and a free room. What was more, he knew the language, he was surrounded by friends and fellow Americans, and he was going to be paid a salary he'd never dreamed of. Twelve hundred bucks a month! If he kept it going, in five years he'd be sitting on a fortune.

Yes. He was lucky, for sure.

In the canteen, Jack felt like he was back in the States. Dozens of his fellow countrymen were crammed into a timber-clad room decorated for the occasion with handmade American flags and paper balloons, making merry like he'd never expected to witness again. The partygoers sang, laughed, and danced to old-time hillbilly music played on a banjo and two fiddles by a trio of drunken musicians who seemed to be competing with the yelps of the dancers.

Jack spotted the Daniels family and started to make his way to them, eager both to share their happiness and the food and bottle of vodka that sat on their little table. Before he reached them, however, a group of workers pulled him into their circle as if he were one of the gang and forced him to sing along to an off-key "Cripple Creek" to which they were making up the words. Finally, he managed to shake off his new friends with a smile and sit with the Danielses. Harry seemed to be enjoying the party and insisted Jack down a cup of vodka in one go, like a *real man*. Jack was soon infected by the merry atmosphere, due in no small part to the copious amounts of sausage, bacon, barbecued ribs, and blinis with cream cheese that the cooks had prepared for the welcome celebration.

After finishing off the cup of vodka, he listened to his belly and set to eating what was left of the feast. He took a bite from some sort of hot dog that Harry offered him, and took another sip of vodka to wash it down as he looked around at the people enjoying themselves. He was surprised not to see Sue, but when he asked Harry Daniels about her, he told Jack that she'd drunk too much and had gone back to her room.

Jack set aside his worries and joined the dancers. He ate and drank as if there were no tomorrow until, at around nine o'clock, the women started to clear up. First the trays, then their husbands, dragging them to their rooms. Jack and the Daniels family were among the last to leave. They could barely speak due to the alcohol, but babbling and laughing, they agreed on their way back to their rooms that traveling to Russia had been the best decision they'd ever made.

After trying to insert it in the lock for the third time, Jack looked with a puzzled expression at the key that Harry had just given him. He held it near the lightbulb in the corridor to make sure it wasn't bent, then tried again. When he thought he was about to manage it, the key slipped through his fingers. Aware of his drunkenness, he smiled like an idiot. At last, he managed to get it in and make it turn. He staggered into the dark room and tripped on his suitcase. He was feeling the wall in search of a switch when a sudden flash lit up the room, blinding him. Jack covered his eyes with his hand, and through the crack between his eyelids, he was amazed to see a figure sitting up in the bed that was positioned in the middle of the room. He was making his retreat when he realized that the person looking at him with surprise was Sue.

He was about to apologize, when she got in ahead of him. "Come in and close the door! You're going to wake the neighbors!"

Jack shrugged and obeyed her without thinking. "What . . . what are you doing here?" he managed to say.

"Well, I was trying to sleep until you came in and woke me up. Has the party finished? What time is it?"

Jack didn't respond. He just looked at Sue, half-naked on the bed. "I don't understand. Harry told me this was my room. He gave me the key, and my luggage is here, and—"

"Sure. The room's for both of us."

"Huh?"

"We're married, remember?"

"But why didn't you explain that we—?"

"That we what, Jack? That we've fooled everyone?"

"No, of course not. Not that. But Walter . . ." Jack couldn't concentrate.

"Come on. Come to bed, and tomorrow we'll see if we can sort something out."

"But Walter . . ."

In reply, Sue turned off the light and took Jack's hand to pull him toward her.

Jack let her do it. He was finding it difficult to think, his senses were dulled, and the contact with Sue didn't help. He wanted to resist, but the *come* that she said softly into the darkness pulled him in like a whirlpool sucking down a drifting raft. Somehow he stripped down to his underpants. Sue wrapped him in the blanket and pressed herself against him. They were in total blackness. In the silence, Jack could only hear the young woman's breathing near his ear. He felt Sue's bare legs, soft and warm, entangle in his, while her arms pulled him closer. He tried to stop and think, but her hands, stroking his chest and hair, made it impossible, dragging him toward a place of confusion and desire, where the faces of Sue, Elizabeth, and Natasha blended into one, appeared and disappeared, offered themselves, then moved away.

He was unable to string together two thoughts. He let himself go.

He couldn't recall ever having such a bad hangover. His head felt as if it were filled with razor blades that cut through his brain with the slightest movement. He lay in silence, trying to remember what had happened, but all he could rough out was a collection of vague images in which the banjo music and the vodka merged with a tornado of kisses and caresses. However, Sue's naked body beside him in the bed left no room for doubt. He got up and woke her. They had to hurry. They had only fifteen minutes before the vehicle that was taking them to the factory set off, and he didn't want to miss it. They quickly got dressed and ran to the communal bathroom in the corridor, which, because of the late hour, was deserted. Then they went down the stairs as they finished tidying their hair and climbed into the van just as it was leaving. Neither of them said anything about what had happened. They endured the drive in silence, saying not so much as a good-bye when they separated to go to their respective destinations, she to a cleaning gang and he to his dangerous undertaking.

The first day of work felt like carting a mountain rock by rock, but at least it meant Jack could forget about the consequences of his encounter with Sue and see the various buildings that made up the gigantic factory.

As instructed by Wilbur Hewitt, he went first to the equipment warehouse to fetch the white overalls that he'd have to wear at all times as a uniform, and which would identify him as an American supervisor. On the apron, which had been used and was made of a coarse fabric, a badge showed the name "George McMillan," the sick engineer he was replacing. They also supplied a notebook, a pencil, a rubber eraser, an articulated wooden ruler, a gauge, some woolen gloves, an *ushanka*, and a pair of felt boots.

From there, accompanied by Anatoly Orlov, the Soviet operative who'd been assigned to him as a guide while he familiarized himself with his duties, he had continued to the press shop, where the stamping took place. Much like at the Ford River Rouge factory in Michigan, the noise from the presses was deafening. Though Jack knew the process inside and out, Orlov insisted on explaining that the steel sheets arrived at the guillotines in huge rolls, before being cut into rectangular plates; then trimmed, pressed, and die-stamped, they were shaped into the parts that would make up the bodywork. However, from that point on, any similarity between the two factories was purely superficial.

The Ford River Rouge Complex in Dearborn was a gigantic miracle of efficiency and technology, where each element—whether man, supplies, or machinery—slotted together with all the other elements with the precision of a clock mechanism. But that was not all. Of the more than one hundred thousand workers employed at the Dearborn installation, five thousand had the exclusive task of keeping the facilities in impeccable condition: hosing down the floors, emptying the waste containers every two hours, cleaning the windows, and repainting the walls and pillars in the company's blue and white. At the Rouge, one could lick the floor without ingesting a single piece of dirt. Doing so at the Avtozavod would be a sure way to poison oneself to death.

Wherever Jack looked, he struggled to find a spot that wasn't a dumping ground. Metal shavings covered the floors, piles of off-cuts and rusty components shared the space with scattered supply carts, and dozens of crates of spare parts were strewn throughout the corridors, as if they'd been abandoned there years before. The Avtozavod's approach to order and cleanliness was like letting a herd of pigs into an operating theater and expecting them to keep it sterile.

And yet, despite the mess and chaos of the facility itself, what really struck Jack most was the inefficiency and lax attitude with which the Soviets seemed to undertake each task. Far from being highly trained operatives, the people responsible for production resembled an army of peasants who handled the welding torches with as much finesse as if they were herding goats.

Amid the flying sparks and the penetrating smell of solder that stuck in the throat, Jack examined them closely. Many of the men were no older than twenty, but their faces, consumed by work, were those of men much older. The women, who were almost as numerous as the men, covered their hair with white scarves to protect it from the dangerous machinery. Near the older men were open vodka bottles, despite the signs that prohibited drinking during working hours and the omnipresent guards, apparently more concerned with other problems. The cold was appalling, to the point that sheets of ice had formed in the corridors where there were leaks.

In America, the iron ore arrived via the River Rouge wharves on Monday morning, and it was turned into a four-cylinder automobile ready for sale by Thursday afternoon. That was efficiency, the meaning of which they did not know at the Avtozavod.

He took note of everything he saw but left his reflections for another day. He went to the warehouse where they'd stored the machines damaged during the storm, and spent the rest of the morning explaining to the operatives what they had to do to repair them.

At the end of the day, Jack found Harry Daniels and his son in the press shop canteen, a vast warehouse-like structure with hundreds of tables set out in lines. While they waited in the line to buy their meal tickets, Jack asked about their first day's work.

"Not too bad," replied old Harry. "Cold as hell, but I'm happy to be manning the presses again."

Jack nodded. He'd persuaded Hewitt to assign Harry and his elder son, Jim, to the mold repair shop, where the most skilled operatives were needed to deal with the faults. It hadn't been difficult. In stamping techniques, the Daniels family was highly experienced. "And your Soviet workmates? Are they friendly?" Jack pressed them.

"They're all just Soviets at the moment; I wouldn't call them *mates*, exactly." They moved forward in the line.

"What do you expect, Dad?" young Jim cut in. "We don't speak Russian, and all they can say in English is *comrade*."

"That's true," Jack conceded. "The language is a problem, but they're offering free lessons in the evenings that anyone can attend." He stopped at the cash register.

"Lessons? Study?" Harry let out a sarcastic guffaw. "Have you seen my hands?" He showed them to Jack. They were callused all over. "I'll be fifty-five in March. When I was six, I learned a few letters, and I've never needed to learn anything else since. My son can study if he wants. When I'm done working, I'll go home to my wife, drink a glass of vodka, and watch the snow fall."

Jack interrupted the conversation for a moment to buy the meal tickets. He was served by a short man with a dark complexion and an aquiline nose, wearing a curious red hat that resembled a sock. Jack said hello in Russian and asked him what kind of food was available.

"Americans, right? I heard you speaking English." He smiled. "I have a few words, from tending to the foreigners, but I see you speak good Russian. You've just arrived here at the Avtozavod, am I right? I haven't seen you before." He smiled enthusiastically again. "You'll like it here. With the kitchens right there, you won't even notice the cold."

Jack realized why they had waited so long in the line. The cashier noticed his expression.

"Oh yes! The food. Of course! It's just you don't often see new faces around here, you know? And I love to talk. Right. You were asking what kind of food we serve. Yes, very good. What chits do you have?" he asked. "Workers? Officials? Party members?" he said, switching to English.

Jack raised an eyebrow, as did Harry and his son. When they'd been given the chits in the morning, they hadn't noticed that there were different types. Jack found his; the lettering said "Supervisor." On the Danielses' chits it said "Operative." Jack asked what each category meant.

"Depending on the chit you've been given, you'll receive either single or double rations. Let's see . . ." He checked the different chits. "For you," he said to Jack, "it'll be three courses for five rubles. The other chits are standard, soup and main course. Also five rubles each."

"Excuse me, but you must've made a mistake," Harry cut in. "Did you just say that me and my son will only receive two courses?"

"That's right."

"So how is it possible that you intend to charge us the same as him, when you're going to serve him an extra course?"

"Oh! I see it hasn't been explained to you. Basically, the government subsidizes all meals, regardless of what they include, so the price is the same for everyone."

Harry Daniels looked at the counter where rows of plates were waiting to be collected. He scratched his nose, struggling to understand. The soup was a greenish liquid in which little else could be seen, and the main courses consisted of some kind of purée accompanied by something resembling salt herring. "All right." He took out two more rubles and added them to the five. "Give me a third course, as well. I've worked nonstop all day, and I deserve a piece of that cow, even if I have to pay its weight in gold."

"I'm sorry, but that's not possible."

"*What?* Can you not see the two rubles I've added?"

"It's not a question of money, sir. The problem is that there isn't enough food."

Harry looked at the row of steaks. "Are you joking?"

"I wish I was, sir, but those steaks are for management only."

Harry broke into a string of protests that the cashier was unable to interpret. The little man reddened but held his ground.

"Please, sir. Do not cause trouble or we will all have problems. It's five rubles each. Take your tickets and hand them in when you collect your dishes."

Harry would not calm down. He left the seven rubles on the money tray, snatched up one of the steaks, and took a bite from it before the massive Soviet guard who watched over the canteen could stop him.

"*Davay!*" the guard yelled at him, grabbing him by the arm.

"Get your hands off me!" Harry wriggled away.

Jack came forward and stepped between Harry's son and the guard, who looked like he was prepared to use force to achieve his objective. "Excuse him, sir. This man doesn't speak your language. It's all a misunderstanding," Jack assured him in Russian.

"A misunderstanding? This American good-for-nothing thinks he can do whatever he wants?"

Jack was glad Harry couldn't understand what they were saying. "I'm sorry if it looked like something else, but this poor man has done nothing wrong. It's just that I wasn't hungry, so I offered him my meat. Look. I'm not lying to you. I'm entitled to that steak." He showed the guard the chit that proved he was a supervisor.

The guard glanced at it without changing his expression. "Is this true?" he asked the cashier.

Jack pleaded with the man with his eyes.

"Yes . . . yes, sir," he said. "That man"—he looked at Jack for an instant—"that gentleman offered his third course to the old man."

The guard grunted. He turned around and returned to his station. Jack sat on the long bench near where Harry had made himself comfortable. The older man was eating as if nothing had happened.

"What did that bozo want?" asked Harry. Jim, his son, was listening, too.

Jack looked at them, not sure how he should answer. "Nothing. Just eat your food."

When they'd finished, the Danielses quickly left the canteen to catch the tram that went from the press shop to the American village. Jack decided to drink his tea without rushing. He was in no hurry to see Sue again, and had work matters that he thought would be better to review near the heat from the kitchens. He lit a *papirosa* and sipped on his tea.

He studied his notes for a long while, until a rasping voice pulled him from his thoughts.

"We're closing."

179

Jack looked up to find a cleaning lady who, rag in hand, was waiting for him to take his notes away so that she could clean the table. He snatched them up and checked the time on the canteen clock. It was seven. Too late to use the services of the crazy driver, and the next tram wouldn't come until the shift change. He was about to leave the canteen, when he heard someone call to him.

"Sir. Here. Your two rubles."

Jack turned around, surprised. It was the cashier. He was holding out his hand, offering Jack the two coins.

"Don't you remember? Your friend paid two rubles extra for his steak, but he really ate yours, so this money belongs to you."

"Oh! It doesn't matter. Keep it."

"Thank you, sir, but I can't accept it."

"You can't? Why not?"

"In the Soviet Union, we don't accept tips. If we did, it would be like saying that we've done an especially good job."

"That's right. And what's wrong with that?"

"Nothing, I suppose. It's just we Soviets should always do our job well."

Jack raised an eyebrow. The constant discovery of so many curious details about the Soviet Union would surely make this his most frequent facial expression. "Well, in that case, there are two reasons why you could accept it. First, because, judging by your accent, you're not a Soviet. And second, because those two rubles aren't a tip, but a reward for helping us. Or have you forgotten that you backed up my version of events with the guard?"

The man stammered, not knowing what to say. Before he could respond, Jack made him close his hand and put the money away.

"Thank you, sir."

"Jack. You can call me Jack. And don't worry. Nobody will know you accepted it," he said, before turning to leave the canteen.

When he stepped outside, a punishing cold struck him in the face. He pulled his overcoat tight to protect himself from the blizzard and looked at the row of streetlamps disappearing into the distance. It was the route the driver had taken, so if he followed it, sooner or later he'd reach the Americans' bunkhouses. He'd started walking in the snow, when he heard some rushed footsteps behind him.

"Mr. Jack! Wait, Mr. Jack!"

Jack turned around to find the cashier in the red hat again.

"Here, sir," he said, offering him a newspaper-wrapped package. "Some steaks. It's not true that there's not enough food. Well, it is, but nobody will miss these steaks."

"Well, blow me down; I knew you weren't a Soviet. What's your name?"

The man smiled. "Agramunt. Miquel Agramunt, sir."

"Well, thanks, Miquel. But don't call me 'sir.'"

Jack had managed to avoid any further encounters with Sue by sleeping on a straw mattress on the floor in Joe Brown's room. It had been five nights, enough for his bones to begin to ache and for him to develop a nasty cough—his lungs were unused to such extreme cold. When she asked him why he had frozen her out, he told her that he valued and admired her as a friend, but that what had happened on the night of the party he could only put down to having drunk too much vodka. She slapped him. From then on, Jack tried to avoid her. When it was impossible, he greeted her curtly, for she seemed to interpret any friendly gesture as an attempt to get close to her. On the sixth night, Jack found her waiting for him outside Joe Brown's room. She was toeing the floor impatiently, and her face seemed to be burning with a dangerous mixture of fury and alcohol. Sue told him to come back to her, or she would tell Walter that he had tried to force himself on her. She was swaying from the drink and slurring her words. Jack ignored her. He wanted to believe that it was the alcohol talking, but it was worrying. He didn't know what he would do about the problem, but decided to say nothing to her until Walter returned.

One person he hadn't seen again was Elizabeth. Through her uncle, he knew that she'd turned down a modest prefabricated house in the American village to move into a mansion in Gorky that the Soviets sometimes lent to foreign executives. According to the industrialist, his niece passed the time going from party to party, which he disapproved of but had little choice but to consent to—she was an adult, after all. Elizabeth's parents had died when she was a child, and Hewitt and his wife, who were childless, had brought her up as well as they knew how. However, after the attack of meningitis that saw his wife end up in a psychiatric hospital, Elizabeth had become rebellious. He didn't blame her for it—she was young and had too much spare time—but that did not stop him from occasionally criticizing her behavior.

As Hewitt had told Jack, her maidservant was the only person able to contain her, and perhaps that was why Elizabeth made no objection when the woman requested to return to the United States.

Jack offered to teach Elizabeth Russian when he was off work, to help her fill up some of her free time, but Hewitt didn't even consider it. His niece knew exactly what she wanted, and it didn't include learning new languages. Not unless the person teaching her was rich enough for her to find him attractive.

"And how rich would that be?" Jack asked.

Hewitt burst into laughter. "More than you could earn in a lifetime, you can be sure of that, son."

His reply didn't impress Jack. He was ready to show Hewitt that, even compared to Smirnov, Jack Beilis was a good catch.

16

Just one in twenty-two.

After studying every word of the reports, Jack had reached the conclusion that, of the twenty-two accidents that had taken place in the various Avtozavod plants, twenty-one seemed to be the result of the factory's abysmal administration. However, for one he had found no explanation.

He informed Wilbur Hewitt of his conclusions.

"Are you absolutely certain?" the industrialist asked him after running his eyes over Jack's report.

"Absolutely. First I separated the incidents in which workers had been involved from those that affected only machinery or production. I was able to consult the files for the injured operatives." He showed them to Hewitt. "Igor Pavlov, twenty-six years old, Ukrainian, left arm amputated when he got it caught in a press while it was running. Outcome: production halted for twenty-six hours for cleaning and repairs to the molds."

"And?" Hewitt felt his arm in its sling.

"Now comes the worrying part. Previous profession: farmer. Experience as operative: two weeks' training and one week as a worker."

"I see . . ."

"Olga Moskovskaya." Jack laid the file on the desk. "Thirty-four years old, Azerbaijani, several cuts to her face and chest that required stitches when her hair was caught in the engine conveyor belt. Outcome: production interrupted for one hour to free her clothing and hair. Previous profession: farmer. Experience as operative: one week's training and one day as a worker.

"Mikhail Lenovski, eighteen years old—"

"Also with no experience, I presume. Is every case the same?" Hewitt broke in.

"Almost identical: peasants, farmers, housewives, herders . . ."

"Good. Nothing more than carelessness, then. And the rest?"

"Sir, I wouldn't call these accidents *careless*, when they could have been prevented if—"

"Sure, sure. But it's not what concerns us. Go on, please."

Jack cleared his throat. He set aside the files on the injured workers and moved on to the incidents that affected the equipment. He explained that most of them could be attributed to a lack of maintenance, misalignments, insufficient lubrication, corroded bearings, belts not being replaced, design faults, or mechanisms not being properly cleaned. "But there's one"—he set aside the rest of the files—"for which I have yet to find an explanation. It happened on January 1, 1933, in the engine plant, the very day that Stalin visited Gorky to inaugurate the production line. According to the official reports, a copy of which you have in your own files, during the afternoon shift, the power supply was cut off when there was a planned outage, but there is no record of this in the fault reports—the basis of the final official report—even though the rules of conduct state that every time there's a stoppage, both the incident and its possible causes must be recorded."

"That's right."

"Well, there is no entry for a planned outage in the incident reports you provided, nor in the power supply register kept at the turbine plant, nor in the records for the transformer that controls the amount of power consumed in the engine plant."

"That's strange, yes. Still, it doesn't prove anything. They could've just forgotten to report it."

"Maybe, but these Soviets record everything. They record your name, the time you arrive, and the time you leave, the machinery you operate, and the number of parts produced on your shift, so it's hard to believe that they'd forget to report something of this magnitude. And it wasn't a brief stoppage. Engine production was interrupted for five hours, with Stalin here, observing everything. The official report attributes the downtime to a planned shutdown of the power plant, but that's not true. My informants assured me that no interruptions were scheduled for that day. Naturally, Stalin was furious and demanded an explanation."

"Oh yes. I remember being told about that." Hewitt clenched his teeth. "They brought the opening of the factory forward to a week before we disembarked so they could take the credit. Are you implying that the factory's bosses made up the excuse of the outage to cover up another problem?"

"I am. And if my theory's right, the only explanation is that they didn't want Stalin to know they'd been sabotaged on such a momentous day."

"It's strange. These reports were provided to me directly by Sergei Loban. He should've told me that the outage was not planned by the management—that the official report was a cover-up. Why would he want to hide it from me?"

"That I don't know. Maybe you should ask him."

Jack smiled with satisfaction as he hid his first pay packet of three hundred dollars in the secret pocket he had fashioned in his belt. Hewitt had explained to him that he would pay him the agreed amount privately every week, without a receipt. Given Jack's rank, he couldn't justify paying him such a large sum. Jack was delighted with the arrangement. He decided to pay a visit to Ivan Zarko, the contact that the smuggler Konstantin had given him at the station in Leningrad, to exchange some of his dollars for rubles so he could spend them. He remembered that Zarko worked as an *upravdom* on Tverskaya Avenue, and he wondered whether that address was anywhere near the mansion where Elizabeth was staying. He also thought that if he was going to see her, he ought to find himself a more appropriate outfit.

Despite the wrinkles on his face, Ivan Zarko proved to be one of those old men who have ice in their eyes and an iron hand, someone who seemed capable of impaling anyone who tried to cross him without blinking an eye. This was clear to Jack as soon as he asked for him, when under Zarko's watchful eye, his two sons frisked him to make sure he wasn't carrying a weapon.

"So Konstantin sends you," the patriarch murmured. "And what in hell does a foreigner want from a poor old man like me?"

Jack explained that Konstantin had assured him that he could get a good price for his dollars on the black market, and that Zarko could help him.

"I haven't been involved in that business for years," the old man said, staring into the distance. "If I was caught trading in currency, I'd never see my grandchildren again. So tell me, how is Konstantin?" he asked from behind a rickety desk in the hallway of the building he managed.

Jack sensed that Zarko's words were those of a shrewd old man dealing with a stranger.

"Konstantin would do anything for me."

"Perhaps he would. But I don't know you. Look, son, if you want some good advice, forget the black market. Tell them at the bank that you didn't know the rules and make do with the rubles they offer you. You'll lose money but keep your health. And health is important in such a cold place."

"It would be three hundred dollars a week," said Jack.

Zarko's two sons looked at each other in surprise.

"Listen to me, American. We don't like jokers—"

In response, Jack took off the belt where he'd hidden the money and deposited a bundle of green notes on the desk. The old man grabbed the cash and hid it under his overcoat.

"Are you crazy? We could be arrested."

Jack looked from side to side to assure himself that the place was deserted. "I never joke. Especially when it comes to money."

For the first time, the old man looked into the blue eyes of the willowy American in front of him. "Damned foreigner . . . How do I know that you're really Konstantin's friend and not an OGPU agent?"

Jack stood in silence, as did Ivan Zarko's sons. He noticed the two of them looking at each other nervously.

"Because he gave me *blat*," he replied, and without waiting for Ivan Zarko to respond, he took the piece of paper signed by Konstantin out of a pocket and left it in the same place he'd deposited the bundle of notes.

With nine thousand rubles burning a hole in his pocket, bought at a rate of thirty per dollar, Jack took in the shop windows on Sverdlovka Avenue like a child left alone in a candy store. The Grand Way, as the locals called it, and which he had nicknamed Rich Street, was an avenue so wide that ten cars could travel along it side by side. Even so, only a few horse-drawn carriages and tramcars were on the street. As he walked, he admired the succession of hotels, churches, museums, and palaces that seemed to be competing for the title of Most Lavish Building. Despite the cold, Jack spurned the tram and climbed on foot toward the former monastery square, in search of a tailor who could make a suit for him similar to Hewitt's. However, none of the three establishments he visited could meet his request.

"How can you not have any fabric?" he'd asked.

In response, the last tailor he called on shrugged and then repeated the same story that Jack had heard from the two previous tailors. "We used to receive musk ox wool and sometimes even cashmere, but for a long time we haven't had the material to make new suits. All we do is repair old suits and sell used garments. We have astrakhan overcoats and one or two *vatniks* that you could wear underneath to protect yourself from the winter."

To Jack, it seemed inconceivable that even when he had the money, they wouldn't give him what he wanted. "And the suits that the Soviet factory bosses wear, don't they have them made here?"

"They do, sir. But they provide the fabric themselves."

Seeing that the tailor's own jacket had been mended, Jack cursed inwardly. After weighing his options, he finally agreed to bring the tailor some garments that he'd kept from McMillan's trunk to alter. He took his leave and returned to the avenue, intending to buy some vodka and a couple of cakes to celebrate his first wage packet with his friends. He'd missed Walter, but in his cable, he'd assured Jack that he would join them soon.

It wasn't easy to find a food store. Finally, he walked into one with meat, poultry, and confectionery filling the window display, only to find a crowd of weary-looking men and women waiting in line at the cashier. He noticed that the shelves contained only a few potatoes, some pots of lard, smoked sardines, and a box of meal. The rest of the shelves looked as if they'd been empty for years. Jack went up to a storekeeper who was cleaning behind a cash register and asked him for some of the products in the window.

"You have to go to the other till. This one's for party members only."

Jack contemplated the endless line. He was reminded of his days of hunger in New York. At least in Russia, even if you had to wait your turn, you could leave the store with food. He was about to join the end of the line when the storekeeper called to him. "You won't be able to buy the food that's in the window."

Jack reddened. He hoped to God that those goods weren't reserved for a privileged few as well. The storekeeper's answer stunned him.

"It's not that we don't want to sell them to you. It's just that the goods in the window are made of painted cardboard. It's only advertising, to make the store look nice."

Two hours later, Jack was on his way back to the American village, carrying a dozen eggs and some sugar. He'd visited at least ten food stores, and in all of them not only did he have to wait in endless lines, but their storerooms were virtually empty.

As the tram clattered through the snow-covered landscape, he wondered what good it was earning pots of money if he had nowhere to spend it. He had no desire to live like a miser, eating black bread, wearing patched-up suits, and traveling on a tram like a sheep on its way to the slaughterhouse. He would never earn Elizabeth's admiration like this. What was he supposed to do? Stick his earnings in a sack and show them to Hewitt's niece to prove his worth? He shook his head and swore to himself. It was so cold, he was afraid to sneeze in case his nostrils froze. He envied the other passengers who wore warm hats. Fortunately, the tram was reaching its destination.

In the communal kitchen, he gave the sugar and eggs to Harry Daniels's wife so that she could prepare something sweet. "I'm afraid I couldn't get flour," Jack said apologetically. "I couldn't find a single place that sold it in the whole damned city."

"And why didn't you buy it here?"

"Here? Where?"

"Where do you think? At the American store!"

Jack felt like someone who had spent the morning trying to pull a door open before realizing that it opened inward. Apparently, the foreign workers had their own stores where there were no lines or lack of stock. He hadn't known. Of course, the prices were three times what they were in the Soviet stores. Mrs. Daniels added that the American store behind the bunkhouses was one of these establishments.

"It's expensive, but at least you can find almost everything there, not like those poor Russian peasants, who only have watery porridge to give their children," said the woman with a sad expression.

It was his day off, so Jack decided to find out for himself what was available in the village store. He said good-bye to Mrs. Daniels and promised her that he'd be back with the best flour in the whole Soviet Union.

The American store proved to be a meager pantry only slightly better provisioned than the stores he'd visited that morning. He wandered between the half-empty shelves, asking himself whether Mrs. Daniels had really meant it when she said that this was the place where he could buy almost anything, until behind the counter he found a Soviet worker who greeted him halfheartedly. Without expecting much, Jack asked him for a pack of flour, but to his surprise, the worker disappeared through a door and returned within a few seconds, the goods under one arm. Seeing this outcome, he added two bottles of vodka, a pack of American cigarettes, a rack of pork ribs, and half a dozen bagels to the order. The Soviet worker disappeared again and returned with the vodka and bagels. The other goods were not available. When Jack asked him if he could order them, the man gave a smug smile.

"Sir, I'm retiring in five years, and to be honest, even if I retired in ten, I doubt you'd see your order arrive at this store." He explained that they sold only essentials, and that, though they had a much better selection than the stores in the city, it was becoming increasingly difficult to get hold of certain foods. "We sold the last sausage two weeks ago, when the welcome party was held. Since then, supplies have been hard to come by."

Jack couldn't prevent a slight shudder. When he asked why they had been cut off, the man shook his head.

"Let's pray it doesn't reach the Avtozavod."

"That what doesn't?"

"The famine, comrade. The famine."

As he left the store, a familiar voice stopped him.

"Mr. Jack! Mr. Jack! Remember me?"

Jack turned around to find a dark-skinned man wearing a sock-shaped red hat. "You're the cashier from the press shop canteen, right?"

"I'm glad you remember me, sir! I haven't seen you in the canteen in a while. Do you take a lunch box to the office?"

"No. It's not that." He avoided explaining that, since the one time they'd met, he had eaten in the foundry canteen. "So what're you doing around here? Have you switched jobs?"

"Oh no, sir! It's just that I also work as a loader. Sometimes we deliver goods to the American store from the central warehouse, or vice versa—we take things from here to our canteen. It depends."

"I see! Well, it was good to see you . . . Michael?"

"Miquel, sir. Miquel."

"That's it, Miquel. I'm going back to the bunkhouse, before I turn into a snowman."

"Yes, sir, of course . . ." He was about to walk off, but seemed to change his mind. "One second, sir!" he called to Jack before he disappeared.

"Yes?"

"I heard you before . . . when you were ordering in the store, and well . . . from what I could make out, you seem to have money."

Jack was suspicious. He'd heard about professional con men, and it seemed too much of a coincidence that this man was taking an interest in his money. "I don't think that's any of your business," he said, turning to go back to the bunkhouse.

"Sir, I'm sorry if I've bothered you. I just wanted you to know that I might be able to get hold of that rack of ribs you wanted."

Jack stopped to look at the little man who was proposing what nobody in that remote place was supposed to be able to do. His smile seemed sincere. Jack pursed his lips and gave himself a moment to reflect.

"Tell me one thing. Is that strange hat that falls over your ear some kind of symbol of the OGPU?"

"Ha ha! The secret police?" He burst into laughter. "By Lenin's whiskers! No, sir! This is a *barretina!*"

"And what does that mean?"

"If I had to tell you my life story out here, we'd freeze to death before the end of the first chapter." He gestured unsubtly toward the canteen in the American village.

"All right. We'll have a drink and talk about those ribs. But stop calling me *sir*; it makes me uneasy."

On the third vodka, the little man moved on from small talk and began to explain how gunmen had forced him to flee his beloved Barcelona. He revealed that as a teenager, he had mixed with people with anarchistic tendencies, people with whom he fantasized about a future that was fairer for everybody. He was not yet eighteen, and every evening, when he came out of the libertarian institute he attended, he would dash off to trade union meetings or rallies to enjoy the fiery speeches on solidarity, equality, and the struggle of the working classes. At those gatherings, his heart would burn, and he would rail against the employers like the rest of the workers who surrounded him, even though his only work was helping his father sell beans from the family store on the Rambla de Catalunya. But that detail didn't prevent him wanting to help his comrades defeat the bosses who oppressed them.

"In time, I gained some prominence in the CNT, and I was active in important strikes like the Canadiense, in which we managed to make the employers accept an eight-hour workday. But then things turned ugly. Some low-life bosses hired gunmen to murder our union comrades. They would appear from nowhere and shoot them in the back of the head. They told me I'd be next. Some people I knew decided to flee to Paris and persuaded me to go with them. There I met a Russian girl who worked for Comintern, you know, Communist International. I fell in love and came to live with her. In the end, she left me for a Soviet soldier, and I stayed here, doing more or less the same job I did in my store back home."

Jack had to stop himself from yawning. Miquel seemed like a nice guy, but he talked too much about matters that didn't interest Jack. "And the hat? Don't you ever take it off?" That was all he could think to say.

"The *barretina*?" He smiled and removed it to show it to Jack. "It belonged to my grandfather. It always catches people's attention, they ask me about it, and it gives me a chance to tell them about my home."

Jack filled Miquel's glass again, hoping he'd at least be quiet while he drank. He took advantage of the pause and asked him about the cost and provenance of the rack of ribs he'd assured him he could supply. Miquel moved closer and whispered in Jack's ear.

"That's my secret," he said quietly. "If I give it away, I'm done for." He added that he had contacts in some of the farming cooperatives that supplied the Avtozavod kitchens, but that trade of that kind was strictly forbidden. If caught, one was sent to a prison camp in Siberia. "That's why it's so expensive," he added.

"How much?"

Miquel pretended to do the sums. "Two hundred rubles."

Jack looked at him. Though he had money to burn, two hundred rubles was more than an ordinary worker's monthly wage. He decided to try his luck. "I can offer you a hundred."

Miquel shook his head. He took another sip of vodka, looked from side to side to make sure no one was listening, and moved in again until he was almost kissing Jack's ear. "Make me a better offer."

"But in the American store, they said it'd cost fifty!" Jack complained.

"Then order it there, and wait a couple of years for it to arrive. Look, Jack, the problem isn't the cost of the pork. It's paying the guys who have to look the other way and keep their mouths shut, and just that will cost a hundred rubles, whether it's a rack of ribs or a chop."

"And you pocket fifty. That doesn't sound very Communist."

"You don't know my problems. If you're not interested . . ." He finished his drink and stood up.

Jack stopped him. "Four hundred rubles. But I want the whole pig, from snout to trotters."

17

For the next few weeks, Jack felt like a rat lost in a maze.

Every morning he donned his white overalls to go on his inspection round. He started in the turbine plant, where the power used in the foundry was generated, and from there he went on to the engine factory, where they forged the motors and gearboxes, before continuing to the press shop, where they molded the various parts of the body that, after being painted, were taken to the assembly line and mounted on a chassis to which the wheels had already been coupled. However, despite the frenetic pace of the work, Jack was barely able to complete his inspection of the four areas before the end of the week. In the Soviet Union, the workweek consisted of five working days followed by one day off, so his downtime was not always on a Sunday, but rotated. Since Joe Brown and the Danielses had different shifts, his days off never coincided with theirs, so he used his time away from work to go over the reports compiled during the week.

He felt he was making little progress.

Most of his reports pointed toward the conclusion that the factory's problems arose from the introduction of an industrial process in a country with a language and culture stuck in the Middle Ages. The absurd situations—like the fact that some extremely expensive presses imported from the United States were taken to be filler and used as reinforcement in the construction of a railway station, or that an entire set of punches had succumbed to rust because, not knowing how to work them, the Russians had simply left them outdoors—were an everyday occurrence. In his research, he'd learned that Ford had experienced similar difficulties when setting up its subsidiary in Berlin in 1926. However, the German character—organized, methodical, disciplined—along with a state of technological development similar to the Americans', had ultimately led to success.

It was in stark contrast to what, in Jack's view, was happening in Gorky, and not because the Soviets were less hardworking than the Germans. The problem was that, while the Germans had met the challenge like an army of bees, the Russians seemed to be doing it like a herd of goats.

He poked the brazier he'd bought to ward off the cold and continued to examine his papers.

If the reports were anything to go by, everything seemed to stem from the stubbornness of Stalin himself; after disregarding the advice of the experts, he had ordered a carbon copy of Ford's gigantic complex in Dearborn, including factories, sewerage, schools, hospitals, social facilities, and accommodation, all to be built in one go, and on a site with very little preexisting infrastructure. What was more, the rushed opening, pushed through to mark the end of the five-year plan, meant that the construction of the Avtozavod was far from complete.

A simple figure confirmed his analysis: not a single Russian automobile had yet come off the Soviet production lines. The small number of units produced was from the stock of seventy-five thousand broken-down Model A Fords that Stalin had purchased in order to cannibalize them.

The other big problem was that 90 percent of the thirty thousand workers at the industrial complex were farmers and herders with no comparable experience. On several occasions, during his inspection rounds, Jack had caught workers lighting fires on the floor to cook food, or wearing bearskin while they handled machinery in which baggy clothing could easily get trapped, or leaving their stations to relieve themselves on the nearest piece of open ground, rather than use the latrines. Trying to make the workers from the steppes follow the rules on safety, cleanliness, and discipline was a thorny business, and it was no surprise that so many accidents happened. However, there were incidents that were difficult to classify as accidents.

Every night, Jack set aside the files related to errors or negligence, and focused on the more mysterious incidents that could have been caused by sabotage. The most curious thing to him was that they'd all taken place in the press shop.

The first incident was caused by a broken chain belt on the chassis line. In the maintenance reports, it was stated that the belt had been replaced by a qualified operative before the accident, so its deterioration was surprising. Though nobody was harmed, production was interrupted for two days. But the strange thing was not so much that a new belt had broken, but that it happened to be the only type of belt for which there was no replacement in the entire factory.

The second incident was a broken hook on one of the cranes used to move engines. The motor that was swinging in the air when it happened fell to the ground from a height of ten feet, crushing two workers. Jack was sad for the two men who died and their families. He knew those cranes, and knew that the case-hardened hooks with which they were equipped wouldn't break under the weight of a steamroller. Also, the maintenance checks, according to the records in his possession, were satisfactory.

The final incident involved an acetylene canister that had exploded. Most events of this nature occurred when novices without welding experience left oxygen canisters open and lit a match, but that night, the person handling the equipment happened to be an operative with ten years' experience in metalwork and mining. The woman died two days later from third-degree burns. Though Jack had no proof, the terrible way she died and her expertise made Jack include the file among the potential cases of sabotage.

Unfortunately, due to the slovenly Soviet bureaucracy, Jack found that there was little more he could do than read his reports. Wilbur Hewitt couldn't provide all the information he needed, nor could Jack go around questioning those involved without arousing suspicion. This meant that there were days when all he could do was put the investigation on ice and devote his efforts to repairing the machines and solving more everyday problems.

Among these, the one that worried him most was Sue.

Because Walter's fiancée worked in a cleaning gang, Jack and Sue rarely saw each other. However, the biggest problem for Jack was that they were still ostensibly married. Jack had confirmed that, as long as he was registered as married, he couldn't request a single room. He coveted one, but if he admitted that the marriage certificate was false, he risked being uncovered and deported. That was why he'd persuaded Joe Brown that his marriage was a mess and that he needed the peace and quiet of a single room to reflect on things at night while the divorce was being processed. Joe Brown was especially understanding when Jack offered the amount of thirty rubles a month in exchange for the loan of his room. The Soviet regulations specifically forbade subletting, but fortunately, within the American village, some things still functioned as if they were in the United States. Joe Brown was happy to use half of Jack's fee to fund a shared room with another factory colleague. From that moment on, Jack was able to sleep alone in a bedroom only a little bigger than a wardrobe that stank of horse dung.

When he asked the bunkhouse receptionist about the smell, she explained that, when the buildings were constructed, they filled the cavities between the wooden partition walls with a mixture of straw and excrement. Despite the smell, she said, it provided excellent insulation.

Once the issue of his accommodation had been resolved, all Jack had to do was wait for Walter's arrival. The last they heard, he was still in Moscow, where he'd apparently found a role as an assistant to the OGPU.

Other than that, Jack had spent his free time planning his future. Since his arrival at the Avtozavod two months earlier, he'd managed to save two thousand dollars, of which he'd used two hundred to cover the three months' rent on his new room that he'd paid in advance, as well as to purchase a couple of used overcoats and a rudimentary stove to help him through the harsh winter.

He felt satisfied. If he carried on like this, in a year he'd amass a fortune of twelve thousand dollars, or roughly 360,000 tax-free rubles if he exchanged them on the black market. With those prospects, all he had to do was choose a European country to move to and spend his mountain of money.

And until that day came, he'd make sure he ate well.

Though he was entitled to the better meal tickets, he'd found that the portions that they served in the Avtozavod canteens were diminishing not only in size but also in variety, until all that was available were pots of *balanda*, a vegetable soup that consisted mostly of salty water; pies containing a ground meat, the origin of which nobody dared guess; and omelets made from powdered eggs. Jack didn't know which of these dishes it was that gave him diarrhea, so he decided to play it safe, avoid them all, and pay astronomical prices for the cooked sausages and chops that Miquel was able to supply at the end of each shift.

What bothered him most was having to hide in order to eat. He ate surreptitiously, praying that his neighbors wouldn't smell the food when he heated it on the stove in his room. Fortunately, the stink from the partition walls seemed to cover up the aroma. He did it so that his companions wouldn't be envious, because slowly, day by day, they were losing weight, while he remained strong.

It seemed inevitable that the famine would finally reach the Avtozavod, where thousands of souls waited patiently to be consumed.

Soon Jack would reach the end of his third month as a supervisor in Gorky, and everything continued more or less in the same way. Everything except the message that had been slid under his door that night. It was in Sue's handwriting. The note announced that Walter would arrive the next day.

He took a deep breath. He wasn't afraid of working under the scrutiny of thousands of watchful eyes, or acquiring food illegally, or trusting a black-market dealer to exchange his dollars for rubles. None of that scared him. But his heart skipped a beat when he thought about looking Walter in the eye as if nothing had happened.

When Walter arrived the next day, Jack found his friend looking very unwell. He didn't know whether Sue had told him anything about the *dalliance* they'd had on the night of the party, but he did know that his friend's face had become even more gaunt and pensive. Jack avoided any mention of Sue and focused on finding out about Walter's employment while they drank tea together in the canteen. "Three months! We've barely heard from you. We tried to contact your friend but couldn't locate him. You had us worried," said Jack, unable to hold his friend's gaze.

Walter downed the cup of tea in one gulp, as if it were the first he'd had all week. Jack asked him if he wanted to share the last piece of cake that was on the counter. His friend nodded. "I should've called you, but communications with Gorky are difficult, and I only speak a few words of Russian. I wrote to you both. I spent a couple of weeks in Moscow, going here, there, and everywhere with Dmitri."

He gobbled his piece of cake in one mouthful, so Jack could only just make out what he was saying. "He was trying to find work for me at the Comintern, as a liaison with the Communist Party USA, but all the positions were taken."

"So why didn't you come to Gorky?"

"Because I'm stubborn. You know me. Dmitri assured me it was just a matter of weeks before a vacancy came up. I had a pretty rough time, Jack," he concluded.

"God, Walter, believe me when I say I'm sorry. If I'd known . . ."

"No. Don't apologize. It was my own fault. I don't know why I felt intimidated by what you did in Moscow, when you found better jobs for everyone than I did. My stupid pride . . . I was a fool to think you were trying to make my life miserable."

Jack felt his stomach tighten when he remembered his night with Sue. He finished off his tea in an attempt to undo the knot. He waited for it to ease before continuing. "So, what's your situation now? I'm sure I could still speak to Wilbur Hewitt and—"

"That won't be necessary. In the end, Dmitri managed to get the People's Commissariat of Heavy Industry to reconsider the offer that I'd turned down. It was difficult—the Soviets are very strict when it comes to labor matters—but in the end, we managed to make arrangements, and I'm going to work as an administrative liaison between the Soviets and the Americans. A pencil pusher's job, but a job all the same."

"Even so, if it's for the regular salary, we could try to negotiate another role."

"No. Really, Jack. Maybe later. Fifty rubles here and there isn't gonna change my life, and I've already begged for too many favors to go asking to switch jobs now. I'm just grateful to you for taking care of Sue. I heard you've applied for a divorce, and paid for a room so she could be by herself. You're a true friend."

"Oh, well, it was nothing." Jack was glad he'd found the courage to go to the Zapis Aktov Grazhdanskogo Sostoyaniya, the Russian registry office, to file for a divorce. "So, I guess now everything can get back to how it was."

He hadn't finished the sentence when Sue appeared from nowhere. Jack, surprised, felt as if she were staring at him like a stalking feline. Walter looked at both of them, in silence.

"I hope so, Jack. I hope so."

With the arrival of spring, life at the factory took a turn for the worse. The Soviet high command had ordered that the Avtozavod be running at full capacity by the summer, which had led to an increase in workload that had not been matched by an increase in rations. The infirmaries were gradually becoming swamped with legions of increasingly emaciated workers who were given a restorative, along with a warning, before being sent back to their posts. Harry Daniels had been one of the latest operatives to need medical attention, but what ailed him couldn't be treated with pills. What he needed, his wife said, was a good plate of stewed vegetables, and that was what she asked Jack for after knocking on his door.

When he heard her request, he didn't know what to say.

"For the love of God, Jack," she insisted. "My Harry barely has the strength to breathe. In the morning, he throws up God knows what, because all he has for dinner is the colored water they give him at the factory. He has a cup of tea for breakfast and refuses to eat more than his cookie so that I won't go without. Please, I beg you. In Boston, I saw my brother starve to death, so I know what I'm talking about."

"But, Mrs. Daniels, you know as well as I do that the company store's practically out of stock. I can't—"

"Son," she cut in, "I'd know the smell that comes out of your room anywhere. And look at you. You might not have fat to burn, but you're strong as an ox. You know how to get food, and you must be able to spare some. Listen," she said, her eyes beginning to well up, "we send everything we have to my mother, who's sick in Detroit, but even so, we've saved two hundred rubles. It's all we have. Here. Take it." She held out the money in a crumpled ball.

Jack took a deep breath, trying to stifle his shame. He refused to take the notes and offered a handkerchief to the woman to dry her eyes. Money was not the issue. The problem was that if he helped Mrs. Daniels, word would spread that he could get food, and then everyone in the village would be begging him for the same thing. He pursed his lips and bemoaned the day he'd had the idea to treat everyone he knew to a hog roast.

"Mrs. Daniels, if I look well, it's because I had this suit mended. And in the canteen, they give supervisors special treatment. I'm . . . I'm sorry, but I can't help you."

The woman went down on her knees in front of Jack before he could stop her, bursting into tears. "In the name of God, I beg you! Think of your parents. If they were here, you would help *them*."

Hearing her mention his parents, Jack shuddered. It occurred to him that, were they still alive, he wouldn't even be here, freezing to death, with an old lady kneeling in front of him and begging him for food. He helped the woman up and showed her to the door. He told her to wait outside. Then he went to his trunk, removed five hundred rubles, and went out into the corridor to give them to her. "Here. It's all I can do for you."

"But what're we going to do with this money?" the woman sputtered with tears in her eyes. "We don't know—"

"I'm sorry, Mrs. Daniels. Ask around. I'm afraid there is no way I can help you."

A minute later, Jack slumped onto his bed and closed his eyes in an attempt to block out Mrs. Daniels's wails that he could make out in the distance. It was impossible. He pictured his mother's face on the body of the old woman on her knees, and his heart trembled. He mumbled a curse. He'd have liked to help those poor people, but if he did, he'd ease their suffering for a day, and the next day he'd be in jail. He went to pick up the bottle of vodka from his table, beside which were the remains of the beef stew he'd had for dinner. Suddenly, he retched, vomiting on the plate and his clothes. He cleaned himself as well as he could; then he opened the bottle and began to drink.

18

Jack had never imagined that simply having a hot meal every day and earning good money could weigh so heavily on him. He finished washing in the communal bathroom just as Mr. Daniels came in. The man greeted him in a wisp of a voice. When he took off his vest, Jack could see more ribs in his back than he would've liked. He returned the greeting and left.

On the way to his weekly meeting with Wilbur Hewitt, he tried to figure out how he could help Mr. Daniels without compromising himself, but as much as he tried, he couldn't think of a way. Through the great iron window of the office building, he could see a timid sun competing for space in the sky with the storm clouds that seemed to always hang over the Avtozavod. He gathered the reports he'd prepared throughout the week and knocked on the industrialist's door. It was ten o'clock on the dot, and as on other occasions, the young nurse who checked the progress of Hewitt's arm every morning emerged from the office. Jack returned the smile that she gave him as soon as she saw him. He remembered her name was Natasha. For a moment, he felt the urge to know more about her, and he wondered for how much longer she'd be treating Hewitt.

The industrialist's voice suddenly made Jack jump as if he'd been caught stealing apples. Jack took out his notes and arranged them on the desk. Hewitt laid his monocle on an old copy of the *New York Times* and waited for Jack to fill him in on the results of his inquiries. However, Jack set aside the reports and looked Hewitt in the eye. He pondered whether he should inform him about what was happening to his compatriots. He made up his mind.

"Mr. Hewitt, if I may, before we discuss the investigation, I'd like to bring a matter that concerns all of us to your attention."

"All of us? Gosh! Well, let's have it, then." He stubbed out his cigarette and leaned over the table to listen.

"It's about the food rations. I don't know if you're aware, but they're dwindling fast, and the American village store is also short on supplies."

"No, I didn't know. I always have lunch here, in the office, and, frankly, the offering seems just as plentiful and as awful as it's always been. But if that's the problem, I'll see if I can get them to provide you with a couple more tickets, and—"

"Pardon me, Mr. Hewitt. Perhaps I haven't explained myself well. The problem's not mine; like I say, it's something that's affecting all the workers."

"Oh! In that case, the best thing to do is lodge a complaint. I'll give you the name of the proper official. These matters are beyond my remit."

"Excuse me if I'm speaking out of turn, sir, but I don't think seeing fellow Americans growing sick from hunger is beyond your remit."

Hewitt's expression of disbelief was like that of a sergeant being insulted by a new recruit. He coughed as if he'd been dealt a punch, and stood over the desk. "Let's get one thing straight, Jack. This is how it works: we don't sniff the Russians' butts, and they don't sniff ours. I don't know why they're cutting rations, but if they are, I can assure you they'll have their reasons. Anyway, it sounds like the cuts are affecting everyone the same, and I doubt the Soviets enjoy seeing their own compatriots going without, so I don't think there's much I can do about it."

"So, that's it?"

"That's it."

"But—"

With a quick swat, Hewitt sent Jack's stack of reports flying. "Listen to me, kid, and listen hard, because you only have two choices!" he said, waving his forefinger in front of Jack's nose. "If you like our arrangement, carry on working with your mouth shut, taking home a salary that most people can only dream of. If you don't like it, take your reports, leave through that door, and then experience hardship like the rest of your workmates."

Jack fell silent, seeing Hewitt's flushed face. He'd never seen him like this. He swallowed and carefully reorganized his files. "I'm sorry if I've overstepped the mark."

"You darn well have overstepped it!"

"I understand, sir. If you want, I can still fill you in on my latest discoveries," he said quietly.

Hewitt pursed his lips while he straightened his vest with his good arm. He looked at Jack as if judging him, before slumping back into his armchair. "OK, kid. Tell me one thing. Do your conclusions this week shed any light on this business?"

"I believe they do."

"Then let's take a look, and I hope they do, because this conversation has delayed me, and in ten minutes, I have to report to Sergei." He started gathering up the notes that Jack had brought him.

"I hope it goes well, sir."

"You hope it goes well, kid? Well, you'd better, because today it's going to be *you* who informs Sergei of your progress."

Though he was going to see him with Hewitt, Jack couldn't avoid feeling the same shudder he'd felt running down his spine the first time he'd walked into Sergei Loban's office. As he sat in one of the red leather armchairs, he breathed in the smoky, damp, wood-scented atmosphere of an office that didn't appear to have been aired in years. Unlike on his previous visit, the curtains were drawn. A bulb, its filament as dull as Sergei's eyes, lit the room weakly. The rest of the paraphernalia—a typewriter with two sunken keys, a black Bakelite telephone, and a pair of metal filing cabinets—took on a sinister appearance in the half-light. Once they'd sat down, Sergei slumped into his own armchair and exhaled like an old horse tired of pulling a heavy cart. Behind him, the ubiquitous portraits of Lenin and Stalin kept a watchful eye on the room. The Soviet put a cigarette in his mouth and offered one to Hewitt. He didn't so much as look at Jack.

Hewitt inhaled as if he really needed it. Then he took out the yellow folder containing Jack's notes and proceeded to describe their contents in detail. When he finished, he took another puff and waited for Sergei's approval.

"An excellent job. Except all you have given me are figures. What I need are the culprits," Sergei murmured.

Hewitt looked at Jack, prodding him to give the Russian an explanation. Jack took the notes and went over them.

"Sir, the conclusions I've reached suggest that there's a high percentage of accidents caused by errors, and—"

"I'm not interested in accidents."

"All right." Jack cleared his throat. "As for the cases of sabotage, we need to separate two types of action with completely different objectives and methods. On the one hand, we have minor faults: screws coming loose, machines not working properly, or materials disappearing. If they didn't occur so frequently, we could put them down to human error. This kind of sabotage tends to cause small amounts of damage and is difficult to prevent. Like I say, the perpetrators are opportunistic, disgruntled workers who—"

"In the Soviet Union, there are no disgruntled workers!" Sergei broke in again.

Jack frowned. For a moment, he considered arguing with him, but he knew that following that path would only take him down a blind alley. "As for the second type . . ." He cleared his throat again while he rearranged his notes. "The second type is totally different and involves trained workers who plan their actions meticulously to cause maximum damage." He handed Sergei a file. "Look: batches of bearings manufactured out of tolerance, the devastating effects of which wouldn't be discovered until thousands of engines blew." He handed him another. "Metallic impurities welded into the steel molds during the stamping process, rendering them useless." He passed him a third file. "Or damage to manufacturing components, for which, curiously, there are no spares in the warehouses."

"Interesting . . ." Sergei took some battered spectacles from his drawer. Putting them on, he read the reports closely. "And the culprits?"

"That's the problem. Like I said, these people know what they're doing. The sabotage doesn't cause immediate damage, which makes it more difficult to identify the perpetrator."

"So we're talking about highly trained operatives?"

"Without a doubt."

"Well. In that case—"

He didn't manage to finish his sentence, because the door to his office was flung open and a man wearing a tight brown army jacket burst in without even glancing at Hewitt and Jack. "Sergei! I need a damned mechanic to fix the Buick once and for all," he blurted out.

Sergei snorted as if the person who'd just interrupted him were his rebellious teenage son. However, it was Viktor Smirnov, the finance commissar whom Jack had met at Elizabeth's birthday party. "I've told you a thousand times to knock before you come in!" bellowed the director of operations.

Viktor gave a start but didn't apologize. With a self-satisfied look at the Americans, he left, slamming the door behind him.

"By Lenin's whiskers! I'm sick of inept bureaucrats. Let's see . . . Where were we? Oh yes! Highly trained operatives. Good. Well, let's leave it here. Thank you, both. Jack, you've been a great help." He held out a hand to congratulate him.

When they left the office, Jack and Hewitt found Viktor Smirnov waiting for Sergei, pacing the hall like a caged cat. Jack knew he was about to be indiscreet, but he couldn't help himself. "Would your Buick be the 1928 Master Six Roadster?" he asked Viktor.

Hearing him, the official stopped dead. "That's right, but how did you—?"

"Six-cylinder engine, forty-eight horsepower, convertible . . . I couldn't help admiring it when I saw it parked outside."

"You know cars?" Viktor's eyes gleamed.

"It's my job. I worked on that very model for a while in the United States. A beautiful vehicle, but as delicate as a damsel, Mr. . . . ." He pretended he couldn't remember his name.

"Smirnov. Viktor Smirnov. Have we met?" He clearly hadn't paid much attention to Jack at the Hotel Metropol.

"No . . . I don't think so. Anyway, enjoy your car before it falls to pieces."

"What a coincidence! The cylinder head's gone on mine. Would you know how to fix it?"

Jack thought of Elizabeth before answering. "Of course. I could strip that Buick down blindfolded."

Back at his office, Hewitt, who had remained silent all the way there, slammed the door and threw Jack's reports into the wastepaper basket.

"What were you thinking? All Sergei needed was any excuse to blame the American workers, and you gave it to him on a platter. Why the hell did you tell him the sabotage was done by experienced operatives? I warned you not to divulge anything like that."

Jack stammered. He'd thought Hewitt would congratulate him on his investigation, but instead, he was yelling at him. "I . . . I didn't accuse anybody," he said in his defense.

"Don't you see? The Soviets will never admit that there are traitors in their ranks. Now Sergei will take your report, present it to his superiors, and blame the Americans for the sabotage." Hewitt collapsed into his chair. He pulled a bottle of vodka from a drawer and took a long draft. Then he offered the bottle to Jack. The young man copied him. "Sergei's a sly old dog," Hewitt went on. "He needs to show that he's got the factory under control, and he knows that the best way to do that is to divert attention from the real problem."

"But if he knows what the problem is, why doesn't he deal with it?"

"Because he can't. The saboteurs are spread throughout his own workforce: people tired of being exploited, peasants taken away from their land and forced to work at the Avtozavod, people who are just goddamned hungry. When the sabotage started, they tried to contain it by repressing the workers, but it only made matters worse. Now Sergei will have an excuse to start arresting Americans."

Jack didn't buy Hewitt's argument. The industrialist was blaming discontented Soviet peasants for the sabotage, but his findings showed that the perpetrators had technical expertise that the Soviets undoubtedly lacked. When he said as much, Hewitt became furious.

"Well, if you don't want to see your fellow countrymen dropping like flies, you'll have to prove yourself wrong. Oh! And one other thing. Your salary. I'm sorry for the inconvenience, but the Soviets are checking my accounts, and it's difficult to justify cash payments. I'm not saying I'm going to withdraw your wages . . . but you'll get them when you've earned them."

19

The young man in the red hat made sure nobody saw him unloading the last sack he'd carted to the American store. "I don't know why you're fixing his toy for him," Miquel muttered when he heard that Jack had agreed to repair Smirnov's Buick. "That Smirnov's a disgrace, an arrogant snake. They say that Stalin himself protects him. I don't know whether it's true, but it's obvious he's very well connected within the party. Just look at him strutting around like a peacock all day in his fancy car and his immaculate uniform, as if he owned the place."

Jack ignored the chatter. All he cared about was the chance to get closer to Elizabeth. "Well, the best thing you can do with a good-for-nothing is keep him entertained," he said, hiding the rack of ribs in the tool cart he was going to use to shift the meat. "Same as usual?"

"*Da*. Same."

Jack paid Miquel the agreed amount and said good-bye. Then he pushed the cart to the woodshed, where Harry Daniels's elder son was waiting for him. Jack had persuaded him to help sell the goods in the American village in exchange for some of the food.

After Hewitt told him about the difficulties paying his wages, Jack had decided that dealing in contraband was the best way to bridge the gap. Profiting from people's hunger might not be viewed favorably, especially by Walter, but in his mind, everyone was a winner: he provided an essential service, made a reasonable profit, and his fellow Americans received a little pork belly to make up for the alarming decline in food rations. He guessed that sooner or later Hewitt would resume paying him, but in the meantime, it would do no harm to cover his back. Jack had planned the operation to avoid any slipups that might alert the Soviets. Since the guards were stationed at the entrance on the fenced perimeter, he'd arranged for payment to be made in the dormitories, while the food would be dispensed in the courtyard latrines, through a cavity made in the sewer wall where neither the buyer nor the seller could see each other's face.

He and Jim finished butchering the pig and buried the cuts in the snow.

"You know what to do. Take the money first, and sell the portions one by one," Jack reminded him.

"The Robertsons haven't managed to raise the money. What should I do about their order?" said Jim. He was nineteen years old but thought like a much older man.

"How's their daughter? Has she recovered?"

"Nah. She can't shake off the pneumonia."

"Then give them the girl's share, and sell the rest to the Phillipses." Jack usually gave priority to workers with families. "And tell him, if she doesn't improve, to come and see me. I know a nurse; I could see if she would help."

Jim followed Jack's instructions to the letter, word got around, and for the next few days Jack supplied the village with fresh and cured meat. Unfortunately, news spread beyond the confines of the American village, and before long, the Soviets stepped up security, searching residents for suspicious goods.

Though he still had not received his wages from Hewitt, Jack decided not to continue dealing in contraband goods. However, when he told Jim he was shutting down the business, the youngster reacted as if he were taking away his last possession.

"You can't do this! Look at us." He showed Jack his undernourished arms. "I need those ribs. My parents need them."

Jack stood his ground. It was true that the American village was growing hungrier by the minute, but the Soviet workers were suffering the same hardships without complaining. At any rate, he couldn't even remember why he had decided to start smuggling food in when he already had a privileged position. "You'd do the same if you were me," he said in his defense.

"Sure. And if you were in my shoes, what would you do?" the young man shot back. His face was red with desperation.

Jack looked at him. He really had lost weight, as had the others in his family, whereas Jack had gone up a hole in his belt. He would have liked to help the youngster, but he didn't know how to do so without putting himself in danger. Miquel wouldn't do business with anyone but him. He pondered for a moment. He cursed himself and spat out the piece of smoked meat he was chewing. "All right. I'll tell you what we'll do. I'll keep the business going with the same terms, but you'll be in charge. If for whatever reason we get busted, you'll take the heat. It's the best I can do."

Jim stammered a thank-you, and Jack nodded firmly. He left the youngster to clean up and went up to his room to wash. He was late for his engagement. As he dried his hair, he told himself that he'd just made the most stupid mistake of his life.

With its blue domes set on top of two little towers, Jack thought that the dacha where Viktor Smirnov lived could not have looked more like a Byzantine church. While he waited for someone to come to the door, he admired the gardens and fountains that surrounded the impressive two-story building. Looking down the hill, he could see the point where the Volga took in the waters from its tributary, the Oka. Beyond the river, the frozen expanse seemed to stretch endlessly to the horizon.

He was about to ring the bell again, when Smirnov, wrapped in a striking red silk dressing gown, came out of his mansion to invite him in. "Magnificent views, aren't they, Jack?" He greeted him with a handshake.

Inside, Jack was captivated by the array of paintings and tapestries that lined the walls, giving the room the appearance of a palatial parlor. He sat on a velvet-lined sofa by a side table with an old gramophone on it, and savored the cup of tea a servant had brought to him, while Viktor crowed about the stove in the middle of the room that heated the entire building.

The Soviet official described the dacha as his redoubt. An old mansion that had belonged to a relative of Tsar Nicholas II, the place was little more than a stable when he had occupied it after the revolution. "But gradually I turned a pigsty into a palace. Just look: Bohemian crystal, genuine French furniture, Ziegler Persian rugs, canvases by Levitan, Serov . . . Costly, yes, but extraordinary. Not everyone knows how to appreciate such treasures, of course, but if you've owned a Buick Master Six, you'll know exactly where I'm coming from," Viktor said, taking it for granted that Jack was a man of refined tastes.

Jack was glad he'd put on McMillan's suit, which the tailors on Sverdlovka Avenue had made to fit him like a glove. Viktor noticed it.

"Bird's-eye?"

"Pardon me?"

"The fabric of your suit. It's bird's-eye, is it not?"

"Oh yes!" Jack said through sheer reflex. "Do you like it?"

"Of course! Not very appropriate for this climate, but elegant nonetheless. I buy my suits from the GORT, our private store. Now look, drink your tea and let's talk about the car. That's what you came for."

Viktor didn't wait for Jack to finish his tea before he asked him to follow him to the garage, where he kept his most treasured possession. With its gleaming beige paintwork, the Buick was immaculate, as if fresh off the production line. Viktor proudly informed Jack that he had it washed twice a day with water from the Oka. Jack saw that next to the

Buick was an old Ford Model A covered in dust, as well as a burgundy Ford Model B, freshly imported.

"I have the tools you requested," Viktor informed him.

Jack examined them. In addition to the usual sets of socket wrenches, on the workbench were a torque handle, some pliers, and several screwdrivers. He turned his attention to the Buick, and while he opened the hood, he asked Viktor to describe to him again what was wrong with the automobile. When Viktor had finished, Jack examined the engine.

"The heating and water consumption suggest there's a leak in the cylinder head." Jack unscrewed the radiator cap and looked at it. He ran his finger inside it and collected a blob of an unctuous substance the color of milky coffee that had accumulated at its base. "This confirms it."

"That's what my mechanic told me."

"No doubt. And I guess he suggested taking out the cylinder head and repairing it by soldering it."

"He did. But he assured me that the repairs wouldn't take long, so I decided to postpone them."

Jack inspected the rest of the engine's organs. He pretended to think for a moment. "It's a design fault. The cylinder head on this vehicle's susceptible to corrosion because of the diameter and position of the cooling ducts. Even if we milled a new cylinder head, sooner or later the problem would return."

"So what does that mean? Can it be fixed or can't it?" Viktor waited anxiously for Jack's reply.

Jack paused before responding. Given Viktor's obsession with his Buick, perhaps he'd struck gold. "The repairs can be done, of course. But we'd need several things that are hard to find, and, honestly, I doubt you could afford it." He waited for Smirnov to take the bait.

Viktor responded to the challenge as if Jack had doubted the authenticity of his lineage. "No one's said anything about money. Tell me what you need," he demanded.

There was a long silence. Finally, Jack looked Viktor in the eye. "What I'd need would be time to work, the right tools, a means of transportation to get around in . . ." He paused. "And somewhere quiet to do the repairs."

Back at the American village, Jack couldn't believe what he'd achieved. Miquel had told him about the intricate web of contacts that enabled Viktor Smirnov to enjoy his luxurious lifestyle without the Soviet machinery coming down on him. But the reality exceeded his expectations. Or at least, that was what he surmised from the extraordinary benefits that he was going to enjoy merely for repairing his car.

When he told Joe Brown that he was giving him back his room because he was moving to one of the family homes in the American village, Joe couldn't believe his ears. "They're reserved for the big bosses!" he exclaimed in surprise.

Jack smiled and winked, and added that his own vehicle was waiting for him at the door.

Joe let out a sigh of wonder when he saw Jack load his bags into an old Ford Model A to head off to his new home.

With the excuse of needing a quiet place where he could repair the Buick, he'd persuaded Viktor to allow him to stay in one of the empty houses, and since, every time he needed materials, he'd have to travel the six-plus miles between the American village and Gorky, he'd also convinced him to lend him the Ford that he didn't use.

The news spread like wildfire, and to Jack's pleasure, he soon noticed that his fellow countrymen began to show him the respect normally reserved for the men at the top. Little things like taking their hats off as he passed, making an effort to be more friendly than usual, or taking an interest in his life became the norm. Along with his position as a supervisor and his control over the illicit trade in food, his newfound status led his fellow Americans to see him as the village chief. What Jack didn't know was that alongside the admiration that he aroused among his friends grew a dangerous dose of envy.

For a short while, Jack enjoyed what anyone at the Avtozavod would have described as a pleasant life. Despite his initial objections, Viktor had persuaded Wilbur Hewitt to temporarily relieve Jack of some of his duties, enabling him to have breakfast in the social club surrounded by admirers who showered him with flattery. There, with the room heated and without the coats that masked their starved bodies, the difference between the fortunate and the deprived was clear. Jack shared his breakfast with everyone, but he would gulp down his coffee and rush to lock himself away in the garage of his new home and work on the Buick, repairing it with surgical precision. At noon, dripping with sweat, he would stop for lunch, before heading to the Avtozavod to complete his rounds and look for leads in his investigation. At sundown, he'd give Viktor Smirnov, his new ally, a progress report, and talk sports cars over dinner, taking the opportunity to extract as much information as possible, as Hewitt had ordered him to do in exchange for his free time. He discovered that, in addition to being the finance commissar, Viktor held a position within the OGPU that he described as *symbolic*.

At one of those dinners, Elizabeth was present.

When they ran into each other, they were both left speechless. Viktor introduced Jack as the Avtozavod engineer who was repairing his Buick, and she understood immediately that the Soviet official had completely forgotten their meeting at the Metropol. During dinner, Jack and Elizabeth kept up appearances until the instant that Viktor went upstairs to find the micrometer that Jack had requested. As soon as he left the room, the young woman confronted him.

"Engineer? I thought you were just an operative."

Jack responded by depositing a bunch of keys on the table. When he smiled at her, Elizabeth raised an eyebrow.

"What are *they*?" she asked with feigned indifference.

"What do you think? The keys to my car and my new home. Maybe one day we could go for a drive?" He held up the keys and jingled them.

Elizabeth heard Viktor coming back down. "Maybe," she whispered, and turned her attention back to her sea bass.

20

Five months after Jack Beilis's arrival in the Soviet Union, the first American disappeared from the Avtozavod.

It was Alex Carter, a powerfully built assembler on the morning shift, whom everyone knew as the Milwaukee Express, the nickname he received as a worker at the Harley-Davidson motorcycle factory. His wife, Harriet, reported his disappearance, but the authorities hadn't paid her much attention, so she had come to the canteen to ask Jack to help her find him.

Jack fidgeted in his seat, remembering Hewitt's warning to avoid sticking his nose where it didn't belong. "Truthfully, I don't know why you've come to me for help. Maybe you should ask his workmates. Sometimes, after a hard day's work, the men head downtown to spend their pay on booze and . . . entertainment." Though Jack was thinking of a brothel, he thought better than to mention it. Still, the woman reddened.

"My Alex would never go with some floozy, if that's what you're suggesting."

Jack pursed his lips. He disliked feeling like someone to whom everyone thought they had the right to turn when they had trouble. He took a deep breath, wolfed down his slice of black bread, and stood. "All right. If I hear anything, I'll let you know right away."

The woman let a tear escape and squeezed Jack's hand in gratitude. When she'd left, Jack wiped the palm of the hand in which Harriet had placed her last hopes.

Though Alex Carter's disappearance was the talk of the American village, none of his workmates deigned to answer the questions that Jack asked them on his evening rounds. Tom Taylor, the Express's best friend, turned to him with a monkey wrench in his hand and gave him a shove.

"Why don't you ask your Soviet friends?" he said, spitting on the floor.

"Yeah. Why don't you ask them?" said another American operative.

"*Ruki nazad!*" yelled an armed guard.

"Hands off," Jack translated for his fellow countrymen, retreating.

"Sure. Go with them. But watch your back," Tom Taylor threatened. "Your money won't protect you forever."

On May 28, the second American citizen disappeared, and on June 6, a third went missing. The rumor spread around the village that the Black Crows, as the Soviets nicknamed the OGPU henchmen, had come at night and taken the workers who protested too much. Apparently, all three of them had complained that their wages had been short. When Jack questioned Wilbur Hewitt about the disappearances, the engineer merely shook his head. "I warned you that if you blamed the sabotage on specialized operatives, Americans would end up paying the price," was all he would say on the subject.

Jack was hurt that Hewitt seemed to hold him responsible for something that had nothing to do with him. In his mind, there was no connection between his report to Sergei and the disappearances. At any rate, the three missing Americans were not involved in any of the incidents that he'd investigated. He was about to argue his point, when the office door unexpectedly opened. Jack fell silent when he saw Natasha, the young nurse. She apologized for interrupting and said that she was just delivering Hewitt's painkillers. The industrialist growled, but accepted the pill and swallowed it. Then he asked Jack and Natasha to leave him be.

Outside the office, Jack remembered the Robertsons' daughter, sick with pneumonia, and seized the opportunity. "Sorry to be so forward, but the girl's been sick for months, and her parents are worried. I wondered whether you knew how I could get someone to help her, even if I have to pay."

"She hasn't been visited by the doctor assigned to the Americans?" asked the nurse.

"I guess she has. But I'm not sure she's had the right treatment."

Natasha gave him a comforting look. "Don't worry, Mr. Beilis. These things take time to subside. Give her this." She took some candy from her pocket and handed it to him. "And trust our Soviet medicine. That girl's in good hands," she added, saying good-bye with a smile.

Jack stood watching the young woman walk away. He was surprised by her friendliness, but even more so by the fact that, after so long, she had remembered his surname.

Jack kicked a stone when, as he came out of his new home, he found his car rendered useless once more. It was the second time that he'd woken up to find that the Ford Model A's tires had been slashed, but on this occasion someone had painted "Soviet Lover" on the windows in red paint. Jack did what he could to wash it off, changed the wheels for some spares that he kept in the garage as a precaution, and started the car. Then, making sure everyone present could hear the engine's roar, he sped off toward Walter's workplace.

Jack's friend was surprised to see him walk into his modest office in the OGPU headquarters. He moved aside the mountain of papers on his desk and offered Jack a chair. Jack refused the invitation and remained standing, pacing from one side of the room to the other. "You have to explain to me what's happening. You work with the Russians," he snapped.

There was nobody else in the office, but Walter looked from side to side, as if afraid he was being spied on. He gestured to Jack to be quiet and went out into the courtyard with him. Outside, the loudspeaker was broadcasting the same propaganda that was blared all day at the factory.

"What do you think you're doing coming here and asking me that?" He brushed aside a few strands of hair that had fallen over his spectacles.

"Damn it, Walter! Three guys have disappeared in two weeks, and everyone's treating me as if it were my fault. They've slashed the tires on my car. If this carries on, any time now they'll be breaking my legs."

Walter bit his lip. "And why do you think I might know something?"

"Come on, buddy! If you'd stayed with us in the village instead of moving to the city, you'd know that it's all anyone talks about. The OGPU showed up at midnight in their black cars and arrested two men, just like that. And we've still had no news of Alex Carter, the first guy who disappeared."

Walter exhaled. "I saw their files," he admitted in a tiny voice. "My Russian isn't great, but their names written in the English alphabet jumped out at me, and I asked a comrade to fill me in."

"Comrade?"

"That's what we call one another."

"Sure . . . and what did the reports say?"

"He didn't give me all the details, but it seems they've been accused of being involved in several acts of sabotage."

"What a load of crap. They're just fathers who want their kids to be able to eat a decent meal every day. Who in their right mind would think they'd sabotage the very people who put food on their tables?"

"Shhh! For God's sake, keep your voice down!"

"And where've they been taken? To the labor camp?" Jack had heard there was a gigantic correctional facility on the outskirts of Gorky.

"I can't tell you that."

Jack raised his eyebrows. He asked Walter if he could at least let him know whether they'd be tried, and his friend nodded, but when Jack asked in what court, he fell silent. "They'll be put on trial by the OGPU itself," he finally said without looking up.

"But that's illegal. How can the people who arrested them be their judges as well?"

"Wake up, Jack! This ain't America. There's a revolution going on here, and we have many enemies."

Jack hawked. He was growing ever more confused by the stance that Walter had adopted. When he reminded him that they knew the people who had disappeared—their wives, their children—his friend became distant, as if he were suddenly being reminded about something from the past.

"I had to leave the village for the same reason you should leave. The Americans are a bunch of deadbeats. They complain about how little food there is and how hard they have to work, without considering that it's the same for everyone. They've forgotten that they fled their country for a reason. The Soviets welcomed us with open arms, and now, if we get along with them, our compatriots brand us as enemies."

"Listen, Walter." Jack laid his hands on his friend's shoulders. "This isn't about how discontented these men are with the working conditions or lack of food. We're talking about the fact that our fellow countrymen are disappearing!"

"No, Jack." He removed his hands from his shoulders. "They might be your fellow countrymen, but they're not mine."

Jack fell silent for a moment. "I don't understand. What do you mean?"

"I've given up my passport. I'm a Soviet citizen now," Walter said firmly.

Word soon spread that the *disappeared* had been sent to Siberia, though nobody was able to corroborate the rumor. The men's families were informed that they had been accused of counterrevolutionary activities and sentenced to hard labor, adding that anyone protesting would be given the same punishment. For the time being, the Americans in the village continued to treat Jack as an ally, even if it was only because he could help them get food. Still, the attacks on his car had been warning enough to make him understand that he had to look out for his own safety, and he expressed his concerns to Ivan Zarko, the money changer who bought his dollars.

Zarko didn't hesitate to offer him his services. "I'll send you Yuri, my nephew. Not even a bear would dare to come up behind you with Yuri by your side," the old man assured him. When Jack met Yuri, he couldn't have agreed more. Zarko's nephew was huge, and if not for the monosyllables he let out from time to time, he could easily have been mistaken for a bear. They agreed that Yuri would guard Jack's home at night, but, during the day, they would pretend that he was an assistant mechanic for as long as it took to repair Viktor's Buick Master Six. After that, they'd find him another role.

As the days went by, Yuri proved to be not only effective as a security guard but also adept at dealing in contraband, and he suggested some ways that Jack could build up his business. "Shoes! People will kill for shoes."

Jack was surprised when he heard the idea, and for a moment he thought that, had he not had such a well-paid position as a supervisor at the Avtozavod, perhaps the skills he'd learned from his father as a boy could have come in useful after all.

21

In late June, the Buick Master Six was cranked up for the first time, and Jack was glad that Viktor Smirnov wasn't there to witness it. The engine purred for a few minutes, ticking over like a clock, but then the copper gasket that Jack had fashioned blew, and the motor let out a snort and died. Yuri raised an eyebrow and laughed. "What a heap of junk."

Jack didn't see the humor. He'd promised Viktor that he'd have his automobile ready for the grand opening of the firing range that the Soviets had built near the Avtozavod, and he was no longer sure he'd be able to pull it off. Fortunately, Viktor and Sergei had gone to Moscow for political business and would not return until September, so he hoped he had enough time to repair the Buick and make some progress with the investigation. He left Yuri to clean up and went out for a walk. For the first time in months, the sun was shining brightly. *What a perfect day,* he thought, *to enjoy with Elizabeth.*

As soon as he learned of Viktor's departure, he had taken the opportunity to arrange a date with the young woman, and he didn't want to arrive late, so he accelerated his newly washed Ford Model A through Gorky's narrow streets.

He found her sitting on her mansion's porch, busy untangling her hair. With the mild temperature, Elizabeth had shed her overcoat, showing her figure. Jack honked his horn and held up the picnic basket he'd prepared. She smiled and approached to inspect the freshly cooked pork chops. She said hello, opened the passenger door, and took her seat.

"Where're you taking me?" she asked.

Jack didn't hesitate. "Let's go to the river."

"I ain't got my bathing suit," she replied, winking, aware that, even in summer, nobody in their right mind would swim in the Volga's icy waters.

"Then we'll have to bathe naked." He smiled and started up the car without waiting for a response.

They stopped on a hill near the Oka River from which they could see Gorky like a distant park dotted with little white bricks. The temperature was so pleasant that if not for the bottle of vodka that poked immodestly out from the basket, Jack would've sworn he was back in America. Elizabeth laughed as she told him about the progress she'd made learning Russian, which her teacher described as backward steps, if anything. Jack was happy. Elizabeth felt close and relaxed, as if they'd been going out together forever, and he loved the feeling. They chatted for hours about their lives, their routines, their projects. Finally, she admitted that she was sick of the Soviet Union, and that all she wanted was for the factory to start running smoothly so that her uncle Wilbur would be transferred back.

"And when you return to New York, what'll happen to Viktor?" asked Jack, instantly realizing the poor timing of his remark.

"Nothing. Why does he come into it?"

Jack cleared his throat. He admitted that he'd assumed she and the official were engaged. She burst into brazen laughter. "Oh, don't be so old-fashioned, Jack. We're in the country of liberation! Haven't you seen that you don't have to be married to have children?"

Jack felt even more confused. "You're thinking of having children?"

Elizabeth looked at Jack as if he understood nothing.

"Come on, let's get back to Gorky," she said, straightening her hat. "I don't want you thinking we really are going to bathe naked."

They met several times over the next few weeks. On Jack's days off, they frequented the cool banks of the Oka, strolled through Gorky's shopping quarter, and went to the parties that senior officials held at their homes. Whenever they met, Jack would try to take their relationship further. Yet she seemed to change her mind for no apparent reason, as if her desires shifted depending on which way the wind was blowing. No sooner did she seem to be interested and warming to him than she would become distant and speak to Jack haughtily, treating him like a stranger. When that happened, it riled Jack, making him question why he was even bothering with such a fickle young woman. But the moment Elizabeth gave him a smile, he was disarmed by her beauty.

"So, when will you go back to the States?" she asked him when they came out of the theater. That Saturday they'd seen *The Cherry Orchard*.

Jack had asked himself the same question a thousand times. He longed for New York's nightclubs, its hustle and bustle, its avenues packed with colorful cars, but as a fugitive, he was aware that he'd never be able to enjoy them again. Elizabeth's question made him wonder why he was staying at the Avtozavod when he already had enough money to move to any other European country. He guessed he was still in Russia because life was simple there, but that answer didn't satisfy him. After all, the only things he liked about the Soviet Union were going out with

Elizabeth and continuing to amass his fortune. "When I have enough so that you'll agree to marry me," he said without thinking.

She laughed as if he'd cracked a joke. Then she adjusted the emerald necklace that Viktor had given her and looked him in the eye. "Jack, honey, if I wanted to marry an aging millionaire, I could do it right now."

To Jack's surprise, on the last Sunday of August, Elizabeth agreed to have dinner with him in the American village. When he went to her mansion to fetch her, she appeared on the porch wearing a simple close-fitting dress and holding a bottle of vodka. Jack took the bottle and kissed her hand. Then he helped her into the car and drove slowly toward the village.

He'd offered Yuri the day off in exchange for giving the house a thorough clean and decorating the living room with flowers, but seeing the results, Jack realized the young man hadn't quite understood the word *thorough*. As for the flowers, Jack wouldn't have noticed the difference had Zarko's nephew left a dish of salad on the table. Fortunately, Elizabeth seemed to pay no attention to it, and she made herself comfortable in a chair while Jack lit some candles. He poured her a glass of vodka and raised his own decisively. "To love in the Soviet Union," he toasted.

"To love, plain and simple." She drank her vodka in one shot.

They had drunk half a bottle by the time they set the main course aside and Jack got up to serve dessert. He took the chance to brush his lips against her neck.

Elizabeth stood to return the gesture, but he held her from behind, stopping her from turning around. As he kissed the back of her neck, he heard her breathing deepen. He prolonged the moment until she couldn't hold on any longer and turned to seek out his mouth. When their lips met, Jack thought he would go crazy. He pressed her against him. He kissed her vigorously, then delicately, delighting in the flavor of her mouth, which half opened to allow their tongues to meet.

They let themselves fall onto a sofa in each other's arms and continued to kiss, biting each other, caressing, searching with their hands for the regions of the other's body they didn't yet know. Jack slid his fingers under a dress that seemed to be shrinking away from his grasp, as if desire were making it move by itself. He unbuttoned her dress and searched for her breasts with his mouth. She offered them to him and groaned when he took possession of them. They slid onto the woolen rug as Elizabeth, anxious and evasive, nevertheless pressed her bare skin against Jack's torso.

When Jack entered her, he thought he would die. He wanted to pinch himself to make sure it was really happening, but her groans were as real as her mouth, as the hands that pulled him closer and held him, as real as the slender legs that were wrapped around his waist and the fresh sweat that pearled on her face. He kissed her until his lips hurt, and kept kissing, kept moving, madly and then slowly, with fire and then tenderness, with love and with desire, while their bodies blazed, reared, and convulsed, faster and faster, until they exploded together. Then, exhausted, they fell asleep, holding each other.

Jack had never desired anybody so much. He would wake up dreaming of Elizabeth and go to sleep remembering her. The rest of his waking hours were a torment from which work couldn't rescue him. In the mornings, he wandered around the assembly plants, trying not to make any more enemies among his fellow Americans, but it was difficult. The discontent in the Avtozavod was spreading like water from a burst pipe, dampening the spirit of the ever more hungry and exhausted workers. But Jack barely noticed it. His senses were dulled to the world around him, captivated by a woman whose almost unreal beauty seemed to be pulling the strings of his destiny. He was constantly imagining her beside him, naked; he remembered every look, every groan, every kiss, and the memory tortured him every empty, endless hour that he was not with her. Then, when he was by her side, desire gnawed at him, hungry and desperate, but she was distant, as if she'd erased the night they'd spent together from her mind; or worse still, as if it had never happened. Elizabeth laughed and spoke to him in a friendly way, with the empty amiability that she would offer an acquaintance, but not with the passion of a lover. Jack didn't know why, but Elizabeth had erected a wall between them. And Jack suspected that Viktor's imminent return was the cause of her remoteness.

22

The summer flew by. Gradually, shoes were replaced by felt boots, and thick *ushankas* were donned instead of summer hats. And when the cold arrived, more workers began to disappear.

The most conspicuous disappearance was Harriet Carter's. Convinced that the Soviets had murdered her husband, the Milwaukee Express's wife had launched a desperate protest campaign, which, though initially ignored, eventually found a response. One morning Harriet went out for a meeting with Sergei Loban and never returned. Something similar happened to Robert Watkins. In his case, word was that he'd caused a scene in the foundry after hearing that the Soviets were refusing to return his passport. That night, he was arrested by the Black Crows and never seen again.

They weren't the only ones. The entire Collins family was arrested and charged with counterrevolutionary activities. Yet, in the American village, everyone knew that the Collinses' only crime was trying to inform reporters from the *New York Times* in Moscow about their desperate situation.

Jack observed the events in silence. It was what Hewitt had advised him to do, and following his advice to the letter seemed like the safest course of action. He had put off the repairs on Smirnov's car to concentrate on his work at the factory after Wilbur Hewitt warned him that if he didn't make some progress in his investigation, they would be forced to revise the terms of his contract. Still, though it was true that there had been few developments, Jack wasn't allowed to nose around during the night shift, when most of the suspicious incidents had taken place.

Hewitt remained firm. "I've told you a thousand times." He set aside his newspaper, fed up with the young man's excuses. "A night inspection would attract attention, and the last thing Sergei's going to authorize is something that could alert the saboteurs. And if the head of security says *niet*, then it's *niet*."

"But while Sergei's in Moscow, maybe you could find a way to—"

"To buy us a one-way ticket to jail? Is that what you want?"

Jack thought he had reason to suspect that Sergei himself was implicated in the sabotage, but without hard evidence, there was no point in telling Hewitt.

He was certain that if he wanted to make progress in his inquiries, he would have to find a way to get around Sergei's rules. The opportunity arose when Viktor Smirnov, on his return from Moscow, turned up at the American village to check on his Buick's repairs.

"What do you mean it's not ready? You've had it for months!" the Russian yelled.

Jack assured him that he would have repaired it by now had he been in possession of the right equipment, but the problem was the copper gasket. "I tried to fabricate one using the materials you provided, but with the first explosion, it melted like butter. At the Avtozavod, there's a machine that would solve the problem, but they won't let me use it. That's why I was waiting for you to get back."

"I see . . . and what machine would that be?" Viktor grumbled.

Jack explained that he would need access to a specific press in the assembly section. "I'd only need a couple of hours. The problem is, it's always operating."

"Then I'll make them stop!" the Russian decided with the expression of a dictator being contradicted.

"I'm afraid it's not that simple. This machine's one of a kind, and taking it out of operation would affect production. However, there is one thing . . ." Jack pretended to mull over an alternative.

"Yes?"

"Once a week, during the night shift, they stop the machine to change the molds. If I could use it then, I'd have enough time to get your Buick ready before the grand opening of the firing range."

"Without fail?"

"Without fail."

"And when do they next stop the press?"

"Tonight, as it happens."

The moment he went through the factory gate, Jack realized that he was walking into the lions' den. All hope of escaping unharmed after flouting Sergei's orders lay with Viktor Smirnov, who walked beside him, one pace behind the armed guard who was leading them to the assembly plant. He hoped that the Soviet official's presence would free him of any responsibility, though it meant he had to attempt to lose Viktor for long enough to find the evidence that would confirm his suspicions.

Via the endless corridor that ran parallel to the assembly line, they reached the location of the press that Jack had mentioned. The armed guard warned them not to leave without his permission, and then he left them alone to work. Jack pulled on some regular overalls instead of his own white ones, opened his kit bag, and took out a micrometer, the ruined gasket, and a wooden template that he had previously perforated, making holes that lined up with the cooling ducts. Viktor asked about the procedure.

"This machine can be used to press or punch, depending on the mold. We need to punch holes in the gasket aligned with the combustion chambers and cooling ducts. But to make the material harder, first I have to reduce its thickness. Compress it."

Viktor looked perplexed.

"Let me put it another way," Jack said. "Imagine you're using a rolling pin to spread out the dough for a rectangular pastry. Suppose we use the rim of a glass to cut out six holes in the dough and take out their centers. Follow me?"

Viktor nodded.

"At that point, you might think the gasket was ready, but if I press it with the roller again, not only will it become thinner, but it will also expand, including into the holes, which would reduce their diameter. Right?"

"I guess so."

"Right. If it was a gasket, in reducing its diameter, the explosion from the cylinders would burn the projecting rim and totally destroy the part. However . . ."

"Yes?"

"If I change the order of operations and press the gasket before making the perforations, the part won't go out of shape however hard I stamp it, because it will already be fully compressed."

"Very clever, but you're boring me to death! Will it work or not?"

"Yes, if I do it carefully. This press has a micrometer gauge that will allow me to measure any deformation, but it's a delicate task that will take time to do right."

"Then don't let me keep you. We have two hours until the next shift."

Jack got to work. After Viktor had watched the procedure for an hour, his interest began to wane. "This is torture!" said the Soviet.

With greasy hands and a sweat-covered brow, Jack looked at Viktor. "Well, the most boring part's still to come. Out back there's a heated room where you can help yourself to some tea. I'll let you know if I need you."

Viktor didn't think twice. He nodded and, yawning, went off to seek refuge in the staff room. As soon as he'd left, Jack took a finished gasket from his kit bag and switched it for the one he was making. Then he took the micrometer and a notebook, and disappeared among the mass of automobiles that filled the plant.

He was inspecting one of the bearing assembly machines that had been sabotaged, when a guard appeared and aimed a rifle at him. "What are you doing in this sector?" he demanded, his finger on the trigger.

"I have authorization from Viktor Smirnov. I'm—"

"American? Step back. Move away from that machine and empty your bag."

Jack spread its contents on the floor. With his foot, the guard separated the tools and the unusable gasket. "Like I say, I have authorization. You can ask—"

"Lower your weapon! What's the meaning of this?" Viktor broke in. Seeing that Jack was no longer at the press, he had set out to search for him.

"This man claims he has your authorization, sir." He stood to attention when he recognized the official.

"That's right. Though he should have stayed at the other end of the corridor."

"I'm sorry. I had to test the gasket with the gauge on this machine, and I didn't want to bother you," Jack explained, seeing a hint of suspicion in Viktor's eyes. "But it doesn't matter anymore, because this clown just wrecked it."

As Jack had guessed he would, when he heard about the part being damaged, Viktor flew into a rage. "What's your name, you bumbling fool?" he yelled, gripping the guard by his jacket.

"Relax," Jack interrupted. "I took the precaution of making a spare gasket."

Viktor sighed with relief. What the Soviet official didn't know was that Jack at last had the evidence he needed to prove his theory.

◆ ◆ ◆

Jack had given himself a week to organize the evidence before presenting it to Wilbur Hewitt. But he never had the chance. A few hours after his clandestine visit, a black vehicle pulled up in front of Jack's home, and two uniformed men dragged him inside the vehicle before heading at full speed to an office at the OGPU headquarters.

He spent an hour in total bewilderment before the door to the room they'd locked him in opened with a squeak, revealing Sergei Loban. Recognizing him, Jack gave a start and stood up. He didn't know that Sergei had returned from Moscow. Nobody had explained to him why he'd been arrested, but one didn't have to be a genius to work out that it was something to do with his nocturnal investigations. Sergei's deep voice confirmed it. The OGPU chief sat in one of the chairs and fixed his eyes on Jack's, which glimmered in the dim light from the single bulb in the room.

"You can sit down," said Sergei. Jack obeyed. "Let's see. I've just got back, and you Americans welcome me with problems. According to this report, last night, in my absence and going against my orders, you entered the factory in the early hours and used a bearing assembly machine. Correct?"

Jack had already prepared his defense. "Yes. But I didn't violate any orders. I went there with Viktor Smirnov's authorization for the sole purpose of fabricating a gasket for his Buick. You can ask him, if you want."

"I already have, and he confirms that point. But he says that you went to the bearing machine in his absence, when he had only authorized you to work on the gasket."

"I wanted to check that the part was—"

"Let's cut the bullshit! You might be able to fool a fairy like Smirnov, but I'm an engineer and I know that to make a copper gasket, a bearing assembly machine is about as useful as a napkin on a pig."

Jack swallowed. He cursed himself for believing Hewitt when he'd told him that Sergei was nothing more than a bureaucrat. He tried to think on his feet. "I never said I wanted to use that machine to manufacture the gasket. I needed to use the gauge to confirm the accuracy of my micrometer. I'm sure your report will show that I had a defective one in my bag, that is, if the guard who pointed his rifle at me even knew what it was."

"Of course he knew." Sergei checked his notes and gnashed his teeth. "And in fact, he mentions it. But it seems too much of a coincidence that you happened to be handling the same gauge involved in some of the worst sabotage in the Avtozavod . . . unless you were doing it on purpose."

"Like you say, it was a coincidence."

"You'll see, then, why I don't believe you."

"Frankly, I don't believe you, either."

"Ha! You Americans are so full of yourselves. Even when you're one wrong word away from being sent to Siberia."

"Now that you mention it, I'd like to ask you about them. About the Americans who've disappeared without a trace," Jack challenged him.

"That's where you're wrong. The detainees have left behind a stench of betrayal so strong that you could follow it all the way to the prison where they're going to pay for their crimes."

"What crimes? Being American?"

"No, Jack. Most of your compatriots whom we've taken have been charged with counterrevolutionary activities that have nothing to do with this investigation."

"What activities? Protesting against taxes they hadn't been told about? Asking for food for their children? Wanting to return to their country?"

"Those men have betrayed our trust. What does it matter if they're charged with sabotage? Either way, they're enemies of the people. Don't forget, you gave me the justification to do it. You assured me that the sabotage was so sophisticated that it could only have been perpetrated by skilled workers!"

"But you know it wasn't them. The reports show the times the accidents took place, but not the moment the machines were tampered with. Like the gauge, for example, the first problem was detected in a routine maintenance operation performed on February 6 at eight ten a.m."

"That's right."

"But what you might not know is that to decalibrate that machine, a qualified operative would need at least twenty minutes. It would take that long to cause a fault subtle enough so that the damage wouldn't be immediately detected, but bad enough to ruin the parts after a few hours of use."

"What are you insinuating?"

"That the machine must've been tampered with in the early hours of February 6, sometime before the shift change."

Sergei gave Jack a puzzled look mixed with resentment. "That doesn't free any Americans from suspicion."

"I beg to differ. I'll remind you that, on your orders, at that time all Americans were forbidden from working the night shift, so it's impossible any of them caused the damage."

Sergei pursed his lips and stood, casting aside the chair. "Arrogant Americans! You think you're better than everyone else. You take us Soviets for fools, without realizing that we're the ones with the intelligence, the courage, and the determination that you lack. And why should I believe a word of your reports?"

"I don't care whether you believe them or not. Wilbur Hewitt hired me to find out the truth behind the sabotage, and that's what I've been doing. If you'd rather close your eyes and ignore the evidence, perhaps it's because that's what you want."

"How dare you? Do you know who you're talking to?"

"Until a moment ago, I thought it was Sergei Loban, upholder of Soviet justice. Now, I'm not so sure."

◆ ◆ ◆

The morning was as cold as it was overcast.

Jack got up with a sore back. As he pulled on the white overalls that identified him as a specialized operative, he shook his head. He was more convinced than ever that Sergei was hiding something, even if he had encouraged him to continue his investigations with the support of a Soviet assistant.

When he reached the foundry, he was received by the official whom Sergei had ordered to accompany him. It was Anatoly Orlov, the Soviet who'd acted as his guide on his arrival at the Avtozavod. Jack greeted him coldly and got to work. Sergei had ordered him to inspect the furnaces, the boiler section, and the mineral wagons. He spent half the morning completing the first tasks. But when he was about to inspect the molten mineral conveyor, Jack stopped.

"What is it?" Orlov asked.

"I can't inspect them while they're moving. You'll have to shut it down."

"Impossible. Production can't be halted."

Jack stood firm. The mineral conveyers consisted of a suspended rail from which metal buckets hung, transporting the molten ore from the crucible. Examining them while in operation was reckless and risky, because the molten material could splash onto anyone underneath.

"To see it properly, I'd need to go through the safety barrier and into the pit," Jack explained. "I'm not going to do that with molten metal raining down on me."

"All right. I'll order them to stop," Orlov muttered.

Jack waited for the conveyor to come to a complete standstill. He asked an operative for a protective apron, pulled on some gloves, and opened the door to the pit. Though stationary, the buckets of liquid metal swayed dangerously overhead. Jack protected his eyes and looked up toward the buckets. Though they seemed secure, they creaked menacingly. He went carefully forward, making sure he didn't tread on the pieces of metal that were still hot, before heading back to the door.

"All in order. I'm coming out!" he yelled to the others.

Suddenly, before he could reach the barrier, the conveyor jerked into motion without warning, pulling along its deadly load.

Jack screamed like a man possessed when a splash of white-hot liquid missed his face by only a few inches, but the conveyor, relentless, continued moving, spitting out pieces of molten metal that forced him to retreat. "Stop the conveyor, you bastards!" he cried from the temporary shelter he'd found under a metal support.

Nobody seemed to hear him. The noise from the foundry was deafening. Jack tried to think—the support wouldn't protect him forever. If he stayed there, he would be burned to death. He looked around. At that moment, a shower of incandescent projectiles lit up a piece of discarded rail. It might be his salvation, if he could reach it. He looked toward the conveyor and saw the buckets swinging overhead. He tried to synchronize his movements with the splashes by counting to himself: *One . . . two . . . three.* He got ready. On three, he leapt from his shelter and swooped on the metal bar, grabbing it and quickly returning to the support. But before he reached it, he felt a searing pain in his left hip, making him howl in agony.

Jack looked at the place where the molten metal had missed the apron and eaten into his flesh. With the red-hot fragment devouring his flesh, he took a penknife from his pocket and cut his pants until his hip was exposed. He roared when he inserted the sharp point between the flesh and the hot metal. As he extracted it, he felt a pain so unbearable that for a moment he wished he could tear his leg clean off. Curling up under the support, he screamed for help again, but there was no response. He took a deep breath and focused on not passing out. He could barely hold himself up because of the pain. He glanced at his hip again and saw a hole like a volcano's crater. He looked away. He had to get out, but fragments continued to pour down, and right above the door they formed an impassible curtain of fire. He knew that what he planned to do was crazy, but he had no choice. He positioned the apron over his shoulders, took a deep breath, and gripped the metal bar with all his might. Then, without thinking, he left the shelter and ran with a limp toward the chain that drove the conveyor. With burning ingots whistling past him, he inserted the bar between two links and returned to the support. He prayed as the chain carried the metal bar toward the drive gears. Finally, the bar jammed between the cogs, the chain tensed, and there was a horrifying screech as the links bent and vibrated.

Jack knew he had only a few seconds before the bar broke. He adjusted the apron and ran toward the door. When he reached it, he found it closed. He tried to open it, but it wouldn't budge. Over him, the conveyor shook as if about to come down at any moment. "Sons of bitches! Open the door!" he yelled. Suddenly, the conveyor creaked; then it writhed as if it had taken on a life of its own. "Open this door right now, you bastards!"

Jack decided to try to make it over the barrier before the entire framework collapsed, but when he attempted to climb up, the chain shattered into a thousand pieces and the entire scaffold with the buckets filled with molten iron came down with a deafening crash.

He felt a blow to the head just as a pair of black hands grabbed him and pulled him out. Before fainting, half asphyxiated by the smoke and ash, he recognized Joe Brown calling desperately for help.

23

Had it not been for the discomfort in his hip, Jack would have thought he was in heaven. With barely the strength to move, he saw a young blonde smile at him as she applied an ointment to his forehead. Then a deep drowsiness slowly overcame him until he slipped back into the realm of dreams.

"Jack, can you hear us? Say something, Jack."

He struggled to open his eyes. His head was spinning. When he managed to focus his vision, at his feet he thought he could make out Joe Brown and Walter. He looked around. To each side of him there appeared to be dozens of patients in a row of beds. He had the impression Joe Brown had a bandaged hand. Seeing Jack move, Walter took off his glasses.

"Where am I?" Jack asked, trying to sit up. An intense pain in his hip stopped him.

"Try not to move. The doc says you need rest," Walter said.

"What happened? Shit! I feel like a herd of bison ran over my head."

"A girder hit you on the temple. It was a good knock. They must've used all the arnica in the hospital on you," Joe Brown said with a smile.

"They took some X-rays, and there's nothing broken. Just little burns all over your body. The worst is your hip. It's like you have a new belly button down there," said Walter.

Jack smiled. "You saved me, right?" he asked Joe.

"Well, I heard you yelling. At first I didn't know where it was coming from, but when I saw the conveyor shaking, I guessed there was someone underneath."

"And your hands?" He pointed at the bandages covering them.

"Bah! Just a few scratches. I'm back to work this afternoon."

Jack took a deep breath. His arms and head were bandaged, and he had dressings all over his body. A sudden memory of the Soviet official looking at him impassively roused him. "What is this place?"

"It's the Avtozavod hospital. Don't worry. It's the best in Gorky. You're in good hands," said Joe Brown, still smiling. "Well, I have to go. Is there anything you need?"

"No, Joe. Just to get better so I can thank you properly."

"Don't worry about that now. Recover. We're all missing your pork ribs." He winked.

"When I get back to the village, I'll treat you to a whole herd of pigs."

Joe smiled again and left the hospital ward.

When they were alone, Walter took out a cigarette and offered it to Jack. "A good guy, that Joe. It was lucky he was there to save you. Anyway, it's time for me to get back to work as well. I'll bring you some more cigarettes on my next visit."

"Wait! Grab that chair and sit down," Jack said in a thin voice, as if about to tell a secret.

Walter was surprised but obeyed. He moved closer to the head of the bed and sat down. "Why so mysterious?"

"It was Sergei. He tried to kill me," he whispered.

"What did you say?"

"You heard. One of his goons started the conveyor after I went down into the pit."

"But, that's impossible. It was Sergei himself who had you brought to this hospital."

"I'm telling you, he tried to kill me!" He raised his voice and noticed a number of patients turning their heads.

"Think it over, Jack. What you're saying makes no sense. If Sergei had wanted to knock you off, he'd have done it by now. He's the head of the OGPU here. He can do whatever he wants. And he hasn't done it."

"Damn it, Walter! It was no accident!" He thumped the mattress. "For some reason, Sergei must want my death to appear accidental."

"But why would he want to do that?" Walter peered at Jack through his thick tortoiseshell spectacles.

"How am I supposed to know? Perhaps it's because I've discovered that he's having Americans taken away under false pretenses."

Walter sat up, indignant, as if Jack's words were blasphemy. "That blow to the head must've damaged your brain! Sergei's an honest man. He's a representative of the Soviet Union, and therefore all he endeavors to do is protect—"

"For Pete's sake! Look at me! Open your eyes and look around! The Milwaukee Express . . . his wife, Harriet . . . Robert Watkins . . . all the other guys . . . We've had no news of them. They're exterminating us, Walter. You must see it. You have to—"

"All right! Don't get upset. You say Sergei's guy watched you go down into the pit. Do you know his name?"

"I don't know. I can't remember . . . Orlov! That's it! His name is Anatoly Orlov."

"OK. I'll see what I can find out. You rest and get yourself fit again. I bet you'll see things differently when you're feeling better."

As he tried to sleep, Jack wondered why Sergei would have sent him to the hospital when he could have killed him anytime he wanted. He couldn't understand it. His head was still sore, but what really tormented him was the deep burn on his hip, which flared up with any movement he made.

He began to consider whether he should flee Gorky. The Soviets still had his passport, but with the money he'd saved, he guessed he could commission a false one from Ivan Zarko.

He was trying to imagine how he would organize his future life in a country like Britain, when he was surprised by the gentle contact of fingers against his forehead. When he opened his eyes, he saw the kind face of the same young blonde wearing a white uniform he thought he'd seen in his dreams. Her smile soothed Jack for a few seconds, until she ordered him to take off his pajama bottoms so that she could change his dressing. When he realized he had to strip, Jack became alarmed. "Couldn't you do it . . . I don't know . . . ?" He pulled the waistband of his pajamas down to just below the burn, making sure the material covered his private parts.

The young woman smiled again, and then Jack recognized her. It was Natasha, the attractive nurse who'd been treating Wilbur Hewitt's arm. If it had been a toothless old lady, perhaps it wouldn't have unsettled him so much, but her youth and beauty made him feel even more uncomfortable. "Jack Beilis," Natasha read from his medical report. "We meet again."

"Yeah. If possible, I'd rather a male nurse took care of these things," he said in an unexpected attack of modesty.

Natasha gave him a maternal look. "Look, Jack, I need to do my job, but if it's any comfort, when I did your dressing this morning, I saw everything there was to see, and I wasn't especially impressed."

Jack felt almost as embarrassed as he had when his mother caught him stroking his first girlfriend's thighs.

The young woman left the report on the bed, and without giving him time to protest, she lowered his pajama bottoms to the knees. For a moment, Jack held on to the corner of the sheet to keep his privates hidden.

"It's your wound I have to dress, not the sheet," she said, gently moving it away.

Reluctantly, Jack allowed her to examine him. The nurse removed the iodine dressing and checked the rim of the wound, which was still raw. "It doesn't look good. Don't blush. I mean the wound." She smiled and soaked a fresh dressing in antiseptic.

Jack didn't see the funny side. "It feels as if something's burning me," he explained.

"It's because of the fragment that's still inside you. We'll get it out tomorrow," she said while she cleaned the burn with a piece of cotton.

"Tomorrow? And why not today?"

"The surgeons are busy with other patients with more serious conditions than yours. You were lucky. Were it not for the steel trim on your apron, I'd be examining your lungs right now without needing an X-ray." She gestured at the garment full of holes that lay on a chair alongside what remained of his clothes.

"Sure. Really lucky . . . Do you know when I'll be able to speak to the doctor in charge?"

"Of course." She smiled and continued to carefully clean the wound.

Jack pulled up his pajamas, stopping Natasha from finishing her work. "I don't have time to mess around. Please, call your boss and let him know that I need to get out of here as soon as possible."

"Mr. Beilis, no patient's here for the fun of it. You'll have your operation when it's your turn." She smiled at him again, wished him well, got up, and left.

When she'd gone, Jack turned to his neighbor, an elderly Caucasian with two bandaged stumps instead of feet. "What happened to you, friend?" he asked.

"The damned cold froze my feet to the bones. And you, why are you here?"

Jack's only response was to lower his pajama bottoms to show the man his wound.

"Bah! That's nothing, boy. In two weeks you'll be galloping around like a colt again."

"Problem is, I don't have two weeks. Do you know who's in charge of this nuthouse?"

"Sure! Everyone knows."

"And what do I need to do to speak to him?"

"Nothing much, boy. Wait until your next dressing."

"Wait? For whom?"

The mutilated old man gave him a knowing smile before answering. "For Natasha Lobanova, the young woman who just saw to you. She's the head surgeon of the Avtozavod hospital. And the best person I've ever met."

Jack discovered that Natasha Lobanova was like her father, Sergei Loban, in her commitment to the Soviet regime. Both pursued equality, though by different means. In everything else, they seemed to be from two different worlds. In Jack's mind, Sergei was a political fanatic who would lose an arm if it meant his ideology would prevail, just as he would tear both arms from any poor fool who got in his way. Natasha's greatest interest, however, appeared to be in eliciting a smile from every patient she saw. Sergei took meticulous care of appearances, from his impeccable uniform to his scrupulously trimmed beard. Natasha, on the other hand, paid little attention to the way she looked, but her clear skin, along with the innocence in her eyes, gave her an allure unlike any other woman Jack had seen. Sergei was rigidity; she was sweetness. He was fear; she was heaven.

When he had the chance, Jack apologized for mistaking her for a nurse, and admitted to Natasha that he knew her father. However, far from welcoming his friendliness, she responded with suspicion.

"I know. He asked me to take special care of you," she replied curtly.

Jack noticed her expression turning hard. "Why the face?" he asked.

"It's nothing. I just don't like favoritism." She tightened the bandage with more force than usual. Jack grunted with pain.

"How's the wound healing?" he said, trying to change the subject.

"As it should. It's a deep burn. After extracting the fragment, we'll see if any nerves have been affected. Is there still a lot of pain?" She bent over to examine the wound.

"All the time. Except . . ."

"Yes?" Natasha gave him a skeptical look.

"Except when I see you." Instantly, Jack blushed at the inanity of his comment.

Natasha raised an eyebrow and stood. "Right. In that case, I'll see if I can find you a photo," she said seriously, then picked up his medical record. "A nurse will come later to wash and prep you for the operation. However, I regret to inform you that removing that fragment's going to hurt."

Natasha had been right. It appeared that the procaine injected near his hip before the operation had not done its job fully, and the moment the pincers began rummaging in his flesh, he twisted in agony. When she had finally extracted the fragment, the young woman apologized. "I'm sorry to have taken longer than expected. I'd administered enough anesthetic for a short procedure, but the metal was in contact with a crural nerve branch, and I didn't want to leave you lame."

"The way that hurt, I'd say you almost did," said Jack while a nurse dried the sweat from his brow.

"Well, I expect everything will be fine, but it's too soon to say. Tomorrow, when the swelling's gone down, we'll check your mobility and pain levels. Now you must rest."

"But rather than staying here, couldn't I recover at my house?"

"You have a house?" Natasha appeared surprised.

"Is that strange?"

"No . . . well, truthfully, yes. You don't wear a ring, and no women have visited you, so I assumed you were single."

"Is that what you look at when you examine me?" Jack was surprised that Natasha had any interest in his private life.

"Of course not!" She reddened.

"Well, it's true. I'm single." For a moment he forgot about his false marriage.

"So how is it possible that you've been given a house?" She adjusted her bun—a rebellious lock of hair had fallen onto her face. "Single people aren't permitted to have houses in the Soviet Union."

"Let's just say things are going well for me." Jack decided against explaining that the house had a lot to do with Viktor Smirnov.

"Well, you're very lucky. And luck isn't something that's overly plentiful in the Avtozavod." She gestured at the patients who packed the ward. "Anyway, I'll try to get you better as soon as possible. There're plenty of others who need this bed." Her expression hardened again. "Oh! And please, don't complain too much when the anesthetic wears off. Some folks here are *really* sick."

During his convalescence, Jack observed that not only did those he thought wanted him dead seem uninterested in his health, but Elizabeth hadn't deigned to call on him, and aside from Joe Brown and Walter, the only visitor he'd received since his admission had been Wilbur Hewitt, who had only come to the Avtozavod to alert him to the problems blighting the factory.

"We're all anxious," the industrialist admitted in the rehabilitation room where he'd found Jack performing a series of exercises on crutches. "Who'd have imagined there'd be a strike that brought the factory to a standstill? Apparently, Stalin's furious, which means that heads are going to roll soon. And you can bet that the first ones to roll will be American."

Jack was surprised. He took a rest from the walking that Natasha had prescribed and sat on a battered armchair that an elderly man had just vacated. "A strike . . . and the factory's been shut down?"

"Completely paralyzed. The pickets have stopped the workers from going in. They've set fire to cars and cut off the power supply. The Avtozavod looks like a war zone."

"No one's said anything about it in here."

"The workers aren't allowed to talk to outsiders about what's happening, on pain of being sent to a labor camp, and you're a foreigner." There was a worried silence for a moment. "The discontent goes back a long time, but the demonstrations began three days ago. From what I've been able to find out, the OGPU have informed Stalin, and he's sending in the army."

"And what do you plan to do?" Jack noticed that Wilbur Hewitt was sweating.

"I don't know yet. I've sent a wire to Dearborn requesting instructions. I can't leave the factory because our contract with the Soviet government has a penalty clause if we interrupt our technical support. I'm guessing it's what Sergei hopes to do: claim a breach of contract and cancel the payments owed. But I'm afraid for my niece. I've suggested she accept Viktor Smirnov's offer to stay in his dacha until the hostilities are resolved."

The news made him uneasy. "And is there anything I can do to help?"

"Get back on your feet as soon as possible, kid. It's rebellion in the American village. Many are trying to organize themselves to return to the United States, but it's rumored that the Soviets aren't going to give them their passports back. That's why I thought you . . . Well, people say you have contacts."

"I don't know what you're talking about."

"Come on, Jack! You can trust me. Do you, or don't you?"

Jack could see Hewitt was desperate. "I don't know. I might be able to speak to someone who knows someone . . . but it's only a *might*."

"Good. That's what I wanted to hear. When do you think you'll be able to walk?"

"I don't know for certain. The doctor says she'll take the crutches away in a couple of days, but I'm not so sure."

"The doctor?"

"Yes. Natasha Lobanova. The one—"

"Natasha? Well, I'll be damned! You've fallen into good hands! Nothing like that ogre of her father. All right. Get well as quickly as possible. I need you out there, and I'm prepared to pay whatever's necessary."

"What exactly are you planning to do?"

At that moment, Wilbur noticed a patient nearby who seemed to be paying more attention than was warranted. "It's too dangerous to say more now, but when you get out of the hospital, come and see me at home."

"Come on, Mr. Hewitt! What's going on? Don't you think what happened to me was suspicious?"

"You mean the accident?"

"Ha! That's one way of putting it. For God's sake, they tried to kill me! That guy Anatoly Orlov waited until I was under the conveyor and then started it up."

"I'm sorry, Jack. I didn't know the details. Sergei assured me it was an accident. He even showed me the statements of witnesses who said it was you who made the conveyor tip over when you wrecked the gearing with a metal bar."

"But don't you see? Sergei was the one who planned it all. I bet he's put me in here to keep me quiet while he brings charges of sabotage against me."

"That Soviet bastard suspects me. That's why you have to get out as soon as possible. Even so, you need not worry about that Orlov anymore. Apparently, he worked for Sergei, taking care of shady business for him. He was his right-hand man."

"*Worked?* He doesn't anymore?"

"I don't think he's up to the job."

"Why? What happened?"

"He showed up dead this morning in the press shop, with his head caved in. They say it was an accident. Like yours."

24

Though Jack had never set foot in a Siberian prison, he imagined their disciplinary regime was no worse than the one they imposed in the hospital each morning.

Though they'd all been shaved on admission, every day a nurse inspected the patients' heads for lice, to prevent the spread of typhus. The ones who could walk were then escorted to the showers, and the lame patients like Jack were washed by two tough male nurses, who manhandled them like they were sacks of potatoes. Dressings were changed daily, but although they assured Jack they used an autoclave to disinfect them, he didn't believe them.

The lack of resources contrasted with the sophistication of the machinery used at the Avtozavod. To build automobiles, the Soviets had imported expensive machines and foundries, but feeding and taking care of their workers seemed to be a secondary consideration. In Jack's mind, that was the one true cause of the strike that had brought the Avtozavod to a standstill, a strike for which the authorities needed people to blame. That was why he needed to get out of the hospital as soon as possible. For a moment, he thought about escaping, but aside from his limp, there were the ward guards, who, as another patient told him, were OGPU. His only choice was to press Natasha Lobanova to discharge him.

He decided to seize his chance to try to persuade her on her night rounds. Sergei's daughter was on duty that evening, and she seemed keen to chat. However, as much as Jack tried, she was immune to his pleas.

While she examined the wound's scarring, Natasha asked Jack about America. Accustomed to enthralling his Soviet colleagues with wondrous stories, he launched into a description of his country with the cunning of a fox stalking a hen. "You have to see it! In the cities, the buildings soar into the sky, lighting it up with neon; the streets are filled with cars, and on the sidewalks, people go from store to store, where the shelves are packed with anything you could wish for: food, drink, cigarettes, clothes, tools, gramophones. Anything you can dream of, you can buy there."

"But what if you don't have money?"

"Then you have to earn it. You need money to buy things."

"Answer me one question. Do those shelves stock dignity?" She lifted the dressing and applied an ointment to the wound. Jack gave a start when he felt the permanganate sting the burn.

"Pardon me?"

"I was asking if they sell dignity in those marvelous department stores of yours."

"I don't know what you're getting at, but anyhow, what good's dignity if you can't have a decent meal?" He pointed at the plate on which they'd served him a ladleful of *sascha*, or the *revolting oat pap*, as he preferred to call it.

"It allows you to look people in the eye." She gave him a look as pure as water.

Jack cleared his throat. He could see the conversation heading onto rocky ground. "Perhaps, Natasha, you find it difficult to imagine what it's like for the millions of starving people who, instead of a dignified look, would prefer to have a nice plate of lentils in front of them."

"Why would I find it difficult to imagine?" Natasha pulled out a couple of hairpins, and her bun spilled onto her shoulders in a blond waterfall. Jack was struck by her confidence.

"You tell me. A young, good-looking surgeon, with a position of responsibility in the Avtozavod, from a family that no doubt provided you with an education and all the privileges that come with it. You don't seem like the kind of person who could put herself in the shoes of these miserable tramps who can't even choose what they eat."

"Anything else while you're at it?" Natasha leaned back in her chair, striking a relaxed pose that Jack had never seen before. When she crossed her legs, he let his gaze linger on them for long enough to lose the thread of the conversation. He stammered when he tried to take it up again. He was disconcerted by this young woman arguing with him on such fundamental issues. After a few more seconds, he remembered the question.

"Well, maybe the fact that your station means you can have any luxury: you can live in a nice dacha, wear fashionable clothes, or enjoy a good roast with white bread. At least that's what much of your ruling class does."

"Oh, really? You must be better informed than I am. Our leaders are honest people who—"

"Like Viktor Smirnov? Perhaps you know him . . . ," he cut in.

Hearing Viktor's name, Natasha's tone hardened. "Viktor and I have very different ways of seeing life."

"So you know him. How do you know him, if you don't mind my asking?"

"I do mind, but so I don't seem rude, I'll answer simply by saying that I'm not impressed by silk suits or sports cars." A faint smile appeared on her face. "But let's talk about you." She paused. "If you're a visitor to Wilbur Hewitt's office, you must be one of those engineers earning their weight in gold."

"And what's wrong with that?" Jack showed a touch of self-importance. "After all, you Soviets need our help, and we're offering it."

"How? By fleecing a country that's trying to lift itself out of generations of grinding poverty?"

"Do you expect us to cross the ocean for a change of clothes and a bowl of soup?"

"Maybe . . . Some people have. Fellow countrymen of yours who've settled here to help build a fairer world. For a moment, when you poured scorn on me for my training and profession, I thought you might be one of those people. But by the sound of it, you enjoy all the privileges you're accusing me of having. And looking at you, you don't appear to be going hungry. Yet, a moment ago, you spoke to me as if I were a deluded rich person and you were an indignant revolutionary."

Jack fell silent. Briefly, he thought about confessing his true situation to her, but he stopped himself. Though he sensed he could trust her, all he knew about her was that she was Sergei Loban's daughter. "Look, Natasha." He moved as close to her as his position in the bed would allow. "You can't begin to understand what people like me have been through, let alone criticize us. I promise you I've earned the right to enjoy every last ruble your government pays me." He lifted his pajamas to show her the burn.

"Perhaps. But I get the impression that rubles won't solve the problems that you attract."

"What do you mean?" Jack thought Natasha was referring to the attempt on his life.

"That you think money will solve all our troubles."

"I don't *think* it; I know it."

"How can you be so sure?"

"Because there was a time when I had a comfortable life, and I can promise you that I was the happiest man on earth." He clenched his fists. Natasha noticed it. "You can't imagine what it means to have everything taken from you, for no reason, with no right to complain, no compensation. To have everything you've fought for—everything you've achieved through hard work—disappear overnight." He was beginning to lose control of his emotions.

"Oh, but I can imagine it, Jack. I'm surrounded by people who haven't even had the opportunity to fight for the things you lost."

"You don't understand what I'm saying. I'm not talking about some stranger. I'm talking about myself. About what they did to me. For as long as I can remember, I've broken my back to make something of my life, and now that I'm getting somewhere again, a little daddy's girl like you shows up to give me lessons on morality and—"

Natasha stood without giving Jack time to finish his sentence. "All right, Mr. Beilis. Perhaps we'll have a chance to continue this conversation some other time . . . when your wounds have healed."

Jack nodded without paying much attention. He was suddenly lost in thought, remembering the days when hunger was his only companion. Then, he seemed to reconsider. "I'm sorry . . . I don't know what came over me. Yes. Hopefully, I'll be back on my feet soon. The rim around the burn seems to be closing and—"

"I didn't mean your hip. I meant the wounds on your soul."

For the next few days, there was no sign of Natasha.

At first, Jack thought her absence owed itself to the prickly argument they'd had on the last night she saw him, but then it struck him that she was not the kind of woman to abandon a patient over such a trivial matter. Also, the rumor had spread in the ward that, in the clashes that broke out after the strike, many of the agitators who had been sent to the prison camps had been injured, and Natasha Lobanova had traveled there to assist them. At any rate, Jack worried, because he needed her to discharge him from the hospital.

As for his wound, it was improving a little each day. The pain was no longer constant, and though he limped badly, he'd begun to walk with the help of crutches. He spent the mornings doing rehabilitation exercises and hobbling around the little courtyard garden to which he had access. After lunch, they changed his dressing; then he used the rest of the afternoon to study some of the Bolshevik books they had in the library—he guessed that, the more he knew about his enemies, the easier it would be to profit from them. The last work he'd looked through was entitled "Economics and Politics in the Era of the Dictatorship of the Proletariat," an essay by Lenin, the father of the October Revolution, which he'd found tremendously unsettling. It advocated the abolition of all private property, which would come into the possession of the state on behalf of all workers.

Jack thought it over for a while, reaching the conclusion that the idea was madness. It might've been an improvement on a medieval society like the Russia of old, when the landed gentry treated their workers like slaves, but that certainly wasn't the situation in the United States. The Depression would end there, and America would once again be a rich country full of opportunity, where any enthusiastic entrepreneur with two cents in his pocket could build an empire with hard work and daring. And clearly, anyone in his right mind would consider it an injustice if the state then came along and snatched everything that enterprising individual had worked for.

He imagined himself returning to America, his pockets full, to open a repair shop that in time he could expand into a chain of stores. It was just a dream, of course, but dreaming was one of the few things a man could do in the Soviet Union.

He also read a worn volume on the idea of equality between men and women, penned by Lenin and entitled *The Emancipation of Women*, and he was deeply affected by it. It was the first time he had thought about the subject. Women were women, and they seemed happy with their role as mothers and wives. And it wasn't that he was opposed to women working outside of the home: in the United States, they worked as cleaners, secretaries, telephone operators, teachers . . . and these seemed like occupations right for them. What he had never considered was the possibility that women could work effectively as miners, train drivers, aviators, or hospital directors. Yet in Russia, people like Natasha Lobanova, or the large female contingent doing the same jobs with identical salaries as the male operatives at the Avtozavod, proved that it was possible. Seeing the results, not only did Jack agree with Lenin that women should have the same rights as men, but he was also surprised at how quickly and effectively the Soviets had popularized a set of principles that, despite their obvious fairness, had never been adopted in any other country.

He was aware that any knowledge he could acquire might one day get him out of trouble. He asked for paper and a pencil, and devoted himself to writing notes on all of the topics that captured his attention, including those he took issue with. The list grew, as did his interest in some aspects of the revolution.

The last book that fell into his hands was a transcript of Lenin's lecture at the Sverdlov University, in which he analyzed the power relations that had shaped the development of societies through history.

He read reluctantly. Jack had never been interested in history: the past was the past. In fact, all he remembered from his time at school was that the United States had been formed on July 4, 1776, and that after the Civil War, slavery had been abolished. However, Lenin's lecture described situations he'd never considered before, such as the fact that, regardless of the historical era or type of government in question, the people or class in power had always exercised that power for their own benefit.

Though he found his reading stimulating, Natasha's continued absence worried him.

It wasn't until a week later that the doctor finally appeared, her blond braids knotted on top of her head and her fatigue visible on her face. The young woman barely returned Jack's greeting when she removed the bandage from his hip. She just checked that the hole made by the burn was continuing to close. Jack assumed her silence was because of the argument they'd had the last time they saw each other. He apologized for it.

"Don't worry. It's not you. I'm just exhausted. The burn's healing well, and there're no signs of infection. How are you feeling?"

"Much better. The pain's almost gone, and I'm walking without crutches now," he lied.

"I bet you can't wait to be back on your feet." Jack let her put her arms around him to finish bandaging his hip. "Good." She moved away when the dressing was done. "Tomorrow morning I'll sign you out. I'll prescribe some exercises that'll help you regain your strength."

"Wait. Don't go yet. I wanted to ask you . . ."

"Yes?"

"It's about these books." He showed them to her. "I've been reading, and to be fair, some of it makes sense."

"Now, *that* is an improvement."

"Still, there're some aspects I don't understand. Lenin says there was a time when kings, emperors, tyrants, bishops, nobles, and dictators conspired to increase their wealth at the expense of their subjects, but he says those days ended with the French Revolution."

Jack's words seemed to soothe Natasha, her weary face relaxing. "That's right. Until then, the people were prisoners of their own ignorance, but Voltaire, Diderot, and D'Alembert created the *Encyclopédie*, a compendium of knowledge that challenged the political and religious authorities, and which, along with Descartes's treatises, was the spark that ignited a people sick of poverty and oppression."

"Yes, that's what he says. For the first time, the masses united and overthrew the enslavers who'd tyrannized them, and took possession of their own destiny. Yet, how is it, after such a great victory, that the tyrants came to rule the world again?"

"Because of ambition and greed, Jack. Like germs, the exploiters regrouped. They grew, they manipulated, and they flourished; the Industrial Revolution was their ideal breeding ground. And like germs, they infected society in the guise of the bourgeoisie, building factories, monopolies, and banks, the ultimate purpose of which was to seize power and wealth again, while the rest of humanity was enslaved once more. States, even those that called themselves democracies, became the perfect vehicle to support and maintain the obscene balance of power: everything for a few, and nothing for the rest. Sad, isn't it?"

Jack nodded, only half aware of what he was doing. Natasha's conviction was so strong that for a moment he felt trapped. He tried to respond. "But if there are no owners, who will provide us with work?"

"Nobody. That's why a new revolutionary state was needed—to take control of the means of production and share the profits among the workers themselves."

Jack fell silent. He had no doubt that in some respects Natasha was right. But after witnessing the terrible living conditions of the Soviet people firsthand, he was also certain that no American would have immigrated to the Soviet Union if they had known about the true situation. "Will you be back to do another dressing tonight?" was all he could think to say.

"No. I've had a hectic few days, and I need to rest. Dr. Dimitrenko will be covering for me. If there's anything you need, he'll be able to—"

"And tomorrow night?"

"Tomorrow? But you won't be here tomorrow."

"But you'll need to have dinner, I guess."

"Are you trying to flirt with me?" She smiled.

"No, of course not!" he joked. "I just wanted to continue this conversation in order to nurture a better understanding between our two great nations."

"Good heavens, Jack! I'm glad you're concerned about improving diplomatic relations between our countries." She smiled again. Then she paused for a moment, as if considering Jack's invitation, but out of nowhere her smile froze and she stood up. "The truth is I wouldn't mind having dinner with you and chatting for a while, but I don't think it's going to be possible."

"And why not? You'll have to eat, and at my house I can make some fabulous food."

"So, you haven't heard? I assumed my colleagues would've told you." Her face darkened.

"Heard? Heard what?"

"It shouldn't have been me who told you, but . . . I'm sorry, Jack. The reason why I've discharged you early isn't because your wound has improved. It's because tomorrow they're sending you to a labor camp."

25

It was the third day of his detention in Sector One of the *ispravdom*, and Jack still didn't know why he'd been locked up. All he had been able to find out from one of his jailers was that he was one of 250 political prisoners detained there separately from the 3,500 ordinary inmates who lived in the labor camp. He guessed that he must be considered one of the worst of them, for, since his admittance, he'd been kept in solitary confinement, with no medical attention other than the eye test performed by a male nurse on his arrival.

He stood to walk the three paces that constituted the length of his cell, a shoebox-sized cubicle where, on one of its damp, rotting walls, he could make out the place where they had bricked up a window. The cell's amenities consisted of a straw mattress, a blanket, and a bucket in which to relieve himself, as well as a bowl of icy water that they handed him every morning along with a few out-of-date newspaper pages.

He sat again to gaze at the cup of *chai* they'd given him for breakfast. Though it was more barley flour dissolved in dirty water than actual tea, he greedily drank down every last drop. Then he squeezed his stomach, thinking ahead to the usual bowl of *balanda* that they would give him at midday. He hoped that the vegetable broth would offer more nourishment than the oatmeal and herring that had made him throw up the night before. He remembered Natasha. On the one hand, he found it difficult to believe that she could be in any way involved in his arrest, but at the same time, he couldn't help being suspicious of the daughter of the man who'd had him incarcerated.

The sound of the lock pulled him from his thoughts. By the time the guard had opened the door, he was standing at attention. As he straightened, his hip seared with pain. Through the door appeared a uniformed guard, who, with all the compassion of an executioner, ordered Jack to follow him. After making him wash in the communal bathroom, the guard led Jack to an open-air courtyard where a group of Russian prisoners waiting to be assigned work wandered around. They looked half starved, and they scratched themselves as if being eaten alive by lice. Jack limped to a corner where he lit a *papirosa*. A prisoner with a shaved head and dark rings around his eyes approached and asked for a cigarette. Jack examined the man for a moment, then took out the packet they'd allowed him to keep and let him take one.

"Strange getup, my friend!" He patted the shoulder pads on Jack's jacket. "Foreigner?"

Jack nodded. He wasn't in the mood for talking, but it was the first person who'd spoken to him, and he thought he might be able to glean some information. "American."

"I'm Ukrainian. From Odessa. What're you in here for? The Avtozavod strike?" He sat beside Jack.

"I wish I knew. Where are we? They brought me here at night. All I know is that I am at some kind of a work camp."

"That's what they call it, but it's a slave camp. They arrest people, let them out during the day to clear fields, then lock them up again at night. Until they're too tired to work. Then they're sent to rot in Siberia."

"And what about you, why are you in here?"

"Come on." He took Jack by the arm. "Let's get away from the loudspeakers. Listening to the propaganda all day can turn you into a vegetable."

Jack let himself be led. As they walked to the other side of the courtyard, the man introduced himself as Kuzmin, a miner in the Donbass who had been expelled from the Communist Party for planning counterrevolutionary activities. "That's what they accuse me of, but in reality all I did was protest against their exploitative methods."

Jack wasn't especially interested in Kuzmin's story, but the man seemed unable to keep quiet. He explained that, in his old job, all the miners had a basic wage that would increase according to how productive they were. The more coal they extracted, the bigger the bonus.

"It seems fair that you earn more for working harder," Jack conceded. He warmed his lungs with a long draw on his cigarette.

"The problem was that some crazy men worked too hard, and, instead of the seven tons that they were required to extract each day, they extracted almost a hundred tons of coal a day."

"If they worked like dogs, I don't see why they shouldn't be rewarded for it."

"You don't understand. The mine's officials concluded that if some men were capable of digging out a hundred tons, the rest of them should be able to extract at least forty for the same salary. When my workmates and I protested against the increase in the workload with no kind of compensation, we were arrested."

"Hmm . . . Looking at it like that, they did do the dirty on you. And what're you doing here, so far from Ukraine?" He thought that Kuzmin might possess some useful information. He offered him another *papirosa* to keep him talking. When he accepted it, Jack noticed that the man was missing three fingers from one hand.

"I'm awaiting trial." He kissed the cigarette and put it in his pocket. "My workmates were tried right away, and sent to a prison in Odessa, but they brought me to Gorky. I'm convinced I'm going to be shot."

"How long does it take before trials are held?"

"As long as those bastards want. There're people here who've been waiting a year, though usually it takes only three or four months. It depends whether your case is with the People's Court or the OGPU." Kuzmin noticed that his mention of the secret police alarmed Jack. "It was them? In that case, not good . . ."

"Not good? What do you mean?"

"I mean you won't even have a trial. No one has authority over the OGPU. No one! You'll be lucky to get out of here alive."

"But you don't even know what they're accusing me of."

"Look, I'm sorry, but I can't talk to you anymore—OGPU prisoners only bring trouble. If you want some advice, when they interrogate you, do not question their laws or methods. In fact, try to take advantage of them. The OGPU officers are like automatons, following Soviet law to the letter. If you can find a way to make use of their own laws, they won't touch you until they can consult with Moscow, and in the meantime, you'll earn a few extra months of life. In the end, they'll condemn you anyway, but you're better off spending three months in Gorky plowing fields than breaking rocks in a Siberian gulag. Good luck, and thanks for the cigarettes."

After Jack spent an hour pacing alone, another guard led him to the infirmary, where a doctor listened to his chest and asked him about his limp. Jack gave the same answers he'd given on arrival. When the doctor was satisfied, he administered some powder to the wound and ordered Jack to wait in an adjoining room. He sat on the only chair in the space until, half an hour later, the door opened and Natasha Lobanova appeared. Seeing her, Jack stood, but she gestured to him to sit down again.

"Natasha, what're you doing here?"

"Trying not to abandon my patient. How are you?"

"How do you think?" Jack spat at her. "Was it your father?"

"I don't understand . . ."

"I'm asking you whether it was Sergei who ordered my imprisonment. I don't know why I'm here, or what I'm accused of, or when they're going to let me go. A few inmates have told me that if the OGPU detains someone, then he is a condemned man."

"Honestly, I don't know the circumstances surrounding your arrest. I never get involved in my father's business, but I can assure you he's an honest man, and—"

"He is? Then when you see him, please tell him that, *honestly*, he has locked up a man whose only crime was to tell the truth."

"Look, I'm not here to argue with you. I thought you'd appreciate the visit, but if you'd rather I left, I'll get another doctor to tend to you."

Jack looked at her. He didn't know what it was, but there was something about Natasha that he found comforting. He took off his bandage very slowly and sat in silence. She ran her fingers around the rim of the wound, pressing the skin lightly.

"So, you're here for telling the truth," Natasha said.

"Like I said, I don't know why they've locked me up. All I know is that the day after assuring your father that he was arresting the wrong workers, I had molten iron raining on me." He groaned when he tried to move.

"And you think it's connected?" She paused what she was doing. "I mean . . . you think my father was behind the accident?"

"Who else could it be?"

"I can't answer that. But I know my father. You'll have to be patient." She finished the examination. "If you really are innocent, you'll walk out of here. I promise."

Jack couldn't help but feel annoyed. The only conclusion he could draw from Natasha's response was that some people didn't leave this place. The young woman was about to leave when he stood and took her by the wrist. "Natasha, why are you bothering with a foreign criminal?" Her clear face was devoid of malice.

"I guess you don't look like a criminal. And you say you're here only because you told the truth, right?" She smiled, allowing Jack to continue holding her hand.

"Listen. I really appreciate your coming, but I need someone to tell me the truth for once. Why did you insist on visiting me?"

Natasha fell silent, looking him in the eye without blinking. "Honestly, Jack, I feel sorry for you." She freed her hand from his. "Don't take it the wrong way. What I mean is, it saddens me that you're here with nobody to turn to. No family to help you."

Jack felt remorse grip his stomach. Though he'd told her the opposite just a few days earlier, he decided to reveal the truth about his personal situation. Natasha listened in silence. When she learned that Jack had entered the Soviet Union as a married man, she fixed her eyes on the cell tiles. "Heavens! So the reason you live in a house is because you have a wife, after all," she said without looking up. "And . . . you have children as well?"

"I'm sorry. I haven't explained myself very well. The reality is that I don't even have a wife. What I mean is, our marriage was the result of a terrible mix-up. In fact, I've filed for a divorce," he hastened to clarify.

"Sure. Well, we all make mistakes sometimes. Me included," Natasha replied, and without warning, she said good-bye and left.

That night, Jack barely slept. Though happy to have seen Natasha, he was unsettled by her relationship to the man he held responsible for his imprisonment. Before she left, he had asked her to let his friend Walter know that he was in prison, and she'd agreed to do so. The sound of a distant explosion made him jump. It seemed the disturbances at the factory continued. He wrapped himself in the threadbare blanket and waited for dawn.

The jailer's roar made Jack give a start. He stopped reading the *Izvestia* newspaper, and as ordered, stood at attention.

"You have a visitor," the jailer announced.

Jack headed down the corridor that led to the visitors' room, imagining that Walter had received his message. But when the bolts on the door were drawn aside, he was surprised to find Sue standing there in a ragged overcoat. After a few seconds in a daze, Jack sat with her on a bench, under the watchful eye of the guard. He asked her how she'd managed to get in to see him. "I'm still your *wife*, remember?" She showed him the counterfeit marriage certificate.

Jack cleared his throat. It annoyed him that, even though their divorce was being processed, Sue was carrying around a forged document that could potentially get them into trouble. However, he didn't have the luxury of choosing his visitors, and, at that moment, Sue was his only contact with the outside world. He put the business with their marriage to one side and asked her why Walter hadn't come.

"When you disappeared from the hospital, alarm bells went off in the village. Those who think you sympathize with the Russians didn't care, but Walter tried to find you. You know he works for the OGPU now," she said, swelling a little with importance.

"Yeah, I know. But why hasn't *he* come?"

"He wanted to, but he can't risk being associated with someone accused of counterrevolutionary acts. He has no idea why you've been arrested, but he thinks you may have been branded an *enemy of the workers.*"

"And what does that mean?"

"You haven't read the Soviet Penal Code?"

"No. Should I have?"

"Walter asked me to bring you a copy." She took it from a cloth bag. "I think it was given to him by a doctor. Here. It's the 1927 edition. We looked through it last night but didn't understand much, since it's in Russian. Wait, let's see, I'll find it . . ." She opened the volume nervously, in search of the paper bookmark on which she'd noted something down. "Yeah. Here it is: 'Article 58.1. A counterrevolutionary action is any action aimed at overthrowing, undermining, or weakening the power of workers.' There's more, but this is the paragraph they translated for us."

With the guard's consent, Jack took the volume from her and ran his eyes over it. He saw that, in addition to Sue's quotation, Article 58.7 specifically mentioned industrial sabotage, and 58.9 referred to damage. He was surprised to find that both crimes were punishable by death.

"Are you OK?" she asked, seeing him turn pale.

"Yeah, yeah." His throat was dry. "And you two?"

"We're getting by. Walter seems happy in his new job. He says the Russians treat him well. He's thinking about joining the party; it might get us a better ration card and more food."

"Sue . . . This is all a big mistake. If I could speak to Walter, I bet he could—"

"I told you he can't come. Tell me whatever you want to say, and I'll pass on the message." She glanced at the guard, as if worried he could understand what they were saying.

Jack shook his head. He didn't like involving Sue in his problems, but he knew that he had no choice. He revealed to her that Wilbur Hewitt had hired him to investigate the sabotage plaguing the Avtozavod, and that in the course of his inquiries, he'd discovered that Americans were being falsely charged and arrested. "Tell Walter to be careful. I'm convinced that Sergei Loban is behind all this," he whispered.

Sue coughed when she heard him. "Loban? But he's the head of the OGPU."

"Just tell him."

"All right. I'll let him know, but I don't see what he'll be able to do to help. After all, he's just the new boy."

"Damn it, Sue, you have to get me out of here. If not you, then whom can I turn to?"

"Jack, think it over! Walter's just an assistant. Do you want them to arrest all of us? They say they're opening the American embassy in Moscow in November. Maybe they can—"

"They say, they *say*! That rumor's been making the rounds since Roosevelt was inaugurated in March." He thumped the table. "And even if they establish diplomatic relations, he won't be able to get help from the embassy, because in America he's wanted for murder."

"Well, don't worry. We'll find a way to get you out. But I have to go," said Sue, seeing the guard gesturing to them to finish. "I should give you a kiss, or the guard will think it's strange."

Jack nodded, his mind elsewhere. When she kissed him, he was surprised.

"Take care," said Sue.

"Yeah. You, too. Say thanks to Walter for the Penal Code. And remind him to speak to Hewitt! Maybe he can help me."

When Sue left, it dawned on Jack that he would not escape the labor camp alive.

26

Jack would never forget the night when, without saying a word, two Soviet guards came into his cell and dragged him out to the same black car in which, a few weeks earlier, they'd taken him away from the American village. He asked where they were going, but neither escort answered. They just put him in the backseat, and one sat on each side of him. As they drove through Gorky's dark streets, Jack recalled the sinister stories that circulated in the *ispravdom* about the nocturnal outings that the prisoners were subjected to from time to time. Reportedly, they were taken in the middle of the night, put in a car that drove them off, and a flash of light was the last thing they saw. As he imagined what awaited him, his heart skipped a beat.

As the vehicle penetrated the forest and the city's lights disappeared, Jack's fears grew. He didn't know where they would stop, or whether people would be waiting for him when they did, but doing nothing could prove fatal. Though he was handcuffed and hemmed in by two men, presumably armed, he told himself that he had to escape. He was strong. If he attacked the two guards inside the vehicle, the driver wouldn't be able to help them. Maybe he would have a chance.

He looked at his escorts. The one on the left seemed the stronger of the two. He would hit him first with the handcuffs, then the one on his right before he could react.

He felt sweat cover his entire body. The vehicle drove on while Jack delayed his surprise attack, waiting for a good moment that would probably never arrive. He could sense the proximity of death, and he didn't want to hasten it. He didn't consider himself a believer but commended himself to Adonai nonetheless. He was taking a deep breath before he would deal the first blow, when the car suddenly braked hard, stopping on the edge of a precipice, near an abandoned hut where two more men stood waiting, flashlights in their hands. He didn't have a chance to react. The guard on his right grabbed him by the shoulder and dragged him out of the vehicle like a sack of garbage while the beam from a flashlight blinded him. Jack shaded his eyes to try to identify the men, but he couldn't. Then, the Soviets moved aside, leaving a familiar-looking man with a graying head of hair standing in front of him.

"Good evening." Sergei Loban's voice boomed in the silence of the night.

"It might be for you." If they were going to kill him, there was little point in formalities.

"Jack, Jack . . ." He paced around the American. "I have to make a difficult decision, and I'd like you to help me."

"What kind of decision? Whether to shoot me or throw me off a cliff?" He spat into the ravine. He thought he could see Sergei smiling.

"How melodramatic you Americans are! You two. Leave us," he ordered his men. "You see, my choice is very simple, as I hope yours will be. I need to know whether you'll go back to your old job."

Jack was suspicious of Sergei's offer. He found it impossible to swallow that he'd been dragged out of jail to be told in the middle of the night that everything was suddenly going to return to normal. "Is this a joke?" he managed to say.

"I never joke," replied Sergei, his expression serious. "Now listen carefully. I'm proposing that you return to your position as if nothing has happened. If you accept, you must keep this conversation secret. You can tell anyone who asks that we arrested you by mistake and that, with the imminent arrival of Ambassador Bullitt, we decided to let you go."

Jack looked around. The rifles Sergei's henchmen carried gleamed in the moonlight. If he tried to escape, he'd be riddled with bullets before he took a single step. Sergei's offer was his only option, so there was no harm in showing some curiosity. "So what would my job be? To wait for a truck to run me over, or for an iron girder to fall on my head?"

"I guarantee you that nothing like that will happen. One of my men will stay with you at all times."

"One of your men? Like Orlov?"

"Forget Orlov. We'll assign you someone more competent. The only difference between this job and your previous one will be that, rather than taking your findings straight to Wilbur Hewitt, you'll bring them to me. And only me."

"Why the secrecy?"

"We have reason to suspect him. We believe he is using his position to embezzle funds for his own profit."

Jack remembered his conversation with Hewitt at the hospital. The industrialist had told him he was afraid that he would be accused of something. "What makes you think I'm going to betray my countryman?"

"Jack, Jack . . . you're so untrusting. Why not look at it another way? If your investigations confirm our suspicions, then he's a crook who deserves to be punished." He continued to pace around Jack. "And if you find that Hewitt had nothing to do with the sabotage, you'll have helped your friend."

Jack pretended to think it over. He needed time. "But if I don't report to Hewitt, he'll think I'm not doing my job and stop paying me." He had to show that he was worried about appearing credible.

"Then invent faults, make up hypotheses, suggest improvements. Play along for as long as possible. You're a smart guy; I'm sure you'll manage."

"Hewitt's smart, too. Sooner or later, he'll discover what I'm up to, and he'll fire me."

"In that case, you can always carry on working at the Avtozavod as a skilled operative."

"With the same miserly salary that my workmates earn?"

"You were worse off in America. And anyway, you run food on the black market, don't you?"

Jack flushed red. "I . . . I don't know what you're talking about. Contraband's forbidden, and . . ."

"I'm talking about the pork ribs that Miquel Agramunt supplies you with and that an employee of yours sells in the American village. As I've told you many times, we Soviets aren't stupid. If I've allowed your little scheme to continue, it's only to keep in check the discontent that a famine could cause among the Americans." He paced again. "So, if you accept my offer, whatever happens with Hewitt, you'll keep working for me, and I'll turn a blind eye to your black market business. In fact, I could even authorize the sale of your products in the village store. After all, you're all capitalists, so the manner in which you swindle one another is no business of mine."

"And if I refuse?" Jack ventured to ask.

"I don't think you're in a position to negotiate." He gestured at the weapons aimed at him. Jack looked at them.

"I'm not intimidated by you."

"Maybe *you're* not. But you wouldn't want your *wife* and your friend to end up like you, hurled down a ravine."

"You bastard!" Jack went to strike Sergei, but a rifle butt to the back stopped him.

Sergei bent over Jack as he knelt, trying not to pass out from the pain.

"Please, Jack. Don't make me behave like a savage. Decide what you'd rather do. Work for me or share a grave with your friends."

Jack swore. As soon as he'd accepted Sergei's proposal, he knew that he'd sold his soul to the devil himself.

When the Black Crows left him on the central street of the American village, Jack gave a sigh of relief. He waited for the black car to disappear into the distance, and only then did he pick up his kit bag. He turned and limped toward his house. To his surprise, he found Yuri on the steps outside, wearing a fur coat that made him look like a crouching bear. At first, the Russian told him to halt, but as soon as he recognized him, he let out a roar of joy, which soon turned into laughter when Jack invited him in for a drink. Jack needed it, too, and the half bottle of vodka he'd been saving for a special occasion barely lasted five minutes. Once they were warm, they talked about what had happened in Jack's absence.

"Uncle Ivan told me to keep watch on the house in case you were locked up for a long time. He has contacts everywhere, and when he heard you'd been sent to the *ispravdom*, he guessed you wouldn't be in too much danger."

"Oh? And why is that?" he asked, intrigued.

Yuri finished off his vodka and smiled. "Because the other Americans who disappeared never set foot in the *ispravdom*. They just vanished."

When Yuri left, Jack wandered around the rooms of his house, feeling like he was in a palace. He checked that everything was where he'd left it: the reports in the trunk, the food in the pantry, his books stacked up, and the furniture in order. Even the tools that were spread across the floor in the garage were as he'd left them.

He was unable to sleep. He lay on the bed with his eyes open, as if his eyelids had been soldered to the sockets, staring at the ceiling in the darkness of the room. He couldn't understand anything. He still couldn't see why he'd been arrested, let alone why he had been released. He couldn't explain why Natasha Lobanova had showed so much interest in him. And he certainly couldn't grasp how he still had his home.

He found no answers. He closed his eyes and tried to rest, but only managed to toss and turn on the bed until the weak rays of sun filtering in through the window announced the arrival of a new day.

As hard as it was, he had to get up. His job as a traitor awaited him at the Avtozavod.

Wilbur Hewitt stood up from the armchair in his office with shock on his face. He hugged Jack as if he were a son returning from war. The industrialist assured him that he'd tried everything within his power to secure his release. "But it proved impossible. They even forbade me from visiting you," he said contritely.

"Don't worry; you didn't miss anything." Jack hid his discomfort.

"I warned you to forget it!" he yelled. "I told you, kid: we don't sniff the Russians' butts, and they don't sniff ours. Anyway, the important thing is you're back. And you say Sergei himself admitted that it was all a mistake? Unthinkable! But at least you're free. How's the burn?"

"It's improving, slowly. What was it you wanted to tell me? You seemed real nervous at the hospital." He wanted to know whether Hewitt's worries were to do with being under Sergei's suspicion.

"Shhh! Lower your voice!" he whispered, and pointed at a loudspeaker as if it had the ability to hear them. "I don't know if I've told you before, but aside from reading the *New York Times*, shooting is one of my favorite pastimes," he exclaimed, making a point of raising his voice. "Do you shoot?"

"No."

"Not even a revolver? And you call yourself an American? Ah well, it doesn't matter," he said, almost screaming. "I'll teach you. The day after tomorrow, they're opening the firing range, so you'll be my guest. After the ceremony, there'll be a banquet, and at times of shortage like this, you have to make the most of these occasions." He paused, then bent toward Jack's ear to whisper to him. "Try to act normal. Perhaps after the celebration we'll find the right moment to speak without arousing suspicion."

Hearing Hewitt, Jack remembered that Viktor Smirnov wanted to drive to the grand opening of the firing range in his repaired Buick Master Six. He guessed Elizabeth would accompany the official, and his heart thumped. Even if his hip hampered him, he hoped that if he worked day and night, and if Joe Brown lent him a hand, he'd be able to fix the car.

He told Hewitt he could count on him for the event.

On the way back to the factory, it occurred to him that perhaps he really should learn to fire a revolver.

Jack was surprised to learn that the opening of a Soviet firing range could be livelier than an American rodeo. The inauguration of the new facilities had attracted hundreds of people who milled around the open field, enjoying themselves as if at a fair. Yet, in place of midway attractions, there was a collection of cabins arranged in a row, as well as dozens of targets scattered in front of them. Jack soon found Wilbur Hewitt, who, carrying a rifle, was engaged in an animated conversation with Viktor Smirnov near a table loaded with assorted canapés. Elizabeth was with them. When Jack approached, Viktor greeted him as if they were old friends. "Jack! I was just talking about you. I was telling the Hewitts that this morning, when I left the house, I found the Buick with the keys in the ignition. It runs like a dream! You have magic hands."

"He sure does!" Elizabeth broke in, and with a conspiratorial smile she held out her hand for Jack to kiss.

Jack tried to play along. After complimenting the young woman, he turned to Viktor. "I'm glad you're satisfied. Even so, I'd like to keep on top of its maintenance. As you know, it's a delicate vehicle that requires constant attention," said Jack, hoping to prolong the favorable relationship he'd established with the Soviet official.

"Ha ha! Don't worry, you've earned the right to keep that house," Viktor replied, as if he'd read Jack's thoughts. "Now, let's have some fun." He picked up the rifle that rested at his feet and showed it to the others with pride. "It's a modified Mosin-Nagant Model 1891/30. It has a range of nearly two miles and can fire ten rounds a minute. It belonged to my father. In my family, we all shoot." He aimed the gun at a target. "Do you?"

"Afraid not. I confess that the closest I've been to a firearm was at a fairground." Jack chose not to mention the times the Soviets had pointed their weapons at him.

"Then we'll have to put that right," said Viktor, before wolfing down another canapé and leading the others to one of the firing cabins to show them his skills.

After a dozen volleys, as he'd agreed with Hewitt, Jack pretended to suddenly feel unwell, blaming it on the aftereffects of his accident. The Avtozavod's general manager rushed to help him. Smirnov accepted Jack's apology without paying much attention, and he continued to demonstrate his excellent marksmanship to Elizabeth while Jack and Hewitt withdrew. Once they were at a safe distance, Hewitt unfolded a copy of the *Pravda* to feign reading.

"Jack, this is going from bad to worse. I've spoken to the bosses in Dearborn, but all they offered were words, while folks here are still disappearing. I'm afraid it'll be our turn any moment now."

"But what could the Soviets have against you?"

"I mentioned it at the hospital. I suspect they want to blame me for the sabotage. Unlike the utopian Communists who dream of equality among all human beings, Sergei's a pragmatist. He pursues his objectives like a bear hunts its prey. He doesn't just think. He acts. And I believe he's set his sights on us Americans."

"But why? We're the ones helping them build the Avtozavod. Without us—"

"You've got it all wrong, kid! We're no more valuable than an old newspaper to the Soviets. We've been useful to them while they learned; now they're ready to pursue their goals on their own."

"But even if that were the case, why would they want to annihilate us? We can still help them."

"Jack, Jack! You still think the Soviets act according to your logic, but your logic isn't theirs. You need to open your eyes, kid. For them, the American workers have become unwelcome guests. The Americans complain. They ask to be paid what was agreed rather than the measly sum they receive after tax. They insist on decent food, decent clothes . . . Some of them even demand their passports back so they can return to the United States. Do you think they'll allow it? That they'll let a handful of disillusioned workers go and shout about the lies of Communism in their home countries? No, son, they won't. They'll silence them however they have to because, for them, the end justifies the means."

"All right. So the means consists of exterminating the dissident Americans, and blaming you for the sabotage. And the end?"

"I told you at the hospital. The end will be millions of dollars. The money they'll save when they justify canceling the payments owed for the construction of the Avtozavod."

"Simply by pinning it on you?"

"Damn it, Jack! We're not talking about the sale of a patch of land! The agreement reached between Henry Ford and Stalin included clauses on the technical support that the American executives had to provide and massive penalties for failing to fulfill the contract."

"But if the accusation's false, surely Henry Ford will complain."

"Wake up, will you! For Stalin, the Avtozavod's a personal matter. They've overthrown an empire; do you really think a lawsuit will scare them? They'll fabricate false evidence to accuse us all and get what they want! They started eliminating workers they branded counterrevolutionaries to create a hotbed of unrest that would justify their subsequent outrages. And not because they want to safeguard their actions in an eventual lawsuit, which I doubt they give a damn about, but to give them an aura of legitimacy in the eyes of foreign powers that they don't yet have diplomatic relations with."

"I see. But what do I have to do with any of this?"

"You have to help us get out of Russia. Help me and my niece. I have the money, and you have the contacts. I'll pay whatever you ask."

"But why me? Can't you just leave the country? You're an important executive. Henry Ford will help you."

"Ha! Old Henry's a sly fox! He wouldn't get me out of here if I were pointing a gun at his son's head."

"But if you tell him about Sergei's plans . . ."

"That would be my death sentence! As soon as Ford suspects that the Soviets are plotting to break the agreement, he'll make me the fall guy. Don't you see? If he blames a single person for the sabotage, and not the organization, my guilt would be his salvation."

"Then take your passports and escape under your own steam."

"What passports? They took ours, just like they took yours. That's exactly why we need you! Do you really think Sergei would allow us to just run away?" He discreetly gestured at two men shooting at a nearby cabin. "They're watching us day and night. That's why I wanted to meet you here. When they're not following me, they're on my niece's tail, like bloodhounds."

Jack tried to think of a solution that wouldn't compromise him. He already had too much trouble for his liking. "You could go to the embassy. The Soviets say it's opening next month."

"The embassy and Ford are the same hyenas with different smiles. Do you think they'll lift a finger to save someone whose arrest will prevent them from losing millions of dollars?" He let the newspaper drop, defeated.

Jack looked at him in silence. Hewitt had lost all but a hint of his arrogance. "And you don't have friends you can call on?"

"Who the hell am I going to ask for help, Jack? My subordinates? They're all scared out of their wits. None of them will make the slightest effort for me."

"I don't know. Maybe Smirnov can help you." He gestured at the Soviet official. "He seems besotted with Elizabeth, he has plenty of money, and contacts, and from what I hear, he despises Sergei."

"I don't trust him. He works for Sergei. For the OGPU."

Jack tried to think. For a moment, he considered revealing to Hewitt how he was being blackmailed by Sergei. But helping the industrialist could only bring him more problems. "And what if you proved that the person behind the conspiracy is Sergei himself?"

"Prove it to whom? He's the boss. Anyway, do you think it would do any good? The Soviets protect one another. Even if I had proof, they'd fabricate new evidence to cover up their plot."

"So, what's your plan?"

"I wish I had one! All I can think of is for you to obtain false passports for me and Elizabeth."

"Do you know how dangerous that would be for me? And anyway, what makes you think I could get them?"

"Look, Jack. Let's lay our cards on the table. I'm not asking you for charity. I'm offering you money in exchange for your help. Mountains of money. I could pay you more than you've ever dreamed of earning. If you want, I'll even fund your escape to America with us."

Jack fell silent. Mountains of money . . . his dream, within reach. He could flee Russia, and start a new life in which—

A volley of gunfire tore Jack from his fantasy. He turned pale. Since they'd set sail from New York, not a day had gone by without his dreaming of returning, but Hewitt's proposal was absurd. Though he knew he might regret it, he looked at the industrialist with determination. "I'm sorry, Mr. Hewitt, but it's too dangerous."

He stood and limped off toward the exit, leaving the industrialist as wounded as if Jack had placed the targets that the Soviets were firing at over his heart.

27

Through November, the arguments between the Americans who supported the Soviet regime and the disillusioned ones who wanted to return to the United States but were unable to do so intensified to the extent that the American village was divided into two opposing camps. Jack tried to keep out of it, but when Harry Daniels's son refused to sell pork ribs to Paul Farmer, who in response struck him on the head with a bottle, he had no choice but to intervene.

"We can't go home, and on top of that, this bastard's laughing at us!" bellowed the Daniels boy, his face bloody. Jack held him back as best he could. His hip smarted—Jim Daniels had bumped into him accidentally when Jack had tried to separate them.

"Goddamned bloodsucker! That'll teach you for sitting by while we all go hungry!" Paul Farmer yelled.

Jack managed to get the young Daniels to retreat to the latrines near the village store where the argument had broken out. When Jim promised him he'd keep his distance, he limped back to the youngster's assailant. "You think you can go around doing that to a fellow American?" he challenged him. Jack was a full head taller than Paul Farmer, but Paul's arms were two fibrous trunks.

"My son was born here, and his Russian mother has the same right to eat a hot meal as the pikers that want to go back to the United States."

"The same right, huh?" He threw the pack of meat he'd taken from Jim Daniels at Paul. "There. Now get out of here! And if I see you waving a bottle around again, I'll ram it down your throat!"

Paul snatched up the package and clenched his jaw. His defiance lasted a few seconds, long enough to make sure that there were ribs wrapped in the newspaper. Then he turned around and marched off, cursing. Jack returned to the latrines to assist the Daniels boy, who was sitting near a door. When he reached him, he saw a gash on the young man's forehead that would no doubt leave a scar for the rest of his days. He took out a handkerchief and tried to stanch the bleeding.

"Are you crazy? Do you think we can afford to get into fights?" Jack reproached him.

"It was him! The bastard was crowing about belonging to the party. He said we should either become Russians or rot in a labor camp," he argued.

"And do you think you'll achieve anything by getting their backs up?" yelled Jack, exasperated.

"At least I can have the pleasure of leaving him without any ribs." He looked at Jack's empty hands. "Where are they? Please tell me you didn't give them to him."

"Go home and have your mother look at that cut." He helped him get up.

"Don't worry, Jack. I'm fine. I'll pick the glass out and get back to work."

"That won't be necessary, Jim."

"Seriously, boss, it's just a scratch. I'll clean up and—"

"I said it won't be necessary. I'm sorry, kid, but you're fired."

He didn't regret it. He knew that, sooner or later, some Soviet would show up in the village asking for an explanation, and Jim would be in trouble. He wasn't wrong: Walter now considered himself every inch the Soviet, and that afternoon he visited Jack, demanding an apology. Jack remained impassive. He assured Walter that he knew nothing about the reason behind the confrontation between the Daniels boy and Paul Farmer, and that, in any case, everything had been resolved. "All I did was separate them. You should ask them."

"Come on, Jack! The entire village knows you're running the food. The Soviets are starting to fume."

"Really? Then let them fume. Like I say, all I did was stop a fight."

"Maybe you'd be more interested if you knew that I'm fuming, too." Walter gave Jack a recriminating look through the lenses of his metallic glasses.

"Well, blow me down. *You're* fuming? You, who since joining the party, have been on double rations?"

"Look, Jack. I just came to warn you. There are more and more confrontations among the Americans, and the OGPU won't allow a little—"

"Cut the crap, Walter! Let's get things clear, shall we?" He got to his feet with the help of a crutch. "First off, I don't know in what capacity you've shown up here, asking for an explanation. Are you here as an old friend who wants to help, or as a new Soviet who can't stand someone else making more money than he does?"

"Do you really want to know?"

"I'd love to." Jack's tone hardened.

"Then listen up: I've been named head of security for the American camp, and I'm not going to allow anyone in my village—"

"Oh! *Your* village! Maybe I should bow."

"You can be as sarcastic as you want, but better I come than the Black Crows. Damn it. All I want is for everyone in this village to live in harmony. And the way things are, with troublemakers and saboteurs all around, the last thing we need is to start fighting among ourselves."

"Among ourselves? The first thing you and Sue did was leave the village."

"Well, if you want some advice, you should do the same and move to the city. Then you'll stop making people envious, living in a palace when all the other workers are cramped together in rooms the size of wardrobes."

"I see! And who'll pay for that? You, or the guys who've provided those new spectacles and that uniform?"

"It's just a suggestion." He pushed his glasses up his nose with his index finger.

"Great. Then let me give you another: you'd do well to look out for your fellow countrymen more, and less for the Soviets. Since you became an OGPU deputy, it seems to have been smooth sailing for you, but for the Americans being prevented from going home, or the ones disappearing, or the ones dying of hunger because of the miserable rations the Soviets allow them, this is no paradise."

"All right, Jack. So you want to get things clear. Then let's do that, because all these calamities don't seem to have prevented you from turning a buck! Who are you to set yourself up as the champion of the people, when you only remember them when it's time to make money?"

Jack could see that the conversation was only going to lead to a quarrel that he neither wanted nor needed. Like the rest of the Americans at the Avtozavod, Walter probably thought Jack's money all came from the contraband, which must have been what made him very angry. However, he couldn't let on that his income came directly from Hewitt, and that it was his pay in exchange for the dangerous mission entrusted to him, or that Sergei Loban himself knew of his *commercial activities*, as he preferred to call them, and consented to them.

At the same time, and though it pained him to admit it, Walter's accusation was to some extent right. As much as he tried to dress up his black-market dealings as a public service, the fact was that he was profiting from his fellow Americans' needs. And perhaps Walter was also right that he would be wise to leave the American village. He could afford it, and if he struck a deal with Ivan Zarko's nephew, the move wouldn't stop him from continuing his business in the village store.

He guessed that if he humored Walter, his friend would be pleased. "Maybe . . . ," he croaked, as if struggling to get the words out. "Maybe I should think about it. I don't know . . . Maybe moving isn't such a bad idea," he finally said.

"Trust me, it's the right thing to do," Walter replied with the satisfied expression of someone who'd defeated his adversary. "Let me know when everything's done. We'll all be better for it, you'll see."

Two days later, Walter himself helped Jack into the car that would take him to the Avtozavod. Once settled in the backseat, Jack looked out of the window. The day had started wet. The driver cranked up the car, and Jack wrapped himself up in his jacket. "Thanks for coming to get me, Walter. Sergei summoned me urgently. The other day I knocked my wound, and I can barely walk."

"It's no big deal. It was on my way. Have you thought about what you're going to do with your things?" He showed no interest in Jack's hip. "I mean all the stuff you've collected at your house—the heater, the samovar, the billiard table . . . Are you going to sell it or take it with you? When I told Sue you were moving to the city, she thought you might have too much stuff."

Jack shook his head. "Truthfully, I hadn't even thought about it. I might get rid of a few things, but I haven't seen the accommodation they've found for me yet. I spoke to a Soviet friend, and for now I'm going to move into a little house that's empty in downtown Gorky."

"A little house? You should mind the friends you keep. In the Soviet Union, owning your own home's forbidden."

"I don't know who it belongs to, and I don't care. I'm just renting it. But if you're interested, I know a few high-level OGPU officers who live in impressive dachas." The car passed some burned-out warehouses, and he took the opportunity to change the subject. "What happened there?"

"A mob of counterrevolutionaries. The anti-Soviet pickets stopped the factory running for a few days, but the OGPU's militias brought them into line," he said proudly, as if he truly saw himself as a member of the secret police.

Jack gazed at the ruins.

The car stopped in front of Sergei Loban's office, where Jack was going to apologize for his absence from work. Walter accompanied him to the door and waited until the director of operations had invited him in.

"All right, Jack. I have to go. If you change your mind about the furniture . . ."

"Sure, don't worry. And say hello to Sue."

Walter smiled. He said good-bye to Jack and returned to the car. Jack watched from the window as Walter told the driver his destination. He raised an eyebrow. Walter had his own chauffeur. He'd moved up in the world; that was for sure.

"Are you going to stand there all morning? Come on! Come in!"

Sergei's imperious voice made Jack hobble into his office more quickly than was advisable, and he smarted from his physical exertion. Seeing this, Sergei stood up. "Still limping? May I ask what treatment my daughter's giving you?"

Jack thanked Sergei for helping him into his seat. "Actually, I haven't seen Dr. Natasha for a few days. In fact, I was almost back to normal, and I thought I'd restart work today, as we'd agreed, but I injured myself again and I can barely walk."

"By Lenin's whiskers! You Americans are made of butter! I remember the day I was hit three times in the battle for Saint Petersburg. One in the belly, here right in the middle; another in the arm, and another in the thigh. I was tended to by a veteran, and the next day I was back on the front line, drinking vodka and firing at the enemy."

"It's possible we're made of different stuff. The point is that I wanted to explain my situation in person to you."

"There's no need to make excuses," he interrupted. "I knew you were unwell; I didn't make you come here to bid you a good morning. I know you spoke to Hewitt at the firing range. Did he tell you anything?"

"Nothing in particular. It seems he likes to shoot, and he invited me to the grand opening."

"And you separated yourselves from his niece and Viktor to talk guns?"

"I was exhausted. I'd worked all night to finish Smirnov's car, and I needed to sit down. Hewitt was kind enough to accompany me, and I didn't see why I should refuse."

"He didn't tell you anything about the factory? About the arrests? About what's happening with the Americans?"

"Only in passing, just taking an interest in his fellow countrymen," he lied. "By the way, what's their charge?" He took the opportunity to try to glean some information on his compatriots.

"Counterrevolutionary activities," Sergei said with a sour expression as he crumpled up a report. "They are ungrateful people who have tried to slow down the unstoppable progress of Bolshevism!"

"It seems strange. The inhabitants of the American village are honorable people; all they think about is their family and their work."

"What kind of honor are you talking about? The one that puts its own interests before those of the great Soviet family? Because I'm talking about rabble: individuals who use treachery and sabotage to pursue their objectives, siding with the small number of insurgents who still yearn for the days of the tsars."

Jack listened in silence to Sergei's rant. He resisted asking for more details because he knew that doing so would only align him more closely with the saboteurs. "All right. Well, if there's nothing else . . ."

"There is." He smoothed his graying mustache. "I'm putting Wilbur Hewitt under close surveillance, so from now on, if you want to have a conversation with him, whether by telephone or in person, you must have it in the presence of one of my men, or you'll be arrested. As for your sudden inability to work, I think we'll have to find a solution. Although the Soviet Union pays a benefit to sick workers, the amount is little more than symbolic, and it would be difficult for me to justify a wage like the one I promised you."

"I don't understand. You assured me I'd keep—"

"Yes, yes . . . I know what I said. But my daughter also said that you'd recover in a couple of weeks, and you've showed up here a wreck. So to resolve this inconvenience, until you get back on your feet, I'm going to do two things: first, authorize the opening of a Torgsin grocery store in the American village, and second, make you directly responsible for it."

"That's it?" Jack was suspicious. There was no Torgsin in Gorky, but Ivan Zarko had told him about the ones he'd seen in Moscow. They were state-authorized establishments where restricted goods were sold in exchange for hard currency and jewels.

"Well." He smiled. "Between sales, it won't do you any harm to speak to your customers. I'm sure there'll be rumors that might be of interest to me. They may know things we don't, and they won't mind sharing them with you."

The Soviet official waited for a response. Jack contemplated his stony, inscrutable gaze, imagining that, whatever Sergei's plan was, there would be few loose strings that he could pull. But perhaps there would be one or two. He decided to play along. "I'd need help. People I trust. I'm struggling to stand up. If I can't work at the Avtozavod, how will I be able to take care of a store?" he asked, confident that Sergei would agree to his request.

"You have friends. Choose a few who'd be prepared to give you a hand. While you recover, I'll free them of their other duties. They'll receive the same wage, but they'll have a comfortable job and access to the best food. They'll be grateful to you, I'm sure."

"Very well. Give me a week to recover and get everything ready."

"It's yours."

"As for the premises . . . I presume you don't intend for me to do business from the latrines."

"Of course not! I had a spare-parts warehouse in mind; it borders on the American village. I'll have it fitted out. Any other questions?"

"Yes. Stock. Who'll supply it, and at what prices?"

"Stock? There's no stock."

"I don't understand." He thought Sergei was playing games with him. "How do you expect people to do their shopping in an empty store?"

"You tell me. You haven't had any problem with it until now."

When Jack left the building, a car was waiting for him. He was annoyed to find Walter sitting comfortably inside it again, and despite his apparent friendliness, he was beginning to see him less as a friend and more as a guard dog with Sergei as his master. As they drove, Walter asked about the meeting, but Jack was evasive. He was deep in thought when, as they entered the compound, he saw that some of the bunkhouses were being closed down. "What's going on?" He gestured to the structure that a motorized crane was demolishing.

"Rehousing. You chose a good moment to move." He pointed at a couple that two guards were leading to a black car. "John Selleck and his wife, Lisa. They tried to escape yesterday but were intercepted at the first railway checkpoint."

"Where're they being taken?"

"To the *ispravdom*, I guess. Apparently, they'd colluded with some defectors wanting to leave the country. Poor fools!"

Jack watched the couple through the rear window. The woman was crying inconsolably, begging the guards not to separate them, but the men dragged them apart, ignoring their pleas.

Once they were outside Jack's house, Walter opened the car door for his friend. Jack, resting on his crutch, thanked him for his help.

"That's what friends are for, isn't it?" said Walter. He climbed back into the car and closed the door. Before leaving, he lowered the window. "Oh, Jack! One last thing. I told the housing committee that you planned to leave the village, and they asked me to speed up the process. Please, make sure you've gotten your stuff out by tonight. I want to reassign the home tomorrow."

Aware of the problems ahead, Jack slumped into the leather sofa in his home and sat there, exhausted, trying to understand why he was wasting time trying to move house instead of planning an ever more necessary escape. For any American, remaining in the Soviet Union was becoming no less dangerous than stomping barefoot on a nest of vipers. And Sergei, without a doubt, was the most venomous viper of them all.

His head echoed with the wailing that resounded in the American village every night when Loban's men burst in to arrest workers and take them away. The appeals for clemency from the sobbing wives and the children subsided only when the cars started up and drove away. He hated that Russian. Not content with trying to kill Jack, Sergei was shameless enough to ask him to spy on his compatriots in order to find evidence that would justify Wilbur Hewitt's arrest. And all this, according to the American industrialist, was to avoid paying the large sums they still owed Henry Ford for the construction of their factory.

He felt like a dirty rag for not helping Hewitt. He should have accepted his offer and joined him in organizing their escape together, but for as long as the wound on his hip forced him to get around with crutches, any attempt would be insane. Even once he'd recovered, fleeing Gorky would require careful planning, and a lot of money. While he was detained at the *ispravdom*, several prisoners had assured him that the Ukrainian city of Odessa was the best way to leave the country, with ships bound for Europe leaving its port. The problem was getting there. From what he'd heard, the trains were under tight surveillance, and in winter, road transportation was nonexistent due to the frequent blizzards.

Whatever the case, any attempt would require Ivan Zarko's help. He could surely provide Jack with false passports. What Jack didn't know was the cost, or how long Zarko would need to procure them.

While he waited for the right moment to inform Zarko of his intentions, he decided to make a list of allies and compare it to his list of enemies.

First there was Walter. He was his friend, but Jack didn't know what to think about him: he felt in debt to him for helping him flee the United States, but his increasingly unconditional loyalty to the Soviet regime worried him. The same could be said of Sue.

Then he considered Joe Brown. Though he never spoke of returning to America, old Joe was a man he could trust, and his discretion, rather than stemming from suspicion, seemed to be a defensive mechanism. The Daniels family was similar. Harry Daniels had said on more than one occasion that he would cut off an arm to be able to return home. Among his acquaintances, he considered Miquel Agramunt. Despite his anarchist background, Jack's meat supplier hadn't hesitated to propose an illegal activity in order to improve his financial situation, which certainly made him a candidate for escaping. He thought he could sound them out by suggesting they join the team that he'd need to run the new store.

The one person he was certain about was Ivan Zarko. As long as Jack had money, he could count on Ivan's help.

As a member of the OGPU, Viktor Smirnov would fall squarely into the category of enemy, were it not for the hostility he'd expressed toward Sergei on several occasions, which, if it came to it, might make him more of an ally. Moreover, his love of money and luxury meant he leaned more toward capitalist ideals than Communist ones. So perhaps Jack could take advantage of their friendship of convenience.

Finally, there were Sergei and his daughter. He had a clear idea what kind of man Sergei was and preferred not to think about it. But Natasha puzzled him. He often thought of her, and though for the time being he could only say that her care had helped him, something inside told him that she deserved his trust.

He breathed deeply as he reread his list. His enemies were powerful, and paradoxically, the only person with some power to face up to them was the man they saw as the worst of the Americans, Wilbur Hewitt.

He reached the conclusion that he had no choice. He'd confess Sergei's sinister plans to Hewitt and accept his offer to escape. Then he'd negotiate with Ivan Zarko, and while he recovered from his limp, he'd lie in wait, running the store as Sergei himself had ordered him to do, but with a subtle difference: rather than spy on his fellow countrymen, he'd find out more about the head of the OGPU, even if it meant going through his daughter.

28

Holding a colorful bunch of winter flowers, Jack waited impatiently for Natasha to come out of her office. He watched the weak rays of sunlight tinge the hospital exterior in a vain attempt to prolong the fall. The sun's natural warmth contrasted with the cold premeditation behind Jack's arranging to meet the doctor, but though he wasn't proud of it, he could find no better way to discover more about Sergei than by probing his daughter.

When Natasha Lobanova finally appeared, wearing her white uniform with a blue handkerchief covering her head, Jack couldn't prevent a slight acceleration of his heart, which he fought off by quickly handing her the flowers. She smiled and accepted the gift. When she asked him what the gesture was for, Jack returned her smile. In reality, as soon as he saw her, he forgot all about Sergei and his grievances.

"I was surprised when you called. What was it that was so important that you had to tell me?" she said, seeing that Jack was still silent.

"Don't you remember? We still haven't had dinner," he replied. As he said it, Jack thought he could detect a slight redness in Natasha's face.

"Oh! I thought it was something to do with your wound. So, did you want me to eat this bunch of flowers?"

They both laughed. She declined his invitation because she had to collect some new equipment from the post office, but Jack wasn't going to give up so easily. He brought up the conversation they'd had on the French Revolution, telling her that she wouldn't have a better opportunity to gain a new convert. "You can't leave me like this. Look at me, I'm lame!" He smiled, with a feigned expression of suffering.

She looked at him long enough for Jack's blue eyes to make her hesitate, then glanced at her little watch and screwed up her lips. She accepted Jack's invitation, but on one condition. "I choose the place," she said.

Following Natasha's directions, Jack drove the Ford Model A down various roads until they reached a ramshackle farm several miles north of Gorky. When they parked, she quickly got out of the car to greet the farmer, who had stopped digging when he saw the strange car arrive. "By Lenin's whiskers! Natasha! Is it really you?" The man dropped his hoe and hugged the young woman. "Come on, come into the house! Who's your friend?"

Natasha kept smiling as the man bowed in front of her again and again, as if he owed her his life. When he'd finished making a fuss, the young woman introduced Jack. The farmer greeted him and guided them into the little home, where a woman surrounded by small children was busy stirring a stewpot on the fire. When the woman saw Natasha arrive, she took the pot from the fire and ran to kiss her.

"Here. They're for you," said Natasha, handing Jack's bunch of flowers to the woman, who celebrated the gift as if she'd been given treasure. "Sorry, Jack, but it's the price of our dinner," she whispered to him with a smile.

They both sat at the table as the children screamed with excitement at the candy that Natasha brought out from her pockets. As they tucked into a bowl of hot soup, Jack listened to the stream of compliments that the married couple had for the young woman. He was told how the doctor had saved the lives of the youngest kids during an outbreak of smallpox.

"She's an angel!" the farmer couple repeated between spoonfuls.

Jack smiled. As well as sincere, these people seemed happy. The four children never stayed still, playing among themselves while the parents encouraged them with their laughter, and Natasha got involved, sitting them on her lap and tickling them. When they'd finished their dinner, the farmer opened his only bottle of vodka, and though Natasha initially refused, in the end it was impossible to say no. They drank a toast to the future, to the family, and to the children. Natasha laughed as the vodka warmed her stomach. Then, while the woman went to find something sweet, Natasha checked the kids for lice.

"That's how I like it! Clean!" she said with pride.

When the farmer's wife returned with three cookies, she apologized for the lack of treats. Almost everything they harvested from the *kolkhoz* went to supply the Avtozavod.

"The cooperative's left with almost nothing," the farmer grumbled, but instead of complaining, he stood and picked up an old balalaika. "Does your friend know how to dance?"

Without waiting for Jack to answer, the farmer broke into a catchy melody, prompting the children to form a ring and improvise a circular dance.

"Come on, Jack! We can't let those little tykes show us up. Let's show them what we're made of!" said Natasha, and she grabbed Jack by the hands and made him take a few steps. He was still hindered by his limp.

Jack barely felt the pain. He had eyes only for Natasha, who seemed to be enjoying his company as much as the music. He held her close enough to feel her chest against his, and she let herself be led. They danced and laughed until a stab of pain in Jack's hip forced him to stop. Seeing this, she took a step back.

"Are you all right? How daft of me. I—"

"Your daftness is wonderful," he said without letting her go.

"And it's wonderful seeing you so happy, with so little."

"Who says it's 'so little'?"

For a moment Natasha blushed, but then she let herself be carried along by the excitement of the children, who tugged on her uniform to make her keep dancing. Jack sat down and continued to enjoy the spectacle as night fell. When the kids collapsed exhausted, Natasha sat beside Jack, who celebrated her return by offering her a piece of his cookie. Her face flushed and her breathing labored, she nibbled on the treat and drank from her glass of water. She was out of breath but laughing heartily. Jack thought he caught a sense of well-being in her face that he had never seen before. He was about to tell her, when the farmer's wife approached her husband and asked him to play the "Gliding Dance of the Maidens." The woman crossed her hands over her chest and waited.

"Listen to this," Natasha whispered in Jack's ear. "The music's fabulous."

Jack nodded. The peasant farmer was silent while he carefully retuned the balalaika. He took off his hat and stroked the strings with a slight tremor. Then, accompanied by the crackling flames, he began to reel off a torrent of notes that seemed to bounce off one another to create the most nostalgic and heartfelt melody that Jack had ever heard. For a while, the music continued to fill the room with sadness and yearning, as if each chord were imbued with the fragrance of memory. When the farmer finished his performance, his moist eyes sought those of his wife, who was drying her own with a handkerchief. Though age had wizened the woman's face, Jack could see that to the farmer she was as beautiful as the first day they'd met.

"Fabulous, but sad," Jack whispered back to Natasha.

"It's not sad. It's a song about love. Melancholic, perhaps. But full of hope."

"Is that what the lyrics say?"

"There are no lyrics. You hear the hope in your heart."

Jack contemplated the poverty that surrounded him. Even if these farmers loved each other with the immensity of the snowy plains around them, he couldn't see how they could hold out any hope. When he shared his observation with Natasha, she gave him a pitying look.

"That's how we love in Russia, Jack. If you find true love, you never lose hope."

They said good-bye with another toast. The farmers toasted family, Natasha, and the Soviet Union, and Jack raised his glass to Natasha.

Back in Gorky, Jack followed the doctor's directions to central Cooperative Street.

"This is where you live?"

"Yes. It's quite an old house, but pretty." She gestured at the nineteenth-century façade of a two-story building.

Jack nodded and looked at her for a few seconds in silence, not knowing what to say. The more he looked at the young woman, the more she captivated him. She remained in her seat, as if waiting for something to happen, but time just passed. Finally, she went to open the door, and Jack, seeing this, got out and rushed to do it for her.

While she searched for the keys to her front door, Jack asked her when he would see her again. Natasha smiled. "Soon," she replied, and kissed him on the cheek. Her lips burned his skin, and he searched for hers. For a few seconds, he savored them as if they were the first he'd ever kissed. Then they separated, embarrassed, mute.

Back home, still in the American village, Jack was surprised at his behavior. He'd forgotten to ask her anything about her father, but instead had enjoyed one of the best evenings of his life.

With the excuse of delivering a part for the Buick, Jack showed up at Viktor Smirnov's dacha. He knew that Elizabeth was hiding away at Viktor's house, and he wanted to tell her about Sergei's plot against her uncle, thus enabling Wilbur Hewitt to evade the OGPU's surveillance of him. When Jack got out of his car outside the ostentatious house, he prayed that his plan would work.

Viktor, wearing a freshly starched brown uniform, cheered Jack's visit, but paid more attention to the gleaming distributor for his Buick than to the limping American struggling to climb the steps leading up to his house. As ever, he offered him a glass of vodka while he asked about the repair. Jack, settled into an Empire-style chair, went into detail about the difficulties he'd encountered so that Smirnov would have to refill their glasses. He had to keep Viktor talking for long enough to give Elizabeth the opportunity to appear, so he changed the subject to the Russian's love of guns. However, Viktor seemed to want to talk solely about cars. Only after a fifth drink did the Soviet sit on the sofa and rest his feet on a side table. Then he forgot about the cars and sat looking at Jack with a blank gaze, as if his brain had suddenly shut down. Jack supposed it was the effect of the alcohol and the suffocating heat coming from the stove in the center of the room. It was clear that Viktor could end the conversation at any moment, so Jack quickly praised his excellent taste, gesturing at the brightly colored arras that hung from the walls.

"They're becoming increasingly difficult to find," said Viktor, his vanity perking him up. "The bourgeoisie lost everything. Everything, except their devilish ability to hide their wealth!" He roared with laughter.

"I bet," said Jack, humoring him. "And on the subject of bourgeoisie, I hear a true bourgeois gem has moved into your house . . ." He gave Viktor a conspiratorial wink, praying that the alcohol had dulled his senses sufficiently.

"So you heard about it . . . Her uncle sent her here for protection." He laughed. "Can you believe it? The farmer sending his best hen into the fox's den! She is beautiful, but cold as an iceberg. If the truth be told, I wouldn't trade the real gem in this house for that girl." He gestured proudly at the splendid German-made stove in the middle of the room.

"The man's becoming delirious in his old age. All he wants to do is work instead of enjoying life." Jack laughed, and he served Viktor another glass of vodka that he downed before it was filled. "Did you know? Tomorrow he's celebrating forty years with the company."

"That long? Heavens! If I'd known, I'd have told Elizabeth to buy him a gift. Or send him to a madhouse." He laughed.

"Well, from what I hear, Hewitt isn't well disposed to receiving recognition." He laughed along with Viktor. "Which is why some of the guys in the American village are planning a party in his honor. I thought maybe Elizabeth could help us surprise him."

"That seems like an excellent idea! She's resting right now, but I'll let her know when she surfaces."

Jack felt his heart thump. If Viktor spoke to Elizabeth without him there, he'd find out that it was all a farce. "Honestly, I don't know what the guys might do to me if I go back empty-handed. They're excited about the celebration, and if we put off the preparations, everything could fall apart."

"All right. If you insist. I'll get the help to call her down."

Jack let out a sigh of relief. The first part of the plan had worked, but he needed to speak to the young woman before Viktor discovered that Hewitt's anniversary was a fabrication.

When Elizabeth came down the stairs, Jack found her as breathtakingly beautiful as the day he saw her buying caviar at the salt-fish market. She was wearing a burgundy dressing gown that hugged her hips and danced over her knees as she descended. Jack couldn't help remembering the night he'd enjoyed her body. Before Viktor could greet her, Jack approached her as quickly as his hip would allow. "If you want your uncle Wilbur to live, play along," he whispered into her ear.

Elizabeth winced. Viktor, seeing her response, lifted his feet from the side table and approached the two of them. "Is Elizabeth so attractive, she cured your limp?" he joked, switching to English, and he snatched the young woman from Jack's side, holding her around the waist. He led her to the sofa and sat her down beside him. "You hadn't said anything about your uncle's anniversary."

Elizabeth looked at Jack, trying to find an answer in his eyes. "I forgot," she managed to say in a thin voice.

"When it comes to gifts, women only remember their own celebrations!" Jack cut in, smiling in spite of the pain in his hip. "How could you forget that it's your uncle's fortieth anniversary as a Ford executive?"

"Oh! I didn't mean I'd forgotten. I meant I forgot to tell Viktor," Elizabeth replied with such convincing confidence that for a moment even Jack believed her.

"It seems Jack and some guys in the American village want to organize a surprise party, and they want you to help them with who knows what," Viktor explained to Elizabeth. "By the way, if you want music, I could lend you my old phonograph." He pointed at a contraption the size of a sewing machine, a flaring horn protruding from it. "It sounds like a litter of starving cats, but it would liven up the party."

Jack thanked him for the offer. The device was an American Edison model, similar to one he'd owned in Detroit. It had a crank that, by compressing a spring, turned a wax cylinder with grooves inside that reproduced the music. The sound, captured through a needle, was crudely amplified by the horn.

He checked its condition. He'd repaired a number of similar phonographs at the Dearborn Dance Society, so if he needed to, he could probably mend Viktor's device. The problem was that he hadn't planned to hold a party at all, but with Viktor insisting, and so that his ruse wouldn't be discovered, he accepted the offer good-naturedly.

The opportunity to be alone with Elizabeth presented itself when Viktor announced that he was going upstairs to find some old cylinders. As soon as he was gone, Jack quickly whispered Sergei's plans for her uncle Wilbur. The young woman listened openmouthed to his every word.

"I swear it's true. Sergei wants to lock up your uncle, and he's hired me to find the evidence to justify it. I can't speak to him, so you have to warn him as soon as possible."

"And what're we going to do? This is awful, Jack."

"I don't know yet. Tell your uncle to gather as much money as he can without arousing suspicion, and to carry on as normal, as if nothing were happening, until I can speak to him. I'll contact some friends to see if they can get us passports."

"And the party you were talking about, what's that for?"

"I needed an excuse to speak to you without making Viktor suspicious, and it was all I could think of."

"But Viktor's protecting us. That's why I'm staying here."

"We can't trust anybody. As well as he's treating us, Viktor is still OGPU," he whispered in her ear. "Careful, here he comes!"

The Soviet official came down carrying a box full of cylinders about the size of cans of vegetables. "There's a bit of everything: waltzes, jazz . . . It's been a few years since I used it."

"They'll do just fine. Thank you," said Jack.

"Good. And as for your uncle's party, what idea for a surprise have you suggested to our good friend Jack, honey?"

Elizabeth was at a loss for words.

"I haven't asked her yet," Jack cut in, "but with the phonograph and his niece in attendance, I'm sure Hewitt will enjoy it."

"Perfect! Then I'll have it sent to the village. In the meantime, we'll have some fun choosing what to wear to the celebration, right, Elizabeth? We'll finally be going to one of those American parties you so sorely miss."

Back in the American village, Jack cursed himself for being so stupid. He now had less than twenty-four hours to organize a fake party right under the nose of an officer of the secret police.

29

To organize the party, Jack decided to call on the same gang that he'd chosen to set up the store. Joe Brown, Miquel Agramunt, Harry Daniels, and his son Jim all accepted the job offer as if they'd won the lottery. Sergei Loban had them relieved from their previous duties without losing their salaries, and they would receive a small daily supplement and a special discount on the food sold at the store. As for the reason for the celebration itself, Jack had pretended that it was for the opening of the store to make sure that enough guests attended. Once they were all drunk, he would be able to get a toast to Wilbur Hewitt out of them with little trouble.

Joe Brown soon showed his worth in the role of store manager that Jack had assigned to him. Within ten minutes of his appointment to the position, he'd already organized a cleaning crew to clear up the old spare-parts store, the contents of which still needed to be moved out. He then improvised some display stands using wooden crates, and placed on them a couple of butchered pigs that Miquel Agramunt had obtained from his contacts. For his part, Harry Daniels, his wife, and his sons prepared the wooden chairs, the central fireplace for an enormous gridiron, and garlands made from strips of cardboard and pieces of colored sacking. Despite the cost of the occasion, Jack thought it was money well spent. He'd invited Ivan Zarko to the party, and if he could distract the Soviet guards, he would take the opportunity to introduce him to Wilbur Hewitt so they could discuss the cost of the counterfeit passports.

Though the party was advertised for six o'clock, a group of onlookers had already gathered at the door to the warehouse in the icy November cold before five. Jack saw through the window that the partygoers included some of his fellow passengers on the SS *Cliffwood*, and seeing them huddled together to ward off the cold, their gaunt faces brightened by the touch of excitement they felt at attending a party where they could put something hot in their bellies, he wondered how many of them dreamed of being back in America at that moment.

He went over the final details. After burning for a few hours, the fire lit over some sheet metal positioned on the ground had warmed the inside of the warehouse and was beginning to turn into a mountain of embers like little volcanoes bursting with lava. Miquel Agramunt had steeped the pigs in oil, pepper, salt, and rosemary, ingredients from his homeland that he'd managed to find in Ukraine, and which, according to the Catalan, would give the pork an excellent flavor. To accompany the food, he had made a drink typical of his country, consisting of a mixture of red wine, baking powder, lemon rind, sugar and cinnamon, and which he called by the strange name *sangría*. It was delicious. While the Daniels family busied itself putting up the last homemade garlands, Jack inspected the music cylinders that Viktor had supplied. The oldest ones, made of solid carnauba wax, reproduced tracks just a minute or two long, but the newer ones, made of Bakelite, contained modern hits and extended to four minutes. He inserted a Bing Crosby cylinder in the phonograph, turned the handle to wind up the mechanism, and positioned the needle on the helicoid groove that turned at a hundred revolutions a minute. The powerful voice of the American singer suddenly flooded the warehouse, for a moment turning the drab building into a Detroit nightclub. Only the dancers were missing.

He thought of Natasha. He'd have loved to spend the party with her, but when he called to invite her, he was told that she was operating on patients that evening. As he listened to the music, he couldn't help remembering their kiss, fleeting yet intense and true.

At exactly six o'clock, Jack adjusted his bird's-eye jacket, took one last glance at the gigantic "American Store" sign, which Jim Daniels had neatly written in the red, white, and blue of the national flag, and drew back the bolt to officially open the shop. The guests waiting outside, enticed by the lively music and the smell of barbecued meat, greeted their host and poured in to claim a spot near the fire.

Before long, the haggard forms that ten minutes earlier had been waiting outside were transformed into a merry band of compatriots who sang and smiled again. The main topic of conversation was how much they missed their country. Dances from the hills played on the fiddle alternated with the American tunes that emerged as if by magic from Smirnov's phonograph. As he mingled among the guests, Jack came across Walter and Sue holding hands. When he saw them, he greeted them warmly and encouraged them to dance, but Sue barely smiled and Walter looked away. Jack kept trying, but he was unable to break through their coldness.

"You haven't moved yet," were his friend's first words.

Since Walter had begun working for the OGPU, it was as if he hardly knew Jack. Perhaps he was bitter at Jack's financial success, or maybe he'd never been as good a friend as he made out. Ultimately, their friendship was that of two classmates, and that had been ten years ago. Jack looked at Walter's new Soviet jacket on which he'd pinned a little cardboard tag that read "Fordville Head of Security." He didn't know what to think.

When they turned away from each other, he tried to push those thoughts from his mind. Walter was his friend, he'd saved him in New York, and he didn't deserve Jack's suspicion.

Half an hour later, Ivan Zarko and his nephew appeared. Following the agreed-upon script, they quickly intermingled with the relatives of some of the Soviet women who'd married American workers. Soon after, Wilbur Hewitt arrived, accompanied by his niece, Elizabeth, and her protector, Viktor Smirnov. Unlike on other occasions, Elizabeth's presence barely registered with Jack: he put it down to his feelings for Natasha. As for Hewitt, Jack saw that the industrialist would play his role to perfection, returning the affection and greetings from the other guests. After a prudent length of time, Jack went to meet him, wearing a salesman's smile. "Forty years of service! I hope to be able to say the same one day!" he said to Hewitt, giving him a firm handshake.

"It's an honor to have worked for a great American company for so long. Some party you've organized!"

"I hope you enjoy it. Come in and try some of Miquel's specialties. Viktor, welcome."

Viktor Smirnov returned Jack's greeting and went to mix with the guests with a look of disdain, as if just brushing against them would forever ruin his immaculate uniform. Hanging from his arm, Elizabeth accompanied him, sporting a stunning cobalt-blue dress that contrasted with the modest attire of the rest of the partygoers. Hewitt let them go ahead and took the chance to approach Jack, who walked behind them with the help of a crutch. "Where did you get this harebrained idea?" he whispered. "If the Soviets dig up my professional background, they'll see that I've been at Ford for only twenty-five years."

"I just blurted it out. It was all I could think of to be able to speak to you alone. I thought that, it being a party, Sergei would pull the guards off and entrust Viktor to watch you. Anyway, the important thing now is to get you out of here as quickly as possible."

"My niece told me that they're planning to lock me up. Is it true?"

"Yes. Sergei's going to accuse you of being behind the sabotage. He even blames you for the attempt on my life. He thinks that you're working for your own benefit, embezzling funds from the factory, or worse still, doing it for the capitalist US government in order to delay Soviet industrialization."

"That man's insane! No one's keener than I am to avoid any disruption at the factory. It's my responsibility to—"

"I know. And that's precisely why I felt obliged to tell you."

"But how did you find out?"

Jack was silent for a moment. He looked at Hewitt and finally let out a sigh. "Because Sergei's forcing me to spy on you."

Hewitt stopped in his tracks. "I don't understand. What do you mean?" His face hardened.

Jack took a deep breath. "I just said it. He's making me find out whether his suspicions are correct."

"So you were already working for him when I asked you for help at the firing range?"

"Let's leave the lectures for another day," said Jack. "What's really important is to get you and Elizabeth out of here, before Sergei tires of waiting and fabricates evidence."

"I warned you! That son of a bitch is intent on laying the blame for his own incompetence on someone else! That's what happens when you put peasants and goatherds in charge!"

"Goatherds? Ha! Sergei's a graduate of the Saint Petersburg State Institute of Technology. If you'd warned me, I could have saved myself from a whole lot of trouble."

"And who taught him? Probably someone carrying a gun."

Jack saw Viktor in the distance searching for them with his eyes, and he led Hewitt to the junk room where they stored potatoes.

"Did Elizabeth mention the money?"

"She did. I have ten thousand dollars that I've been taking bit by bit from my account."

"That's good. Wait here. I'm going to fetch my friend. I'll be right back."

After looking through the lock to make sure nobody was watching, he opened the door and slipped out of the junk room. Shortly after he returned with Ivan Zarko and his nephew, Yuri, who stood guard on the other side of the door. After the introductions, Jack explained the situation superficially to Zarko. They needed three passports and a safe escape route. He refused to say how much money they had, though the Russian asked him several times.

"Forget the price for now and tell us whether you can help us escape," Hewitt said in broken Russian.

"Who does this sack of shit think he's negotiating with? A railway station clerk?" growled Zarko.

Jack didn't bother to translate. "Please, Mr. Hewitt! Keep quiet," he said. "This man isn't one of your employees!" He turned back to Zarko. "Excuse him. He doesn't speak the language very well," he said on Hewitt's behalf. "We'll pay what you consider fair."

"Why?" said Zarko, his expression ill-tempered. "Why should I be fair with him? I respect you because of my long friendship with Konstantin. He gave you *blat*. I owe your friend nothing."

"I'll vouch for him," Jack said to settle the matter.

"Hmm . . . I don't know if I'll be able to help you." He shook his head. "If you want to get out of the country without too many checks, you'll need a Polish, Romanian, or Bulgarian passport, for instance. But if they arrest you, the first thing they'll do is interrogate you in the language of your passport."

"The girl and her uncle speak German, and I can get by, too." Jack was glad he'd had lessons for his trips to the machinery fair in Berlin. "Will that do?"

"I don't know, but it's your money. It'll cost you three thousand dollars, twenty-five hundred for theirs and five hundred for yours."

"Including transportation?"

"No. For transportation expect to pay the same again. It will take me about three weeks to get the documents. Maybe four. But before spring it will be impossible to leave."

"Too long. I can wait, but these people need to go right now."

"Impossible. The railway's a ticket straight to the gulag. The checks are constant. Two, even three times between each station. If the fugitives were anonymous citizens, they might be able to slip through, but as Americans reported missing, forget it. They'll arrest you as soon as you set foot on the train. As for road transportation, it disappears in the winter."

"Damn it! Then find a private vehicle."

"Ha! And how will you refuel? Vodka and piss? You won't find a gas station open for at least another six hundred miles. Trying it would be suicide."

Jack remembered the American couple he saw being arrested and shook his head. There had to be a way.

"All right. You get the passports. We'll take care of the rest ourselves."

Zarko agreed. He said good-bye to Jack with a squeeze of the hands, and gave Hewitt a disparaging look. Then he left the room and disappeared with his nephew. The industrialist waited to be filled in. "He'll get us the passports. It'll cost you six thousand dollars."

"Six thousand? That's daylight robbery!"

"Three thousand is for Zarko. In advance. The rest is what I've estimated we'll need for bribes, lodging, transportation, and unforeseen expenses."

Hewitt looked at Jack with a tinge of distrust. Nonetheless, he put his hand in his pocket. "Six thousand!" He handed the money to the young man. "I hope you know what you're doing."

Jack wandered around the warehouse, feeling six thousand dollars more obligated and six thousand dollars less safe. He wasn't sure he was doing the right thing. He knew he had to escape, but the image of Natasha in his mind was holding him back. As he served himself a shot of vodka, he felt as if all the guests had suddenly stopped dancing and fixed their eyes on him. Flustered, he made his way through the crowd to the corner where Viktor and Elizabeth were standing near the phonograph to better hear the music. He was surprised not to find Hewitt with them. Viktor seemed to have drunk too much and was struggling to remain steady. Jack filled his glass and drank a toast with the couple to hide his nerves. "To the American party!"

"The American party!" they replied in unison.

Viktor chinked his glass so hard that he splashed vodka on his uniform. When he moved away, he backed into the phonograph and made it fall on the floor.

Jack picked up the contraption and put it back in its place, but when he tried to make it work again, he found that it was broken.

"I'm sorry, I . . . ," Viktor sputtered.

"Don't worry. Let's hear the fiddle!" Jack yelled at the musicians.

"You've got it all over you, too," Elizabeth noted.

"Huh? Oh yeah." Jack gave his lapels a shake. "What a mess! I'll go home to change, and while I'm there, I'll try to fix the phonograph."

Viktor agreed without caring much where the device ended up, and he turned toward Elizabeth to kiss her. Her lips were unresponsive.

"Have fun. I'll be right back," said Jack.

Jack told Harry Daniels to take care of the guests and remind them that, in the new store, as well as potatoes and pork ribs, they would have a shoe repair service, and offer credit. He asked Jim to help him transport the phonograph. When they reached his house, Jack thanked the youngster for his help.

"Leave the gadget there and get back to the party. I can manage on my own." He closed the door and went to look for a clean suit.

In his bedroom, he took the six thousand dollars from his jacket pocket and separated the wet bills. While they dried in the heat from the stove, he went to the wardrobe to change his suit. However, when he opened the door, he remembered that Yuri had stored his evening jacket in McMillan's trunk.

He looked up at the top of the wardrobe. The trunk was still there, too high to reach with his hand. He dragged a chair over and positioned it beside the wardrobe. Then he put his left foot on the seat and lifted himself until he could reach the trunk's handle. However, as he tried to pull it, he wobbled, and the trunk crashed to the floor.

Jack swore to himself. As much as he tried to ignore it, he was infuriated by his hip injury. He got down from the chair and opened the lock, but as he did so, he saw that, with the impact, a panel inside the trunk had become detached, revealing what looked like a false bottom. Amazed, he used a coat hanger as a lever to tear out the panel, and saw that, sure enough, the trunk contained a hidden compartment. He quickly emptied it and tipped it over. The items concealed there included a notebook full of jottings, accounting documents, and plans of the Avtozavod. However, they were not the finds that made his heart stop.

Almost reluctantly, he set aside the plans and picked up the red booklet marked with the gold letterhead of the United States.

Jack looked at it openmouthed, unable to believe what he was reading. It was George McMillan's passport. According to Wilbur Hewitt, McMillan, the engineer, had remained in New York due to a sudden attack of appendicitis. So why would his passport be in his trunk, ahead of his arrival in the Soviet Union? Incredulous, Jack carefully flicked through the booklet. When he read the last page, he let it drop as if he'd been shot. His heart pounded.

On the last page, stamped in black ink, was an entry visa for the Soviet Union dated December 26, 1932, a week before the SS *Cliffwood* disembarked in Helsinki. And if George McMillan had entered the Soviet Union, Wilbur Hewitt had been lying to Jack since day one.

30

Though the evidence implicated Hewitt, Jack wanted to believe that there was a simple, innocent explanation.

Certainly, the date stamped on the passport proved irrefutably that McMillan had entered the Soviet Union. However, he couldn't understand why, after crossing the border, McMillan had hidden his passport. And even more of a mystery, where was the engineer now?

Jack examined the face in the passport photograph: scholarly spectacles, wide-set eyes, a curly mustache—a distinguished countenance that, given the uniqueness of its features, he was certain he'd never seen before.

Then he remembered Sergei's suspicions. The OGPU boss claimed that the nature of the sabotage proved beyond a doubt that the perpetrator must have experience working with complex machinery, a description McMillan fit to a tee. Perhaps he was the man whom Sergei was looking for, and Wilbur Hewitt was the person hiding him.

One fact was clear: Hewitt had lied to Jack when he told him that McMillan hadn't left New York. However, there was one piece that didn't fit. If Hewitt knew that McMillan had entered the Soviet Union, why would he have allowed Jack to keep his trunk and belongings? It made no sense, unless Hewitt was certain that McMillan would never reclaim it.

He couldn't find a logical explanation for Hewitt's lies. He held the papers under a lamp and examined them minutely. His hands trembled as he leafed through each page of notes and read each transaction, unable to make any sense of it. He set them aside, angry with himself. Had his vanity and ambition blinded him? Could he really have been so stupid as to think that someone like Hewitt could hire and pay outrageous sums of money to a complete stranger? Unless, as it seemed, Hewitt needed a total imbecile for his plans.

He couldn't think straight. However, he still had enough wit to understand that the reason Hewitt was so afraid and so keen to escape was his guilt. The dilemma was that Jack couldn't blow the whistle on him without implicating himself. He had just revealed his contacts to Hewitt, he was going to provide him with false documents, and he'd taken payment for it. If Hewitt went down, he would bring Jack down with him. And then there was Elizabeth; it wasn't her fault if her uncle was corrupt.

The only solution Jack could find was to leave things as they were and wait. He would persuade Hewitt that their escape would be impossible until spring, and in the meantime he would try to find his own way out. Until then, he'd look after himself. He'd work in the store, recover from his injury, earn money, and plan his escape. Now that he knew he was completely surrounded by vermin, it was all that mattered.

December brought as much snow as it did bad news. The famine, fueled by shortages in Ukraine, the granary of the Soviet Union, was spreading its tentacles over the Avtozavod in the form of severe rationing. Fortunately, Jack's store provided some relief for the Americans, not so much because of the meager provisions of the official store as because of the food that Miquel was able to procure on the black market.

With Sergei's acquiescence, Jack had managed to turn a cockroach-ridden warehouse into a grocery store that offered not just potatoes, beans, and pork belly, but also the tasty marinades that Miquel prepared, and the dishes that Harry Daniels's wife cooked for those who preferred to work overtime. Harry and Jim washed and prepared the food rations from the general store to make them more appealing, and offering credit had attracted customers from the first day. With Joe Brown acting as bookkeeper and recording every last ruble, Jack soon became a seasoned and successful businessman.

But the only person Jack wanted to impress with his acumen was Natasha.

When his duties allowed it, he would go to see her. Most of the time, their meetings were limited to a short walk on the hospital grounds, but, work permitting, they would climb into the Ford Model A and escape to Gorky to enjoy its monuments and avenues. By her side, Jack found that his difficulties seemed to vanish. The problem was that, as soon as he returned home and closed the door, they all returned.

His main cause for worry was his relationship with Hewitt, even though he had tried to think about him as little as possible since he discovered the industrialist's deception.

Another problem that he had to solve in December was moving to his new home. Though Walter had kept his distance, and the distrust of his fellow Americans had waned, Jack still felt it wise to move. Ivan Zarko had found him a house in the city, and he didn't want to delay.

He was trying to decide what furniture to keep when an insistent rap on the door tore him from his thoughts. When he opened it, he found Ivan Zarko's nephew, whom he'd sent for the previous day to help him with the move. He let him in and showed him the belongings that had to be taken out to the horse-drawn cart that they were going to use for the move. While Yuri got to work, Jack put his final possessions in McMillan's trunk and prayed that the palace that Zarko had promised him would live up to the description.

However, when he found the colony of bats that flew in through the holes in the roof of his new home, he wondered whether Zarko knew the difference between a *palace* and a *dunghill*. Yuri had assured him that he'd see it differently once it had been given a good cleaning, but Jack doubted it. When the Russian had finished unloading, Jack limped up to the little balcony on the second floor that looked onto Alekseevskaya Street, near Gorky's kremlin. From his viewpoint, he could see the towers of the old fortress built by the tsars, its majestic appearance a clear sign of the power that they once held.

He turned to look at the adjoining homes, on two floors like his own and of similar appearance. According to Yuri, most of them had belonged to members of the bourgeoisie before they were turned into warehouses and workshops after the revolution. He closed the balcony door and went back inside to say good-bye to Yuri. Once alone, he sat on a chair and uncorked a bottle of vodka. He drank, the heat reviving him. On the third draft, he began to see the house in a different way. Perhaps, to avoid arousing suspicion if he was visited, he should give the walls a lick of paint. It would make the house look more like a proper home, where escape was the last thing on the mind of its tenant.

What unfortunately he could not change was the steep staircase that had made him groan with pain as he climbed it.

He applied the lanolin cream that Natasha had given him to the scar and flexed his leg. Then he tried to lift the knee to the height of his navel, but before he reached it, he felt as if a blade were piercing his belly.

He breathed hard before swallowing another draft of vodka. Hewitt, a traitor; Sergei, a fanatic; McMillan, missing; Anatoly Orlov, dead . . . It all swirled around in his head. He decided to sleep and wait for dawn.

He was woken by an unbearable pain in his hip, which he attributed in part to the terrible cold of mid-December. However, the air felt strangely warm. When he sat up, he found Yuri wandering around the room. Apparently, the young man had a key and had risen early to clean the house. Jack put on a dressing gown, washed his face with the water he found in a basin, and looked around. Now that it had been washed down, the place looked better, though it could still easily be confused with a pigsty. Yuri, who was devouring something, greeted him with his mouth full and offered him some kind of roasted sausage sandwiched between two pieces of black bread. Jack took it and wolfed it down without complaint. He was so hungry, he could have eaten the bats that still flitted in the roof.

"Bath?" asked Yuri, and without looking away from his sausage, he gestured at a wooden tub full of steaming water.

"You Russians know how to survive the winter." Jack's smile lasted as long as it took for the effects of his hangover to set in.

He looked at the bathtub and hesitated. He felt like submerging himself in hot water and forgetting about his problems for a while, but he wasn't sure his wound would welcome it. Since the attack, he had kept the area dry.

He saw that Yuri was about to go downstairs. "Are you going?"

"I left some of your things in my uncle's warehouse. I'll fetch them. He needs the space."

"All right. But don't be long. You'll have to help me get down the stairs. Yesterday it hurt like crazy." Jack regretted deciding to spend the night on the upper floor.

When he was alone, he took off his underwear and the bandage that he'd put back on after his relapse. Then, slowly, and despite the discomfort caused by his movements, he lowered himself into the water. The wound bothered him, but the warmth was soothing. He found a comfortable position in the tub and closed his eyes, breathing in the steam as if it nourished him. For a moment, while his whole body relaxed, his mind traveled to Detroit, and he saw himself in America again. A bathtub full of hot water . . . a job that fulfilled him . . . a hassle-free life . . . and Natasha. He was surprised by how little he would need to be happy.

He was on the verge of falling asleep again, when he heard knocking on the door downstairs. His comfort disappeared, turning into alarm.

It couldn't be Yuri because he had a key. He shouted out, receiving no response. He tried to sit up, but an intense pain ran down his spine. Gripping the edge of the bath, he gathered in his legs and rolled to one side. Then he heard footsteps coming up the stairs.

"Yuri?"

The footsteps continued. There was no reply.

He tried to get up. Despite the pain, he managed to get himself onto his knees. Then he leaned back until he was squatting. He was on the verge of standing, when he noticed a figure before him. Jack stammered when he saw that the person looking at him naked, water up to his calves, was Natasha. Very slowly, cursing continuously, he submerged himself in the bath again.

"No!" she said, and ran to stop him.

With the young woman's help, Jack got out of the tub and tried to cover himself with his underwear, but she made him lie on the bed, and felt the scar with a worried expression.

"What possessed you to take a bath? I told you not to get it wet."

"What're you doing here?" he said, covering himself with a blanket. "Did your father send you?"

"My father? Of course not! Well, he mentioned your relapse, but it was my idea to come. I asked for your address at the American store. I knocked, but you didn't answer. The door was unlocked, and I was worried you might need help."

Still in a daze, he looked at Natasha, whose face was even more beautiful with her hair unbraided. "You came here from the factory just to see me?"

"Not exactly. I live just a few blocks away, remember?"

"Well, no, not really. The time I took you home, I remember parking in front of an old building, but I'd had one drink too many. I still don't know how I made it back to the village. But let me think . . . Ah, that's it! Cooperative Street! That's where your house is."

"A house, me? No such luck. Just a room with a shared bathroom and kitchen, like any other single girl."

"But, for someone in your position, isn't living in a shared house a little, er, stifling?"

"Why?" She smiled. "I don't have more hands, legs, or heads than anyone else."

"I don't know. You're an important surgeon. You should have the right to—"

"To a house like this?" She looked around. "It certainly is big. And if properly cleaned, it would even be quite nice, but it would be even better if a couple of families that needed it lived here, don't you think?"

Jack was surprised by the willingness with which Natasha accepted living conditions that didn't match the importance of her role. He wasn't sure what to say, so decided to remain silent and let the young woman tend to him. She was applying a dressing that she'd taken from her case, when Jack decided to be bold. "You look . . . I don't know . . . different."

"Oh! And is that a compliment?" She gave a start, surprised.

"No. I mean . . . I don't know. It's just seeing you like this, without your uniform . . ."

"Is it that bad?" Natasha got up, laughing. She did a twirl.

"No. You look lovely," said Jack. "It's just . . . today you look like a normal young woman!"

"What do you mean?" She feigned anger. "So what did I look like before?"

"Well . . . er . . . a Russian doctor!" he replied. "No! That's not what I meant. It's just that it's the first time I've seen you being a doctor without your coat," he said, quickly trying to dig himself out of a hole.

"Oh, I think you did mean it." She was still smiling.

"Really, I'm sorry. This . . ." He cleared his throat. "Do you mind turning around?" He motioned that he wanted to get dressed.

Natasha obeyed, the smile still spread across her face, while Jack pulled on his pants.

"So. How's the burn doing?" He finished dressing.

"Well, this Russian doctor doesn't think getting into the bathtub was the best idea. Let's take a look." She undid his pants and pressed gently. "Fortunately, the scar hasn't softened too much. I imagine you'll be walking unaided in a couple of weeks."

"It's still damned painful."

"The fragment damaged the nerves. You might have to get used to it. What's the smell in here?" She turned around to where Yuri had left a plate of leftover sausages.

"Breakfast. Will you join me?"

"I'd love to. It's been ages since I've had a good meal, but I don't know if I have time."

"Come on! Help me. I won't be able to cook them on my own." He pretended to be in pain.

Natasha couldn't refuse, and she helped him roast a couple of sausages from the package that Yuri had left, and toast some slices of black bread. The aroma spread through the house, mixing with the heat from the embers. They sat together by the fire and savored the food.

"You're slimmer out of your uniform." Jack examined her.

"I don't think I'm all that skinny. It's the rationing," she replied, seeming embarrassed. "And work!" she quickly added.

"And what does your boyfriend think about it?" Jack joked.

"Boyfriend? What makes you think I have one?" she said, playing along.

"Well, I don't know. It just seems strange that such a pretty girl, and someone so accomplished, could live in a shared apartment and think only about work."

"Well, maybe I'm strange. But I can promise you that, if I had a boyfriend, he'd kiss me even if I were the skinniest girl on earth." She laughed, and when Jack put his arms around her, also laughing uncontrollably, she let him kiss her. "And you? Haven't you had a girlfriend? I mean . . . apart from your wife."

"Sure. Come here, I'll introduce you to her." He pulled her toward a mirror so she could see herself.

"No. I mean an American girl." Her expression turned serious. "My father said you'd been seeing Wilbur Hewitt's daughter."

"He said that? Well, you don't need to worry. She's water under the bridge."

"So, it's true."

"What does it matter? Hey, what's with the twenty questions? You wouldn't be jealous, would you?"

"Me? Are you kidding? Oh wow! You even have a phonograph!" She broke off the interrogation and headed cheerfully toward the device. However, when she saw it close up, her expression changed to one of astonishment. "Where . . . where did you get this?"

"Do you like it? It's an Edison, from—"

"I know what it is! I'm asking where you got this contraption from."

Jack noticed a sudden hardness in her tone.

"Um . . . an official gave it to me to repair," said Jack, feeling as if he were being accused of an unknown crime.

"An official?"

"Yes. Viktor Smirnov. He's an OGPU officer under your father's command. Is there something wrong?"

"No . . . it's just that . . . you'd do well to keep away from that man." Her voice faltered.

"Viktor? Since I arrived, he's done nothing but help me."

"Viktor doesn't know how to help anyone but himself."

"How would you know? Do you know Viktor well?"

"Sorry, but I'd rather not talk about it. I shouldn't have mentioned it."

Jack had to swallow his curiosity. He didn't know what to say. All that occurred to him was to ask about the people wounded in the recent demonstrations. Natasha seemed to relax again.

"It was terrible," the young woman said. "There were dozens of casualties: young, old, women . . . I don't understand how the police could have responded so brutally." She took a last bite of her breakfast.

"They may have had their reasons. I mean, it's possible those young men, old men, and women were so desperate they didn't fear whatever retaliation came their way. That, or . . ."

"Or?"

"Or quite simply, the police overstepped the mark."

"You and your prejudices against the Soviet Union!" Natasha stood up. "Those who died were counterrevolutionaries trying to destroy everything the country has built. And my father would never authorize—"

"All right, all right! But do you know what? This whole *counterrevolutionary* thing is starting to sound like a chorus you've all learned, as if it's been drilled into you since kindergarten. I hear it from you, from Sergei, from Viktor, from the police, from officials, from operatives . . . and from that irritating radio channel they broadcast in every corner of the Avtozavod day and night!"

"I have to go. Thanks for the sausage," Natasha said.

"Wait! I didn't mean to upset you. It's just . . ."

"What?"

"That when it's not counterrevolutionaries, it's the capitalists, or failing that, the imperialists. You see enemies everywhere and . . . damn it, some of us have come to help you!"

"Sure. Anyway, Jack. It was a pleasure getting you out of that bathtub." She gave him a fleeting kiss.

"Wait. You're leaving, just like that?" he yelled when he saw her starting to go down the stairs.

"No. We Soviets aren't as rude as you think." She smiled at him. "Come by the hospital whenever you like," she added, before turning around again and leaving the house.

31

Jack spent some of the next week tidying up his house. He cleaned and organized it, and the repairs carried out by Yuri on the carpentry work finally made it look like a proper home. However, most of his time he dedicated to running the store, which, with the arrival of the festive season, was in full swing.

On Christmas Eve 1933, Joe Brown cashed up and showed Jack their earnings. After adding up the total again, Jack shook his head.

"What's troubling you, Mr. Beilis? It's quite a lot more than we expected."

It was a while before Jack answered. He was remembering his father. It was exactly a year since his death. "It's not that, Joe. And I told you not to call me *Mister*."

"If it's about the customers again, let me tell you that if not for this store, even more of them would go hungry. And you won't stop me from calling you *Mister*, sir. You're my boss now, and for as long as you are, you'll have to put up with it."

"I see. Here." He handed him the bonus he'd decided to share among his staff. "But Mrs. Newman can't feed her sick kids, and Burton's caught typhus, and—"

"And you looked the other way when you caught his eldest son stealing four pieces of meat. Do you think I didn't notice?"

"They would've rotted anyhow."

"Sure . . . well, I know people who'd kill for that *rotted* meat."

Jack decided the conversation was over and continued stacking empty crates. The exercise was strengthening his hip, and as Natasha had predicted, he could now manage without crutches. However, his memories were still plagued by old wounds.

He longed to see Natasha. After the episode with the bathtub, they had continued to meet, and though the young woman was friendly, for some reason their encounters felt clandestine. Natasha always chose solitary parks for them to walk in, where they could kiss and fondle without being seen, huddling together to keep out the cold. But she refused to go to his new house, giving him excuses that he didn't understand. However, the young woman asked him to trust her, so he did.

That was why he was surprised when, that evening, just before they closed the store, Natasha showed up at the door wearing her overcoat and *ushanka*, her blond braids falling onto her shoulders.

"Hello!" he said, startled.

She waited for a few seconds in the snow, until he invited her in.

"I thought I was going to freeze to death!" she said with a smile. "How's it all going?"

"Fine, fine. Come in and sit near the barbecue. We've just put it out, but it's still warm." He pointed at the terra-cotta grill that Miquel and Joe Brown had built in a corner. "What a surprise. What brings you here?" As she took off the *ushanka*, Jack admired her bright, affable face.

"It's the twenty-fifth tomorrow. It's just another day here, but I guessed it would be different for you. That you'd miss your family, and the gifts, all those things." She took a package wrapped in newspaper from her case and handed it to him. "I thought you'd like this."

Jack unwrapped the package with curiosity, without admitting that he didn't usually celebrate Christmas, either. When he tore away the last piece, he discovered the beautiful cover of a copy of F. Scott Fitzgerald's *The Great Gatsby*.

"Heavens! Thanks a lot. But, how . . . ?"

"I remembered you reading in the hospital to keep yourself amused. A few years ago, an American patient gave me this novel, hoping that reading it would help me love his country, but I've never had time. And anyway, even if I'd wanted to read it, I only understand a little English." She laughed. "He told me it was a wonderful story about New York, and I thought you might like to remember your city. And maybe you could read it to me."

"Well, thanks again. I must say I was surprised to see you here, in the village. Lately, with all the hiding away we've been doing, I've gotten used to having a secret lover."

She smiled when she heard Jack's description of their relationship. Though it had been half in jest, she planted a kiss on his cheek as a reward and sat beside him. "So, will you read it to me?"

"I'll do better than that." He set the book aside and returned her kiss. "I'll take you to New York so you can see it for yourself."

Natasha laughed like a little girl. "I don't know if I should. I hear people eat disgusting things there, like hot dogs."

"Bah! You shouldn't listen to that Communist propaganda." He laughed. "Anyway, after trying those sausages the day you surprised me at home, I doubt anything will frighten you. My God! I don't think I've ever eaten such disgusting sausages."

"Ha! I didn't want to say anything, but me neither!"

Jack didn't let her finish. He gave her a kiss that came from his soul. As their lips touched, he started to slowly undress her. One button followed another, and another. And with each button he kissed her, and with each kiss, the caresses were more eager. When he opened her white coat and brushed against her chest, he stopped, as if suddenly sensing he was about to commit a forbidden act. Yet Natasha's eyes remained closed, and her mouth waited for him, half open. Jack kissed her again and closed his eyes. His heart fluttered. That kiss was followed by hundreds more, on her neck, on her chest. He savored her nipples, which responded by straightening and offering themselves to a tongue that grew ever more hungry, more daring. Jack explored her body, sampling it as if it were the first and the last he would ever taste, and embraced her with abandon. Their bodies melted together as they held each other, their moans growing bolder, and when he sensed her breathing, hoarse and frantic, when her soft body arched against his, Jack let himself go, forgetting everything he knew and losing himself in the depths of her emerald eyes, in the redness of the cheeks that, for an instant, he thought belonged to him.

Jack was still sleeping when Natasha woke at dawn. She looked at him affectionately, noticing the medallion that hung over his powerful chest, and she took it between her fingers, smiling as she remembered how, while they made love, it had hit her several times on the chin. As she rested it back on his chest, Jack woke up.

"Do you never take it off?" she asked.

"I'd sooner die."

"It has a curious engraving. What does it mean?"

"I don't know. My mother gave it to me when I was a boy. At night, when she tucked me in, I remember her stroking the medal on my neck and saying . . ." He fell silent.

"What did she say?"

"Nothing. Forget it. It's stupid."

"Come on, Jack! I'm sure it isn't. What did she say to you?"

Jack was silent as he fixed his eyes on Natasha's. "Well, she would say . . . She'd say that, without love, life wasn't worth living. There you go. Maybe that's why she died. Because I wasn't there by her side to love her."

"Don't say that."

"*Without love, life isn't worth living* . . . I told you it was stupid."

"No. No, it isn't."

"Yes, it is." He abruptly got up.

"I'm sorry. I shouldn't have asked."

"No, I'm sorry. It's a sad story. Do you know what? I've often thought that if I lost this medallion, I'd lose the only thing of value in my life."

"Really, I'm sorry. I—"

"No. Don't worry." He smiled. "Apart from asking me to take it off, you can do whatever you want with me."

Jack was overjoyed to find that there were other ways to have fun in the Soviet Union in addition to drinking vodka, and he loved that Natasha was the hostess revealing those ways to him. Every evening, when she'd finished seeing her patients, the young woman would take the tram to the store in the American village, and though by that time night had fallen, to Jack it was as if the sun had just come up. Every minute with her was the equivalent of months of happiness stored up. They chatted, laughed, cooked, or kissed. And then they played, and were dragged along by a torrent of caresses filled with feelings as intense as they were new to them. For as long as their bodies were intertwined with each other, they were oblivious to the cold and the solitude that enveloped the Avtozavod. They existed only for each other, and they wanted to remain like that, skin against skin, their breathing labored from tiredness, as the hours passed deep into the night. Only laughter interrupted their kisses, and only kisses interrupted their laughter, until the moment their serenity ended because Jack had to take Natasha home. Then, when he returned to his own house, he wondered why she never agreed to stay with him, and at those moments, the injustice of it tormented him.

Jack often ordered a special dinner from Miquel to surprise her with, and in the warmth of the embers, they spent the hours in the store, sampling the tasty food while she remembered her young days as a member of Komsomol, the Communist youth organization, where she discovered her calling for medicine, or told him about the efforts of her father, who after being widowed, had striven to make her a good Soviet.

On one of those nights, Jack asked about her interest in shooting. "Do all you Russians shoot in your spare time?"

"As much as you Americans eat hamburgers," she countered mischievously. "No. But it was a popular activity among the Komsomol kids. In fact, I'm a crack shot!" she boasted.

Jack thought he would dazzle her with tales of New York. He described the massive structures of steel and concrete that at that time of year would be glittering like giant Christmas trees, shedding their light on the busy crowds crawling down Broadway's boulevards looking for premieres, stopping at the hot dog or donut stands, enjoying the Christmas carols and the lights, or the endless shop windows displaying festive garlands and gifts.

Natasha sensed that Jack's words came from an immigrant's homesickness, not from boastful vanity. "So if you miss it so much, why don't you go back?"

At that moment, Jack remembered his parents, and his face darkened. He pursed his lips before sighing. "For the same reason I came here, I guess. No one leaves their home because they want to." He avoided telling her the real reason for his flight. "But do you know what? I'd love to show you America. In the end, we have more in common than you think. Have you not heard of the Marx Brothers? You have Karl, and we have Groucho." He looked her in the eye, as if searching for something more than an answer in them.

"I . . . well . . . I have to go home." She laughed without understanding the play on words, and got up to say good-bye.

"Wait!" He took her hand. "What about my hip? You promised you'd take a look."

"Does it hurt now?" She kissed him lightly on the lips.

329

Jack looked at Natasha's bright face again. "Your kisses are the best medicine," he said, before turning off the light to lose himself in her burning lips.

In late February 1934, the success of the store in the American village and his ever closer relationship with Natasha began to make Jack doubt his need and desire to escape. For the first time in his life, he felt as if he could have everything he wished for: work that earned him enough to enjoy the luxuries he wanted; a woman he not only loved but also admired; and though it was a paradox, a feeling of security. And yet, the more he persuaded himself that there was a future for him in the Soviet Union, the greater was his longing to return to the United States. He missed the little things, like wandering down avenues packed with busy pedestrians, being able to spend a few cents at a hot dog stand, admiring a shop window crammed with goods, or attending the latest premiere from Metro-Goldwyn-Mayer. Perhaps his nostalgia was irrational, but when he remembered the United States on freezing Gorky nights, he was filled with an energizing warmth.

He missed his country. The land of freedom.

America might not be the perfect country. In fact, the crisis brought about by a financial system of insatiable greed had ended the hopes and dreams of millions of families, including his own. But Jack still believed in the land where he was born.

That didn't stop him from appreciating the good things about Russia. Foremost among these, Jack recognized, was how quickly its leaders were lifting people out of poverty. After spending the year surrounded by Soviet workers, he'd learned that the revolution had transformed a medieval nation of nobles and serfs into a powerful state in which everyone, regardless of race, religion, or birth, had the right to a job, to a home, and to food. However, he also saw that the same leaders who so willingly shared out land and work among the dispossessed were fanatics who made the Soviet Union a dangerous place for anyone who dared take issue with their ideology.

Ordinary Russians were indefatigable workers—reserved, honorable, committed, and honest people. At least, that was how he saw Natasha Lobanova, the Soviet citizen he knew best and the woman he loved . . . Yet, despite loving her deeply, sometimes he was troubled by thoughts of Elizabeth Hewitt.

He couldn't understand why it happened. Now and again, her image would suddenly appear in his mind like a slap in the face. It was as if for some inexplicable reason he was still attracted to her, not because of her beauty that he'd experienced for himself, but because of everything that surrounded her. He envied her position, her friendships, her upbringing; even her ridiculous manners and affected mannerisms were as seductive to him as they were impenetrable. He knew it was stupid, but despite being aware of his stupidity, he couldn't prevent her from tormenting him.

He hadn't seen Elizabeth since the night he discovered McMillan's passport. He knew she was still living with Viktor Smirnov, and though he'd suggested to Natasha that they visit them, she had refused. He still hadn't been able to uncover why she was so against the idea, but every time he mentioned Viktor's name, Natasha's expression turned dark. One person he had seen again was Walter, who seemed to have regained his old jocularity since he learned that Jack was going out with the OGPU boss's daughter.

One night when his friend was doing a round of the village, he came into the store to suggest they all have dinner together at his house. "You have to try Sue's cooking. You can't imagine how much she's learned."

Jack tried to make his excuses, but Natasha, who was helping Jack cash up, got in ahead of him. "Tell Sue we'd love to come."

When Walter left, Jack berated Natasha for accepting the invitation. "I don't like you making decisions for me," he said in a tone that took the young woman by surprise.

"I was just being friendly! You've often complained that you miss your life in America. It's always just the two of us, and I thought you'd like it if we all spent an evening together. And I want to chat with the woman who was your *wife*, now that I know it was all a sham."

Jack scowled as he padlocked the store entrance. He couldn't explain to her that, though they'd processed their divorce, Sue's presence still made him uncomfortable. "I'm sorry; it's just that you always seem to be the one that decides whom we see. You got very worked up when I suggested meeting with Viktor Smirnov," he said to vent his frustration. "That man could help me in the future. He's very well connected and—"

"No! I've told you what I think about him. You don't need that man's help. If you need anything, my father—"

"Your father! And what would happen if your father changes his mind one day and decides to take the store away from me, or they transfer him to a different factory, or he gets annoyed over any little thing and sends me back to the *ispravdom*? Damn it! He doesn't even know I'm sleeping with his daughter." He opened the Ford's door to take her home.

"But don't you see? Viktor will never see any farther than the end of his nose!"

"How can you be so sure? It was thanks to him I was able to live in a proper home while the other Americans huddled together in pigsties. And the car I drive you back and forth in is his. You should be grateful."

"I should? Well, look what I'm going to do with your car!" She got out of the vehicle and slammed the door. "Enjoy it, but count me out if you want to visit him." She walked off in the direction of the tram.

That night, Jack could barely sleep. He didn't like arguing with Natasha, but having to go along with her wishes without knowing why she was so angry annoyed him even more. He poured himself some vodka to calm himself down. The heat from the alcohol burned his throat but soothed him. As he served himself another glass, he wondered why women were so complicated. He had tried to understand their behavior, breaking everything down like he would with a complex mechanism, but as much as he tried to take them apart and reassemble them he never got the machine to work.

He turned his thoughts to Wilbur Hewitt, who, two days earlier, when he'd managed to slip away from his escorts, had shown up at the store to ask about the passports.

Jack had fobbed him off. He still didn't know whether Hewitt was really to blame for the sabotage, though it didn't make sense that he had hired Jack to investigate crimes that he had committed himself. Unless, of course, he was looking for someone on whom to lay the blame. Jack finished his vodka, put the bottle away, and slumped onto the sofa near the hearth to gaze at the little embers that floated like fiery sprites. It worried him that he'd reached such a simple conclusion that hadn't occurred to him before. A scapegoat . . . and McMillan . . . where was he? And what connection did he have to the sabotage? He considered reexamining the documents he'd found in the trunk, but his head ached. Vodka and arguments were not a good combination. He slowly closed his eyes and let his mind drift with the anxiety of not knowing what direction his life would take.

An insistent banging as if his head were being drilled woke him. Jack sat up and checked his watch. It showed 5:00 a.m. His temples throbbed, but the knocking persisted, unrelenting. He pulled on a dressing gown and went down the stairs as quickly as he could to prevent whoever it was from smashing down his door. He had no idea who it could be. When he opened up, he found Elizabeth Hewitt, soaked through, her makeup running and her eyes red from crying. Before he could ask her what was happening, the young woman came in, and, with no explanation, threw herself into his arms, sobbing inconsolably. Jack tried to calm her down, wrapping her in a blanket. When Elizabeth managed to speak, she told Jack that they'd arrested her uncle. "We were sleeping, and the telephone woke us up. Viktor took the call, then quickly got up. He didn't want to alarm me, but his face gave it away. I insisted he tell me what was happening, and finally he explained. Oh, Jack! It was Sergei! He's sent Wilbur to the *ispravdom*, charged with counterrevolutionary acts. I . . . Viktor wouldn't tell me anything else. Oh God! I'm afraid something dreadful has happened to him."

"All right. Calm down. Why did you come here? I'm sure Viktor will be able to—"

"Viktor threw me out."

"What?"

"He told me I had to leave, that he couldn't harbor the niece of a capitalist traitor."

"And he threw you out? In the middle of the night?"

"Well, no. I left. I called him everything under the sun. I didn't know who to turn to, so I came here. I don't know anyone else. You have to help me, Jack! You can speak to Sergei."

"Me? But I just run a store. I don't know why you think I could—"

"Jack! Please, I'm begging you! You go out with his daughter. He'll listen to you."

Jack blushed. "Are you forgetting who you're talking about? In matters of the state, Sergei Loban wouldn't listen to his own mother. And anyway . . . if they've arrested him, they have their reasons."

Elizabeth separated herself from Jack.

"Why . . . why do you say that?" she stammered.

Jack tried to calm her down, but she retreated again. "Please, relax. From what I know, Sergei's been investigating your uncle for some time, and if he's finally decided to charge him, it must be because he's found proof. And . . ." Jack remembered how Wilbur Hewitt had deceived him with the McMillan business. "And there're things you don't know," was all he finally said.

"I'm begging you for your help, Jack! What am I going to do on my own?"

"I understand, but I don't see how I can—"

"Please. If you don't want to compromise yourself, at least help me find a lawyer. I don't speak the language, and I don't know who else to turn to."

"That's not the problem. It's simply that I—"

"What is it, Jack? Have you forgotten me already? What is it you want? Do you want *me*? I'll do whatever you ask, do you hear? Whatever you ask," she said with determination.

Jack was convinced that Elizabeth really meant it. He remained silent for a few seconds while he considered his options. Taking Elizabeth in would put him in a delicate situation as far as Sergei was concerned. And as for Natasha . . . Natasha knew he had been seeing Elizabeth, and she wouldn't approve, either. But he couldn't leave her out on the street.

"All right. I'll go to see Loban in the morning. You can stay in my room until you find somewhere else. I'll make do here," he said, gesturing at the sofa in front of the hearth.

Elizabeth nodded, sighing with relief. Jack contemplated her in silence. She, though still beautiful, looked like a broken doll. He made her some of the valerian-and-lemon-balm tea that he took for his pain, and he showed her upstairs. Elizabeth sat on the bed and drank the infusion like an automaton. Jack took the cup from her hands and helped her lie down. Then he covered her and turned out the light. When he was leaving, he heard Elizabeth say good night.

"Please, Jack. Get us back to America."

Before dawn, Jack was already waiting impatiently in the hall outside the office of the director of operations. He hadn't slept. If they were capable of imprisoning Hewitt, no American could consider himself safe. When he saw Sergei appear, he finished his cup of coffee and swallowed his nerves. The Russian greeted him with a glimmer of surprise, opened his office door, and invited him in. While Jack sat down, the OGPU boss left a folder of reports on the desk and took off his old hat. His face seemed more serious than usual, as if he bore a heavy burden that he was unable to lift. He sat and studied Jack in silence.

"So?" He said nothing else.

"Thank you for seeing me without an appointment, sir. I know you're very busy, but as I said to your secretary, it's an urgent matter."

"Yes?"

Jack cleared his throat. No doubt Sergei had guessed the reason for his visit. "In the early hours of this morning, Elizabeth Hewitt came to my house. She said that last night some thugs showed up at her uncle's home and took him away without explanation."

"Right. Do you suppose those thugs were following orders?"

"I suppose so. I'd be grateful if you could tell me who gave them those orders and what he's accused of."

"I don't mind satisfying your curiosity." He looked up from the report that he'd taken from the folder. "I gave the order."

Jack raised an eyebrow. For a moment, he considered arguing with Sergei but held back. In truth, he didn't even know what he was doing there, trying to call the head of the Avtozavod secret police to account, much less when it was about Hewitt, the man who'd tried to deceive him. Upsetting Sergei could only bring trouble, so he'd try to learn the whereabouts of the industrialist and leave the rest of the questions for Elizabeth herself. "You'll understand my position. I in no way intend to question you, but I feel an obligation toward that family. Hewitt's niece is desperate. She just asked me to find out about her uncle's situation and if it's possible to visit him. It was Hewitt who hired me, after all," he said in an attempt to justify his actions.

"Hewitt hired you? Ha!" Sergei stood, thumping the table. "How deluded you are! Do you really think the Soviet state would have allowed a newcomer like you to stick his nose in our business, just like that, however qualified he was? Or that Hewitt himself would have paid a stranger to play such an important role?"

"I . . . I don't understand," Jack sputtered.

"Hewitt had nothing to do with hiring you. I ordered him to do it in Moscow, when I discovered that McMillan had disappeared."

"Disappeared? But wasn't he confined to a hospital in the United States?" He tried to act surprised.

"So that's what Hewitt told you? Look, Jack. Even though you're an American, I have always believed you to be an honest man. Otherwise, I can assure you that I wouldn't have let you within ten miles of my daughter. And for the same reason, I think I owe you an explanation." He took a puff on his cigarette, as if weighing carefully what to reveal to him. He took a deep breath and continued. "I started suspecting Wilbur Hewitt not long after he was assigned to this factory. I'm talking three years ago, when the construction of the Avtozavod first began, and he was chosen to oversee it. Hewitt was very enthusiastic; I won't deny it. His team worked day and night, and in a few months they transformed a piece of wasteland into the impressive complex that is now the pride of the Soviet people. But when the first machines were commissioned, the problems started, too." He took another puff. "At first, Hewitt blamed the incidents on the Soviet workers' lack of skills. To solve the problem, a group of technicians traveled to Dearborn to be trained, while some American operatives were brought to the Avtozavod. However, far from improving, the problems worsened, and the sabotage started. The OGPU and Ford agreed jointly to appoint two special supervisors with the mission of uncovering the criminals. For the Soviet side, the designated man was Anatoly Orlov, and for the Americans, it was George McMillan. The two of them would work side by side, and their findings would be reported directly to me."

He checked that Jack was following him before continuing. "McMillan was an oddball, a bookworm who spent entire months neck-deep in accounts and reports. He was suspicious of everyone, he barely spoke to Orlov, and he kept his discoveries secret. I imagine that, at some stage, McMillan found out that Hewitt was responsible for the sabotage, and realized he was out of his depth. He must have guarded the information for a while, but when I was in Moscow, not long after your arrival in the capital, I received a call from him admitting that he'd found the evidence I was looking for."

"And now he's handed it to you."

"Not exactly."

"What do you mean?"

Sergei Loban's only response was to open a drawer and take out a red folder, which he dropped onto the desk. Jack picked it up and opened it. Inside, he found a clipping from the *Pravda* newspaper, dated January 6, 1933, the very date when Wilbur Hewitt offered Jack the role of supervisor. He read the headline in bold:

UNIDENTIFIED MAN COMMITS SUICIDE BY THROWING HIMSELF INTO MOSKVA RIVER

And under the text appeared a photograph of a body, the face identical to the one Jack had seen on George McMillan's passport.

32

When Jack confessed the outcome of his meeting to Elizabeth, the young woman retreated until she bumped into an armchair into which she slumped like a marionette whose strings had been cut. Jack hesitated before kneeling to take her hands in his and console her. When he lifted her chin, he could see barely a wisp of the beauty that had captivated him in her reddened eyes.

He made tea for both of them. While he heated the water, he felt sympathy for her but also felt sorry for himself. Elizabeth was clearly forlorn, but Wilbur Hewitt had left Jack in the lurch, too. He waited for the young woman to take a couple of sips before telling her that Sergei had authorized a visit to see her uncle. Elizabeth seemed to come back to life. "I don't believe him. I don't believe that bunch of lying Soviets. Where are they keeping him?"

"He told me they've taken him to the *ispravdom*. Don't worry. They took me there, too, and it's a safe place," he lied to ease her worry. "Wrap up warm. It's out of town."

As he drove in the direction of the labor camp, Jack reflected on the macabre plot that Wilbur Hewitt had devised, and on the attempt in the factory with which, according to Sergei, the American executive had tried to murder him. His accompanying Elizabeth at that moment was less to do with kindness than out of a desire to confront the industrialist face-to-face. He accelerated hard, and the Ford lurched forward on the icy road before going into the final bend before they reached the sinister barbed-wire fencing that surrounded the *ispravdom*.

When they showed him Sergei's letter of authorization, the guard let them through and led them to a small, bare room, with no furniture other than a metal table screwed to the floor, and four chairs arranged around it. While they waited, some gut-wrenching screams made Elizabeth jump.

Ten minutes later, a bolt was drawn across, and a guard emerged through the door at the other end of the room. He was followed by a wreck of a man dragging a leg. Seeing that it was Hewitt, Elizabeth ran to help him, but the guard yelled at her to keep her distance.

"What's he saying?" she asked Jack.

"He's telling us to sit down and remain seated. Do what he says."

"You have five minutes," the guard said in English, and he positioned himself beside the table.

Elizabeth looked at her uncle with wide eyes, as if she were looking at a stranger. "Uncle Wilbur? Oh God! What have these savages done to you?"

Wilbur Hewitt pressed his lips together and raised his head, trying to preserve some trace of dignity. He glanced sidelong at the guard. "Don't worry. These Soviet sons of bitches only—"

"Silence!" the guard shouted in English. His voice made him as threatening as someone aiming a pistol at them.

Hewitt looked at the guard again and spat on the ground. "Sorry . . . What I meant to say was, these kind hosts are treating me excellently," he blurted out with irony. "Listen carefully. I've asked to speak to the ambassador, with no success. They say the telephones don't work, but they've allowed me to give this letter to you. You have to get it to him."

He took a crumpled handwritten note from one of his pockets and handed it to Jack.

Jack took it and passed it to Elizabeth.

"Uncle Wilbur, Jack says they're accusing you of conspiracy, sabotage, embezzlement . . ."

"Yes, yes . . . and of killing my fellow Americans. Nothing would make these bastards happier," he said while the guard was speaking to a comrade. "I'm innocent! I swear to you that—"

"Mr. Hewitt," Jack cut in, "Sergei Loban says he has proof."

"Sergei's a compulsive liar who could have made anything up. Look, son—"

"I'm not your son, sir," Jack interrupted again. Elizabeth looked at him in surprise.

"Silence!" the guard yelled, having turned his attention back to them. "If prisoner continue to slander our leaders, visit will be canceled."

Despite Jack's repulsion at Hewitt's hypocrisy, he stood up to show the guard the order issued by Sergei authorizing a private conversation. The guard looked at him out of the corner of his eye as he read it.

"And I have order to oversee conversation," he replied, unimpressed.

Jack, after a moment's hesitation, nodded and returned to his seat.

"All right, Mr. Hewitt. It seems we can't stop this man from interrupting us every time he hears us criticize his superiors. However . . ."

"Yes?" the industrialist asked.

"However, there's no reason why we can't continue this conversation in German," Jack said in that language. "I doubt the guard will understand it. Don't waste any time, just answer my questions."

"Of course," Hewitt replied, also in German.

"Good. Why did you lie to me?"

"Me? I don't know what you're talking about. I haven't—"

"Mr. Hewitt, I don't have time to play games. Why did you tell me that McMillan had stayed in the United States?"

"Listen, boy. That has nothing to do with—"

"*Niet!*" yelled the guard. "Conversation is finished!"

"Not so fast!" Jack said, standing up. "The commissar himself, Comrade Sergei Loban, has stated that we can speak for ten minutes, ten, without specifying what language we communicate in, and you have made me waste two of those minutes. If you think you can prove that we're criticizing the regime during our conversation, then go ahead, interrupt it. But if you don't know German, I advise you to refrain or find someone who does understand it. Anything other than contravene an order from the head of the OGPU." Jack prayed that the Soviet custom of following any order received from a superior would work in his favor.

The guard reddened. Jack, seeing him hesitate, saved him the effort.

"Thank you," he said. "I won't mention to Comrade Loban that we wasted those two minutes." He quickly sat down again.

"Please, Jack! Can you explain to me why you're attacking my uncle?" asked Elizabeth.

"Mr. Hewitt, that guard's making a telephone call. In very little time, a Russian who understands German will appear through that door, and our chance will be gone, so listen: I know that McMillan entered the Soviet Union on December 26, 1932, one week before the SS *Cliffwood* arrived in Helsinki. Why did you lie to me?"

Hewitt bowed his head.

"Hewitt!" Jack insisted.

"It wasn't me, damn it! It was Sergei's idea." He paused, blowing out. "McMillan traveled on the SS *Leviathan* a week early to reach Russia before us. He had work to do in Moscow, but mysteriously vanished. When he didn't show up, Sergei suggested I hire you to replace him."

"But why did you deceive me? Why did you hide McMillan's disappearance from me?"

"That was Sergei's doing, too. That Russian's a wily old fox. He said to me that if I told you the truth, if I mentioned McMillan's mysterious disappearance, it would scare you off. He would never have allowed a stranger to prowl around his factory, and I had my hands tied." He fell silent for a moment. "Look . . . Do you remember when I introduced Sergei to you as a liaison officer on board the SS *Cliffwood*? Well, I lied. Sergei was never an official there to escort me. That was his cover during his journey to the United States; in reality, he belonged to the OGPU. He forced me to fool you for the same reason. So you'd take the job. That's why I told you at the Metropol that they'd just appointed him as head of the Avtozavod security."

This time it was Jack who was silent. For a moment he began to doubt who it was that was deceiving him. "Damn it! You lied to me! You haven't stopped lying to me since I met you!"

"For God's sake, Jack! What choice did I have? Everyone here does what the Soviets tell them to do. You, me, that guard, everyone! You have to believe me, Jack. You have to!"

Jack looked him in the eyes. The old industrialist was trembling, unable to hold his gaze. "Sure . . . And according to you, why do you think Sergei wanted to hire me?"

"How do I know? Sergei's paranoid. He sees enemies everywhere. In me, in the Americans, in the counterrevolutionaries . . . He might've thought I was responsible for the sabotage, or he might not, who knows? Perhaps he was looking for a replacement until McMillan appeared. Damn McMillan! I don't know what in hell's name could've happened to him."

"Well, it seems strange that you don't know, because Sergei assures me it was you who killed him."

"What? McMillan's dead?" he stammered.

"Come on, Hewitt. Don't pretend to be surprised."

"McMillan, dead . . . My God!" His monocle fell onto his chest.

"Enough! Nothing you say makes sense, much less the excuse that Sergei forced you to hire me. With McMillan dead, why would he want a replacement?"

343

"My God. McMillan dead . . . Now it makes sense."

"What does?" Jack stood up, exasperated.

"Everything, Jack. Why he hired you, why he didn't want me to tell you about McMillan's disappearance, your accident at the Avtozavod."

"Really? Tell me, in that case." He raised his voice.

Wilbur Hewitt pocketed his monocle and pulled at his hair. He was silent for a few seconds. Then he looked at Jack wide-eyed. He was about to reply, when an officer burst into the room, and with a great deal of bluster ordered the guard to stop the conversation immediately.

"Why did Sergei hire me? Why?" yelled Jack in German.

The newcomer grabbed Hewitt by an arm and made him stand. Then the industrialist came out of his daze and turned to Jack. "Don't you see? He didn't care what you'd find out. He hired you to use you. If McMillan's dead like you say . . . you were the bait to catch his murderer. You're his decoy."

Back in the city, Jack tried to calm Elizabeth down, promising her that her uncle would be safe until the trial.

"My suspicion is that they're trying to legitimize terminating the contract with Ford in order to save millions of dollars."

"And what can we do?"

"I don't know. If they have irrefutable proof, as Sergei says, I don't think we can do anything. If I were you, I'd travel to Moscow immediately to deliver your uncle's letter to the ambassador."

"And leave him here alone?"

"Look, Elizabeth. Stick by him, and all you'll do is put yourself in danger. Go to Moscow, let the embassy take care of this, and don't come back to Gorky until it's resolved."

"I'm not going to do that. I'm sure between us we can find a way to . . . What is it, Jack? Why are you lowering your head?"

Jack didn't respond. He took out a cigarette, lit it, and took a puff. He remained silent, but the young woman insisted.

"What is it? Are you not going to help me?"

"That's what I've been doing, isn't it?"

"Jack, I don't have anyone else! You know he's innocent, right?"

Jack took another puff. Then he stubbed out the cigarette and clenched his teeth. "I'm sorry, Elizabeth. You do what you have to do. I've already done everything I can."

Jack stacked the four frozen sacks of potatoes yet again, before accepting that repeating the same task over and over again wouldn't solve his problems. He looked at what remained of the stock on the shelves. In January, supplies had all but dried up, and the store survived only by selling the shoes that Jim Daniels, Joe Brown, and Miquel Agramunt made from scraps of leather and worn tires as he'd taught them to do. He cursed his bad luck. With Hewitt in prison and hunger taking hold, his future seemed bleak. It was only a matter of time before Sergei fired him.

He threw one of the sacks on the floor and sat on it while he wondered what action he should take. He was sorry for Elizabeth, but couldn't help feeling manipulated by one and all: Sergei, Hewitt . . . Even Elizabeth had come to him only when she'd needed someone. He didn't know what to do. If he tried to help Hewitt, Sergei would see it as an affront to the Soviet regime and take reprisals, but on the other hand, if he refused to meet Elizabeth's demands, sooner or later Hewitt would reveal his involvement in acquiring false passports and organizing their escape. As for Natasha, he knew only that he missed her.

He went outside to enjoy the peace and quiet of the open area at the entrance to the village. He wrapped himself in his coat, then filled his lungs in the hope that the icy wind would help clear his head. Though he longed to be with Natasha again, he'd decided to stop seeing her until the situation improved. He wasn't in the mood to share his worries with her, knowing that at any moment either Sergei or Elizabeth could come between them. He climbed into the Ford and turned the ignition. It sputtered like a sick man before his heart was resuscitated. He put it in gear, hit the gas, and made it slide over the ice in the direction of his house. For now, keeping Elizabeth happy would give him time to think, even if it meant being away from Natasha for a time.

He found the young American huddled in front of the fire in the living room. She looked as if she hadn't left the chair all day. Her face was stained with eye shadow, like dirty drips on a whitewashed wall. Jack placed a piece of newspaper containing a portion of black bread on her lap, and she gazed at it with about as much interest as if he'd laid a pebble there. Finally, she turned to look at him. Her moist eyes shimmered in the light from the flames. "What am I going to do, Jack?"

He didn't respond. He didn't even know how to deal with his own problems. He sat beside her, contemplating the fire that was turning the logs to ash, and he saw a metaphor for what the Soviet Union was doing to their lives.

"I thought I'd ask a friend to get the message to the embassy. He works for the OGPU, but he's American. I guess he'll know how to do it."

"What friend? The one you spoke to at the opening of the store?"

"Yeah. Walter."

"Good idea," she said without conviction.

Jack observed her. She looked like a broken toy. His watch showed 8:00 p.m. "Come on! Wash your face and wrap up warm. We'll make the most of the darkness and go take a look around your uncle's house. Maybe we can find something there that'll help us."

"The Soviets will have turned it upside down already."

"We have nothing to lose by trying." He helped her decide by taking her by the arm.

Fifteen minutes later, Jack stopped the car a block away from the mansion assigned to Hewitt. They covered the remaining distance on foot. After checking that nobody was watching the house, he wrapped himself in a sheet to camouflage himself in the snow, ran to the door, and signaled to Elizabeth to approach. The young woman rushed to join him, but slipped on the icy road and cried out when she hit the ground. A light came on in a nearby window. As quickly as he could, Jack swooped on Elizabeth to hide her.

"I'm sorry," she whispered, huddled under the sheet. "Have they seen us?"

"Shhh." He peered out from under the sheet to check. "They've turned off the light. Let's go!"

They ran to the threshold of the house. Jack warned Elizabeth to breathe lightly in case their breath gave away their presence.

"The key!"

She took it out, opened the door, and they went in. Feeling his way in the dark, Jack checked that all the shutters on the windows were shut. Even so, he drew all the curtains before turning on the flashlight.

"Jesus Christ!" she exclaimed.

Jack remained silent and continued to shine his light around the house. "The hyenas haven't even left the bones," he said.

The room looked more like a battlefield than a parlor. Moving the toppled chairs aside, Jack walked among sofas and armchairs that had been cut open. After inspecting one of the bedrooms upstairs, he decided that, had Hewitt hidden some valuable document, Sergei would now have it. He went back down to the ground floor to join Elizabeth again. "At least we've tried," he murmured, and turned off the flashlight.

"Wait! Shine it there." She held Jack's wrist to guide the beam of light into a corner, beside the fireplace.

"It's just a bunch of old newspapers."

"They're my uncle Wilbur's newspapers!" she said, as if Jack's comment were an insult.

"We have to go now."

"Let's take them. It will comfort my uncle to be able to read a paper the next time I visit him."

"Are you crazy? We'd need a wheelbarrow to carry that mountain. If you want, take a few and let's get out of here."

"We can do it. We'll put them on top of the sheet and drag them to the car."

Jack saw Elizabeth's face and knew she wouldn't give in. The last thing they needed was to have an argument in the house. He swore and pointed the light at the stack of newspapers again. There weren't as many as he'd thought. "All right. We'll take them."

Between the two of them, they made a bundle with the sheet and dragged it to the door. Jack opened it carefully. There was nobody outside. On his signal, they ran, crouching, pulling the bundle to the car. It started on the second attempt, and they drove home.

Jack rose early to take the tram that went up to the office that the OGPU had set up at the entrance to the kremlin where he had been informed Walter was now stationed. He found his friend in a temporary hut, wearing a brown uniform and buried under a pile of reports. He guessed Walter would be glad to take a break, but when Jack greeted him, his friend, far from seeming pleased, took off his spectacles and jumped up as if he'd seen the devil in the flesh. Without giving him time to speak, he grabbed Jack's arm and dragged him out of the hut, much to the surprise of the Soviet clerk who shared his desk.

"What possessed you to come here without warning?" he spat out when they were outside in a courtyard.

"Sorry. I didn't know I had to request an audience with a friend!"

Walter looked from side to side. "Don't get me wrong, Jack, but this isn't the Avtozavod. I'm sorry it's me who has to tell you this, but you're not exactly popular right now."

"What do you mean?"

"Your relationship with Hewitt. The OGPU think you might be connected to his counterrevolutionary activities."

"Well, fortunately, you're not like those OGPU guys, right?" Jack gave him a smile.

Walter maintained a circumspect expression. "Why are you here? I have a lot of work to do."

"It's about Hewitt. I went to visit him yesterday with his niece, and he asked us to get this letter to the new American ambassador."

"Put that away!" said Walter when he saw an officer approaching. "Come with me."

Walter led him through an endless dingy green corridor furnished with only a pair of wooden benches. He opened a rickety door and ushered Jack into an office. Once inside the little room, he adjusted his glasses and asked Jack for the letter.

"It doesn't say anything in particular," said Jack, trying to keep Walter on his side. "He just maintains his innocence and asks for a lawyer to be sent to represent him at his trial."

"Nothing in particular? Here he labels his accusers as schemers! And you want me to send this? You must be out of your mind!"

"That's precisely why I've brought it to you. If you think it's unwise, imagine what the OGPU would do with the letter."

"So why don't *you* send it?"

"You said it yourself. I'm not well regarded at the moment." He took it for granted that Walter would understand the dangers of his position.

"And all you can think of is to pass the risk on to me."

"No, Walter. I'm just asking you to help make sure a fellow American gets a fair trial."

"I don't understand your obsession with that man. Getting involved will only bring you problems, you can be sure of that."

"Look, if you don't want to do it for Hewitt, do it for Elizabeth. His niece is innocent in all of this."

"Oh really? Judging by her jewelry, I'd say she's profited very nicely indeed from everything her uncle has stolen."

"You should try to be more impartial. He hasn't been tried yet, and you're already sentencing him."

Walter exhaled dramatically. He read the message again and looked at Jack, who held his gaze. Finally, Walter pocketed the letter. "I can't promise anything. In the Soviet postal service, any suspicious letters are vetted. As soon as they see that it's addressed to the embassy, they'll intercept it, and if I send it to someone else to send on to the embassy, they'll open it as soon as it's delivered." He paused to think. "The only option would be to send it to Dmitri, my contact in Moscow, and ask him as a special favor to hand it personally to an American official coming out of the embassy."

"Thank you, Walter. I'm—"

"Don't thank me. But please, don't ask me for any more favors." Without giving him a chance to reply, he rushed off, leaving Jack standing alone in the little room.

33

The news of Hewitt's arrest spread like wildfire through the American village, causing fear that led to a slump in sales at the store. Jack couldn't have cared less about the company accounts. His only concern was to get his hands on the passports that Ivan Zarko had promised him, and though he'd paid in advance, there was a delay. According to Zarko, the OGPU had stepped up surveillance, and his supplier said he thought he was being watched. With no option but to wait, Jack passed the days with the same sense of unease that he'd felt in the *ispravdom*. He spent his time behind the counter in the store, studying the Soviet Penal Code that Sue had given him, cleaning and recleaning the ever-emptier shelves, and trying to find a way to prevent Natasha from turning up at his house without warning and discovering Wilbur Hewitt's niece sleeping under his roof.

"Why don't you want me to come? You used to invite me to your house every other minute, and now when I suggest it, you always say no," Natasha said after hearing yet another one of his excuses.

Jack took a deep breath. Until then he'd managed to avoid making her suspicious, saying that work was being done there and the house was a mess, but Natasha insisted that it didn't matter how it looked.

"It's chaos there at the moment. What's wrong with wanting you to be comfortable?" answered Jack.

"And this hovel's comfortable?" She waved her hand at the storeroom where Jack had set up the mattress they were lying on.

Jack raised his eyebrows and got up to poke the fire that was beginning to die down. It was true that the American store was anything but romantic. He tried to distract her with a kiss, but she moved her lips away.

"No, Jack. Last week you promised that we could go to your house this week, and . . ." She fell silent.

"And . . . ?"

Natasha burst into tears. Jack flushed red. It was the first time he'd seen her cry. He tried to console her, but Natasha moved away from him.

"No! I've wanted to believe it wasn't true, that it was just gossip, that I didn't care, I don't know . . ." A sob stifled her.

"I don't know what you're talking about, Natasha," Jack sputtered.

"You know perfectly well!" She stood up and began dressing. "I'm talking about that American whore! The one you're hiding in your house! The niece of that corrupt capitalist!"

"I'm not hiding any—"

"Oh no?" She picked up Jack's pants and threw them in his face. "Then let's go there now. Let's go there and see whether I'm right!"

Jack looked at her, incredulous. He sputtered again. "You don't understand . . . ," he finally managed to say.

"It's true, isn't it? You lousy bastard!" she sobbed.

"For heaven's sake! Don't be hysterical. Elizabeth is sleeping at my house, but not for the reason you think. I . . ." He held her to try to stop her from leaving.

"Let go of me! Ugh! I don't know what I saw in you that made me . . . What an idiot I've been!"

"Will you do me a favor, Natasha, and please calm down?" beseeched Jack. "I took Elizabeth in because she had nowhere to go.

They've arrested her uncle. She came to me, desperate, in the middle of the night, and I didn't have the heart to leave her on the street."

"And that's why you didn't tell me anything? That's why you lied, saying you were doing work on the house?"

"What the hell did you expect me to do? Tell you I'm protecting the niece of the man your father considers to be a counterrevolutionary criminal? I'll be damned! You're all crazy! Your father, you, Hewitt, Elizabeth . . . Tell me, what should I have done?"

"What you should have done is trust me! Why is that so difficult?" She freed her arm from his grip.

"Look who's talking! The perfect Soviet, lover of honesty, but capable of deceiving her own father to avoid the shame of admitting that she's sleeping with an American—"

A slap in the face cut him off. Jack fell silent. He'd never expected Natasha to react in this way.

"Get out of here!" he said.

Natasha didn't reply. She finished getting dressed, picked up her case, and left the warehouse, giving the door such a slam that every shelf shook.

While he waited for the passports that Zarko was going to supply, Jack spent the next few nights going over the documents he had found in McMillan's trunk.

There were reports on the most skilled workers, detailing their education, experience, and specializations. The list comprised the names of 150 American citizens, along with another twenty Russian nationals who'd received training in the United States. He studied the Americans' names one by one and compared them to his own reports. The list confirmed what he'd previously concluded: there was no link between the American workers and the sabotage. Though all the Soviet names were unknown to him, a little dot over one of them caught his attention. It was so tiny that he thought at first that it was a speck of dust, but when he tried to brush it away, he realized that it was a pencil mark. He read the marked name: Vladimir Mamayev. He hoped it would have some special significance, but without Sergei Loban's cooperation, it would be impossible to find out.

There were also accounting documents listing money transfers made by the Soviets that corresponded to shipments of machinery from Berlin and Dearborn. Only one entry drew his attention, a payment from a different source from the rest, which all seemed to come from a single organization.

He hid the documents and slumped onto the sofa.

Vladimir Mamayev.

Why had McMillan marked that name with an almost imperceptible dot? He might never know. At any rate, he didn't much care. According to Walter, Hewitt's trial would take place at the end of May, and by that time, Jack would have fled to England, the country he'd chosen as his next destination.

Elizabeth was little trouble. She stayed shut away in his room waiting for news, passing the time choosing issues of the old American newspapers for her uncle Wilbur to read. Until he fled, he would feign an interest in the industrialist's case and try to keep the earnings he'd saved up safe.

That night, he dreamed of Natasha. He woke in the early hours, longing for her. He regretted hiding Elizabeth's presence from her. He tried to sleep, but it was impossible.

The thunder of the engines of the vehicles speeding through central Gorky made Jack leap to the window. Elizabeth came down the stairs in her nightgown, looking shaken. They weren't the only ones unsettled. All the neighbors seemed to be doing the same thing.

"What's going on?" she asked. She observed the constant stream of trucks packed with soldiers. Jack had never seen so many armed men in one place.

"I don't know, but judging by the size of the entourage, nothing good. Get dressed and be ready! I'm going to the kremlin to speak to Walter."

Despite introducing himself as a friend of Walter Scott, he was stopped at the entrance to the OGPU offices, and he had to wait outside until he was able to persuade a soldier to take a message through. Before long, his friend appeared, looking concerned.

"What's happening, Walter? They're saying reinforcements have arrived to contain some riots, and everyone's running around like crazy."

"Sorry, Jack. We're very busy, and I can't see you now."

"And so am I. For God's sake! Is it so difficult just to tell me what's happening?"

Walter couldn't hold Jack's insistent gaze. "Look, I can't say much, but I'll tell you one thing." He lowered his voice so nobody would hear him. "Hewitt's trial's been brought forward, so I doubt the letter I sent to the embassy will be of any use."

"Brought forward? To when?" He thought of Elizabeth.

"I'm not sure. Tomorrow, or the next day."

"But you said it would be held in May."

"That was the plan. But that was before Stalin showed up out of the blue to find out in person what's happening with the sabotage incidents. You can't imagine the fear that man instills in people, Jack. Everyone in the office is running about like frightened rabbits."

"But you're the cops."

"Stalin doesn't spare anyone. Last time he was in Gorky, he ordered a hundred counterrevolutionaries to be shot, along with ten members of the OGPU who had been accused of counterrevolutionary tendencies by their own comrades. Look, they've given us a little reminder of it." From his jacket, he took a clipping displaying photographs of the executed policemen and showed it to Jack. "I guess there are black sheep in every flock."

After hearing the news, Jack tried unsuccessfully to see Sergei Loban. According to a subordinate, the head of the secret police was in a meeting with Stalin, and he would remain by his side for as long as the Father of Nations was in Gorky.

Jack went home to tell Elizabeth what he'd discovered. He found her behind the door, her breathing agitated and her face pale. When the young woman learned that, with the trial happening early, there would be no American lawyer coming to defend her uncle, her head dropped and she began to cry, as if she finally understood that nobody would be able to save Wilbur Hewitt from the firing squad.

"Don't worry. I'll speak to Natasha. Maybe she can get her father to see me," said Jack without thinking—he knew very well that nothing he could do would help Elizabeth's uncle.

He didn't dare leave her alone. He dug out the notes in English he'd made from the Soviet Penal Code and gave them to her, pointing out the paragraphs that might prove useful. She waved them away and started sobbing again.

"Read it," Jack insisted. "They'll probably call you to the witness stand. It might not get him released, but you could prevent yourself from being implicated."

Elizabeth didn't seem interested. "And you, what will you do?"

"I want to get to the store to stock up on food. I doubt the OGPU will go there, but given the situation, we can't be too careful. I also forgot to ask where the trial's taking place, so I'll take the opportunity to find out how the jury and the defense work. I'll come back as soon as I'm done. Until then, don't even think about opening the door to anybody."

The young woman nodded without much conviction.

Jack wrapped up and then headed to Ivan Zarko's house to ask him to hide the Ford Model A somewhere safe. He might need it at some point, but with the place teeming with police eager to make arrests, being an American driving in a private vehicle could only bring him trouble. "It's just until things calm down," he explained to Zarko.

The old man spat out a stream of abuse before agreeing to lock the car up in an abandoned repair shop, but he warned Jack that, if the OGPU found it, he would sooner tell them who its owner was than be interrogated. Jack didn't bother arguing. He nodded, said good-bye, and took a tram that was unusually packed with civilians all wearing their Sunday best.

At the Avtozavod, he couldn't find Walter, so he headed to the hospital entrance, where two policemen were asking everyone going in or out for identification. Jack let some people go in ahead of him while he deliberated how best to avoid unwelcome questions. He was aware that if he asked outright for Dr. Lobanova, he risked being fobbed off or having Natasha herself refuse to see him. When he saw a little group of people waiting to visit their sick family members, he decided to ask one of the last in line for help, feigning his old limp. "Cigarette?" Jack said, offering one to the well-built man who'd agreed to let Jack lean on his shoulder to take the weight off his painful leg. "This damned cold cuts my hip like a knife!"

The stranger celebrated the offer of a cigarette as if he'd just struck gold, and thrust the *papirosa* into the gap between his teeth. Jack held on to the man as if he really needed the support, and limped forward toward the policemen, striking up a conversation with such familiarity that anyone seeing them would have sworn that they were close relatives or old friends. Once in front of the police officers, they both showed their papers. The well-built man was visiting his son and was allowed straight through. However, hearing Jack's foreign accent, one of the guards ordered him to stop.

"American?" he asked, reading his name on the old prescription that Jack had offered as proof.

"By birth, unfortunately," Jack replied in perfect Russian. "Luckily, I was able to return to the motherland."

"This is just a prescription," said the Soviet guard. His eyes remained hidden in the shadow of his visor.

"Yes. I forgot to bring my pass. With this limp . . ." He felt the man he was resting on trying to set off into the hospital, and he held him to make him wait.

"Well, I'm sorry, but your name isn't on the patient list," the young man said.

"Listen, I'm freezing to death, and I can barely walk. The truth is I was supposed to come next week, but the pain . . ."

"Like I said, you're not on the list. You'll have to come back another day."

The well-built man attempted to go in again, but Jack held him more firmly than any recovering patient would. "Wait a minute!" Jack said to the man, before turning back to the guard. "Look, perhaps you haven't read the letterhead on the prescription properly, but Natasha Lobanova isn't just the director of this hospital; she's also the daughter of Sergei Loban, the highest authority in the OGPU for sixty miles around. And I can assure you that if you don't let me in, Dr. Lobanova will be more than happy to recommend to her father that you patrol those sixty miles day and night."

The young guard lost his confidence and looked to his comrade for help. Not finding any, he turned back to Jack. "All right. But hurry up," he said, then snatched the document from the next person in line.

As soon as the guards were out of sight, Jack parted company with his sturdy new friend and headed down the corridor that led to Dr. Lobanova's office. He was about to go in without knocking, when he heard someone arguing bitterly inside. He recognized Natasha's voice, its tone rising in response to the angry words of the other speaker. He waited outside, unable to make out what the dispute was about, until a crash of glass shattering into a thousand pieces made his heart thump. He heard the latch on the door moving, and he quickly hid behind a nearby screen. Through a gap, he saw a uniformed officer come out of the office. He tried to see the face, but the man had his back to him. At that moment, someone tapped Jack on the shoulder, making him spin around. He found himself face-to-face with an elderly woman in need of directions to the rehabilitation room. He gestured in its direction and turned back to the crack in the screen. The officer, with a fist in the air, seemed to be threatening Natasha. Jack couldn't believe what he was seeing. It was Viktor Smirnov, rage contorting his face.

He waited behind the screen until he was certain that Viktor wouldn't return. Then he came out from his hiding place and walked into Natasha's office without knocking. He found her squatting on the floor, picking up the remains of several flasks and test tubes.

"I told you to get out!" Natasha yelled, before realizing who it was. Recognizing Jack, she tried to compose herself. "Oh! What're you doing here?"

"I'm sorry to show up unannounced. What happened?"

"Huh? Oh . . . nothing. I bumped into the sample trolley. Why are you here?" She finished cleaning up, sat herself in an armchair, and tried to act normal.

Jack felt hurt that she was lying to him. He sat opposite her, pondering whether to ask her what really happened, but he decided to be prudent. "I wanted to see you." He'd promised himself he wouldn't talk about his feelings, but he found it impossible. "How are you?"

"Busy, like everyone in the Avtozavod."

"Yes. I heard about Stalin's arrival, but I mean, apart from the disruption, how are you doing?"

"In relation to us?" She took out a cigarette and lit it. Jack was surprised—Natasha smoked only when she was under a lot of stress.

"Yes, us."

"Well, to be honest, Jack, not great." She took a puff that consumed half her *papirosa*. "But with all these sick people around me, wasting my strength worrying about my own unhappiness is a luxury I can't afford." After a long pause, she said, "And you?" She drummed her fingers on the chair's arm.

"The same, I guess. I miss you." He hadn't realized how unhappy he'd been until the moment he saw her again.

"You'll get used to it. I have. I have my work, and you have your girlfriend."

"Please, Natasha! Let's put that behind us. I told you Elizabeth had nowhere to go. As soon as this business with her uncle's been resolved, she'll go back to him."

"And then I'll go back to you?"

"Look, this is a stupid argument. What is it you think I should do? Tell me! I'll follow your advice to the letter."

Natasha was silent. She took a draw that finished off the cigarette, and got up to consult some X-rays hung on an illuminator. "Anything else? I have a lot of work to do," she said to end the conversation.

Jack also stood up. "Now that you mention it, I need you to tell me about the usual procedure for counterrevolutionary trials—time frames, defense, appeals . . ."

"Why? Are you afraid you'll be arrested?"

"It's not for me. It's for Wilbur Hewitt. A friend's told me his hearing will be very soon."

"Sorry, Jack, but I don't know anything about it."

"You haven't spoken to your father? Hewitt's trial is all anyone is talking about."

"No, I haven't. And I couldn't care less about that American's court case. I have enough to worry about with my patients."

"Do you know who could give me some information? Please . . ."

"Tell me one thing, Jack. Why should I help that American?"

"All I can think of to say is because it's me asking you." His voice trembled slightly.

Natasha looked at him. She approached in silence and kissed him lightly on the lips, in a way that seemed to Jack as if she were saying good-bye forever. Then she wrote the name and address of a party lawyer on a piece of paper, handed it to him, and with tear-filled eyes, asked him to leave her office.

When he was outside, he wondered why Viktor Smirnov had threatened Natasha and why she had concealed it from him.

34

Jack didn't know whether to hide the store's stock or take it to his house. In the end, he did neither. He took the essentials, left some provisions on the shelves, and shared the rest with Joe Brown, Miquel, and the Daniels family, advising them that, to keep up appearances, they should continue to come to the store even if it was almost empty.

One week. That was the time that the lawyer Natasha had recommended had estimated the trial would last. According to the attorney, it couldn't go on much longer because Stalin had to return to Moscow for affairs of the state.

The lawyer also warned him of the particular circumstances that could work against Wilbur Hewitt. "Usually, common criminals are tried by a committee of citizens made up of twelve people elected in a public assembly, but counterrevolutionary cases are settled behind closed doors by the local OGPU branch. However, with such a high-profile defendant, I imagine Stalin himself will preside over the trial and open the hearing to the public to make an example of him."

Jack explained this to Elizabeth.

"A public defender belonging to the party? Would anyone in their right mind think that a paid-up Communist will take the side of an American against Stalin and half the Supreme Soviet?"

Jack shrugged. It was what he had been trying to make her understand all along. "The other possibility is for Wilbur to turn down his public defender and choose someone he considers more appropriate. Problem is, I doubt anyone will be prepared to take that risk."

"Then we'll do it!"

"What?"

"You and I. We'll defend him! Let's do it ourselves!"

Jack slowly shook his head. Elizabeth was clearly out of her mind. "Are you serious? You'd be signing his death sentence, and ours. We don't know—"

"You just said nobody will want to defend him. You've studied the Penal Code. We'll pay that lawyer to advise us in secret. With the six thousand dollars my uncle gave you, we could—"

"I don't think it's a good idea. Anyway, that money was for our passports."

"Who cares about the passports? We haven't seen them, and we don't need them for the time being."

"Elizabeth, we don't have that money anymore. I paid in advance. I can't go to my supplier now and demand he return what he'll already have shared out. And that lawyer you mention helped me because Natasha asked him to. For no other reason. He wouldn't agree to advise us for all the gold in the world. Don't you see? Whoever does it will be a marked man."

"Give me his name."

"Who?"

"Your supplier. I'll speak to him. Or I'll speak to your friend Walter. Damn it, Jack, I swear to you that if I have to move heaven and earth, I'll get that money back!"

Jack clenched his fists. He could see that, if he didn't help Elizabeth, she'd end up dragging everyone down with her. The problem was that he had no idea how to defend a man who deep down he believed was guilty. He sighed loudly before asking her to bring him the Penal Code that he'd left upstairs. By the time Elizabeth returned, Jack had brought McMillan's documents out from their hiding place. He looked at her imploring, hopeful face. "I'm not promising anything," he said.

"Well, I am promising *you* something. If you help me save my uncle, I'll give you whatever you want. Do you understand? Whatever you want."

Neither Elizabeth's pleading nor her tears affected the policeman on guard at the OGPU offices. The man, who looked like a woodcutter wearing a faded uniform, told her that he wouldn't disturb Sergei Loban by order of the devil himself, but when the policeman stuffed an envelope containing five hundred rubles that Jack had dropped on the ground into his jacket, he knew there wouldn't be a problem. The man telephoned his superior and passed on Elizabeth's request. After a brief conversation, he hung up.

"You'll have to wait for Comrade Loban to finish some business," was all he said.

Jack and Elizabeth waited, each deep in thought. After several long minutes, the telephone rang. The policeman took the call. Then he turned to them.

"Comrade Loban authorizes Wilbur Hewitt's niece to defend her uncle and Jack Beilis to act as interpreter. He asked me to inform you that the trial will begin this afternoon, at three o'clock at the Soviet Palace of Justice in Gorky." He cleared his throat. "If you wish, I will notify the *ispravdom* so that you can visit the prisoner before appearing before the commission." Without waiting for an answer, he patted the jacket pocket where he'd stashed the envelope of money.

There was no need for further explanation. Jack took another five hundred rubles from his wallet and handed them to him.

35

At half past two, a pair of guards opened the courtroom at the Palace of Justice. Jack and Elizabeth had to wait for the Soviet delegation to take their seats. Sergei Loban, the head of the OGPU, would lead the prosecution. He was followed by a large group of senior figures in the secret police from Moscow, representatives of the Komsomol, and the lucky trade unionists and local party members who had received clearance to share the stage with the Supreme Soviet Leader, Joseph Stalin. Among them, Jack caught a glimpse of Viktor Smirnov. Once they had seated themselves on the rows of chairs that seemed to have been arranged for the occasion, an OGPU officer showed Elizabeth and Jack to a table positioned to the right of the dais, directly opposite Sergei Loban.

From his seat, Jack observed the sobriety of the courtroom, its only adornment a gigantic portrait of Stalin on the wall behind the dais. The executive body, made up of a large contingent of OGPU commissars and members of the Communist Party Committee, sat on two banks of chairs arranged on either side of an empty central seat that he assumed Stalin would occupy. Jack searched for Natasha's face, hoping to see her in the audience, but the only person he recognized was Walter, who was seated at the back of the room.

Moments later, a Red Army soldier led the American business-man to a chair midway between the defense's and the prosecution's tables. Jack gestured to Hewitt, whom he had managed to speak to briefly before they moved him from the *ispravdom*. However, the lack of time had prevented him from finding a Soviet lawyer to advise them on their defense. Last, an official in uniform approached the dais and announced the arrival of Joseph Stalin. He was received with deafening applause.

Jack could not help but feel awestruck in the presence of the man who, as everyone he knew kept saying, would burn his own family alive to further the revolution. He wore a brown military jacket with red epaulettes, and his decisive manner seemed only to confirm that anyone who did not fear him was either crazy or foolhardy. When the applause subsided, the official introduced the remaining members of the jury, but Joseph Stalin interrupted him and motioned with his hand for Sergei Loban to read out the charges being brought against the prisoner.

Sergei stood, thanked Stalin, and addressed the room. "Comrade Stalin . . ." Another long round of applause interrupted the beginning of his speech. "Comrade Stalin . . . comrades of the Joint State Political Directorate, Soviet commissars, representatives of the Komsomol, distinguished members of the OGPU, people's counsels . . ." More applause. "Before beginning my address, I must inform you that the accused, an American national, Wilbur Hewitt, has, voluntarily and in writing, relinquished his right to be tried in his own language. He has also rejected the public defender who was assigned to him, and desig-nated as his defender his niece, Elizabeth Hewitt, who will defend her uncle with the assistance of Jack Beilis in the capacity of interpreter. I state for the record that, in this trial, charges are being brought against the industrialist Wilbur Hewitt only, and therefore any other culpability that may derive from the case is excluded."

Hearing him, Jack let out a curse. His main line of defense was going to center on showing that the upper management of the Avtozavod had plotted to annul the agreement entered into with Henry Ford, waive the millions of dollars owed, and avoid a penalty.

While Sergei listed the crimes that Hewitt was to be tried for, Jack went over his notes in search of a new strategy.

"As everyone in this courtroom knows," Sergei went on, "the vital work that the state police carries out includes pursuing, detaining, trying, and sentencing all anti-Soviet elements that threaten the rule of the proletariat. However, considering the special nature of this case, its potential international repercussions, and above all, the presence of our leader, Comrade and General Secretary Joseph Stalin, it has been decided that the proceedings will be brought publicly." He paused to receive Stalin's assent. "Notwithstanding, since his crimes are so numerous and the damage caused so extensive, this does not prevent the prisoner from being accused of counterrevolutionary scheming, for which the penalty is immediate execution."

Jack understood that after such a description, Stalin would never allow the sentence to be reduced. He cleared his throat and signaled to Elizabeth to set out the arguments for her defense. The young woman followed the instructions they had agreed on and stood so that everyone could see her contrite face, without a trace of makeup, and with her hair gathered up in a Soviet-style bun.

"Dear sirs. Mr. General Secretary . . ." As she'd agreed with Jack, the young woman paused for dramatic effect. Stalin was unmoved. "I . . . I'm not able to express myself as eloquently as you." Jack translated each sentence, leaving enough time for the men and women who packed the courtroom to notice Elizabeth's fragility. "My uncle, Mr. Hewitt, came to the Soviet Union in the hope of doing his job well. Perhaps it wasn't to help you, or help your revolution—that I don't know. But I can assure you that he was prepared to sweat blood to make this factory the pride of the Soviet Union." She looked at Jack for his approval. "I don't know anything about your laws, but Jack Beilis has studied them, and he tells me that, unlike other legal systems, in this country what is truly important, beyond what the laws say, is that truth prevail." She waited for Jack to interpret her words. "As my uncle Wilbur wishes, I've asked Mr. Beilis to argue his defense without needing to translate every word of mine. However, please consider anything that he says to have come from my mouth. That's all. Thank you for your attention . . . Thank you," she said, her voice trembling.

Stalin accepted the request without a hint of mercy, leafed through the report that one of his aides had just handed to him, and ordered the first witness to be called. It was a Soviet worker who testified that he had suffered the consequences of the sabotage firsthand. When Sergei asked him to show those present the stump that he had in place of an arm, a murmur rippled through the room.

The one-armed witness was followed by sixteen more testimonials from injured workers with similar stories. Jack knew that their statements bore no incriminatory weight against Hewitt, but Sergei was cultivating a feeling of hostility that would soon color the atmosphere of the proceedings if he didn't act quickly to counteract it. When the last witness had finished, he asked to speak, but Sergei interrupted him, requesting an adjournment due to the late hour.

"Permission granted," Stalin hastily replied. "The proceedings will continue tomorrow morning at ten o'clock."

As they left the room, Jack turned to Elizabeth with irritation. "Damned Russian! That bastard drew the testimonies out so that we wouldn't have time for rebuttal, and Stalin consented to it."

"But you can give your evidence tomorrow."

"Yeah. After they've brooded all night over how your uncle Wilbur is a serial mutilator."

Once they were outside the kremlin, Jack asked Elizabeth to go home by herself. He needed to see the legal expert whom Ivan Zarko had recommended, and whom he was required to see alone.

It took an hour to find the apartment building, which was in a state of semicollapse, near Monastyrka, in the south of the city. When he found that the address was a doorless room that a leper wouldn't live in, he thought he'd made a mistake, but a rich voice coming from a shape wrapped in blankets told him to come in.

"Are you the American?" it asked.

Jack saw something resembling the body of an old man emerge from under the blankets. It stank of urine and alcohol. Jack nodded. When the man invited him to sit on a pile of old rags, he declined.

"Have you come alone?"

"Yes. Are you Valeri Pushkin?"

"Silence!" he yelled. "Nobody told you to say my name."

For a moment Jack thought Ivan Zarko had got it wrong. He took out the note to recheck the address, but the old man snatched the piece of paper from his hand.

"Yes, that's me. What did you expect? A slick-haired shyster?" He took off the woolen hat that came down to his eyebrows and revealed a scar-covered face. "Ivan Zarko sent me a message saying you'd pay for my advice."

"Yes, that's right, but . . ." Jack fell silent. He doubted this angry old man could defend himself, let alone Wilbur Hewitt.

"Good. Did he say how much?"

"No."

"A thousand rubles. A thousand rubles and a bottle of vodka. The good stuff, not that crap they sell on the highways." He kicked an empty bottle, which rolled until it stopped near another dozen empties.

"Here." Jack took out a thousand rubles. "And another hundred for the vodka," he said. It was his only option.

"Perfect." The old man stuffed them into his pocket and smiled. "So . . . Zarko filled me in." He searched among the trash for a little vodka in one of the empty bottles. "That American's on trial, and you want to defend him so you can fuck his little niece, am I right?" He found some dregs of vodka and knocked them back.

"No, it's not that." Jack wondered whether he should waste another second with this disfigured old man.

"Well, it makes no difference to the case." He tilted the bottle again in the hope that he could drain a last drop from it. "You want to defend an American who's already been condemned." He laughed like a lunatic. "Tell me one thing, boy, and think carefully before you answer, because your future might depend on it: What exactly is it that you want?"

"I don't understand."

"Americans!" He shook his head with disapproval. "You're lucky it was old Zarko who recommended you. Look, kid, whatever your aim is, you have two options, the second less promising than the first. If you manage to persuade them to declare him innocent, you'll be hated by the entire OGPU. They might leave you be for a while, but as soon as the case is forgotten, they'll come after you. Those people don't forgive a defeat, I can promise you that."

"And if they convict him?"

"If they convict him, they'll execute him by firing squad, and shoot you."

"What do you mean?" Jack wobbled.

"That unless you leave the country, sooner or later you'll meet the same fate. Defending a guilty man before Stalin is not, shall we say, well regarded."

"Look, I'm not sure why I'm wasting my time listening to you, but—"

"Silence!" the old man bellowed. "I haven't finished. Old Zarko asked me to help you, and that's what I'm going to do, so listen closely because there are things you must know if you're to have any chance against those cretins. I know what you're thinking . . . that there's no way a dirty old drunk like me is going to help you, but in my day, I was one of the most successful lawyers in Saint Petersburg. A sad business, but that's another story. Do you have any reports? Any documents that might help us?"

Jack considered telling him about McMillan's papers, but prudence decided him against it. However, he promised that he would provide anything that the old man needed.

"Good. Well, until then, what you have to do is delay the verdict for as long as possible. The secret police will want to close the case while Stalin's here and notch a victory, but Stalin won't stay in Gorky for long. That man's a demon, I can tell you. He appears in the middle of the night, goes for his enemy's throat, and then returns to his lair in Moscow to continue his plotting. If you want to find him, all you have to do is follow the trail of corpses he leaves behind." He coughed. "To slow the proceedings down, ask for witnesses that are difficult to find, cross-examine witnesses that have already been questioned, ask for written evidence, complain, protest, shield yourself behind legal language, whatever you can think of. Just make sure that Stalin has to leave the city before the verdict, or you'll watch your friend Wilbur be shot to pieces, and the same thing will happen to you."

Suddenly, as if by magic, Jack's opinion of the drunk had completely changed. "All right. Anything else?"

"Yes. The Communists are masters of propaganda. *Pravda, Izvestia,* Radio Moscow, pamphlets, posters, rallies, union meetings . . . If they used their skills to sell by mail order, they'd be the best businesspeople on earth. And if you want the slightest chance of winning, you should do the same."

"Me? How? Stick posters up on the walls of the kremlin?"

"Drop the sarcasm," the old man spat out. "A Soviet trial's unlike any you've ever seen. Forget laws and evidence, because they won't help you. They'll do whatever they want, however they want. Try contacting your fellow countrymen in Moscow. Maybe that will help."

"It was the first thing I did. I sent a message to the American embassy, to—"

"By Lenin's whiskers! Who said anything about an embassy? They've only just opened it; the diplomats won't move a finger because they won't want to upset Stalin. Call the journalists. Those people are made of sterner stuff. Get the American journalists posted to Moscow interested in the case. Only if they report it in the United States will the embassy even consider stepping in."

Jack was left openmouthed. He couldn't understand how a man with so much common sense could be living like a beggar. He guessed the vodka had been responsible for his decline, and the fact that he'd run out, the reason for his temporary lucidity. He remembered his father's last days, and what alcohol had done to him.

He didn't know how to put into practice the old man's advice. He was trying to explain the difficulties, when he suddenly remembered the little man with the bow tie. "Hang on! Maybe there is one possibility. I met a Louis Thomson on the ship that took us to Helsinki, and again later, in Russia. I know he works for the *New York Times* in Moscow, but I wouldn't know how to locate him. Perhaps you could help me."

"Sorry, kid. If the OGPU found out I was back to my old ways"— he pointed at the scars on his face—"what they did to me then would be child's play compared to what they'd do now."

Jack took out another five hundred rubles and showed them to the man. The lawyer licked his lips when he saw them. When he finally agreed to help, Jack knew they would be the best five hundred rubles he'd spent since he arrived at the Avtozavod.

Back home, while they ate dinner, Jack agreed to a new strategy with Elizabeth. When she went to bed, he remained awake, thinking of Natasha, longing for her touch, cursing himself for falling in love with the daughter of his enemy.

36

The second session began with the same protocol as the day before. Jack waited impassively for the parade of officials, the salutes, and the applause for the Supreme Leader, followed by the ominous silence that spread through the room when Stalin ordered the resumption of the trial. Beside him, Elizabeth's chair remained empty. When Sergei asked for her whereabouts, Jack took the opportunity to ask for an adjournment.

"Honorable representatives of the Soviet people, I regret to have to inform you that Miss Elizabeth Hewitt has suddenly fallen ill, seized by an attack of hysteria caused by the unexpected arrest of her uncle and the ordeal of the trial. She is prostrated in bed today and unable to speak, so she has requested the adjournment of these proceedings until she has fully recovered."

Sergei seemed unmoved. He smoothed his graying, perfectly trimmed beard, and looked at Stalin, who shook his head.

"Mr. Beilis, I understand your reasons for making such a request, but the events are of such gravity that any delay to their resolution would not be tolerated by the Soviet people."

"Mr. Loban, I'll remind you that your country's Penal Code lays down the principle of the right to a fair trial."

"And I will remind you that the principle of a defendant's right to a fair trial is subject to, and subordinate to, the principle of national security."

"You mean then that the session should continue even though Wilbur Hewitt has no defense?" Jack hoped his presumption would make Sergei reflect. However, it was Joseph Stalin who stood up from his chair, his face red with rage.

"Mr. Beilis!" he bellowed. "Perhaps you are accustomed to the American legal system, in which individuals' rights are respected above all else, but now you are in the great nation of the Soviet Union. Here, the collective prevails over the individual, social interests over private ones, national law over the abominable ambitions of the counterrevolutionaries. Yesterday, Miss Hewitt stated that she had agreed to defend her uncle alongside you, and that you would be the one to make her arguments without needing to consult her directly. I find no reason why this should not continue to be the case now. Moreover, I warn you that I will interpret any time-wasting tactics as an affront to the interests of the state, and if you persist with them, I will have you arrested."

Jack looked at Wilbur Hewitt sitting in his chair, oblivious to the threats that Stalin had just made. Everything was becoming increasingly complicated. He supposed that his only chance was to discredit Sergei. He organized his papers and turned to the Russian. "Mr. Loban, Wilbur Hewitt is an American citizen. The principle of extraterritoriality guarantees that certain citizens are tried in their own country, even if the crime they are accused of has been committed on Soviet soil. Wilbur Hewitt—"

"Mr. Beilis! Wilbur Hewitt is no diplomat, so the principle you mention is inapplicable. Article Four of our Penal Code is crystal clear about the scope of our jurisdiction."

"It's true, he's not a diplomat, but since the commercial relationship between the Ford Motor Company and the Soviet Union predates any diplomatic relations between our countries, and given his position and the type of professional and commercial relationship that he has been engaged in, Wilbur Hewitt's status is comparable, under the principle of analogy, to that of a bona fide diplomat, with all the considerations due to it."

Sergei smiled. "Forgive me if I laugh at your ignorance. The principle of analogy is not applicable here because it refers to the crime and not the jurisdiction. Perhaps you should stop making incoherent requests and start defending your client, or we will be obliged to end your involvement."

Jack sighed. He took out a cigarette and lit it. He looked at his notes, filled with stupid ideas. He didn't even know what he was doing, trying to defend the same man who had lied to him when he'd hired him. He remembered the advice of the drunken lawyer, and addressed the jury. "Very well. I call Stanislav Prior to the witness stand."

Hearing the name, Wilbur Hewitt could not prevent a look of astonishment. Stanislav Prior was the mutilated witness who had begun the round of testimony the day before. Jack gestured to him to relax.

Once he was in the witness box, Jack made Stanislav Prior recount in minute detail every event that led up to his accident. It took fifteen minutes. When the testimony was over, Sergei stepped in.

"Don't make us waste time with statements we've already heard. If you want to review them, request the court records," he warned him.

"Mr. Loban, I need the jury to keep fresh in their minds all of the details of your relationship with the accused." Without giving him a second to respond, he turned to Prior again. "You say that the press that mutilated you, an American model acquired by the Avtozavod from the Ford Motor Company, unexpectedly discharged a stroke, cutting off your right arm. Is that right?"

"I just said it," the man answered.

"According to Mr. Loban, the machine was part of a batch that initially should have been supplied from Dearborn, but that was ultimately replaced by a batch from the dismantled Ford factory in Berlin. He attributes the fault that caused your terrible accident to the deterioration of the machine. Tell me, were you aware that this replacement was carried out to save costs with the agreement of the Avtozavod's Soviet directors?"

"No. I just operate the machinery. Well, not anymore . . ." He showed Jack the end of his stump.

"I see. And tell me, the press that cut off your arm, does it not have a safety mechanism that obliges the user to simultaneously activate two buttons, set at a distance from each other, so that when the stroke is discharged, both hands are clear of the impact zone?"

"Yes, that's right."

"So, how is it possible that it trapped you?"

"Like I said, the machine failed."

"Yes. But what was it that failed? I know that press, and if the safety procedure is followed, it's impossible for such an accident to happen. Both buttons must be pressed—"

"No, sir."

"What do you mean? I can assure you, that press—"

"That machine had two buttons, at first. Later, it just had one."

"A single button? I don't understand. Allow me to consult my notes . . . According to the report provided to me by the prosecution, it was a Cleveland Z25."

"I don't know. I don't know anything about the model."

"But did you write this damage report?" He took it to the man so that he could read it. Jack had found it among the documents that he'd compiled during his inspections as a supervisor.

"I can't remember."

"Here it says *Stanislav Prior*. My knowledge of Cyrillic script is limited, but *Prior* can be read very clearly. In this report, you informed your superiors that the safety mechanism had broken, on a date prior to your accident. A week before, if I'm not mistaken."

The one-armed operative looked to Sergei for help, but Jack instructed him to respond.

"Yes. But the machine was repaired," the operative said.

"Ah! Excellent. And what did the repair consist of?"

The man looked at Sergei again.

"Please, answer the question," Jack insisted.

The operative cleared his throat. "The broken button was bridged to remove its function, so the press worked with a single button."

"And why was the old one not replaced with a new one?"

"Because there were no spare parts."

"Oh! And do you know who was responsible for supplying the spare parts?"

"No. I don't know." His face turned pale.

"Mr. Loban." Jack turned to the Avtozavod's head of security. "Do you know who was responsible for supplying spares? Do you know whether it was Mr. Wilbur Hewitt?"

Sergei reddened. He eyed Jack with contempt.

"It fell to a Soviet employee who has already been purged. But if that's the entirety of your argument, I advise you to explore other avenues. This is just one of many witnesses who have testified to the poor condition of the machinery supplied by Wilbur Hewitt."

"I understand, but if the button had been replaced, none of this would have happened."

Sergei considered his response carefully before replying. He looked at Jack challengingly and pointed at the accused. "And if instead of enriching himself, Wilbur Hewitt had supplied equipment fit for use, that button would never have broken, and today Stanislav Prior would be able to hold his child in both arms," roared Sergei to thunderous applause.

Knowing the risk to his own safety that he was taking, over the course of the morning Jack tried to draw out his strategy for as long as possible, but when he called the fourth witness, Sergei exploded.

"That's enough! I ask our great Supreme Leader to put a stop to any further statement that, rather than provide new information, merely slows the progress of the trial."

"Esteemed representatives of the Soviet people," Jack countered, "yesterday, nothing stopped Mr. Loban from boring us with testimonies that only demonstrated the occurrence of a series of unfortunate accidents, without at any time proving any connection between those accidents and the accused. This is what I intend to illustrate, and therefore I request—"

"Mr. Beilis!" The courtroom fell silent when Stalin himself stubbed out his cigar and stood. "I do not have all day to listen to testimonies that are already transcribed in the records, so end your turn or I will order your silence by other means."

Jack could see that if he pushed it too far, Stalin would end the proceedings. However, he had no choice but to continue. The suspicions of the drunken lawyer had been right. If they were allowing him to defend Wilbur Hewitt, it was only because Stalin wanted to legitimize this farce of a trial. But, as soon as it was over, they would do away with him. He set aside his witness list and tried to apologize. "Mr. General Secretary, I can assure you that my only interest is to defend the truth, unlike Mr. Loban, who seems intent on laying the blame on Wilbur Hewitt, without providing even a shred of evidence to support his serious accusations. Broken machines cause accidents, interruptions, or failures in production. But these machines are broken"—he brandished his reports—"not because of some nefarious actions on the part of the accused; rather, the cause was an inexcusable lack of maintenance, negligent handling, or total ignorance of the safety warnings, the responsibility for which, under the agreement, falls to the Avtozavod itself."

He took a volume from his case and turned to Sergei. "You accuse Mr. Wilbur Hewitt of counterrevolutionary actions, of fraudulent enrichment, and even of deliberately injuring workers he has never seen. Well, are you familiar with this manual?" He showed him the volume with a brown cover, the title in English reading *Maintenance and Safety Procedure for Employees of the Ford Company Factories.*

"Of course."

"Of course. And you know it, because Wilbur Hewitt handed it to the factory's Soviet directors in person, am I right?"

"Yes, that's right."

"Good. Where is its translation?"

"Pardon?"

"Where is its translation into Russian? This is an original copy, in English, and I don't think the Avtozavod's operatives are capable of reading it."

"There were problems understanding certain terms. But the translation is under way." He cleared his throat. "At any rate, its contents do not alter the crimes Mr. Hewitt is charged with."

"They don't? All right. Do you know what this is?" He took another similar volume from his case, this time with a green cover. "It is the *Verordnung über Wartung und Sicherheitsmassnahmen für die Arbeiter in den Ford-Fabriken*, the translation of the same manual into German, which the German government made available to all of its workers in May 1928, three months before production of the Ford A began in Berlin."

"That's irrelevant."

"Irrelevant? Do you consider it irrelevant that the Germans' adherence to the maintenance schedule and the rest of the safety measures outlined in this manual meant that, in the four years during which production was maintained in Berlin, there were only three serious accidents, almost the same number of incidents that take place here each week? Do you consider it irrelevant that those accidents could have been avoided?"

Sergei frowned, but more out of surprise than concern. "Are you accusing us of something, Mr. Beilis?"

"I merely asked a question. If there is anything that might accuse you, it will be your answer."

"Comrade Loban." The commissar responsible for administrating the sessions stepped in. "Do you wish to take a break from the proceedings? Perhaps you should consult—"

"Sergei does not need to consult anything!" Stalin broke in. "Arrogant Americans!" he growled. "Very well, Mr. Beilis, since you insist, I will answer your question." He raised his voice, and the courtroom fell silent. "The Soviet Union has built an immense factory from scratch. We have invested vast sums of money to transform a frozen wasteland into a technological center that will power the proletarian awakening. We have taken thousands of peasant farmers from their barren fields, their poverty, and their dismal future, and brought them here, to a place where they can shape their own future. Where before there was despair, exploitation, and death, now there are cities, factories, wages, hospitals, schools . . . All of this requires sacrifice. And now you, an immigrant who left his country because it was dying of hunger; you, an immigrant whom our government welcomed with open arms; you, who were given work and a home for the simple reason that you needed it, dare to question our methods?"

Jack swallowed. Stalin was making the dispute personal. Making Jack seem like an enemy to Communism's achievements. If he didn't counter it, the rest of his defense would have as much weight as a speck of dust in the wind. "In that case, I suppose all these mutilations were among the sacrifices that were expected," said Jack.

Stalin gave him a murderous look. The young American was proving to be a skilled adversary.

"Mr. Beilis . . . Your arguments are pathetic. You compare Germany with the Soviet Union, invoking their translation of a manual and their observance of the maintenance schedules. However, you go to great pains to conceal the other facts."

"Which facts?"

"The ones that make your defense a fallacy. You avoid mentioning the differences between the Gorky and Berlin factories, but I know them well, because I signed every last contract myself. You forget to point out that the Ford A manufactured in Berlin was not the first vehicle that Ford had produced in Germany. You forget to report that in 1912, the first trade delegation was set up in Hamburg; that Ford tractors have been sold in Berlin since 1925; and that in that same year, a factory was opened in the Westhafen district to manufacture the Model T. You hide the fact that the Model T was produced in that Berlin factory until it was replaced by the Model A in 1928. And you intentionally hide from this courtroom the fact that the brand-new machinery they used, which was so perfectly maintained, is the same machinery that, after running without rest for four years, was dismantled and sent to Gorky's Avtozavod. So do not speak to me about German maintenance, or German translations, or German workers. They had years of experience, with new machines and manuals inherited from old models. Do not make demands on us like a capitalist country, when your defendant, Wilbur Hewitt, sold us scrap metal at steel prices."

37

Jack used the recess to go to the American store. He found Joe Brown and Miquel Agramunt there, frightened as rabbits. Neither Harry Daniels nor his elder son had shown up for work.

"We think they've been arrested," Miquel told him. "The Black Crows turned up this morning and took about a dozen Americans."

Jack kicked a half-empty sack. That he hadn't also been arrested only confirmed that everything was part of a plot to give the trial a veneer of legitimacy. In any case, everything was beginning to fall apart. He advised Joe and Miquel to stay at home until things calmed down. Then he rushed off to meet Ivan Zarko. It was obvious now that his only hope was to escape the Soviet Union before the verdict was reached.

He found the man eating with Yuri, his nephew, in a warehouse near the repair shop where they'd hidden his old automobile. When Ivan saw him, he made a face. Still, he invited Jack to join them, and asked about the case.

"Things are complicated," Jack replied. "Thanks for putting me onto that lawyer. Shame he's an alcoholic . . ."

"Alcoholic? Even drunk, that old man's head and shoulders above any of the lawyers who buzz around like fleas trying to get a seat in the party. Anyway, in the Soviet Union, drinking vodka's no disgrace; it's a privilege!" He served himself a glass. "Tell me, Jack, what can I do for you?"

"I need the passports. I don't know how long the trial will go on, but things might turn ugly sooner than expected."

Zarko shook his head. "I was about to send Yuri to speak to you."

"Oh?"

"It's about the price. The passports are almost ready, but my supplier says he's had unexpected costs."

"What kind of costs?"

"I don't know. A thousand. Maybe two."

Jack scowled. He rummaged in his jacket and took out fifteen hundred rubles. "Here. It's all I have on me. I'll give you the rest tomorrow."

Ivan Zarko exploded with laughter. Yuri gave him a puzzled look, then followed his lead, guffawing even louder than his uncle. Jack thought both of them were out of their minds.

"Not rubles. Dollars. Two thousand dollars, boy," Ivan explained before taking another swig of vodka.

Jack clenched his teeth. He had no choice but to trust Zarko. He agreed to bring the required amount. "When will you have the passports?"

"In a week," Ivan replied. "And the money?"

"In a week. When I'm holding them in my hands."

He was about to leave the warehouse, when he suddenly stopped to think over what he was going to do. He turned to the crook again, looking him in the eyes. "And get another one ready for a twenty-five-year-old Russian woman. I don't care what it costs. I'll send you the details."

The trial resumed with Elizabeth absent. She'd wanted to attend, but Jack had made her see that such a sudden recovery from her illness would arouse suspicion, making their defense less credible. However, the real reason was that he didn't want her to witness the railroading of Hewitt that he knew would take place. Elizabeth agreed in the end and busied herself organizing the newspapers she'd rescued from her uncle's mansion.

The session began with the usual avalanche of cheers to mark the arrival of Stalin and his cronies. Once they were seated, Jack returned Viktor Smirnov's greeting when he approached to ask about Jack's role as Wilbur Hewitt's defense attorney.

"I didn't know you were a lawyer as well as a mechanic," the Soviet official said to him, less dressed up than usual to avoid clashing with his comrades.

"Me neither. I'm just doing it to help Elizabeth."

"I see! You rascal. A tasty morsel . . . but mind you don't choke on it."

By the time Jack arrived, Sergei was already on the platform, organizing his notes. The OGPU head asked General Secretary Stalin for permission to proceed and began his harangue. Jack barely paid attention; he was still worried about the Daniels family's whereabouts. However, his anxiety turned to despair when he realized that though the session had started, Wilbur Hewitt hadn't yet taken his seat.

"Esteemed comrades," exclaimed Sergei, "I hope today that I have shown the lack of evidence in the arguments of the defense. Mr. Beilis has tried to lay the blame with the Soviet people, with us, his customers and hosts, for the outrages committed by his own American bosses. He has accused us of a lack of foresight, of negligence and neglect, and a thousand other things, knowing—and I repeat, *knowing*—that most of the sabotage must have been perpetrated by highly specialized personnel, as he himself admits in this report *he signed*." He showed the courtroom a document on which Jack Beilis's signature was clearly visible. "It's curious: he brands us as inept, guilty of negligence, and yet he has no qualms about holding us responsible for the actions of American experts trained and overseen by Wilbur Hewitt himself.

"Comrades, the time has come to prove every last crime committed by the accused, so that we are left in no doubt as to his complete and utter culpability. I will do so beginning with the gravest of these crimes: conspiring to profit from the public resources of the Soviet Union. Resources that its sons and daughters have paid for with blood and sweat." A burst of applause obliged Sergei to break off. He took the chance to drink from a glass.

"Wilbur Hewitt"—he pointed at the industrialist's empty chair without the slightest tremble in his finger—"devised a Machiavellian plan in which he involved some of his compatriots who are at this very moment under arrest. Wilbur Hewitt plotted, lied, and bribed to replace a batch of machinery from Dearborn, paid for on the assumption that it was new, for another of a similar appearance, but used, damaged, and dangerous, from the dismantled factory in Berlin where he had previously worked. The difference in the price, millions of Soviet rubles, ended up in his own pocket and those of the traitors who helped him."

At that moment, Jack thought of the Daniels family again. He prayed that Sergei's insanity hadn't touched them as well. The OGPU officer took out a note and went on.

"To prove it, I am going to read the transcription of a telephone conversation that I myself had with Mr. George McMillan, who at that time was Wilbur Hewitt's head supervisor and engineer, but whom I hired behind his back to investigate the irregular activities of his superior the moment they were first detected. The transcription is of a telephone call from the Hotel Metropol in Moscow on January 5, 1933, just over a year ago, received at my office at the OGPU's kremlin headquarters."

He read it out loud:

Good morning. Could you put me through to Sergei Loban's office, please?

Who's calling?

George McMillan. It's urgent.

One moment, sir. I'll check and put you through . . .

Sergei Loban speaking. How may I help you?

Mr. Loban. It's George McMillan. I've found the proof you were looking for in relation to the misappropriation of funds.

Do you have it with you?

Yes. I have everything. Records of the transfers, the amounts, everything.

Very well. Where are you now?

At the Metropol.

Good. Stay where you are. I'll send a vehicle to collect you immediately.

"As you can see, the conversation unequivocally incriminates Wilbur Hewitt, whom McMillan was investigating. I concede the floor to the defense, should he wish to make any further statements or attempt to rebut the People's evidence."

Jack stood up. He looked at the accused's empty chair, and turned to Sergei. "Thank you very much, Mr. Loban. Yes. I would certainly like to raise a point that no doubt many of you will have noticed. Why is Mr. Hewitt not here?"

"The defendant is indisposed. It must be a family trait," Sergei responded with irony.

"Do you not intend to question him?"

"It won't be necessary for now. The accused has already made a full statement in writing."

"Oh, I see!" Jack prayed that Hewitt hadn't implicated him in the business with the false passports. "Excuse my ignorance, but what if the accused wished to retract his statement?"

"Mr. Beilis," Stalin cut in, "if his previous statement were retracted, it would mean that in one of his two accounts he was lying, whereby any testimony of his would be invalidated."

"And what if I wished to question him?"

"It would be taken into account. But continue with your questions for now; in view of the evidence, you might not consider it necessary."

"Very well, Mr. General Secretary. In that case I will follow your advice." He looked at his notes and turned back to the head of the OGPU. "Mr. Loban, I've listened carefully to your description of what you call *proof*, but from your reading of the telephone conversation that you claim to have had with Mr. McMillan, I cannot infer Wilbur Hewitt's involvement. His name is not mentioned at any time. How can you therefore be so sure it was him?"

Sergei smiled, as if he had an ace waiting up his sleeve. "For two reasons. First, because the transfers that George McMillan refers to in his call were to Wilbur Hewitt's personal account: fifty thousand dollars from the coffers of the Soviet Union." He showed the room a copy of the accounting records. "And second, and more important, because a witness saw Wilbur Hewitt murder McMillan and throw the body from the Bolshoy Kamenny Bridge into the Moskva River on the same afternoon as the call."

Jack let out a sigh of astonishment. "And may I ask who that witness is?" he sputtered.

"Of course. He's sitting in this room right now. Officer Viktor Smirnov."

Jack could barely contain his shock. As he gathered his notes at the end of the session, he understood that Hewitt's fate was sealed. All the evidence incriminated him: McMillan's telephone call, the accounting records, and above all, Smirnov's unexpected testimony. He found it hard to believe that the wealthy idler had witnessed McMillan's murder. But that was precisely what he said in a sworn statement. However, if, as Viktor claimed, Sergei had possessed the incriminating evidence for a full year, why had he waited so long to arrest Hewitt? It made no sense. The only explanation Jack could think of was they had been buying time to root out Hewitt's Soviet accomplices. After all, that was the reason Wilbur Hewitt had given him when he hired him to replace McMillan with the hidden motive of using him as bait.

The courtroom gradually emptied out. Jack collected his copies of the court minutes and stored them in his case. He didn't know what he was going to tell Elizabeth. The only thing he knew with certainty was that the permission-granting process they'd gone through to act as Hewitt's defense had been a farce with which the Soviet regime could legitimize a trial, the verdict of which seemed to have already been decided. Indeed, it had been as farcical as the part played by Viktor Smirnov as a frivolous dilettante.

He knew that Elizabeth would refuse to admit that in the best-case scenario, her uncle Wilbur would spend the rest of his life imprisoned in a labor camp. If she insisted on remaining in Gorky, he knew that sooner or later they would arrest her, too. There was no longer room for half measures. Either Elizabeth fled with him, or he'd escape without her. He still had a chance, though remote, to begin a new life with Natasha.

He was about to head to see Elizabeth, when he spotted Walter walking along on the opposite sidewalk, chatting with a comrade. Jack shouted to him, and Walter hastily parted company with his companion and approached.

"Please, don't compromise me!" He wouldn't even accept the hand that Jack offered him in greeting.

"Sorry. I just wanted to ask you about the letter."

Walter gave a bad-tempered sigh. He looked around him.

"All right. Let's go down that hallway. But only for a moment."

Before speaking, Walter made sure there was nobody within earshot. Then he reassured Jack that he had sent Hewitt's message, but he still hadn't received confirmation that Dmitri had delivered it to the embassy.

"But the trial's going to end soon and they'll sentence him. Maybe if you called the American journalists posted to Moscow, they could—"

"I can't do any more. I've helped you too much already."

"And what happened to your solidarity? To your principles? A capitalist he may be, but Wilbur Hewitt's innocent."

"Don't you see? What's at stake here is much more than the life of a single citizen. What's at stake is the success of the Soviet Union. The success of our struggle and our revolution depends on our strength. If we waver, the imperialist countries will pounce and devour us."

"I . . . I don't understand," Jack muttered.

"Look, Jack. I don't know why you insist he's innocent. Forget Hewitt, or you'll end up like him. Take some friendly advice."

Walter didn't let Jack reply. He opened the hall door and left without saying good-bye.

Back home, Jack found Elizabeth sitting by the fire, leafing through an old copy of the *New York Times*. Seeing him, the young woman left the newspaper on the pile that she'd already inspected and asked about her uncle. When Jack told her he was absent from court, her face darkened.

"They've submitted overwhelming evidence. They're accusing him of some very serious crimes," he gently tried to explain.

She barely paid attention. Her mind seemed to be somewhere else.

"The trial will likely end tomorrow," he added. "I guess they'll bring your uncle to make a statement. You should go."

"Yeah . . . of course."

"And be prepared. Before coming home, I spoke to my contact. The passports aren't ready, but he's offered to hide us in a safe house until they are. We can stay hidden there and then try to reach Odessa."

"You've planned all this without considering my uncle? Without waiting to hear his sentence?"

"Elizabeth, did you not hear me? I'm just trying to carry out your uncle's wishes. If they declare him innocent, there won't be a problem, but if they don't . . ." He shook his head. "If they condemn him, there won't be anything he can do to help you."

Elizabeth cut him off. "I don't know what you're trying to say, Jack. Do you really think I'd abandon him?"

"No. Of course not." He cleared his throat. "Walter sent the letter to the embassy. I'm sure they'll be able to get his sentence reduced—"

"You say it as if they've already found him guilty! What was the new evidence?"

Jack fell silent. He took a deep breath and searched for a cigarette that he didn't find. He didn't want to tell her that her uncle was accused of murder. "Technicalities. It's all right. I'll go over my reports one more time," he said. "Maybe I've missed something. In the meantime, we should have some dinner."

Elizabeth accepted his suggestion. She got up and headed to the little kitchen to stir the soup she'd made from some leftovers she'd found. She served Jack a bowl while he took the court transcripts from his case. Jack saw that there was barely even one piece of potato floating in the broth.

"You forgot to bring supplies from the store," she explained. "I'm not hungry."

"It's not that I forgot—they've all but run out," he murmured, and he spread out the records he'd been given in search of the accounting transactions. He studied them between spoonfuls and made notes in the margins. When he'd finished, he asked Elizabeth to go up to the bedroom.

"I'm not tired," she said.

"Please. I need to be alone."

Elizabeth reluctantly obeyed. When she'd gone, Jack went up to the hearth and suffocated the fire with a wet blanket. Then, using a poker, he pushed aside the embers, before placing a wide wooden board on the ashes to protect himself. He lay on top of the board, and from that position rummaged inside the chimney. He put on a pair of safety gloves he'd brought home from the factory and slowly removed some firebricks to gain access to a cavity that he'd fashioned as a safe. He took out the reports and replaced the bricks. He brushed himself off, set aside the board, and relit the fire. When it ignited, he contemplated the flames with satisfaction. Nobody would suspect that the firebricks concealed the hiding place where he stashed his money.

He made some tea and began to sip it along with the soup. The drink comforted him, not so much because of its flavor, but because its heat reminded him of the warmth he always felt from Natasha's smile.

He longed to hold her again. Whenever he had a moment of peace, he would remember her kisses, her looks, her caresses. When he saw her, he would plead with her to run away with him. She was all that mattered to him.

When he'd finished his tea and soup, he went over McMillan's documents. Rereading the list of Soviet engineers who'd traveled to Dearborn, he paused at the name that had initially caught his attention.

Vladimir Mamayev

Vladimir Mamayev was the only engineer he had no record of in his preliminary reports. This would have been purely coincidental if not for the fact that, according to those reports, the rest of the listed technicians were on a training course in Moscow on the dates when the most significant sabotage had taken place.

He served himself some more tea while he mulled it over.

He set aside the names and positioned McMillan's accounting records alongside those noted down in the court transcripts that he'd been given. When he compared them, he raised his eyebrows in astonishment.

The two reports matched point by point. Sergei's evidence was solid. However, the numbers corresponding to the account that transferred the fifty thousand American dollars to Wilbur Hewitt's private account differed by one digit. It was the same entry that McMillan had marked with a dot. Jack searched for the identity of the issuer in the court transcript, but found only the word *Confidential* in the corresponding box.

He finished his tea. Something did not add up, and maybe it was simpler than it seemed. Fifty thousand dollars . . . Why would a rich man like Wilbur Hewitt risk his position for an amount that would be small change to him?

He went over the records again. It was true that Hewitt had taken money from his account, but it showed credits and debits that corresponded to orders for supplies made from the Avtozavod, which indicated that the account was not a private one, but a company one. And given the high volume of transactions, Hewitt could easily have missed a payment from a third party.

Jack noted down the numbers and the name Vladimir Mamayev, telling himself that perhaps Wilbur Hewitt deserved another chance. And not just for him, but for Elizabeth.

To avoid having to put the fire out again, he hid the reports under a cupboard. Then he wrapped up as warmly as he could. He had to speak to the only person he trusted who had access to OGPU documents, and that was Walter Scott.

Jack buttoned up his overcoat as the icy cold cut through his lungs like a knife. He coughed from the pain. He made sure nobody was watching the house, and set off, equipped with an old umbrella to ward off the blizzard. He checked his watch again. It was six o'clock in the evening. He guessed that, by that time, Walter would have arrived home. He lived in the *sotsgorod*, a workers' neighborhood.

He knocked on the door and waited. Sue appeared, giving a start when she recognized him.

"Jack! Long time no see!" She cleared her throat. "Well . . . don't just stand there; you'll freeze to death. Come in."

Jack saw that the apartment consisted of a single room that served as bedroom and living room. Sue rushed to pull across the curtain they had in the middle of the room to hide the unmade bed. She didn't look well. When he asked for Walter, she replied that he'd be home soon.

"Place looks comfortable," he lied.

"It's a bit small, but we're happy." She forced a smile while she put up her hair with a bobby pin. "Do you remember when we left New York, thinking that we'd be given a little house with a garden?" She laughed. "Those were the days! Here, sit down." She offered him a rickety chair. "I'm sorry I can't offer you any vodka, but with the famine, there're certain luxuries we can't afford. They give Walter a bottle a week at work, but he trades it at the market for eggs and a couple of bones for making broth. Do you want tea while you wait? That I can offer."

Jack accepted. He hadn't seen Sue since the store's opening. He hadn't noticed it then, but in the weak light of the bulb, her face looked haggard and was marked by little wrinkles.

"So how are you?" she asked him. "Walter told me you're playing the lawyer, defending the capitalist you saved on the ship."

"Yes. It's something I agreed to do." He didn't want to give any more details. "And you two, how are you?"

"Fine, fine . . . Here. Be careful with the tea; it's boiling."

They sat in silence for a while.

"Do you know how long he'll be?"

"No, not really. He's very busy right now. With Stalin here, everyone is. But he'll be home soon. Ah!" They heard a key in the lock. "He's here." She got up to greet him. Jack copied her.

Walter opened the door and took off his woolen *ushanka*, sprinkling the floor with snow. He was still brushing himself off when he noticed Jack. He stopped dead, as if he'd seen a ghost.

"What a surprise! What the hell brings you here?" Walter saw the cup of tea beside Jack and gave Sue a reproachful look. Jack noticed it.

"Don't worry, I won't stay long. I don't want to put you in an awkward position. It's just that I have information. Strange information . . ."

"I see . . . Sue, could you go see the neighbor, ask if they can spare a potato or two?"

"Walter, you know they don't have so much as a—"

"Go find a damned potato!" he yelled at her.

Sue rushed to put on her coat and left the apartment. Walter sat opposite Jack, glowering.

"So? What information is this?"

Jack opened the folder and took out the court transcripts they'd given him. He explained what they were and why he had them in his possession.

"Yeah, yeah, I know. I've been at the sessions, in the audience."

"Well, in that case you'll know that McMillan made a list of bank transfers. This one here. And the one giving the figure of fifty thousand dollars is the one they attribute to Wilbur Hewitt." He pointed at it.

"Yes. At the office today, they were saying that they'd examined the list of transfers, and in addition to verifying that the recipient of the fifty thousand dollars was Wilbur Hewitt, they also found that he'd withdrawn some of the funds."

"And they hadn't noticed it before? I say that because any money going into a Soviet bank is monitored so closely that it's impossible to take it out without the government knowing about it."

"With most transactions, yes. But Hewitt's account, to which most of the money went, was held in a German bank. It was opened to pay for contracts and supplies."

"Wow, Walter, you *are* well informed!"

"Well." He narrowed his eyes. "Though my colleagues would say otherwise, my Russian has improved a lot. Lately, they speak about nothing else in the OGPU. You just have to keep your ears open."

"Anyway, that's not why I'm here. It's something else. Look at this." He indicated the issuer's account number. "I need to know whose account that is. Who ordered the transfer."

Walter scanned the document with reluctance. "It says it there: *Confidential*. They guard that information like treasure."

"Sure, but I'm not asking about the number in the transcript. I'm referring to the one I've corrected underneath, in red pencil."

Walter removed his glasses to read it carefully. "Where did you get this?" He frowned.

"I'd rather not involve you."

"You already have by coming here. If anyone followed you, I'll be linked to someone defending a murderer."

"Think about what you're saying. Doesn't it seem strange to you that the witness to a crime that happened a year ago suddenly appears in the middle of a trial? If he has always had that evidence, why didn't they arrest Hewitt sooner? And it's not just any witness. No. It's someone with status. Viktor Smirnov . . . But why would a guy who's only interested in his cars get involved in this case? It beats me. All I can think of is that they've threatened to take away his privileges."

"Well, since you're asking me to think about it, you could also consider that even if he has complicated reasons for giving evidence, that doesn't mean that Hewitt's innocent. McMillan died, the money disappeared, and there's the recording."

"Damn it, Walter! Hewitt doesn't seem like the kind of guy who throws his employees off bridges. And if they lied about that, they could be lying about everything."

"You don't have the look of someone who would kill his landlord, but you murdered Kowalski. Really, Jack. How easy it is to look the other way when you're defending someone who's provided you with all manner of luxuries!"

Jack was hurt that Walter had chosen to remind him of the landlord's death, but he could sense that his friend was envious of him. For the sake of their long friendship, he tried to be tolerant. "I can see why you might feel sore, but it's not fair for you to look down on me for it. I've worked for everything I have, and your own boss, Sergei Loban, authorized it. And I didn't realize you and Sue were in such a precarious situation. Shit, Walter! If you needed help, a loan, I don't know, whatever. All you had to do was ask, and I—"

"Well, I'll be damned, Jack! Now you're a fucking loan shark? And to think you hated your uncle the banker."

"Please! Don't take what I'm saying literally. I was just trying . . . Well, it's just that I had no idea you were living in these conditions. When you left the American village, I thought you were moving somewhere better."

"Sure . . . A mansion, like Wilbur Hewitt's."

"Give it a rest, Walter! I'm sorry, really I am. Look. Here. It's not much, but . . ." He went to take out some notes from his wallet, but Walter stopped him.

"I don't need handouts, Jack. In fact, I think you need *my* help, otherwise you wouldn't be here." He got up and strolled around the room. "Anyway, let's leave it. Are you going to tell me where you got that number?"

Jack took a deep breath and studied Walter's troubled face. He hesitated as his heart accelerated. It was Walter. His friend Walter. "I found it in a trunk that belonged to McMillan," he finally said. "Hewitt let me have his luggage, unaware that there were dozens of reports hidden inside that contain information on the Avtozavod, including the banking transactions that have been used in the trial to incriminate Hewitt. The records in the court case match McMillan's reports with one exception: the issuer's account number is different. And McMillan's papers are the official balance sheets, stamped by the Vesenkha, the Supreme Soviet of the National Economy."

"And all of that was in a trunk?"

"It had a false bottom. Look, Walter, I'm convinced that the document I've found is the same one McMillan was going to hand over to Sergei when he called him. That's why I don't understand why Sergei would alter the issuer's account number."

"I agree that it's strange." Walter stood up and tugged at his thinning hair. "But, truthfully, Jack, I don't know what significance your discovery could have. I don't even know if I'll be able to find anything out. Where's the original?"

"Hidden."

"OK. Then bring it to me tomorrow, and I'll see what I can do."

"Tomorrow will be too late. I need to know the issuer's identity before the trial resumes."

"I see. Problem is, I'd have to go back out now, find someone at the office, and try to get them to help me by showing them a number written in red pencil. If you'd brought the original, then—"

"Listen, if it's true that Sergei's changed the number, then that report's the only evidence that could prove it. And I'm not about to hand it over to those wolves. I am going to present it in the trial, in front of Stalin, but first I have to know why the numbers were altered."

"The thing is . . ." He shook his head, as if unable to find a solution. "The thing is, I don't think I can help you. Maybe you should speak to someone with more power in the OGPU. When it comes down to it, I'm just a *seksot*, an informer, as much as Sue likes to think otherwise. I'm a nobody."

Jack didn't know what to say. He finished his tea and considered what Walter had said. Finally, he got up to say good-bye to his friend. "One last thing. Does the name Vladimir Mamayev mean anything to you?"

"No." He shook his head. "I've never heard it before. Why?"

"No reason. Thanks anyway. Say good-bye to Sue for me. I owe you one."

"What're you going to do?"

Jack put on his fur coat and pulled his *ushanka* down as far as it would go. "Speak to Viktor Smirnov. I don't know if it'll help, but it's time to find out."

38

Since he'd left Walter's humble apartment block, Jack hadn't stopped wondering what Smirnov's true role was in the whole business. Before the trial, his apathy toward anything other than his own pleasure had freed him of suspicion. However, his sudden emergence as a witness meant he had serious questions to answer.

When Jack banged on the front door of Viktor Smirnov's dacha, he couldn't prevent a shiver from running down his spine. While he waited, he admired the large collection of vehicles parked in front of the house, watched by the guard who a minute earlier had frisked him before letting him pass. The laughter and music from inside reached the garden. Whoever was in there was certainly having a good time. He knocked firmly again and waited.

When Viktor Smirnov opened the door with his dressing gown half open and a glass of champagne in his hand to find himself face-to-face with his unexpected visitor, his smile instantly disappeared. Jack greeted him coldly.

"Jack! What're you doing here?" He looked from side to side, to make sure that Jack was alone.

"I'm sorry to show without warning, but I needed to speak to you about a serious matter."

"Oh. Well, now really isn't a good time. I'm celebrating with some friends from Moscow, and we were about to drink a toast."

Jack could hear heels clicking and women's laughter. "It won't take long."

"What's it about?"

"It's about Sergei's statement. There's something that doesn't add up, and I thought you must know about it."

"Oh?" He looked back into the house, as if weighing whether to return to the fun that awaited him or deal with Jack. "All right. Let's go upstairs, then. We can speak more freely up there."

As they went down the hall toward the stairs, Jack heard the laughter of the women who, scantily dressed, were dancing and exchanging kisses with some officers whom he'd never seen before. One of the young women appeared, her breasts uncovered, and called to Viktor to come down. She stumbled over her words but insisted.

"I'll be right there!" Smirnov replied to the girl. "Old friends," he explained to Jack, as if that could hide that they were prostitutes. "Right. You were saying?" He closed the door to his study and sat in a magnificent leather chair.

Jack accepted Viktor's invitation and copied him. He didn't know where to begin. He took off his *ushanka* and gazed around the room. The music from the gramophone was putting him on edge. "Quite a party. I'm sorry I've interrupted you."

"And so am I." Viktor served himself a glass from the bottle of champagne he'd picked up in the hall. Though there were glasses nearby on a sideboard, he didn't offer Jack one. "So, what is so important that you had to come disturb me at this hour?"

"I think"—Jack took a deep breath—"I think Sergei's lying."

"Oh? And how can you be so sure?" He savored a sip of champagne very slowly, without taking his eyes off Jack.

Jack hesitated. Something inside him told him not to tell the truth. "I don't know. It might be nothing. I . . ."

"Come on, Jack. You can't have come here in the middle of the night just to interrupt our party."

"No, of course not." He dried the sweat from his hands. "I . . . Does the name Vladimir Mamayev mean anything to you?" he finally asked, and Viktor coughed as if the champagne had flooded his lungs.

What was left of his drink spilled onto the desk. Jack hurried to help him. But while he mopped up the spillage with his own *ushanka*, he saw a framed photograph that made his heart freeze.

"Excuse me," Viktor apologized. "I've drunk too much tonight. No. I don't know anyone named Mamayev. Why? Is there something wrong?"

"No, of course not."

Jack fell silent as he gazed at the photograph of a young woman in Viktor Smirnov's arms. It was Natasha, with a gigantic diamond on her finger.

A convenient unbearable pain in his hip had provided the perfect excuse to end Jack's meeting with Smirnov. Now he lurched down Gorky's deserted avenues like a sleepwalker, the snow whipping his face until it was wrapped in a shroud of ice.

He imagined Natasha and Smirnov, plotting together with Sergei. They had all fooled him. All of them. Even Hewitt. *Bastards!* he thought to himself.

On the way home, he wondered why Natasha had hidden her relationship with Smirnov from him. Though he had distanced himself from her in recent days, he couldn't help but feel betrayed. It tortured him to think that her pleasant face—without a trace of duplicity, those honest eyes—was masking a huge lie. That her kisses, embraces, and sighs were those of a fleeting encounter. But then, why had he caught her arguing with Smirnov in her office?

He could barely think. Did it really matter? He was overwhelmed by having reached a crossroads where, whichever path he chose, he would be heading into the abyss. He cursed everyone angrily, then hardened his heart and picked up his pace. If his rage hadn't prevented it, he might have shed a tear for his own soul, but there was no time to cry. Only escape could save him. It was time to flee, or die trying.

He was approaching his house when he came across a wild mob, running down the streets from home to home and vandalizing everything in its path. He tried to ask a passerby what was happening, but the man ducked into a nearby doorway. When he turned to ask someone else, there was a sharp bang. Jack stopped in his tracks. There were some screams, and the sound of a vehicle speeding off. Then there were more cries, followed by more gunshots.

Jack ran to his house and yelled to Elizabeth to come down to the living room. As the young woman dressed, he began to gather the possessions he'd need during his escape: warm clothes, his savings, the incriminating reports, and McMillan's passport. When she came down, she asked what was happening.

"There's no time to talk. Gather your clothes. Only the essentials. And see what you can salvage from the kitchen. Anything edible—potatoes, bread, whatever."

"Now? Where're we going?"

"I don't know. I'll get Ivan Zarko to hide us somewhere safe."

"But why? And what are those bangs?"

"They sound like gunfire. It looks like the OGPU is raiding houses indiscriminately."

"Have you heard anything about my uncle?"

"We can't do anything for him now. Get your coat and do what I say. Quickly. We'll worry about your uncle later."

"I'm not going to flee and leave the only family I have here. My uncle Wilbur hasn't done anything wrong, and—"

"He hasn't? How can you be so sure? Do you know where he got the money for the passports from? What would you know? Wilbur Hewitt lied to me. He got me into this mess. He killed George McMillan, the person I replaced at the Avtozavod, and—"

"What?" Elizabeth's face was twisted with disbelief.

"You heard. I didn't tell you to spare your feelings, but a witness saw your uncle kill George McMillan."

"George? That's absurd! My uncle wouldn't kill a fly. I don't know how you can believe it."

Some nearby gunshots made both of them give a start.

"Well, I believe it because there's a witness who described how, a few days after arriving in Moscow, your uncle strangled that man with his own hands on the Bolshoy Kamenny Bridge and threw his body into the river."

Elizabeth was left dumbfounded, looking at Jack as if he were a ghost. "But, Jack, don't you remember?"

"Don't I remember what?"

"The terrible injury that my uncle suffered on the SS *Cliffwood*? How could an invalid who could barely hold a cup in his hand strangle a man twenty years his junior and hurl his body over a balustrade?"

Jack cursed himself before punching the nearest wall. How could he have been so stupid not to have realized it before? What Elizabeth was saying was so obvious that even a child would have considered it. He cursed himself again. Without question, Smirnov had given false evidence at Sergei's behest in order to implicate Hewitt in a crime so vile that it would dissolve any trace of his innocence in the eyes of the jurors. He didn't know how to respond to Elizabeth, but at that moment, the revelation was irrelevant, as were McMillan's accounting records and the name Vladimir Mamayev. No secret report was going to stop those who had lied and hatched this plot, nor would it prevent them from coming after Jack and Elizabeth. When he tried to explain it to the young woman, she turned on him.

"What secret reports are you talking about?"

"It doesn't matter anymore. Your uncle's condemned. We have to escape."

"Escape? Is that all you can think of?"

"And what would you have us do? Turn up in Stalin's bedroom and demand a fair trial? Don't kid yourself. Come on!" He took her wrist to make her go with him.

"Let go of me!"

"What the hell is wrong with you, Elizabeth? If we don't escape now—"

"All you know how to do is run away. Just like you ran away from New York so you wouldn't go down for the shooting."

"What?" Jack turned pale. He couldn't believe what Elizabeth had said.

"Did you really think nobody would find out? Nobody would know you were a fugitive?"

"But, how . . . ?" Jack imagined that Walter must have somehow revealed the details of his landlord's death to her.

"It's all in here," she said. She took an old copy of the *New York Times* from inside her dressing gown and waved it at him. "In the local news section, dated the day before the SS *Cliffwood* set sail."

Jack was silent, feeling the blood pulse in his temples at a feverish rate. "It . . . it was an accident," he finally managed to sputter.

"Oh yeah? Well, here it says a guy named Kowalski reported you for shooting him and running away with his money."

"What did you say? He reported me?" Jack didn't understand. How the hell could a dead man have reported him? "Give it here!"

He snatched the paper from her and read the article closely. When he'd finished, he slumped into an armchair. It was impossible. The last paragraph of the piece explained that Kowalski had suffered only a minor injury.

The thunder of a burst of gunfire tore him from his daze. He was no murderer! If he'd known that Kowalski was alive, he could have stayed in the United States and proved his innocence; proved that he hadn't stolen from his landlord, much less fired at him on purpose. And if he hadn't killed him, why had Walter lied to him? Why had he told him that Kowalski was dead?

Jack let out a scream that resounded around the entire house. If he'd had Walter in front of him, he would have beaten him to death. He cursed him. That rat whom he'd considered a friend, who had offered to escape with him to the Soviet Union to save him from the electric chair; that heartless bastard had deceived him and made him believe that he was a murderer just so Jack would accompany him on his brainless adventure, to use him for his knowledge of the Russian language, without caring that he was ruining his life.

He had never hated anyone so coldly, so profoundly. He'd never felt so betrayed. He stuffed the article into his coat and roared with fury again, while Elizabeth stared in astonishment at Jack's transformation into a beast thirsty for revenge.

Some bangs on the door made him come around. He jumped up and ran to a window to see who was knocking. It was a stranger begging for help. Jack had no time to react. A car braked sharply next to him; then someone got out and shot the man in the head. Jack closed the window and turned to Elizabeth, who was screaming. "We have to go!"

"No! I'm not going without my uncle," she said, filled with terror.

Jack could see that he'd have to remove her by force, but told himself that it would be sensible to wait until she had calmed down. "All right. I'll go fetch the car, drop by the store to take what's left, and come back for you. You wait here. We'll see what we can do for your uncle," he said to reassure her. "Here. Take this key. When I go, lock the door, hide upstairs, and don't open up for anyone. Understood? *Understood?*"

She nodded, her eyes filled with tears. Jack hugged her. He promised her that everything would be OK, told her again to hide, and left in the direction of Ivan Zarko's abandoned repair shop.

Despite the frost, the Ford Model A rumbled into life. Jack waited for Yuri to open the repair shop door, then slowly rolled the vehicle onto the paved street.

"We'll meet at my house later. I'll pay you the rest there," Jack said to him.

Jack accelerated away. He drove through the night at full speed with the headlamps off, following the dim glow of the moon. The gunfire and screams continued. As he approached the American village, he saw fires blazing. He considered turning back, but he needed supplies, or he and Elizabeth would starve to death. He skirted around the village and headed toward the rear entrance of the store. He parked and went in. Outside, the gunshots reminded him that one false move could be his end. Still, he was driven by a cold-blooded desire. Even if it was the last thing he did in the Soviet Union before escaping, he was determined to find Walter and take his revenge.

He turned on the flashlight he'd brought from the car. The beam illuminated the bare walls. Someone had been there before him. There was nothing left on the shelves. He was about to leave when suddenly he noticed a crouched form in front of him. "Who is it?" he yelled. His heart skipped a beat.

There was no response. He aimed the flashlight at the point where he thought he heard some muttering. He was about to retreat, when a pair of powerful arms suddenly grabbed him from behind and began to asphyxiate him. Jack struggled. He tried to free himself, but whoever was holding him had the strength of a bear. He could barely breathe. He gripped the flashlight like a mace and hit back with all his might, but he missed his target. He was beginning to feel his life force leaving him.

In a final attempt, with a two-handed blow, he made contact with his assailant's head. The man, stunned, released Jack and fell to the ground. Then Jack leapt on him, intending to ram the flashlight into his head. He sat astride the man's chest, about to strike him, when he recognized the man beneath him.

"Joe?" Incredulous, he stopped the deadly blow midswing.

He shone the flashlight around him and discovered the Daniels family and Miquel, cowering in a corner.

They explained to Jack that they'd decided to hide there when the OGPU burst into the village and began firing indiscriminately. "I'm sorry, Mr. Beilis," Joe Brown apologized. "I thought you were one of *them*."

"But what's happening?" Jack asked.

"It was Smirnov. He was laughing and yelling threats," Harry Daniels replied. "This morning we saw him fire on the Petersons when they tried to escape. My God! He shot them down without a second thought, and then finished them off as if they were vermin. This is insane! We ran with only the clothes on our backs and hid in the forest."

"What're we going to do, Jack?" sobbed Mrs. Daniels. She was hugging her younger son, almost suffocating him.

"I don't know. You'll have to escape. No one's safe here."

"But how? To where?"

"I don't know. Here." He took five thousand rubles from his jacket and handed them to them. "It's all I can do for you."

"Jack, for the love of God! We have nowhere to go."

He was silent while he looked at his friends' frightened faces. He realized that their lives were in his hands. He cursed his bad luck. "All right! Do you have food?"

"A bag of kippers, some cookies, potatoes, and turnips," said Miquel. "It's all that was left."

"Good. Then take only what's essential and follow me."

Jack loaded the car with the food that Miquel had managed to save, warm clothes, blankets, a can of gasoline, and a couple of knives, leaving the rest of their belongings on the ground. "Come on, get in!"

Without turning on the headlights, Jack drove the Ford A south. The sound of gunfire was soon replaced by the bang of explosions. In the distance, Jack saw one of the assembly plants go up in flames. When he looked back at the road, to his horror he discovered a barricade that had sprouted from nowhere. He swerved and left the road, fortunate not to hit any trees. A volley of bullets whistled around them.

"Get down!"

He didn't have to repeat himself. He regained control of the vehicle as well as he could and accelerated until they reached the track that he and Natasha used to walk down together. After a few miles, he slowed down. "There's an abandoned cabin somewhere around here. Get out with your belongings, and wait for me. Don't use any lights. I have to go back to Gorky for Elizabeth."

"I'll go with you," offered Miquel.

"No. It's too dangerous. And you're the only one who speaks Russian and knows the area. If anything happened to you, they'd be done for."

Miquel nodded, but Joe Brown offered to come in his place.

"You will help if there is any trouble. I am good in a fight, and, believe me, I drive a helluva lot better than you do," Joe said.

Jack thanked him. "Remember," he said. "Keep quiet. If we're not back by noon . . ."

He didn't finish the sentence. He didn't need to.

Jack stopped the vehicle near his house. There was no time to take precautions. He asked Joe to wait in the car with the engine running. "If you see anyone approach, accelerate as hard as you can."

Joe nodded. He moved into the driver's seat and wished Jack luck.

Jack ran to the house, praying that Elizabeth had changed her mind. The street seemed deserted. When he reached the door, he inserted his key in the lock. But before he even turned the key, the door swung open.

Jack tensed. Gripping a knife in one hand and the turned-off flashlight in the other, he advanced through the living room in the dark. The only light came from the embers that crackled in the fireplace. He was tempted to call out to Elizabeth, but he stopped himself. Suddenly, he walked into a chair that was lying in the middle of the room, and when he stumbled, he lost the flashlight. He crouched down to search for it blindly, crawling forward. When he found it, he decided to turn it on. He heard a noise behind him and turned to shine the light in its direction. The beam illuminated some rough forms. Jack retreated, still aiming the flashlight at them. It was Walter and Elizabeth. He was holding her from behind and pressing a revolver against the back of her neck.

"Walter?"

"Where are they, Jack?"

"What're you doing? Let her go!"

"Freeze or she's dead! The reports. Where are you keeping them?"

Jack cursed himself for leaving Elizabeth alone, and for failing to see Walter for who he really was. He would have enjoyed ripping out his heart.

"Son of a bitch! What are you trying to do? Don't you think you've done enough by making me believe I was a murderer?"

"Ha! So you finally figured it out." Walter smiled. "And you thought you were so smart. Poor, stupid Jack. So smart you thought you could dazzle Sue with your good looks and your money."

"I never thought I was better than you."

"Oh, but you did. Remember when you punched me in the coffeehouse? Ha! I could have laughed for a week when you swallowed the lie about Kowalski. You fell for it like a fool."

"Why did you do it, Walter? You could have left without me."

"You're wrong. When we went to Amtorg, I already knew they'd only accept skilled workers. Saul Bron was just fobbing me off. If you hadn't intervened when you did, I would have brought up that you were a technician. I needed you, Jack. Without you, I would never have achieved my dream."

"Have you lost your mind? How could you? How could you do this to us, Walter? What will Sue say?"

"Don't even say her name!" He aimed the gun directly at Jack's head.

"What will you tell her, Walter? That someone shot us? Will you make up another lie like the one about Kowalski?"

"I told you to shut your mouth!" Walter bellowed. "Do you think she cares about you? She doesn't give a damn about you, Jack. Not one bit."

"That's not true. She helped me when—"

"When she visited you in jail? Is that what you were going to say? Because if it was, you should know that I was the one who sent her to figure out how much you knew."

Jack fell silent. He looked his adversary in the eye. "How much are they paying you? What have they promised you?"

"Do you really want to know? Respect, Jack! Respect! No one laughs at my ideas here. I'm *somebody* here. I've had enough of being the poor idealist they poked fun at in his own country for his beliefs. I've had enough of being a nobody, of being invisible, looked down on . . ."

If he hadn't feared for Elizabeth's life, Jack would have leapt on Walter and ripped him apart with his bare hands. Walter was trembling like a frightened rat. Jack tried to buy time. "For God's sake! Do you really think you're important to them? Do you think you have a place in their history books? Come on, Walter. Let her go. Let her go and—"

"Give me the reports!" he roared, and he cocked the revolver. "Do you think this is a joke? I'll kill her, and then I'll kill you."

Jack believed he would carry out his threat. He lowered the flashlight. Walter was grimacing grotesquely, like someone possessed. "All right! Here. I have them here!" He took the reports from the cupboard and showed them to him.

"Leave them there, on the floor, and step back."

Jack did as Walter asked.

"This isn't the way to build a better world, Walter."

"No? And how would you know? Get back! And you, pick them up," he ordered Elizabeth.

She obeyed and handed them to him. Jack caught a glimpse of her terrified face in the beam of his flashlight. "You have them. Now let her go!"

"Relax, Jack. Let's see what we have here." Walter examined the papers as well as he could to check they were what he was looking for. Then he headed toward the fireplace, dragging Elizabeth with him.

"I'm telling you to let her go!" yelled Jack.

"Oh . . . I'll get around to that." He threw the reports onto the embers. The papers took on an orangey glow, before going up in flames. They were consumed in an instant. When there was little left but ash, Walter withdrew.

"You've got what you want. Now let her go."

"Not so fast, Jack. There are two more things to take care of." He pointed the revolver at Jack.

"Wait!" Jack dipped his hand in his overcoat and pulled out a roll of green bills. "Look! There's a thousand dollars. You and Sue can buy whatever you want. Take it, it's yours."

Walter hesitated. "I don't need your capitalist money," he sputtered.

"Nobody will ever know, Walter. You and Sue deserve it after so many years of suffering. Come on. If you don't take it, someone else will." The flashlight trembled in his hand. Jack was running out of options.

"All right. Leave the money on the floor. No tricks."

"Sure. But first let her go." Jack slowly moved toward the fireplace.

"I said leave it on the floor!" Walter bellowed.

"And I said let her go." Jack took a couple more steps until he was right beside the embers, which he revived with some pieces of wood.

A gunshot rang out in the room. Jack felt the bullet shatter the tiling at his feet, the fragments hitting his pants. The smell caught in his throat. He had to cough before he could speak again. "Let her go, or the money goes up in flames. Even if you shoot me, I swear I'll burn it." He waved the bills over the embers.

"Filthy capitalist! All right. I'll let her go." He aimed his gun directly at Jack's head. "I'll let her go!" he repeated as Elizabeth walked slowly toward Jack. "No! Not to him. To the side, where I can see you. Now give me the money."

"OK, Walter. It's yours. Here." Jack hurled it at him.

Just as he tossed the roll of bills, he turned off the flashlight and threw himself forward. Walter fired twice.

"Sons of bitches! I'm going to finish you!" He fired again. Several flashes lit up the room.

Suddenly, there was silence.

Jack lay waiting in the darkness, his body protecting Elizabeth and his heart thumping. He didn't know what had happened, but Elizabeth was motionless. He was about to get up, when the flashlight illuminated him. He thought he was about to die.

"Are you all right?"

Jack was unable to identify the voice that emerged from behind the blinding beam of light. He slowly got to his feet and helped Elizabeth up. Then the beam changed direction and lit Walter's lifeless body. When he approached the newcomer, Jack saw that it was Yuri.

"We arranged to meet here, remember? That bastard was about to make you burn my money," muttered Ivan Zarko's nephew. "I found Joe Brown outside. We were waiting for you, but you were taking too long, so I decided to come and see what was keeping you. Come on. We have to get out of here before the Chekisty show up."

On the way to the car, Jack asked about the outbreak of violence in the Avtozavod.

"It was just a matter of time. The famine's decimating the Soviet people. They're desperate, and Stalin's presence here incited them. Several groups of armed dissidents have dug themselves in at the Avtozavod and burned some of the buildings; the army will be here soon."

They reached the car and climbed in. Joe Brown revved the Ford into life, and they drove at full speed in the direction of the cabin where Miquel and the Daniels family had taken refuge. Seeing that they were going away from the city, Elizabeth protested. "We can't leave!"

"Staying in the city would be suicide," Yuri promised her. An explosion in the distance supported his argument.

They drove on.

Before long, they turned off down the hidden track that led to the cabin. They stopped the car nearby. The entire place was silent. They cautiously got out and gave the door three quick knocks and two slower ones. The door opened, and they quickly went in. Once inside in the dark, Jack told his companions everything that had happened.

"Sergei Loban! It's that tyrant's fault that we're in this situation," Elizabeth said, cursing him.

"Sergei? I doubt he has anything to do with tonight," Yuri declared.

"How could you defend him? The man's a monster."

Yuri raised an eyebrow, as if surprised by the young woman's opinion.

"Elizabeth's right. Sergei's behind all of this," said Jack.

Yuri scratched his chin and spat. "I don't think you know what you're talking about. Sergei might be a harsh man, but we know him to be fair. Anyone will say the same thing. If not for him, the OGPU would run rife in Gorky."

"And that's why he's overseeing this indiscriminate killing, is it?"

"I'm telling you, he has nothing to do with it."

"And how can you be so sure?"

"I see you haven't heard," Yuri said, giving a long sigh. "Sergei Loban was arrested early this afternoon and accused of high treason. They've removed him from his post and sent him to the *ispravdom*. Viktor Smirnov is responsible for the massacre. He's in charge of the OGPU now."

39

Jack decided to return to Gorky the moment he understood that Natasha Lobanova's life was in grave danger. Perhaps the photograph in which she appeared with Smirnov had clouded his judgment, but something inside him made him believe in her. Yuri tried to make him see that what he was about to do was madness, but Jack wouldn't budge. For the first time in his life, he didn't care what happened to him.

"All right. I'll come with you, then."

Outside the cabin, Yuri stopped Jack.

"I didn't want to ask you before, but what do you plan to do with all these people? You only asked for three passports, plus the one for the Russian girl."

Jack had no answer. In fact, he hadn't thought about it. At that moment, all he cared about was Natasha. "We'll figure something out," he said, starting the car again.

With Yuri giving directions, they reached Natasha's neighborhood without being intercepted. On the way, they had agreed that Jack would wait in the vehicle while Yuri tried to find out where she was. The Russian was convinced that if Natasha was still free, she would have hidden in a nearby house. She knew almost every neighbor, and if she asked, they wouldn't hesitate to help her.

Jack watched Yuri set off into the darkness. When the Russian was out of sight, he kept low while he tried to gather his thoughts, his mind exhausted from so many revelations.

He still didn't know exactly what role both Sergei and Hewitt had played in all that had happened, but that the true criminal was Viktor Smirnov was an irrefutable truth. His false evidence implicating Hewitt in McMillan's murder was just one element in an intricate plot in which Walter had been a pawn.

He thought of Natasha and Smirnov. He struggled to imagine what connection there was between them and why Viktor kept a photograph of the two of them in his study. But the fact was that Natasha had warned him against Viktor, and he hadn't listened.

He wanted to believe that she still had the same feelings for him as he did for her, feelings that tormented him; he wanted to believe that he'd be able to enjoy her skin and her kisses again. He couldn't understand what kind of spell it was that had made him feel so captivated by a woman who was so different from those he'd always dreamed of. Natasha wasn't conventionally beautiful; she didn't enjoy luxury or care about status; she didn't give a damn about mansions, or appearances, or money. She lived her life with no ambition to climb in society; she seemed happy to do her job with honesty, and the gratitude of her patients was, to her, more important than any fee. And yet, when he was close to her, her smile bewitched him, her conversation drew him in, her sighs touched him, and her jokes disarmed him. He knew that he loved her because her mere presence made him a better person, someone different. And because in her absence, the old Jack Beilis, with all his ambitions and frustrations, always returned.

He prayed that Yuri would find her. However, when the Russian's solitary silhouette appeared at the end of the street, he felt his stomach turn. Yuri was still climbing into the car when Jack, fearing the worst, asked him what he had found out.

"She's safe in a neighbor's apartment."

Jack sighed with relief.

In the first light of dawn, the two men made their way through some newly built and still unpainted apartment blocks, and up a dark staircase with chipped walls. As they climbed, they crossed paths with a couple abandoning their home, loaded down with bundles. Yuri urged Jack to keep climbing. On the fifth floor, Yuri approached a door on which the lock had been forced, and he knocked. They could hear whispering. Yuri identified himself, and the groan of a heavy piece of furniture told them that the entrance had been cleared. The door squeaked on its hinges and opened very slowly, revealing Natasha's bloodied face. Jack didn't wait for an invitation. Anguished, he kissed her, and she responded. When they separated, it became clear that the blood that covered her face and hands wasn't hers. Going into the house, he saw several families huddled together at the back of the room. Natasha, without a word, quickly guided him to a little kitchen, where Jack was appalled by the scene he encountered. On the wooden table a young girl with a terrible wound in her stomach was in the throes of death, while a woman who might have been her mother was trying to stop the bleeding with some dirty bandages.

"What is this? What's happening?"

Natasha barely looked at him. She moved the woman aside and tried again to stop the bleeding. The girl, her eyes wide with horror, was shaking and gasping. The floor was a pool of blood. Natasha worked with determination.

"There was an explosion, and these people came to find me. It's madness, Jack," she cried. "Everything we've fought for seems to be crumbling. For pity's sake, help me!"

Jack held the girl to keep her still, while Natasha's hands disappeared into the rush of red liquid coming from the child's belly. Suddenly, the girl called to her mother and gripped her hand. A second later she stopped moving. For a moment there was absolute silence, until it was interrupted by her mother's heartrending scream. Natasha kept bandaging the child, who lay pale and motionless. Jack understood that, though aware of the truth of the situation, Natasha was refusing to accept the girl's death.

"Leave her. She's gone," Jack whispered, and gently tried to move her away.

Natasha sobbed. Jack held her in his arms until she slowly separated herself from him. "Let's go outside," she suggested.

Jack followed her. They left the apartment and headed into the corridor. Natasha, her eyes red, looked through a little window at the columns of smoke rising up from the Avtozavod.

"My father . . ."

"I know. Yuri told me he's been arrested. I'm sorry. I . . ."

"He's dead, Jack. My father's dead." She burst into tears, heartbroken.

Jack felt the blood freeze in his veins. Yuri had only mentioned that he'd been imprisoned. He thought she must be mistaken. However, when Natasha gazed up at him, looking more helpless than he'd ever seen her, he understood the truth of her words. "What . . . what happened?"

"A colleague from the hospital told me. He showed up at my house to tell me that he'd killed himself. That my father admitted his involvement and shot himself at the *ispravdom*. The bastards! They killed him, Jack! They murdered him . . ." The tears stopped her from continuing.

Jack held her again. When her sobbing subsided, he squeezed her hands between his.

"Come with me to America."

She looked at him, as if unable to comprehend his words. "With you?"

"We'll escape this place and start a new life. I've ordered you a passport. I just need a photo of you, and—"

"And abandon them?" She gestured at the room where she'd tended to the girl. "Leave behind everything that my father fought for?"

"It's not safe for you here. Yuri thinks they'll come after you."

"No, Jack. I'm not going to allow those people to sully my father's name. I'll find out what happened. I'll find the evidence and make the culprits pay for their crimes."

"But don't you see? Nothing you do will stop them."

"I don't care!" She freed herself from Jack. "Damn them, Jack! Damn them!"

Jack took a long, deep breath. He saw Yuri's silhouette waiting impatiently on the landing and gestured to him to wait. "They might not be of any use, but I found some documents," he finally said. "Some reports that show the transactions that the supposed traitor made to Hewitt."

"The transactions they're accusing my father of making? That was the lie they used to arrest him. They said he was the one who transferred the funds to Hewitt so they could split the profits later. But it's not true, Jack! I knew my father. As a girl, I saw him go hungry to share his rations with his men. I saw his scars, the ones caused by the explosion when he shielded a teenage soldier. He sweated blood for the revolution. He dreamed of a fair society. A better world. He instilled it in me. My father was . . ." She cried again. "He was a great man, Jack . . . a great man."

Jack remained silent. He looked at Yuri again, who shook his head in disapproval. "The reports I'm talking about, the documents I had access to, they were official records. From the Vesenkha. But with one important detail: the account number didn't match the one they gave in the trial."

"What do you mean?"

"They proved that the issuer wasn't your father. I don't know who it was, but the money definitely came from another account."

"And where are these reports?" Her eyes lit up with hope.

Jack shook his head. "They snatched them from me and burned them." He didn't tell her about the copies he'd made. Giving them to her would only make her put herself at risk.

"God!" She let herself fall, despondent.

"Natasha, now that you know that your father's innocent, there's nothing to keep you here. I can get you out. Let's escape while we can!"

"Don't you understand, Jack? Before I only suspected it, but now there's proof. We can show them that—"

"We can't show them anything! I'm telling you they burned those reports! Who do you think is going to believe you?"

"But you could give a statement saying what you've just told me."

"If I did, all I'd do is get us both killed."

"How can you be such a coward? You can't hide now!"

He knew that Natasha wasn't thinking straight, but Jack couldn't help feeling like he'd been stabbed in the stomach. "Hide? Me? And what've you done all this time? Hide because you're ashamed of me. And hidden me from everyone: your friends, your own father. And you ask me to come out and sacrifice myself to defend the honor of the man to whom you never even admitted we were together? Why didn't you tell anyone? Why?"

Natasha looked at Jack as if she didn't know him. "I . . . I was never ashamed of you, Jack."

"That's what you say now." His expression was bitter. "Do you know what? There've been times when I've dreamed I could be happy by your side. All you had to do was trust me, instead of hiding how you felt."

"It wasn't like that, Jack . . . You don't know—"

"Yeah, there're a lot of things I don't know." He remembered the photograph of her and Viktor Smirnov, an engagement ring on her finger.

"Jack!" Yuri broke in. "We have to get out of here! Soldiers are coming!"

"Look. This has all been a big mistake." Natasha was trembling. "I thought I knew you, but really you were always a stranger."

"Yes. That's what I've been." Jack's eyes filled with tears.

"We have to go!" Yuri urged him.

Jack nodded. He was about to go with Yuri, when suddenly he remembered something and stopped. "Hold on. There's one thing I forgot." He looked at her. "There was a Soviet engineer who traveled to the United States for training; he was the one who I believe carried out the sabotage. I never managed to find him, but if it helps, his name was Mamayev."

"Mamayev? Vladimir Mamayev?"

"Yes. You know him?"

Natasha's head dropped, and it remained there while a gut-wrenching sob shook her body. When she looked up again, her face was twisted with pain. "I had a relationship with that man, and God knows I regret it." She looked at Jack, seeking his understanding. "Vladimir Mamayev was the name that Viktor Smirnov used so my father wouldn't recognize him when he called for me. If I didn't make our relationship—yours and mine—public, it was to protect you."

"Jack! They're coming up the stairs!"

"Shit! I'm coming!" Jack yelled, and he turned to Natasha again. "For God's sake, come with me. There's a new life waiting for us."

"I'm sorry, Jack. I can't."

"Can't you see that if you stay here, you're sealing your fate?"

"No, Jack. It's you who's forgetting that, even if fate leads us into the abyss, there's always hope."

A gunshot rang out on the landing below them.

"Natasha!"

"Use the roof. Go. Go and save yourself. You may not understand it now, but when you're far away and can no longer hear my voice, close your eyes and listen to your heart."

40

Jack drove at full speed. Yuri had gotten out of the car near his uncle Ivan's house to see if more false passports could be supplied, and they'd agreed to meet again at nightfall at the cabin where the Americans were hiding.

When Jack arrived at the cabin, he parked the vehicle in the granary and knocked as agreed. They were all inside waiting, afraid: Elizabeth, the four members of the Daniels family, Miquel Agramunt, and Joe Brown. Eight in all, including Jack. If Natasha came, there would be nine of them. It was a lot of people. Too many.

He updated them on the situation. They would have to stay hidden in the cabin until Yuri returned with news, and they'd remain there until he could provide passports. They didn't ask, so Jack didn't mention how difficult it would be to obtain the documents or what they would cost. They counted their provisions and shared some stale cookies. Four cookies each. They ate with no appetite and sat down to wait, huddled together. Outside, the morning wind roared.

Their Soviet adventure was coming to an end. Jack smiled bitterly. He remembered the old headlines in the *New York Times* that extolled the virtues of a revolution on the other side of the ocean. The headlines that had captivated Walter and thousands of desperate people like him. The headlines that had ended his life and that of so many others.

He wanted to believe that the hell they were in would end. For a moment, he imagined himself back in America, driving through New York in his new car, wearing a hundred-dollar suit on his way to the latest show. Dancing and smiling again. At least that was something he could aspire to with all the money he had acquired. He felt the rolls of bills that he'd distributed around his coat, some near his heart. As he did so, he felt a void right under it, in the place that Natasha Lobanova was meant to occupy. Natasha, the woman he was in love with.

He prayed that she would change her mind. That she would see that staying in Gorky made no sense, and that she'd come with Yuri to the cabin. He imagined her, radiant, strolling through Central Park with her hand in his, going up the giant skyscrapers to look at the horizon, enjoying life, the two of them together.

The trial would have resumed by now. Viktor Smirnov would be bringing the farce to a close, applauded by the same flunkies who, clearly, had supported him in bringing about Sergei's downfall. They would present more false evidence of Sergei's treachery, and Hewitt's, and his niece's, and even that of the translator who'd disappeared.

He looked at the Danielses. They had no passports, no savings, no food. Joe Brown shivered under a threadbare blanket. He had only wanted a fair chance at a better life, and now he was freezing and hungry, dreaming of returning to the country where they had called him *Negro* every day of his life. Miquel hummed a song that Jack guessed came from his homeland. He stroked his red *barretina* as if it were his most treasured possession. Elizabeth sighed. She hadn't stopped sighing for a single moment. Surely her uncle Wilbur was dead. Jack pitied all of them, but most of all he pitied himself. He let his body slide down the wall until his backside found the floor. He longed to be with Natasha. He could only hope that Yuri would bring her to him.

They sat in silence for hours, frightened by the bursts of gunfire in the distance. Not long after nightfall, the sound of footsteps put them on the alert. Jack gripped a knife and approached the door. Joe Brown did the same. They waited, holding their breath as the footsteps neared. It sounded like several people. Jack signaled to Joe Brown to get ready. Joe crossed himself. Knuckles rapped on the door. A few seconds later, they heard Yuri's voice. Jack hoped Natasha was with him, but when he opened the door, he found himself face-to-face with Ivan Zarko. The two men slipped quickly into the cabin. Yuri had a sack of black bread. He opened it and shared out the loaves.

"Do you know anything about the trial?" Elizabeth asked.

Though Jack could guess the answer, he translated the question.

"They've sentenced him. Apparently, Stalin's staying in Gorky until Smirnov has crushed the rebellion, which complicates matters as far as your escape is concerned. And now, if you don't mind, I need to discuss some details with Jack, outside," Zarko said apologetically.

After translating his answer, Jack pulled on his *ushanka* and went out with Ivan and his nephew. Once outside, he asked Yuri about Natasha.

Yuri shook his head. "I tried to persuade her, but it was like talking to a rock. The hospital was full of wounded. Workers shot to pieces, men and women who'd been tortured, burned . . . She spoke to me while she helped a half-dead mother give birth."

"I'll go find her."

"It's pointless. They've issued a warrant for your arrest, and they're watching her. If you go, in all likelihood they'll end up killing all of us."

Jack nodded in resignation. Though he had expected Natasha's answer, he had held out hope for a different one. He asked Zarko for the passports, but the old man shook his head.

"You said four! One for you, one for the capitalist, one for his niece, and another for the Russian girl."

"How much would six more cost?"

"It's not a question of money, Jack. Yours are ready, but the way things are, obtaining more will be impossible. We'd need small photographs, blank passports, new signatures . . . With Smirnov heading the OGPU, any slip would mean the firing squad."

"How much, Ivan?"

"Too much."

Jack looked down at the ground. Then he turned toward the cabin, where six souls waited to hear their fate. "Could you get a camera?"

"I guess so, but the problem's not the photos so much as the passports themselves. Yours are German, but for them we'd need one Spanish and five American. We'd have to order them from Moscow, get the right signatures . . ."

"You find the camera. Maybe we can do something about the passports later on, somewhere else."

Ivan Zarko shook his head, as if implying that trying to escape without passports was madness. Even so, he agreed to Jack's request.

"As for the escape route, you mentioned a freight train . . ."

"You have to forget the railway. They've fenced off the station and stepped up security with packs of trained dogs. They're searching every train leaving Gorky from top to bottom."

"We have the car." He gestured toward it. "Squeezed in, we could—"

"You wouldn't make it sixty miles. They've set up roadblocks, and the secondary roads are impassible because of the snow. Not to mention the issue of fuel. Your only chance is the Volga. Gorky's wharves are heavily guarded, but downriver I could arrange passage for you on a barge that could take you to Stalingrad. There we have friends who could keep you hidden until you are able to take another boat to the Sea of Azov. But there's a problem . . ."

"Yes?"

"There're too many of you. It will be a risky journey . . ." He made it clear to Jack that their chances of success were slim. "And it will cost money." He gestured toward the fugitives. "A lot."

"Damn it! I'll pay! Forget the money."

"It's up to you. I'll get that camera."

"One more thing." He stopped Yuri as he turned away. He took off his *ushanka* and then the medallion his mother had given him. When he handed the necklace to Yuri, he felt as if he were parting with a piece of himself. "Here. It's the last favor I'll ask of you. Give this to Natasha. Tell her that, without love, life isn't worth living."

He told his friends not to worry, that Ivan and Yuri would solve their problems and lead them to freedom.

Elizabeth believed him. The rest of them guessed what really awaited them.

Jack sat down and fell silent. Until the last moment, he had hoped that Natasha would come with him, but she had chosen to fight for her ideals. For an instant, he cursed her integrity, her senseless generosity, and her commitment to solidarity. He cursed them from the bottom of his soul. And yet, he couldn't reproach her for them. She overflowed with honesty, while he, when it came down to it, was just a poor wretch.

He chewed on a piece of black bread and tried to get her out of his mind. He had to forget her once and for all and get used to the idea that he was returning to the United States, perhaps to lead the life he had always wanted alongside a young heiress to a fortune. Her time in isolation seemed to have changed Elizabeth. She now not only accepted her uncle's fate, but in a moment of weakness, had even suggested some future plans for Jack.

He gave a wry smile. Anyone would envy him in his place. In America a wonderful life awaited him, filled with comfort and enjoyment at the side of a rich, intoxicatingly beautiful woman. A wonderful but empty life.

The whole next day passed without any sign of Yuri and Ivan Zarko. While they waited, Elizabeth huddled next to Jack. She barely spoke, but held on to him, as if she knew he was her only support. At intervals she would ask him whether they would be happy in America, and he said yes without conviction. The hours passed slowly, each of them searching the faces of the others for a glimmer of hope. By midafternoon, they gave up waiting. All they could hear outside was the howling blizzard.

On the third day, Ivan returned with Yuri. They arrived at dawn. Jack had been awake for hours, unable to sleep. Hearing them arrive, he separated himself from Elizabeth and rushed to open the door that he'd jammed shut with a pole. The two Russians quickly came in and woke the rest of the group. Ivan and Yuri told them that they had to begin their escape as soon as possible, as OGPU patrols were now searching the forest for fugitives. They all hurried to get ready. They gathered their belongings and left the cabin in the direction of the outbuilding where the Ford Model A was hidden.

While the rest of them loaded the vehicle, Jack stayed behind to make final preparations for their escape. Ivan Zarko gave him the camera, a map with directions to the river port of Lyskovo, and the name and address of the contact who would hide them.

"He will arrange your passage. In Stalingrad, Oleg will be waiting for you. An old acquaintance. He'll identify himself and keep you hidden until you can get on the next boat."

"Thank you for everything. You and Yuri have been true friends."

"You've paid us well for it. Here. The three passports."

Jack embraced him. He knew the old man was taking risks that no money could compensate him for. When they separated, he put his hand in his overcoat. "What we agreed for the camera and everything else." Jack handed him four rolls of bills. "And the six other passports?"

Ivan Zarko shook his head.

"All right. We'll manage," replied Jack, though he knew that those without passports would never escape.

He climbed into the car and turned the key. Yuri opened the door to the granary. Jack was in a daze, staring down the track and waiting for Natasha to appear at the last moment. A few seconds passed. Elizabeth urged him to start the car. Jack seemed to wake up. He stepped on the button next to the accelerator, and the engine roared into life. He was about to accelerate, when Ivan approached to say good-bye. As Jack lowered the window, Yuri dipped his big hand in a pocket, took out the medallion that Jack had given him to pass on to Natasha, and returned it to him.

"I'm sorry," said Yuri. "She had decided to come."

"What?" He thought he had misheard.

"Natasha. She told me there was no need for you to part with your medallion, because she'd already decided that she'd go with you to America."

"She was going to come? So where is she?" He turned off the engine.

Yuri lowered his head. "We waited for her, but she didn't show up."

"What do you mean she didn't show up? I don't understand. She agreed to meet you and didn't arrive? Damn it! Can you explain to me what happened?" He got out of the vehicle.

Yuri avoided eye contact.

"I'm asking you what happened!" He grabbed Yuri by the front of his coat, and the Russian searched for a sign from Zarko of what to do.

The old man approached Jack and made him let go of Yuri. "I warned you not to tell him," he said to his nephew. He spat on the ground, as if the earth were to blame. Then, biting his lips, he looked at Jack. "They arrested her when she was coming out of her house. It was Smirnov. They're sending her to Siberia."

The echo of some distant barking tore Jack from his bewilderment. He didn't think twice. He asked Joe Brown to take his place at the wheel. Joe didn't understand. When he told them to leave without him, none of his friends could believe what they were hearing. But Jack remained firm. His eyes were bright with determination.

Neither the Daniels family's pleading nor Elizabeth's tears persuaded him. Jack remained outside the car and asked Miquel Agramunt to take care of everyone. "Only you can save them. Don't let me down." He embraced the man as if he were saying good-bye to the brother he never had.

Agramunt agreed to do as he said.

Jack gave him the three passports, the instructions for using the camera, and a roll of bills. The barking was growing closer. They could almost smell the dogs. Jack moved away from the car, and they were about to leave when Elizabeth opened the door and climbed out. "I'm staying with you," she said, trying to hide her tears.

Jack shook his head. "It's too dangerous. You have to go with them. I'll catch up with you later."

"You won't make it. Do you think I didn't see you give Miquel the passports?"

"Because of that? Don't be silly." He took George McMillan's passport from his coat and showed it to her. "Do you really think I was going to stay in this filthy country?"

Elizabeth glanced at the document. Something told her not to believe him. "Jack, I'm begging you, get in the car. We'll be happy . . ." Her red, swollen eyelids hid the beauty of her eyes.

"I can't."

"Sure you can! For heaven's sake, Jack! Do you think I haven't seen you? It's because of that woman, right?"

"I have to try."

"And what will you do? Shout from the rooftops that she's innocent? Goddamn it, Jack, don't you see? As soon as you show up, Viktor will kill you."

"I'm sorry, Elizabeth. I can't leave her."

"Just think for a moment! When I asked you to help my uncle, you told me yourself it was hopeless," she implored him. "The Soviets won't believe you. They wouldn't believe you even if Viktor screamed a confession at them." She collapsed to the ground.

Jack was silent. He knew Elizabeth was right, but something inside him more powerful was compelling him to stay. He helped the young woman up and made her get in the car. He kissed her hand and closed the door.

"Go! Drive!"

Joe Brown obeyed. He stepped on the gas, and the vehicle skidded before straightening and heading off down the icy track. When the car was just a dot in the distance, Jack turned to Ivan Zarko, searching for his comprehension, but the man groaned like an old woman.

"What are you trying to do? You know that passport's worthless," he said.

"I know." He tore it into pieces and threw it in a ditch.

"So what're you going to do?"

Jack let the wind whip his face. "First, make sure you get those people to Odessa alive and well. Passports . . . tickets . . . whatever." He took all his savings from his overcoat and handed them to Ivan Zarko. "I hope it's enough."

Ivan blushed as he counted the money. He had never imagined that Jack could have amassed so much, much less hand it over to him. He stuffed it into his coat and nodded. "Sure, it's enough. And then?"

Jack gazed at the wheel marks left by the car as it sped off through the snow. He sucked in air and let out a lungful of breath before looking at Ivan with sadness in his eyes. "Then I'll need your help, one last time."

41

Jack sat waiting in a corner near the fireplace at his house. Despite the warmth from the embers, he was trembling like a frightened child, though he wasn't afraid. His shivering was just the product of nervous energy. He knew his ill-fated journey was coming to an end. He closed his eyes and tried to picture Natasha. Gradually, her face materialized. At first it was vague, pale, languid. Then her eyes came to life, a smile spread across her face, and her white hands stroked his face delicately, as they always did. He felt her love. He smiled.

He rubbed his eyes to fight back his exhaustion. He'd worked through the night to get everything ready. His watch showed ten o'clock. Smirnov would arrive soon. He served himself a glass of vodka, drinking it in one mouthful, and waited patiently. Ten minutes later, Smirnov knocked on the door.

"So, you've been hiding in this pigsty? I thought you had more taste." He gave a cynical smile, brushed Jack aside, and entered the house along with his guards.

Jack followed behind them in silence.

"So?" Smirnov went on. "The message you sent said something about some reports and an account number. Where are they?"

"Somewhere safe," Jack lied.

"Somewhere safe, of course. And may I ask what you intend to do with them?"

"Nothing special. Just use them to make you release Natasha and confess your crimes."

"Ha!" As he laughed, Smirnov revealed a row of perfect white teeth. "My crimes . . . You have a lot of nerve for a poor foreigner destined for the cemetery."

"I can see you still hate the poor. Is that why you got rid of Sergei? So you could enrich yourself at the expense of the Avtozavod? To steal money from the workers?"

"You, wait outside!" he ordered his minions. He drew his revolver and waited for them to obey. When they'd left, he smiled. "Come on, Jack! Have you forgotten that Sergei confessed? It was he who diverted a fortune to Hewitt's account, and allowed the sabotage to halt production. Luckily, I uncovered him."

"Would that be the same luck that got you to America under the name Vladimir Mamayev? It's curious, Viktor, but you were the only man at the Avtozavod who knew enough to cause the defects in the machinery without being detected. The useless Smirnov, who didn't even know how to tighten a screw."

"Such a lively imagination! I love it, Jack! I never would have guessed that you were such a marvelous storyteller." He paced around Jack.

"So, you think I'm making it all up. Fair enough. But then why did you come to my house accompanied by armed men? Stalin's in Gorky. Don't you have anything better to do? Wait! Maybe I can suggest something. Perhaps you could be getting rid of any evidence of account 660598865. The account that identifies you as the real issuer of the transfers and the man behind the sabotage at the Avtozavod."

"Very well. Let's stop playing games." He aimed the gun at Jack's head. "Where are the reports?"

"Tell me, Viktor . . . When did you start hatching this plan? Was it when George McMillan discovered your intentions? Was that why you murdered him?"

"I'm losing my patience!"

"Do you know what? When Sergei recited McMillan's telephone call during the trial, one thing that struck me was that, at the end of the call, the American hung up without saying good-bye. I thought it must have been an omission from the transcript, but I checked it out, and those transcriptions always include the pauses, the sneezes . . . every last sigh. If Sergei didn't read McMillan's good-bye, it was because the person who was spying on the American at that moment ended his life before he could give him away. The same person who accused Wilbur Hewitt in the trial of a crime he himself had committed. Hewitt, an invalid at the time, would have found it impossible to carry his own suitcase, let alone, as you assured us, lift a man weighing more than two hundred pounds and throw him over a balustrade."

"Jack . . . Jack . . . Are you forgetting that it was Sergei who submitted that evidence?"

"Evidence that you provided to him, right when you learned that Stalin would be coming to Gorky. I don't know how you made Sergei believe you, but it was an ideal situation for you, wasn't it? The perfect moment for Sergei, unable to uncover the traitor he'd been pursuing for so long, to receive evidence that until then he knew nothing about. And the perfect time, moments later, to reveal to Stalin that Sergei, head of the OGPU and whose position you coveted, was a corrupt official whose crimes had to be exposed. The perfect moment to put yourself forward as the hero. Was that how you did it? Was that when you altered the accounts again? Was that when you planned to murder him and take everything for yourself?"

"And what if I did?" he yelled. "Sergei believed me when I told him that I'd put off testifying under direct orders from Moscow, and he kept quiet when I threatened to kill his daughter. Sergei was nothing but a pathetic idealist, a self-righteous fool who really believed in equality for all. Equality? For whom? For those miserable peasants who don't know a screw from a lump of dung? What's the point of having power and wealth if you can't enjoy them?"

"And what does that have to do with massacring innocent people, Viktor? Do you really need to exterminate them to achieve your goals?"

"Ha! Those counterrevolutionaries are scum. Soulless scum! Can you imagine the look on their faces if they knew I had funded the sabotage?"

"You?"

"Come on, Jack. I thought you were smarter than this. What better way to discredit Sergei's work?"

"Sergei responded to the sabotage with an iron fist, sending the perpetrators to labor camps. That was why you decided to implicate him in the misappropriation of funds. To free yourself of him and Hewitt. I imagine that it would have been easy for you as finance commissar to take money from the Avtozavod and invent a bogus company in the name of Mamayev to transfer the money to Hewitt and incriminate Sergei. Once they were out of the picture, you could control the Avtozavod and the millions of rubles in its accounts as you pleased."

"Very good . . . It seems the imminence of death has sharpened your intellect. It's just a shame that—"

Suddenly, his eyes seemed to catch sight of something. Still keeping the revolver aimed at Jack, he moved slowly to the fireplace, where he pushed the embers with his boot.

"Well, well, well, Jack . . . what do we have here?" He bent and picked up a piece of singed paper that he'd just noticed in the ashes, examining it in the ray of light from the window. "It looks like the remains of the report I was looking for! Who would have guessed it? It looks like that idiot Walter Scott carried out his mission after all." He laughed and struck Jack with the butt of his revolver.

Jack staggered. Despite the pain, he kept his composure, while a trickle of blood ran down from the corner of his mouth.

"Damned American! I should have had you killed when you escaped the conveyor, like I did Orlov."

Jack spat out a mouthful of blood. Until that moment, he'd believed that Orlov had set the conveyor in motion. "And what stopped you?"

"Your friend Walter. He persuaded me you'd be more useful alive, and to be fair, he was right, because he kept me informed of everything you confided to him." He dealt Jack another blow, making him go down on one knee. "Pretentious fool . . . You thought you were the smart one. You believed you had me eating out of your hand while you repaired the Buick, but you didn't know how quickly I discovered your game. Yes. The young man from the party at the Metropol whom I pretended not to recognize, and who had the nerve to show up at my house wearing a bird's-eye suit. A suit that I would've recognized among a thousand others because I gave it to McMillan as a gift. It was a shame my gifts didn't have the desired effect on him and I was forced to kill him." His laughter was boastful. "Tell me, Jack . . . Did you really think I'd even care that you had some lousy document? Ha! A million reports wouldn't have persuaded Stalin. That cretin would never convict me because he'll always blindly believe every word a relative of his says. You're as arrogant as Sergei and Natasha."

"Leave Natasha out of this. She has nothing to do with it."

"Oh, but she does. She and her father despised me. Did you know Natasha left me? Me! Viktor Smirnov! Stuck-up whore . . . How dare she cast me off!" he cried as if Natasha were in the room and could hear him.

Jack took a step back. "That was why she didn't want you to know about me and her, right? That was the reason. Natasha wasn't hiding me from her father; it was your rage she was trying to protect me from."

"You know what? I think we should continue this conversation somewhere where you can share with us the names of all the people who've helped you." He cocked his weapon. "How ironic, Jack. You came to Russia searching for paradise, and I'm the one who will be sending you there. And, so you see how much I appreciate you, I'll send Natasha with you."

"Goddamned bastard! She's innocent!"

"I'm sure she is," he said with a cynical laugh, "but I can't allow Loban's daughter to run around plotting how to avenge her father's death. Men! Get in here and hold on to him!" he yelled.

Jack felt rage compress his lungs until he couldn't breathe. He thought of Natasha, and her memory urged him into action. Taking advantage of the distraction when Viktor's henchmen entered the house, he swooped on his adversary, dealing him a head butt that made him collapse like a rag doll. Sprawled on the floor, Smirnov screamed at his men to restrain his assailant. One of them grabbed Jack, but he spun around and knocked him down with a punch. He was about to throw himself on Viktor again when, suddenly, he felt a sharp, burning pain in his chest. Then his legs weakened, and he collapsed to his knees. Incredulous, he looked at the dagger that one of the soldiers had just plunged into his chest. When he looked up, he saw Viktor's stunned face.

As his vision went dark, he heard the new head of the OGPU scolding his men for the stabbing. Then he remembered Natasha's sweet, honey-flavored kisses. The sweetness turned sour as vinegar as he fell headlong onto the floor.

42

Two days later, with the rebellion stifled and the insurgents arrested, the courtroom at the Palace of Justice reopened for the public trial of the Soviet people versus Natasha Lobanova. The new commissar in charge of the OGPU, Viktor Smirnov, was acting as prosecutor, with Stalin himself the chair. The leader had decided to remain in Gorky until the trial was resolved. After listening to Smirnov's web of lies about her and her father and his request for a death sentence, Natasha stood impassively waiting for the chairman to give his verdict.

The entire room fell silent when Joseph Stalin stood.

"Natasha Lobanova. You are accused of conspiring against the revolution, plotting with your father, and committing high treason, crimes punishable by death. Do you have anything to say?" the chairman asked.

During the hearing, Natasha had already said everything she had to say. Strong and proud, she fixed her eyes on Stalin's, knowing that there was nothing she could say that would alter her sentence. In other circumstances, she would have defended herself, but after Yuri had told her that Smirnov had killed Jack and taken his body, there was nothing left for her to live for. Without Jack, she no longer cared.

"Very well. In that case, as chairman of this court"—he paused to look at Natasha—"I declare the defendant, Natasha Lobanova, guilty of the crimes of which she has been accused, and sentence her to the death penalty. The accused will be executed as soon as—"

"One moment!" A trembling voice was heard, coming from the back of the room.

The audience turned to see an old man, his face covered in scars, burst in from the corridor, accompanied by another man in a bow tie carrying a varnished mahogany box.

"By Lenin's whiskers!" Smirnov sputtered. "Arrest those men!"

"Mr. General Secretary, I beg you! I am here to prevent serious damage to the Soviet Union!" The two men walked forward until they were even with Natasha.

"Silence! Who are you?" Stalin asked.

"Mr. General Secretary, with the utmost respect, I request permission to speak." He gave something like a bow. "My name is Valeri Pushkin, retired lawyer, and the person accompanying me is Louis Thomson, the *New York Times* Moscow correspondent. We possess information of great importance to this case and—"

"All the statements have already been heard, and the accused has been found guilty."

"Yes . . . but, Mr. General Secretary, if you will allow me, you haven't yet finished meting out a sentence, and as the second paragraph of Article 18 of the Penal Code sets out, all Soviet citizens have the obligation—yes, the *obligation*—to report any crime included in Article 58. It says so here." He opened the copy of the Penal Code that he was carrying and waved it in the air.

"Article 58 refers to counterrevolutionary crimes, and this court has already addressed them," Stalin roared.

"Yes. However, the crime I am referring to, though related to Natasha Lobanova's case, is another. Please, permit me to—"

"What manner of insubordination is this?" Smirnov cut in. "Arrest him!"

"Mr. General Secretary"—the old lawyer knelt in a calculated theatrical gesture—"Article 1 of our Penal Code specifically states that the purpose of the criminal law of the Russian Soviet Federative Socialist Republic is to defend the socialist workers' and peasants' state. If you do not hear me, you run the risk of the Avtozavod falling into the hands of criminals." He saw Smirnov leave the dais and head toward him, pistol in hand. "I beg you, Comrade Stalin. Do not squander the opportunity to let the Americans know that in the Soviet Union, justice really does prevail."

Stalin flushed red. For a moment, he looked as if he would draw his own pistol and shoot the retired lawyer himself. However, he clenched his fists and gestured to Smirnov to stop. "It's all right, Viktor. Leave him," Stalin said. "You said your name was Valeri . . . ?"

"Valeri. Valeri Pushkin."

"Very well, Comrade Pushkin. Show us what you have to show us, and let's put an end to this business once and for all."

Viktor Smirnov returned his weapon to its holster, but before doing so, he aimed it at the old lawyer and pretended to shoot. Valeri swallowed. Then he opened the mahogany box, and with Louis Thomson's help, took out a strange device.

"I need a socket. Aha! There's one . . ."

Smirnov went pale. "Comrade Stalin! Are you going to allow this crazy old man to make a mockery of us?" he bellowed.

"Let him continue. I'm curious. What device is that?"

"It is an American invention, Mr. General Secretary. A *phonograph*, I believe they call it." The lawyer plugged in the contraption and turned it on.

"Are you going to play us all a Russian march?"

"Huh? Oh no, sir. These devices are old, really, but very interesting. Unlike modern gramophones, which can only reproduce sound, these contraptions can also record it . . . I'll show you."

On his signal, Louis Thomson took a can from the box, removed the lid, and extracted a hollow wax cylinder. He positioned it over the phonograph's axis, placed the sapphire stylus on the surface, and turned on the motor. The wax cylinder began to turn on itself until suddenly it filled the room with the refrain from *Polovtsian Dances of Prince Igor*. Before Stalin could recover from his astonishment, the lawyer withdrew the needle and took out a knife. "Now listen," Pushkin said.

Without stopping the cylinder, he applied the sharp edge of the knife to the cylinder to plane off the outer layer on which the music was engraved, until the cylinder was left completely smooth. Then he placed the stylus back on the surface of the wax, activated a lever, and fell silent.

"Comrade Stalin! I told you that this man is a lunatic!" Smirnov yelled, and he came down from the dais to arrest the lawyer himself.

However, Valeri Pushkin, undaunted, stopped the device, changed the position of the lever, and turned it on again. Before Smirnov reached him, a metallic voice rang out in the courtroom.

Comrade Stalin! I told you that this man is a lunatic!

Comrade Stalin! I told you that this man is a lunatic!

Hearing his own voice coming out of the device, Viktor Smirnov stopped in his tracks. While he stood there bewildered, Valeri Pushkin took another can from the mahogany box and replaced the wax cylinder. He restarted the phonograph, and Smirnov's voice once again resounded from the horn. However, now, his words, accompanied by Jack's, were emanating from the horn. Stalin stood up, incredulous.

So you've been hiding in this pigsty? I thought you had more taste.

So? The message you sent said something about some reports and an account number. Where are they?

Somewhere safe.

Somewhere safe, of course. And may I ask what you intend to do with them?

Nothing special. Just use them to make you free Natasha and confess your crimes . . .

The phonograph continued to reel off Viktor Smirnov's confession, to the amazement of the courtroom. Viktor, horrified, tried to interrupt the reproduction, but on a signal from Stalin, several men swooped in and stopped him.

"Comrade Stalin! All of this is a plot!" Smirnov implored as they held him back.

At that moment, with the courtroom in total silence, the phonograph played the final passage.

Tell me, Jack . . . Did you really think I'd even care that you had some lousy document? Ha! A million reports wouldn't have persuaded Stalin. That cretin would never convict me because he'll always blindly believe every word a relative of his says.

While Valeri Pushkin approached the dais to show Stalin the copy of the Vesenkha document that Jack had given to Yuri, he could still hear Viktor Smirnov's final words.

"It's a plot! Damn you all! Damn you, Jack Beilis!"

43

"Dr. Natasha! There's a gentleman outside who would like to see you."

"Please, ask him to wait a moment."

Natasha Lobanova finished bandaging the tiny leg of the baby she'd just operated on and handed the child to its mother. The woman, a peasant wearing a threadbare scarf on her head, was holding another child by the hand while hugging the baby with her free arm as if it were her most treasured possession. Natasha smiled. She washed her hands and walked out of the treatment room. Outside, Wilbur Hewitt was waiting for her. The man took off his hat and left his briefcase on the floor.

"Please excuse my poor Russian, but I didn't want to leave without saying good-bye," Hewitt said.

"I'm sorry I haven't seen you before. I heard that you were acquitted, but there's so much to do in the hospital that I haven't had the chance to—"

"There's no need to apologize." He smiled.

"They tell me your niece reached America."

"Yes, that's right. They managed to get on a ship in Odessa." He paused and adjusted his monocle. "I . . . I'm very sorry about Jack. I didn't know you and he . . ."

"Yes." She bit her lips. Her eyes filled with tears. "Almost nobody knew."

"Well, I'm glad you got your job back. These people need you. Anyway . . . the ambassador's waiting for me. I must go or we'll miss the train to Moscow. Thank you for everything, and good luck."

"To you, too."

Wilbur Hewitt picked up his briefcase and turned around. Outside, surrounded by suitcases, Louis Thomson and a crestfallen Sue were waiting for him.

Natasha watched them leave. When the car was gone, she returned to her office, checked her patient list, and took off her white coat. The sun was setting. With the arrival of spring, the nights were growing shorter again. She said good-bye to her assistants and left the hospital.

She was still living a frugal life on Cooperative Street in a room with a bed, a table and chair, a small wardrobe, and a sideboard piled high with books.

When she closed the door, she walked slowly over to the phonograph that Jack had wanted her to keep. She was glad that Valeri Pushkin had given it to her before leaving for Leningrad with Ivan Zarko and his family. She stroked the mahogany box that protected it and carefully removed it. As if carrying out a ritual, she took the lid off the metal can and removed the wax cylinder. She positioned it over the phonograph's axis and cleaned the surface with a silk handkerchief. When the cylinder began to turn, Jack Beilis's warm voice floated through the room again. Natasha closed her eyes so that she could see him and listen to the sound of his sweet words.

Dear Natasha: I don't know what will happen tomorrow, but whatever happens, don't waste your tears on me. On the contrary: smile. Until today I have drifted through life, trying to run away from poverty as if it were the greatest sorrow, without realizing that the misery traveled with me, in my soul.

Some might be saddened by my fate, but I feel lucky. Few men are able to say that, even if their life turned out to be short, it was really worth living. I have been lucky. Lucky to find you. Lucky to learn that, even if fate leads us into the abyss, there is always hope.

Today, for the first time in my life, I can be the master of my own destiny. And that's why I choose you.

Promise me that you'll never change. That way I'll know that, when you can no longer hear my voice, you will still listen to me in your heart.

When the phonograph let out its final sound, Natasha smiled. Though he was gone, she carried his love with her, so deep inside that nobody would ever be able to take it away.

EPILOGUE

Leonid Varzin set aside the plans for the heat engine and puffed on his *papirosa* as if there were no pleasure more intense. Smoking was one of the two privileges that differentiated him from the other inmates of the Kharkov Prison Camp. The other consisted of staying alive, which was feasible for as long as he and his cellmates successfully developed the prototypes they were working on. While he savored the smoke, Leonid observed the willowy prisoner hammering the fixtures of a frame in the workshop. One after the other, the blows were angry, relentless, each stroke seemingly aimed at the chains of his captivity.

"You should save your strength. At that pace you won't last another six months, and I asked them to keep you alive because we need your skills," he called out.

The prisoner didn't answer. He kept his eyes on the fixture and continued hammering. Leonid and his pals might find respite from the monotony of imprisonment in developing their projects, but for the man with the hammer, helping them was only a means to survive another day, as he had been doing for two years.

When he finished with the rivet, he stood and fixed his blue eyes on the bars over the windows. Outside, it was snowing hard, and the cold numbed his chest in the place where a dagger had once been lodged. He rubbed the scar, and without intending to, brushed his hand against the medallion that still hung from his neck. When he gripped it, the bars slowly vanished.

He kept hammering, with the same determination as on the first day he arrived. For him it was just another day. But when the sun went down, it would be one fewer day until he was reunited with Natasha. One fewer day until, finally, he could enjoy the last paradise.

Author's Note

In the summer of 2011, I began to draft the first pages of this novel. At the time, I was in New York, where I'd traveled in search of rest and inspiration. Each morning, before sitting in front of my laptop, I'd go for a walk in Columbus Park, two blocks from the apartment where I was staying. During one of those walks, I stopped at a colorful market where books were sold by the pound at a price so ridiculous it was as if they were giving them away. I had been browsing for a while when an old essay entitled "Working for the Soviets" caught my attention; it was about the large numbers of Americans who had immigrated to Russia during the Great Depression. I bought it without hesitation. That night, for the first time in many years, I thought of my grandma Bienvenida.

My siblings and I enjoyed a fortunate childhood. Perhaps we didn't have the best toys or go on vacation every summer, but we always had two adorable old ladies by our side, with their curled white hair and their felt slippers, with which they'd briefly threaten us when they grew sick of our mischief. There were two of them, Bienvenida and Sara, and they were twins—twin sisters and twin grandmas.

Bienvenida never married. When Sara was widowed, Bienvenida went to live with her to help her with her small children. Many years later, when we were born, Sara and Bienvenida cared for us with that love and tenderness that only grandparents know how to give. Bienvenida was actually my great-aunt, but in my heart, she was my grandmother, and I only ever thought of her as Grandma Bienvenida.

Sara had her favorite grandchildren, and Bienvenida had hers. I was Bienvenida's.

As I grew up, I became ever more intrigued as to why Grandma Bienvenida never married. She was a sweet and caring woman, with a pleasant face and an enormous heart, and at ten years old, I couldn't understand why she'd remained alone. One winter's night while she rubbed my joints with alcohol to bring down my fever, I dared to ask her. She replied that she'd never found the right man. However, there was a sadness in her face that I'd never seen before, and without knowing why, I knew she was lying to me.

I wasn't wrong. Years later, I caught her crying while she read an old letter. When I approached to console her, she pressed the letter against her heart, and holding back tears, she told me that if I ever fell in love, and however difficult the circumstances, I must fight for that love as if my life depended on it.

We never spoke about it again. Bienvenida died at age ninety-three, when I was seventeen, and it was one of the saddest days of my life.

Years later, my father told me about the fleeting relationship that had marked Grandma Bienvenida. He revealed to me that she once met a young man with whom she fell hopelessly in love. He was a livestock trader and had just returned from the Soviet Union. During the months they spent together, the young man captivated her with his amazing tales of the nation of the Bolsheviks. He described the places where he worked, the immigrants from other countries he met, the wonders he discovered, and the horrors that forced him to flee Russia.

When the Spanish Civil War broke out, he enlisted with the Republicans, and their paths separated. The last Bienvenida heard of him was a letter from the Ebro front, in which her sweetheart repeated that he loved her more than ever, and bemoaned the absurdity of war.

This story was archived in my memory, and remained there until the day I stopped at that colorful market in New York.

That night, in my rented apartment in Brooklyn Heights, I imagined the thousands of desperate people who, like that livestock trader, immigrated to Russia in search of a better future. Those who embarked on a journey to a place where everyone had the right to be happy, without suspecting that they were heading toward their ruin. The lives and deaths of all of those people inspired me to write this story about hope and egotism, about innocence and evil, about ideals and love—a tale of the consequences of fanaticism and poverty, but also, at the same time, a tribute to the sacrifice and fortitude of a group of courageous people who, thrown into an alien world, fought to be the masters of their own destinies.

I didn't want to end this reflection without borrowing the words of an old writer friend, who once assured me that if you search deeply enough, every life contains the inspiration for a beautiful novel. I don't know whether he was right, but what I can say without fear of being mistaken is that this novel was inspired by a beautiful person, my beloved grandma Bienvenida.

A Genuine Story

Regardless of the necessary degree of truthfulness required from any novel inspired by real events, determining the balance of reality versus fiction on each of its pages always puts the writer in a predicament. When I embarked on writing this novel, the options I toyed with brought uncertain rewards. If the documented facts outweighed the fiction, it would enjoy the credibility bestowed by historical rigor, but at the risk of infecting the book with the dryness of a novelized essay. Conversely, if the emotions of the characters took precedence over the facts, it could arouse the suspicion of historians.

For the layperson, an approach based entirely on the facts seems the less risky alternative. However, I was preparing to spend three years of my life writing a novel, so the choice could not be based so much on these considerations as on what I honestly felt the reader deserved. And the reader deserved not so much a true story as a genuine one.

The macroeconomic data that politicians bombard us with does not reflect the reality of an economic depression. A depression is the poor woman whose desperation leads her to throw herself from a balcony because she cannot see a future for her children, or the thousands of destitute people rummaging through waste containers in search of something to eat. Equally, love is not the pleasure of a passing conquest, or a Valentine's Day gift wrapped at the last minute. Love is a widow's gaze as she caresses the photograph of her sweetheart and longs for the embraces they shared, or the throb you feel when you are near the person who makes you want to live every second as if it were your last.

This is why, instead of writing about historical figures, I preferred to tell a story about characters. After all, all I knew about the real figures were their deeds; I knew nothing of their feelings, their fears, their ambitions, the hatred they harbored in their hearts, or their darkest desires. In which case, what should I do? Invent their thoughts, fictionalize their feelings, and fabricate their actions? Would that be honest? Would it be right to put words that they never said in the mouths of historical figures, or describe feelings they never had? Rather than lie, would it not be preferable to create fictitious people of flesh and bone, whose actions could be shaped by those exceptional circumstances that really did change the lives of millions? How would I make readers more realistically experience the terrible events that took place, and what, in short, would be more real?

The decision meant choosing between reason and emotion. The judicious me said, *Play it safe*, but my heart compelled me to lay myself open. In the end, the decision was dictated by feeling. I wanted to write a novel, and a novel is, by definition, fiction. And why do we love fiction? For its unique ability to trigger emotions, to captivate, to make us dream of characters who love and feel just like we do. Their problems interest us because they are our problems, and we are moved by their lives because they are our lives. And because if reason is what makes us human, then feelings are what make us people.

The process

Though this was to be a novel, the complexity of the historical setting of the 1930s required me to redouble my research efforts to ensure that every last detail of my depiction of a period as enthralling as it was heartrending was imbued with plausibility. It was arduous and treacherous work, hindered by the contradictory nature of the records, which varied substantially depending on the source. As clear as the water from a spring may seem, it always carries sediment from the place from which it emerges.

To determine the accuracy of the facts, I classified the documentation according to the political affiliation of its authors, weeding out any documents of a propagandist nature produced by biased factions on whatever side. I did this with the large number of essays and chronicles published in Europe at the time—the contents of which reflect the sentiments of those who saw Russia as a beacon of freedom and hope—and with those who viewed her only as an imminent threat. It is also worth mentioning the large collection of reports, essays, and analyses produced after the advent of glasnost, which were a ray of light in this long and murky tunnel.

As for the thousands of immigrants who, without intending to, became the protagonists in a horror movie not of their making, we can differentiate between three groups. First, the technicians and specialized workers who provided their services in exchange for advantageous remuneration. Second, the handful of idealists who, identifying with the principles of equality and solidarity that underpinned the Soviet Union, left behind everything they had to begin a new life that was as hard as it was altruistic. And finally, the largest contingent and the one that suffered the most hardship as a result of the events that unfolded: the legion of dispossessed Americans who, dazzled by the promises of prosperity advertised in the *New York Times*, left the United States in search of the work and sustenance that their own country denied them.

For this dispossessed group, the adventure proved particularly painful. Most of the Americans who traveled to the Soviet Union did so before the United States established diplomatic relations, which in practice meant that, when their visas expired, they were left with a choice between being expelled from the country or renouncing their US citizenship and accepting Soviet nationality. Faced with this predicament, many decided to return to their homeland, but when they tried, the Soviet authorities stopped them. The Stalinist purges put an end to the exploits of these workers who went in search of prosperity and ended up the scapegoats of Soviet totalitarianism.

In some of them I found inspiration for the protagonists of my novel.

Wilbur Hewitt's alter ego is found in Charles Sorensen, the Ford production manager in Detroit responsible for the contract that bound the Soviet state corporation for the motorization of the nation, the Avtostroy, to Henry Ford. To set up the Avtozavod, Sorensen traveled to the Soviet Union, where he studied the specifics of the construction of the factory in Gorky on-site alongside Joseph Stalin and Valery Mezhlauk. Later, back in the United States, he requested authorization from Henry Ford to return to the Soviet Union and solve the problems plaguing the Avtozavod, but Henry Ford didn't allow it. His very words were, "Charlie. Don't you do it! They need a man like you. If you went over there, you would never come out again. Don't take that chance!"

In the case of Sergei Loban, I drew inspiration from the figure of Valery Mezhlauk, engineer and vice chairman of the State Planning Committee who was responsible for the agreement for the construction of the Avtozavod, signed in Dearborn on May 31, 1929, in the presence of the president of the American corporation, Henry Ford, and the Amtorg chairman, Saul Bron. A few years later, both Mezhlauk and Bron were summarily executed under the unfounded accusation of "enemy of the people" during the secret police's reign of terror.

Viktor Smirnov could be seen as a reflection of the sinister director of the secret police Genrikh Yagoda, a figure described by his contemporaries as vain, corrupt, and sycophantic, a lover of luxuries and women. During his early years as a member of the Cheka, the Soviet secret police, he formed a network of spies and hired killers that infiltrated the NKVD, the People's Commissariat of Internal Affairs, until they gained total control. After allegedly murdering his immediate superior, Vyacheslav Menzhinsky, Genrikh Yagoda was appointed People's Commissar for Internal Affairs. It is thought that he then ordered the death of the celebrated Bolshevik leader Sergei Kirov, and unleashed a political bloodbath that would later be named the Great Purge, in which thousands were executed. During his time in power, Yagoda set up a secret laboratory in which he experimented with chemical products, poisons, and other instruments of torture that he used against his enemies. With the money taken from the accounts of the deceased, he built himself a sumptuous home with a private swimming pool in the center of Moscow. Ultimately, Yagoda met the same fate as his adversaries, and was shot in the back of the head in the same prison that was the site of many of his own horrific crimes.

Finally, Jack Beilis, though distinct in personality, shared some traits with Walter Reuther, who began his career with the Ford Motor Company, where he became an expert in molds. In 1932, he was fired as a result of the Great Depression, and traveled to the Soviet Union to work as an expert at the Avtozavod factory in Gorky. During the two years during which he offered his services, Walter Reuther experienced many of the blessings and evils of the Soviet political machinery. In the end, he made it back to the United States, where after a long period as an activist for workers' rights, he joined the Democratic Party.

Soon after the Soviet factory was opened, commercial relations with Ford began to deteriorate, until in 1935 they completely broke down. In the words of Natalia Kolesnikova, director of the Gorkovsky Avtomobily Zavod Museum of History, it is highly likely that, had the Reuther brothers, who were managers at the time, remained in the Soviet Union, they would have been victims of Stalin's purges. In 1938, the first director of the Gorkovsky Avtomobily Zavod (GAZ), Sergei Dakonov, was executed. All of the workshop managers were arrested. Numerous foreign workers, primarily Americans, suffered reprisals, and some disappeared forever into concentration camps or gulags.

ACKNOWLEDGMENTS

During the time I devoted to writing this book, many people were kind enough to share their knowledge and affection with me. To all of them I owe my sincere thanks, for without their selfless help, it would not have been possible to write this novel.

First, I would like to mention Professor Boris Mikhailovich Shpotov, member of the Institute of General History of the Russian Academy of Sciences in Moscow, and a Fulbright-Kennan Scholar at the Woodrow Wilson International Center for Scholars. Professor Shpotov was kind enough to reply in great detail to many questions on the existence of sabotage, sporadically attributed to the foreign workers posted to the Avtozavod factories. I am equally grateful for the generous contribution of Dr. Heather D. DeHaan, associate professor of history, director of the Russian and East European Program, and academic vice president of the Binghamton Chapter, UUP, Binghamton University of New York, with whom I had in-depth conversations about the location and peculiarities of the American village in Gorky. I would also like to extend my thanks to Dr. Edward Jay Pershey, project manager at the Western Reserve Historical Society in Cleveland, and Natalia Kolesnikova Vitalievna, director of the Gorkovsky Avtomobily Zavod

Museum of History in Nizhny Novgorod (renamed Gorky in late 1932) for their help answering similar questions. Finally, I must also thank industrial design engineer Bernardo Tórtola, an expert in concept car styling and design, and a passionate collector of historical vehicles, who conscientiously advised me on the various specifications of the immaculately maintained Ford Model A that he owns.

As for those who have supported me day to day with their warmth and affection, I would like to mention my parents, of whom I am tremendously proud. Together with my siblings, my daughter, and my grandchildren, they are the people who complete my happiness and provide the stability that I need to write for such long periods without once feeling dispirited. These special individuals complete my happiness, but this happiness would not exist were it not for my wife, Maite, an exceptional person whom I love deeply and whom I consider to be the most wonderful woman on earth.

Glossary

Amtorg: Acronym for the Amerikanskoe Torgovlye (American Trading Corporation), the New York office responsible for Soviet trade relations in the United States. Established during the absence of diplomatic relations between the two countries under the auspices of the Soviet intelligence service, the OGPU, Amtorg combined its trade activities with espionage, gathering intelligence on corporations like the Ford Motor Company.

Avtozavod: Russian term meaning automobile factory widely used to denote the Gorkovsky Avtomobilny Zavod, or the Gorky Automobile Plant. As a result of a personal interest in Taylorist production methods, Joseph Stalin, through the Soviet state corporation Avtostroy, backed an agreement with the Ford Motor Company for the construction of a replica of the American factory in Nizhny Novgorod (renamed Gorky in late 1932). It was agreed that Ford, in addition to supplying the required materials, would send American technical personnel to set the factory in motion, along with a large number of discontinued Ford Model A cars from the company's German facilities. Although the first stone was laid on May 2, 1930, the lack of training among Soviet staff, the standardization of inefficient bureaucratic processes, and the use of low-quality materials to cut costs led to delays in production, for which the secret police sought culprits. Sending 230 Soviet technicians to Dearborn for training proved fruitless. Sporadic sabotage and intermittent strikes were the excuses used by the Joint State Political Directorate (the OGPU) to accuse a large number of American operatives and technicians of negligence and espionage, arresting and executing them. The operation cost a total of 41 million dollars in gold. There were many disputes over the fulfillment of contracts.

Blat: Term used to refer to the use of informal agreements, personal connections, and exchanges of services and contacts within the bureaucratic structure of the Communist Party of the Soviet Union (CPSU) to obtain rationed products or goods unavailable to the general public on the black market.

Bolshevik: A member of a radicalized political group within the Russian Social-Democratic Workers' Party, led by Vladimir Lenin. The term is often used as a synonym for Communist.

Breadline: During North America's Great Depression, this was the name given to the endless line of starving people who waited every day at the doors of the soup kitchens. Most of these centers were run by religious and philanthropic institutions, though there were some cases like the breadline in Detroit funded by the gangster Al Capone in an attempt to improve his public image.

Cheka: The first of the Soviet political and military intelligence organizations. Its mission was to "suppress and terminate," with extremely wide-ranging powers and almost without legal limit, any "counter-revolutionary" or "deviationist" act. By extension, various secret police forces that later emerged in other countries were referred to as *chekas*. In February 1922, the Cheka was restructured and renamed the State Political Directorate (the GPU) under the People's Commissariat for Internal Affairs (the NKVD) of the Russian Soviet Federative Socialist

Republic. After the formation of the Soviet Union in 1922, the GPU became the OGPU, under the Council of People's Commissars of the USSR. The NKVD, in addition to other responsibilities, controlled the *militsiya*.

Dacha: Country house used seasonally. The dacha became fashionable among the Russian middle class from the late nineteenth century. In the former Soviet Union, the dacha was associated with the luxurious homes used by the high-ranking officials of the Communist Party.

Fordville or the American village: The "American village" was the term used to denote the complex of bunkhouses built some two miles from the Avtozavod to house the American immigrants working in the factory. The accommodations consisted of prefabricated buildings of one or two stories built from timber, plywood, and mud. Most of the workers had a single room, though families with children could opt to have an extra room. The bathrooms and kitchens were part of the communal facilities. In addition to the bunkhouses and the individual homes reserved for senior staff, the village had sports facilities, a social club, and its own store, where its inhabitants could buy food and other goods. In 1937, the village, which no longer housed any American residents, was demolished.

Great Depression: Also known as the Depression of 1929, it was a global economic crisis triggered in the United States by the Wall Street crash of 1929, which spread until it affected almost every country in the world, and lasted until the late 1930s. The Depression had devastating consequences. The most seriously affected sectors were agriculture, consumer goods production, and heavy industry. This meant that cities like Detroit and Chicago, which relied on heavy industry, suffered the effects of the crisis more intensely. Unemployment reached 25 percent of the population, and with no welfare for the unemployed at the time, all those affected were left destitute.

Great Purge: A series of campaigns of political repression and persecution undertaken by Stalin in the Soviet Union during the 1930s. Hundreds of thousands of members of the Soviet Communist Party, the army, socialists, anarchists, and opponents of the regime were hunted down, summarily tried, and sent to concentration camps. Hundreds of thousands more were executed. Other sectors of society that suffered persecution were the white-collar professionals, members of religious orders, *kulaks* (landed peasants), and certain discontented ethnic minorities. Most of these arrests were made by the People's Commissariat for Internal Affairs, also known as the NKVD.

Holodomor: The Soviet famine of 1932–33 affected the major grain-producing regions of the USSR, and in the Ukrainian Soviet Socialist Republic (UkSSR), it was known as the Holodomor. It is estimated that it killed eight million people, 80 percent of them Ukrainians.

Intourist: The state travel agency of the Soviet Union. Founded in 1929 by Joseph Stalin and run by NKVD officials, its purpose was to control foreigners' access to Soviet territory and travel within the state. In 1933, it merged with the Soviet state company Hotel, adding hotels, restaurants, and transportation to its services.

Ispravdom: Meaning "house of correction" in Russian, *ispravdom* referred to any of the correctional facilities, prisons, and labor camps that the Soviets set up in order to carry out penitentiary sentences. Although the Soviet Penal Code envisaged forced labor not as a punishment but as a means to reform the individual, in practice, the labor camps proved to be extermination facilities. The Gorky labor camp, built for eight hundred inmates, housed 3,461 prisoners in 1932. This increase was due first to the long preventative prison sentences meted out; second to the fact that sentences were determined according to the type of offense, rather than its magnitude, so that a sentence for the theft of hundreds of rubles was the same as for stealing five; and third to the mass influx of prisoners from other parts of the state. In time, the attempts to instill civic-mindedness among the inmates through education and labor policies (in 1932, in the Gorky *ispravdom*, the state provided 760 newspaper and 110 journal subscriptions, instruction to 350 illiterates, and vocational training to 263 inmates who requested it) gradually gave way to mass transfers by the OGPU of political prisoners to the forced labor camps, known as gulags. These were mostly located on the Siberian steppes, where the extreme weather, food shortages, disease, and hard labor decimated the prisoner population. The total number of documented deaths in the correctional labor camps and colonies from 1934 to 1953 stands at 1,053,829. Aleksandr Solzhenitsyn, the historian and Nobel literature laureate, estimated that the Bolsheviks murdered some 70 million people, excluding those killed in war, a further 44 million—a total of 114 million people from the Bolshevik revolution of 1917 to Stalin's death in 1953. Just in the year from 1937 to 1938, more than 1.3 million people were sentenced to death.

NEP: The New Economic Policy was proposed by Vladimir Lenin, who defined it as state capitalism. The state continued to control foreign trade, the banks, and heavy industry, but allowed some private enterprises and businesses to be established. The decree of 1921 required farmers to hand over a certain quantity of their produce to the government as a tax in kind. Other decrees perfected the policy and expanded it to include some industrial enterprises. The New Economic Policy was abolished and replaced by Stalin's first five-year plan in 1928.

Prohibition: The term commonly used to denote the ban on the manufacture, importation, and sale of alcoholic beverages, in force in the United States from January 17, 1920, to December 5, 1933. Since the law did not penalize consumption, people found ways to continue drinking alcohol, whether through the lucrative black market, or by collecting prescriptions authorizing the use of alcohol for medical purposes.

Sabotage: In 1928, the OGPU launched its first major anti-sabotage operation in the Donbass, implicating eleven operational managers and 20 percent of the engineers and technicians. Most of them were sentenced to death. Thereafter, the secret police centered its attention on the more than two thousand members of the Industrial Party (Prompartiia), trying its leaders in 1930. Most of its members were incarcerated. Foreign workers were a common target of these accusations. In 1934, Andrey Vyshinsky, the state prosecutor, was forced to issue an order to stop the local prosecutors from making scapegoats of the factories' engineers and managers because production was being affected. The detained technicians were sent to *sharashkas*, laboratories staffed by prisoners under the strict control of the secret police within the Fourth Special Department of the NKVD. Previously termed Experimental Design Bureau, they received more than a thousand scientists, engineers, and technicians who worked in them, chained to drawing boards.

Torgsin: The Russian acronym of *torgovlia s inostrantsami*, meaning "trade with foreigners." The term referred to the network of state-run stores where foreigners could buy goods that were banned or restricted for Soviet citizens. These products included food and other rationed essentials, as well as luxury items. Although the vast majority of the customers of these stores were foreigners, their products could also be sold to Soviets, provided that they paid in jewels, gold, or dollars, since the purpose of these establishments was to obtain hard currency for the state. This led to the development of a black market for currency as a means to gain access to restricted goods.

Working hours: From 1929 to 1931, in the Soviet Union the weeks were changed from seven to five days. Sunday, the traditional

Christian day of rest, was eliminated, and instead, workers were organized into five groups, each assigned a roman numeral (I to V) or a color (yellow, pink, red, purple, and green), with each group allocated a different day of the week to rest. A year consisted of seventy-two five-day weeks plus an additional period of five public vacations, making a total of 365 days. The change was intended to improve productivity and working conditions. A working week consisted of four days on and one day off. In 1931, the week was changed to six days, a system later abandoned to return to the seven-day week in June 1940. The working day was eight hours, including a one-hour lunch break.

BIBLIOGRAPHY

Baker, V. *American Workers in the Soviet Union between the Two World Wars*. Morgantown, WV: West Virginia University, 1998.

Cahan, A. *Yekl: A Tale of the New York Ghetto*. New York, NY: Dover Publications, 1970.

Castro Delgado, E. *Hombres Made in Moscú*. Barcelona, Sp.: Luis de Caralt, 1963.

Cuello Calón, E. *El derecho penal de Rusia soviética. Código Penal ruso de 1926*. Barcelona, Sp.: Librería Bosch, 1931.

Dillon, E. J. *La Rusia de hoy y la de ayer*. Barcelona, Sp.: Editorial Juventud, 1931.

Filene, P. *Americans and the Soviet Experiment, 1917–1933*. Cambridge, MA: Harvard University Press, 1967.

Fitzgerald, F. S. *El Crack-Up*. Barcelona, Sp.: Bruguera, 1983.

Hidalgo Durán, D. *Un notario español en Rusia*. Madrid, Sp.: Editorial Cenit, 1931.

Katamidze, S. *KGB. Leales camaradas, asesinos implacables.* Madrid, Sp.: Editorial Libsa, 2004.

Kucherenko, O. *Little Soldiers.* New York, NY: Oxford University Press, 2011.

Lee, A. *Henry Ford and the Jews.* New York, NY: Stein and Day, 1980.

Maltby, R. *Cultura y modernidad.* Madrid, Sp.: Aguilar, 1991.

Ministry of Defense of the USSR. *The Official Soviet Mosin-Nagant Sniper Rifle Manual.* Boulder, CO: Paladin Press, 2000.

Montero y Gutiérrez, E. *Lo que vi en Rusia, Imp.* Madrid, Sp.: Luz y Vida, 1935.

Orjikh, B. *Cómo se vive y se trabaja en la Rusia soviética.* Santiago, Ch.: Editorial Bola, 1933.

Oroquieta, G. and C. García. *De Leningrado a Odesa.* Barcelona, Sp.: Editorial Marte, 1973.

Prójorov, A. *Bolshaya Soviétskaya Entsiklopédiya,* BSE, vol. 24. Moscow, CCCP: Soviet government publication, 1969–1978.

Répide Gallegos, P. de. *La Rusia de ahora, Renacimiento.* Madrid, Sp.: Compañía Iberoamericana de Publicaciones, 1930.

Reuther, V. G. *The Brothers Reuther and the Story of the UAW: A Memoir.* Boston, MA: Houghton Mifflin, 1976.

Rigoulot, P., S. Courtois, and M. Malia. *The Black Book of Communism: Crimes, Terror, Repression.* Cambridge, MA: Harvard University Press, 1999.

Rio, P. *The Soviet Soldier of World War Two.* Paris, Fr.: Histoire & Collections, 2011.

Rukeyser, W. *Working for the Soviets: An American Engineer in Russia.* New York, NY: Covici-Friede, 1932.

Salisbury, H. *American in Russia.* New York, NY: Harper & Brothers, 1955.

Schultz, K. "Building the 'Soviet Detroit': The Construction of the Nizhnii-Novgorod Automobile Factory, 1927–1932." *Slavic Review* (Association for Slavic, East European, and Eurasian Studies, Pittsburgh, PA) 49, no. 2: (1990).

Scott, J. *Behind the Urals: An American Worker in Russia's City of Steel.* Cambridge, MA: Houghton Mifflin, 1942.

Shternshis, A. *Soviet and Kosher: Jewish Popular Culture in the Soviet Union, 1923–1939.* Bloomington, IN: Indiana University Press, 2006.

Timbres, Harry, and Rebecca Timbres. *We Didn't Ask Utopia: A Quaker Family in Soviet Russia.* New York, NY: Prentice-Hall, 1939.

Tzouliadis, T. *Los olvidados.* Barcelona, Sp.: Debate, 2010.

Vallejo Mendoza, C. *Rusia en 1931. Reflexiones al pie del Kremlin.* Madrid, Sp.: Editorial Ulises, 1931.

Witkin, Z. *An American Engineer in Stalin's Russia: The Memoirs of Zara Witkin, 1932–1934.* Introduction by Michael Gelb. Berkeley, CA: University of California Press, 1991.

Zemtsov, I. *Encyclopedia of Soviet Life.* Piscataway, NJ: Transaction Publishers, 1991.

ABOUT THE AUTHOR

A native of Spain, an educator, and an industrial engineer, Antonio Garrido was inspired by the stories of Jules Verne and Sir Walter Scott as a child. Although in his early career Garrido focused on technical writing, the discovery of a forgotten manuscript in 2001 led him to write his first novel, *The Scribe*, a finalist for the Fulbert Prize.

Since then, he has become known for novels that reflect deep study of the cultural, social, legal, and political facets of specific historical eras. *The Corpse Reader*, a fictionalized account of the Chinese founding father of forensic science, won the Zaragoza International Prize and the Griffe Noire prize. *The Last Paradise*, a historical thriller, is his third novel and a winner of the Premio Fernando Lara de Novela. His work has been translated into eighteen languages.

Garrido currently combines writing with teaching at the Polytechnic University and the Cardenal Herrera-CEU University in Valencia, Spain.

About the Translator

Photo © 2013 Thomas Frogbrooke

Simon Bruni is the translator of more than a dozen fiction and non-fiction books from Spanish, including Paul Pen's *The Light of the Fireflies* (AmazonCrossing, 2016) and Antonio Garrido's *The Scribe* (AmazonCrossing, 2013). In a career that has seen him translate everything from video games to sixteenth-century Spanish Inquisition manuscripts, Bruni has found the pull toward literary translation irresistible. He has won two John Dryden Translation Prizes, in 2011 for *Cell 211*, Francisco Pérez Gandul's cult prison thriller, and in 2015 for "The Porcelain Boy," Paul Pen's harrowing short story.

Printed in Great Britain
by Amazon